W9-AYD-679

A Brew to a Kill

Berkley Prime Crime titles by Cleo Coyle

Coffeehouse Mysteries

ON WHAT GROUNDS
THROUGH THE GRINDER
LATTE TROUBLE
MURDER MOST FROTHY
DECAFFEINATED CORPSE
FRENCH PRESSED
ESPRESSO SHOT
HOLIDAY GRIND
ROAST MORTEM
MURDER BY MOCHA
A BREW TO A KILL

Haunted Bookshop Mysteries
writing as Alice Kimberly

THE GHOST AND MRS. MCCLURE
THE GHOST AND THE DEAD DEB
THE GHOST AND THE DEAD MAN'S LIBRARY
THE GHOST AND THE FEMME FATALE
THE GHOST AND THE HAUNTED MANSION

A Brew to a Kill

Cleo Coyle

BERKLEY PRIME CRIME, NEW YORK

THE BERKLEY PUBLISHING GROUP
Published by the Penguin Group
Penguin Group (USA) Inc.
375 Hudson Street, New York, New York 10014, USA
Penguin Group (Canada), 90 Eglinton Avenue East, Suite 700, Toronto, Ontario M4P 2Y3, Canada (a division of Pearson Penguin Canada Inc.) • Penguin Books Ltd., 80 Strand, London WC2R 0RL, England • Penguin Group Ireland, 25 St. Stephen's Green, Dublin 2, Ireland (a division of Penguin Books Ltd.) • Penguin Group (Australia), 250 Camberwell Road, Camberwell, Victoria 3124, Australia (a division of Pearson Australia Group Pty. Ltd.) • Penguin Books India Pvt. Ltd., 11 Community Centre, Panchsheel Park, New Delhi—110 017, India • Penguin Group (NZ), 67 Apollo Drive, Rosedale, Auckland 0632, New Zealand (a division of Pearson New Zealand Ltd.) • Penguin Books (South Africa) (Pty.) Ltd., 24 Sturdee Avenue, Rosebank, Johannesburg 2196, South Africa

Penguin Books Ltd., Registered Offices: 80 Strand, London WC2R 0RL, England

This book is an original publication of The Berkley Publishing Group.

FIRST EDITION: August 2012

Library of Congress Cataloging-in-Publication Data

Coyle, Cleo
A brew to a kill / Cleo Coyle.—1st ed.
p. cm.
ISBN 978-0-425-24787-7
1. Cosi, Clare (Fictitious character)—Fiction. 2. Coffeehouses—Fiction. 3. New York (N. Y.)—Fiction. I. Title.
PS3603.094B74 2012 2012014539
813'.6—dc23

PRINTED IN THE UNITED STATES OF AMERICA

10 9 8 7 6 5 4 3 2 1

This book is dedicated to the hardworking street chefs who run the food trucks and carts of New York City. Long may you roll!

Acknowledgments

A Brew to a Kill is the eleventh book in the Coffeehouse Mystery series, and as many of you know, I've written all of them in collaboration with my very talented spouse, Marc Cerasini—a better partner a girl couldn't ask for. He and I both owe a debt of gratitude to our publisher. First and foremost, we'd like to recognize our editor Wendy McCurdy for her unflagging support and professionalism. We'd also like to thank her son, Alex Schoch, for suggesting this book's clever title, which set the perfect tone for the story.

The staff at Penguin's Berkley Prime Crime is among the best in the business, and we sincerely thank them for shepherding this beautiful book into publication, including assistant editor Katherine Pelz, production editor Megan Gerrity, copyeditor Jessica McDonnell, and art director Rita Frangie.

The research behind *A Brew to a Kill* emerged from our decades of living and working in New York City. More recently, we credit a fast-moving culinary odyssey that began on Governors Island at the Vendy Awards, which annually honors the best street chefs of New York. Our voyage continued through the dynamic Asian community of Manhattan's Chinatown, the eclectic peninsula of Red Hook, Brooklyn, and the polyglot neighborhoods of Queens, especially the warm and welcoming Filipino community of Little Manila in Woodside.

More specifically, we'd like to thank all twenty-two finalists in the 2011 Vendy Award's cook-off competition for inspiring many of the culinary aspects of this mystery, especially the Cupcake Crew truck (www.cupcakecrewnyc.com). Please note that the members of this Cupcake Crew are kind, generous, and creative—in short, nothing like the completely fictional Kupcake Kween and her mischief-makers.

Thanks also to the La Bella Torte truck (www.labellatorte.com) for their delicious Italian pastries, good humor, and the saying on their truck. More than a famous movie quote, "Leave the gun, take the cannoli" pretty much defines what our Coffeehouse Mysteries are all about.

From our gastronomic research in Lower Manhattan's Chinatown, we'd like to thank the very talented pastry chef John Wu and his Everything Frosted on Mosco Street (www.everythingfrosted.com/about_us.html). Another inspiration for the Kaylie express, this wonderful establishment also inspired Mrs. Li's kitchen.

Our egg custard tart research included many bakeries in Chinatown, and we'd like to single out happy stops at Golden Manna Bakery on Bowery Steet and the Lucky King Bakery and Natalie Bakery Inc. on Grand. Thanks to all for the kind service and excellent tarts!

In Woodside, Queens's Little Manila, we found valuable inspiration in Filipino cuisine at the beloved eatery Renee's Kitchenette and Grill, as well as Engeline's restaurant, and the East Coast outpost for Red Ribbon Bakery. You can find them all, too, via New York's 7 train above Roosevelt Avenue.

As for the coffee research in this book, aspects of Matt's Brazilian Ambrosia came from two superb offerings of San Francisco's Ritual Coffee Roasters (www.ritualroasters.com): the Santa Lúcia and the Sao Benedito, both produced by the Pereira Family of Brazil. For barista background, we extend ongoing java thanks to one of the nation's top coffee bars Joe, based in Greenwich Village, NYC (www.joetheartofcoffee.com).

With the utmost respect, we tip our hats to the NYPD in general and the Sixth Precinct of Greenwich Village in particular. Our interaction with New York's Finest has been nothing but the finest. As to the Ps and Qs of police procedure, this is a light work of amateur sleuth fiction. In the Coffeehouse Mysteries, the rules occasionally get bent.

A "federal case" thank you to Coffeehouse Mystery reader

"Barbara C." whose own official work planted the seed of an idea in this one.

For consultation on matters medical, special thanks goes out to the best doc in the West, Dr. Grace Alfonsi, M.D. (If there are errors in this book, they are entirely our own.)

It's no "co-inky-dink" that we're also thanking CM reader Nancy Prior Phillips once again. Her wit and good humor continue to inspire us, as do so many of you who read our series and leave notes and messages via e-mail, our website's message board, and the social networking sites. Your kind words keep us going as writers, and we can't thank you enough for that.

Finally, we'd like to recognize our agent, John Talbot, for providing the kind of support and encouragement that keep authors moving forward.

To everyone else who we could not mention here by name, including friends and family, please know that your comments and heartfelt messages have kept our spirits up and fingers pressed to the keyboard. Our virtual coffeehouse is always open. You are more than welcome to join us online at www.CoffeehouseMystery.com.

—Cleo Coyle
New York City

Coffee . . . makes the politician wise,
And see thro' all things with his half-shut eyes.

—Alexander Pope, *The Rape of the Lock,* Canto III

Prologue

I feel . . . that I would like to wallow in crime this evening.

—"THE COMPANION,"
***THE THIRTEEN PROBLEMS* BY AGATHA CHRISTIE**

PEERING *through the sooty windshield, the Driver surveyed the scene. Not a thing was moving below the halogen halos of city streetlamps. No cars. No pedestrians. No witnesses. Only the lone cyclist on his two wheels and these four wheels stalking him.*

Perfect, *thought the Driver.*

When the traffic signal slipped from red to green, the cyclist swung onto West Twentieth, his shiny red spandex vanishing in the predawn fog. The Driver counted to ten and rolled the battered van after him.

Not too close. Not yet . . .

With clueless passion, the cyclist pedaled, oblivious to the twin beams stabbing inexorably toward him. His destination was the Hudson River Greenway, thirty-two miles lapping the island of Manhattan. This personally prescribed route to the perfect body was a triweekly workout set in stone.

The Driver's path was set, as well, the course conceived months ago, a map years in the making.

He's moving faster. Don't lose him . . .

With itchy anticipation, the Driver picked up speed. Out of the shadows darted a perky young jogger, shapely legs pumping. The Driver cursed, hit the brakes.

The cyclist slowed to ogle the girl, but the Driver knew this man—and his rapacious gaze. He would see only the girl's flaws: breasts too small, nose too long, first hint of muffin top. All quite fixable—for the right price.

When the pretty runner reached the corner, the street was clear again. Closing the distance, the Driver waited one last time—for the bastard to turn, to look, to see exactly what was coming.

The engine roared, the tires spun, and the van leapt forward. With a shuddering thump, two tons of hurtling steel crushed man and bicycle.

"Not enough. Not nearly enough!"

The Driver braked, shifted into reverse, hit the gas once more. Another thump, and the van rocked. After a pause, the vehicle shot forward again.

"There you go, Doc! How's that for a three-in-one?"

As the van sped away, a trail of sparks followed, a fiery display that ended with the dangling muffler breaking free. The Driver barely noticed. All that mattered was the course ahead.

The next deadly outing would require an audience. A far riskier prospect, but the plan was in motion; the truth inevitable: On the road to a better place, you had two options when something got in your way—

Change lanes or run it down.

With concrete resolve, the Driver had made that choice. "And now there's no turning back. No matter who has to die . . ."

One

> ***This seems to be the basic need of the human heart in nearly every great crisis—a good hot cup of coffee.***
>
> —*I SHOULD HAVE KISSED HER MORE* **BY ALEXANDER KING**

"In times like these, Clare, failing to take a risk is the biggest risk of all."

Across the café table's cool marble surface, Madame Dreyfus Allegro Dubois pinned me with her near-violet eyes. "Don't you agree?"

Of course, I agree. I wanted to shout this, scream it. Risk and I were old friends, and if anyone knew that, my octogenarian employer did.

"Investing in the new coffee truck was my idea," I reminded her between robust hits of espresso. "I know it's a smart idea."

"Good. Now all you must do is convince him."

Him was Mateo Allegro—due to arrive within the hour. An international coffee broker, Matt was the Village Blend's coffee buyer, Madame's only child, my ex-husband, and the father of my pride named Joy.

"Like I told you, I tried to convince him . . ." (Half a dozen e-mails worth of "try" to be precise. When text didn't work, I placed calls overseas. Lengthy calls. Enriching AT&T hadn't helped, either.) "The man doesn't listen, and he's still in a state."

Beneath the mauve silk of her mandarin jacket, Madame's narrow shoulders gave a little shrug. "What can I say? He's his father's son. All that passion, all that intensity, all that tenacity—"

"Tenacity?" I knocked on the coral-colored tabletop. "Matt's head could break this."

"I wouldn't count on it, dear. For one thing, that's Italian marble. Very *old* Italian marble. Old things tend to be stronger than you think."

Sitting back in my café chair, I ran my hands along the thighs of my blue jeans and attempted to fill my lungs with a healthy dose of equilibrium. It wasn't easy. The sun may have set, but our coffeehouse commerce was far from winding down. A line of caffeine-deprived customers hugged the espresso bar, and beyond our wall of wide-open French doors, laughing latte lovers still packed our sidewalk tables.

The city was enjoying one of those glorious stretches of early summer weather, before the high humidity hits, when afternoons are sunny and clear, and nights are pleasantly temperate. Madame and I were perched between the two—the warmth of midday and the chill of midnight, when the sun clocks out and a magical light seems to soften New York's hard edges.

I tried my best to drink in that gentleness, that calm. All day long I'd been on my feet, dealing with bickering baristas, demanding customers, and low stock. With the arrival of my assistant manager, Tucker, I finally took a load off, along with my Village Blend apron, to welcome the coolness of early evening with warm sips of caramelized peaberries.

Unfortunately, a single shot of espresso would not be enough caffeine. Something blacker than nightfall was headed my way, and before I knew it, the business troubling me would be murder.

At the moment, however, the business on the table (literally and figuratively) was coffee—and the question of how best to keep this business selling and serving it through the next century.

So far, Madame had seen things my way. And why not? Despite appearing as starched and restrained as a Park Avenue blueblood, Madame was a bohemian at heart, embracing the odd and offbeat. To her, authenticity mattered more than money. Flouting convention was a virtue, taking risks an asset.

"When you're a war refugee," she once told me, "you learn to take chances, to cross boundaries. If you don't dare, you don't survive . . ."

The woman had done more than toil when she'd arrived on Manhattan Island. New York City ground up polite little girls like beans through a grinder, and Madame quickly understood that working hard was not enough.

After her Italian-born husband died young, she learned how to maneuver and strategize. In order to ensure the survival of herself, her son, and this landmark business, she outwitted the scoundrels who thought they could swindle or crush her. And she'd won. This century-old business was still thriving.

As for me, I was no war refugee. I'd come to New York from a little factory town in Western Pennsylvania. But I shared Madame's admiration for the virtue of daring—and she well knew of my long-standing relationship with the "R" word.

At nineteen I risked my future by quitting art school to have my (surprise!) baby. At twenty-nine I risked my security by leaving my marriage to an incurably immature spouse. At thirty-nine I risked my sanity by returning to my old job of managing this coffeehouse, which required working with said spouse. Since I'd turned forty, I'd risked even more to ensure the safety of my friends, my family, and my staff (a redundant mention since I considered them family, anyway).

Spending my energy reminding Madame of all that, however, would have been a waste of good caffeine, so I returned my cup to its little round porcelain nest and tried a new tack.

"You know what I think?" I said.

"No, dear. I only read minds on weekends."

"I think we're missing the simplest solution."

Madame's elegant silver pageboy tilted in question.

"You're still the owner of the Village Blend," I pointed out. "You can break your son down with one firm conversation. Please. When he gets here, talk some sense into him."

"I'm his mother, and he respects me. And I could do that—"

"Thank you."

"But I won't."

"Why not?"

"Because, my dear, I won't be around forever—"

"Oh, no. Don't start that kind of talk—"

Her gently wrinkled hand waved me silent. "One day you and Matt will own this building and this business. You must learn how to handle him."

"*Learn* how to handle Matteo Allegro? I've been handling your son since I was nineteen!"

"You handled a boy, Clare, then a man. A lover, then a spouse. You managed your relationship through a divorce and even his remarriage. But handling a man as a romantic partner is not the same as handling him as a business partner."

Ready to argue, I opened my mouth—and closed it again.

A single imperious head-shake from my former mother-in-law was reminder enough that further protests would be pointless. This I knew after having spent so many years being a part of this small but remarkable family (my daughter included): Matt wasn't the only Allegro with a head harder than millennial marble.

"Just remember, Clare, conversations about money are never easy when emotion is involved, and in any long-term business relationship, emotion is always involved. But a good relationship isn't about making things easier."

"It's not?"

"No."

"Then what is it about?"

"Making things *better*."

Expelling a breath, I rose to fetch more caffeine. "You'll stay for our meeting, at least, won't you?"

Madame passed me the cup and smiled, an insightful little expression that implied her words carried more than one meaning.

"I'm not going anywhere just yet."

"You must be crazy, Clare! Out of your managerial mind!" Matteo Allegro's Italian-roast eyes were wide with indignation, his voice loud enough to startle my baristas and disturb the peace of my late evening customers.

"You're overreacting, Matt. Calm down." I lowered my own voice an octave or twelve, hoping he'd take my cue. "This is simply an expansion. It had to be made."

"You threw hard-earned capital out the window to purchase a food cart?!"

On a long exhale, I threw a desperate look his mother's way. *Help.*

Across the table, Madame allowed her gaze to meet mine, but her jaw remained set. *I warned you, dear. You want this business decision to stand? Prove it should. Handle him.*

Shifting in my chair, I stared at the man.

Matt stared back—*after* swiping aside a dark swath of low-dangling fringe. For years, my ex had kept his hair cut Caesar-short. These days, he wore it longer than a Musketeer. With his return from this coffee-hunting trip, the locks were downright shaggy, plus he had face fur.

I knew Matt loathed shaving in hot climates, but now he'd finally pushed the "devilish rogue" thing too far. The trimmed goatee had sprouted into a caveman beard. Not that it was any of my business if he looked like he was about to plant a suitcase bomb, but I did think it time he made a date with a barber—or a Weedwacker.

While he'd let his hair go, I had to admit, the rest of his body appeared fitter than ever. Under an open denim shirt, his tight white tee outlined his broad shoulders and sculpted chest. Encircling one wrist was a braided leather bracelet given to him by a coffee-growing tribe in Ecuador; fastened around the other, a costly Breitling chronometer.

Such was the recipe that defined Matteo Allegro: one part daring java trekker, one part slick international coffee buyer. Not that there wasn't more to my ex, but that paradoxical blend epitomized Matt's addictive appeal. At nineteen, I got hooked on the guy. By forty, however, I found him harder to swallow than a doctor-prescribed horse pill.

"I'm going to say this again. Try to listen this time, okay? What I invested in was a truck. Not a cart. A gourmet coffee and muffin truck—"

"Not only are you squandering capital, but you actually took on *debt* to seek out some magical customer base that might not even exist? That's risky, Clare. Risky and reckless!"

Okay, that tweaked me. Matt never held back an opinion, especially a negative one, but a sudden aversion to risk? *This* from a man who thought nothing of traveling deep into lawless regions of Africa, trekking Central American mudslide zones, diving off the cliffs near Hawaiian volcanoes?

"The Village Blend coffee truck has been up and running for almost a month. And guess what? We haven't lost our shirts—"

"Yet," he said.

Pushing aside my empty espresso cup, I rested one arm on the marble tabletop (and yes, I was betting I could break it with his head).

"In this competitive environment, you either expand or perish." By way of a truce, I rested a hand on his muscular shoulder. "I promise you, Matt, I'm trying to save the Blend, not ruin us."

My soft touch appeared to have a favorable effect. The tension in the man's body slackened, and his booming voice finally came down to a seminormal decibel level.

"Clare . . . We tried expanding once. Remember my kiosks in high-end clothing stores? I do, and not with feelings of nostalgia, either. We lost a bundle."

"So we failed once. That's no reason not to try expanding our customer base again."

"Did you consider advertising?"

"Ad campaigns are ephemeral. What the Blend needs is a long-term strategy for our modern market—although, technically, we're *post-postmodern . . .*"

I handed him a spreadsheet of stats tracking profits since I'd resumed managing his family's coffeehouse. With hard work and discipline, I was able to keep costs low and squeeze more profit from every ring of our register. The baristas I'd painstakingly trained were making higher amounts of sale to every customer, but the overall number of patrons was not growing.

"I considered opening a second store, but rents are outrageous. The truck solves the problem of choosing a dud location or having a hot neighborhood go cold. If one area doesn't produce a steady customer stream, we simply drive to a new one."

Matt reviewed the data, exhaled. "What's your strategy?"

Ignoring the man's skeptical gaze, I mustered the same polite but firm tone I'd used on our paper cup supplier when he announced the third price hike in as many months and said—

"Proselytizing."

"That's a business strategy?"

"It's a philosophy *and* a business strategy. We have faith in our Blend, in the quality of our coffee, the commitment to our customers, the century-old tradition of family ownership. We're simply going to spread the word."

"How?"

I flipped to a customized map of New York. "There are five boroughs in the Big Apple, right?"

"Last I checked."

"Well, there's no way we can get everyone in New York to come to this Manhattan shop, even if it is a landmark business. So Esther and I worked out a day and time schedule for our Muffin Muse truck to go to them. We serve commuters during morning and evening rush. On weekends, there are parks, fairs, and flea markets. We track the revenue at each location, test new locations daily—"

"On paper, it seems reasonable . . ." The man actually sounded conciliatory.

I glanced at his mother. She slipped me a fleeting wink. Then Matt looked at her and she raised her demitasse, hastily hiding her pleased little smile with a sip of espresso.

"You could have tested this theory out some other way, Clare. A cheaper way. Did you have to invest in a food truck that cost nearly one hundred thousand dollars?" Matt's shaggy head shook.

"Believe me, I did my homework on median costs and earning potential. You need to start trusting me on things like this. Have a little faith. You know I'm the one who's a better judge of it."

"You?"

"Yes, me. We each have our strengths. I don't tell you how to source coffee—"

"You don't know how to source coffee—"

"And you don't know a thing about managing at retail."

"That's a load of crap!"

The roar came back, and now he was turning on his mother. "Why are you so quiet tonight? Don't you have an opinion? Can't you talk some *sense* into her?!"

Ack. Little more than an hour before, I'd asked her to do exactly the same thing—*with him.*

For an agonizing minute, Madame sat completely still. My spirits began to flag. *Is she going to take his side?* Tensely, I watched as she set her demitasse down with a click.

"Clare is not wrong about your lack of experience on the retail end."

Matt gawked. "I've worked in this shop since I was nine years old! Bussing tables, pulling espressos; you're the one who taught me to be the best."

Madame's features softened at that, but her tone remained resolved. "You're an exceptional coffee buyer and a fine barista. But Clare is a better shop manager. She's constant and committed yet innovative; fair but firm with staff and suppliers. Clare is also an artist at heart, which means she knows how to see and how to *listen*."

The effusive praise struck me numb for a moment. But only me.

"I listen!"

"What you do is hear, Matteo; it's not the same thing. Clare is also a genius at artful critique."

"*Artful critique?*" Matt echoed. "What the hell is that—a neo-management term? Sounds like a cross between Vincent van Gogh and Donald Trump."

"It's to do with *insight . . .*" Madame exhaled. "My dear boy, you are an excellent coffee hunter, and you clearly adore circumnavigating the globe. But this little patch of ground needs a sovereign, not a Magellan. Clare is here, day in and day out. Business may be good at the moment, but each month brings new challenges, and the broader economic picture is far from stable."

"I assure you, Mother, things are tough all over this planet." Matt's expression clouded. "I know that better than anyone—"

The passing shadow may have been momentary, but I knew my ex-husband. His words weren't rhetorical. Before I could press the man with questions, however, an amplified voice interrupted him, a noise so loud it rattled the spotless glass of the Blend's French doors and startled my evening customers.

"Chocolat! Ooooh la la, chocolat!"

Blasting at maximum volume was a musical cliché—the Francophile classic "La Vie en Rose," rendered via tinny instruments, the usual lyrics replaced by an infantile caricature of a French woman's voice reciting (hard to believe, but . . .) a cupcake menu.

"Straw-*bear*-wee! Lee-*mon*! Butt-*tair* cream!"

All three of us stared as a long, rainbow-colored food truck came into view. Festooned with sparkling lights and capped by a Vegas-worthy Eiffel Tower, the vehicle made its turn off Hudson to pull up beside our sidewalk café tables.

Matt turned toward me. "What is *that*?"

I closed my eyes. *How to answer?* The phrase "my new arch-enemy" wouldn't do much to back my argument here.

"Ooooh la la! Chocolat!"

Like a neon shark, Kaylie Crimini's famous Kupcake Kart had arrived for its second obnoxious feeding of the day. I told Matt as much.

"Feeding?" he repeated. "Feeding on what?"

It pained me to say it, but Matt had to know. "Our customers."

Two

"CLARE, I have never seen anything like this . . ."

With a kind of bewildered horror, Matt stared at the sideshow next to our sidewalk. The truck's service window clanged open, revealing Kaylie Crimini's honey-hued beehive bouncing among her staff inside the vehicle. Suddenly a sign appeared: *Twilight Special, 50% Off!*

With the Kart now ready for cut-rate business, passersby began lining up.

The tinny faux-French music continued pouring from Kaylie's truck speakers as the annoying menu recitation played on: "Fla-*vours* for *vous*! *Chocolat* fooge! *Chocolat* ship . . ."

With the Blend's peace shattered, a dozen of my patrons closed up their books and laptops and began packing up. Matt watched in disbelief as many of these exiting customers stopped to purchase cupcakes before heading home.

"She's baa-*ack*," sang Nancy Kelly, approaching our table with a new round of espressos.

Nancy was the newest and youngest member of my barista staff. A fresh-faced farm girl from "all over," as she put it, Nancy was a reliable opener and a constant source of good cheer—no mean feat in a fast-moving city whose demanding, overanxious customers could reduce courteous countergirls to tears. As she cleared our empty cups and handed out new ones, Matt frantically jabbed the air.

"That truck . . . it's actually selling pastries and coffee in front of *our* shop! What is this? *Who* is this?"

Nancy answered for me (with a slight crushin'-on-you batting of eyelashes—an affliction of which I had yet to cure her). "She's our nemesis, Matteo . . . er . . ." She threw him an apologetic smile. "I mean, Mr. Allegro."

"Nemesis?" he repeated. "Nancy, what are you taking about?"

"Kaylie Crimini is crazy jealous because our Muffin Muse is the talk of the foodie blog world and her cupcakes aren't anymore!"

Matt's face went blank. "What's a Muffin Muse?"

"The name of our coffee truck," I reminded him flatly. "Do you have selective hearing? Maybe I should have tried PowerPoint."

"It's like this," Nancy tried again. "The Village Blend's one-two punch of espresso drinks and muffin awesome-isity has beat the Cupcake Queen at her own game."

"Game?" Matt said. "What game?"

"The street food game," I said. "Last summer Kaylie Crimini's Kupcake Kart was the star of the food truck world, but this year we're getting the attention."

"That's right!" Nancy flipped back one of her wheat-colored braids and grinned with home-team pride. "Our truck has been stealing Kaylie's spotlight. How cool is that?"

"We're stealing her spotlight, so she's stealing our customers!" Matt turned to face me. "Great, Clare. You launch a food truck and gain a predator?"

"*Peer*, Matt. Kaylie is simply a business peer, a competitor in a big town with plenty of other competitors and literally millions of potential customers to go around. I'm sure she'll grow up and get over these childish stunts soon." At least, I hoped she would.

The bell over the front door jingled again, but this time it wasn't a patron departing. An attractive Filipina woman entered our shop: Lilly Beth Tanga, my new business associate.

In her late thirties, Lilly was built much like me: petite but with a mature, shapely figure that nicely filled out her jeans. She was a hard worker, too, with a constant surplus of energy and ideas, and from the sparkling look in her beautiful, almond-shaped eyes, I could tell she was brimming with more.

"Kaylie Crimini *again*!" Lilly cried, approaching our table with a grin. "*Diyos Ko!* I think the Kupcake Kween is stalking me. She and that diabetic coma on wheels!"

After a quick, warm hug for me and another for Madame, she pulled up a chair to join us—and I was very glad that she did. Earlier today, I'd asked her to stop by and help me convince Matt to get on board the Muffin Muse truck (so to speak). With the sugar queen's arrival, I could use all the help I could get.

"So good to see you again, Lilly," Madame said. "How is little Paz?"

"Up to his tricks, as usual. He's barely done with fifth grade, and he's ready to program network television. He actually got his friends to help him organize a weekly recess variety show."

"What do they call it?" I asked. "*Playground Idol?*"

"Close!" Lilly laughed. "*P.S. 11's Got Talent.*"

Matt actually cracked a smile. "And you are?" he said, his mood obviously improving with the arrival of an attractive female.

"Lilly Beth Tanga," I jumped in, "meet my business partner, Matt Allegro. Lilly is—"

"Filipino, right?" Matt extended a hand. "*Magandang araw,* Ms. Tanga."

Lilly Beth took Matt's hand. "*Sandali lang,* Mr. Allegro. But honestly, you'll make more points speaking with my mom. I was born in Jackson Heights and my Tagalog is very rusty."

"No problem," Matt said. "My own's pretty rusty these days—although I do remember *sarap nito*."

"*Sarap nito*? Then you must enjoy Filipino food, *oo*?" Lilly Beth cocked her head and her sweet smile turned slyly flirtatious. "Or are you maybe referring to something else?"

I raised an eyebrow. Lilly once told me that *sarap nito*, the Tagalog word for "delicious," had a literal translation of "that feels good," which meant it also described sensory delights *beyond* the dining room.

Either my new friend wasn't listening when I warned her about Matt's open marriage and womanizing ways, or, with one look at my muscular, attractive, albeit overly-hairy ex, Lilly decided the best way to persuade the man was with a little flirtation.

I cleared my throat. "Lilly Beth is an expert on delicious things. Her mother, Amina, runs a popular Filipino eatery in Queens. Lilly is also a registered dietician. That's why I hired her. She's consulting with me and our baker on cutting some of the fat and calories out of our popular pastries."

"And I brought some new samples for you and Madame to taste tonight . . . and Matt, too, *since he's here . . .*"

She smiled at him again, very sweetly, which, I had to concede, wasn't exactly hurting the *Sway Matt* campaign.

"Do me a favor, Matteo," she said, pulling a small bakery box out of her tote. "Take a taste of these donut bites. They come in two flavors: cinnamon sugar and pumpkin spice. I've got a low-fat mocha muffin, too, with dreamy chocolate cream cheese filling and chocolate *fooge* frosting . . ." She threw a wink my way.

We all dug in, sampling in silence and glancing at each other with wonder.

"These are really low fat?" I asked, mouth still full.

Lilly Beth nodded. "The donut bites are baked, not fried, and I've cut the fat in the mocha muffins by using skim milk ricotta. The filling is low-fat cream cheese and high-quality cocoa powder."

"What about this chocolate fudge buttercream?" I asked.

Lilly Beth smiled. "No butter."

"You're kidding."

"Melted semisweet chocolate blended with thick, Greek-style yogurt, a little vanilla and a pinch of salt for balanced flavor."

"Okay, these are good," Matt admitted, reaching for another donut bite, "but will this 'healthier' stuff sell?"

I nodded emphatically. "Our Cakelet-and-Cream Sandwiches and 'Healthified' Blueberry Pie Bars are the talk of the foodie blog world. Our truck can't keep them in stock."

"The Nutella-Swirled Banana Muffins and low-fat Strawberry Shortcakes are winners, too," Lilly added. "The customers will enjoy these new donut bites even more. Consider all those moms, Mr. Moms, and nannies out there, pushing strollers on sidewalks, hanging out with their kids in parks and playgrounds. Treats like these are just the right portion size for little ones—without a crazy amount of fat and calories from copious amounts of butter or shortening."

"Be careful, Clare," Matt warned. "You don't want to be labeled the diet food truck."

"You've been in the bush too long, Matt. By law, New York City requires its restaurants to post calorie counts. With federal regulations on their way, much of the food world is paying attention. Almost everyone is searching for ways to add nutritious to delicious—"

"Well, maybe not *everyone*." Lilly Beth jerked a thumb toward the circus outside. "That woman parked in front of my son's school today. She's actually peddling that slow-death monstrosity she calls the Three Little Piggies to children!"

"Three Little Piggies? What? It's got bacon in it?"

"No, that's her Maple-Bacon Cupcake, in which she whips solid bacon grease into butter at the start of the recipe. The Piggies is a giant coconut cupcake stuffed with a mini cheesecake topped by a chocolate-fudge cupcake with whipped cream and a little pink plastic pig on top." Lilly Beth threw up her hands. "There should be a law!"

Matt crossed his arms. "I'm not a big fan of laws, Lilly—not that I'm happy this cupcake truck has planted itself beside our café, but all this woman's peddling is a boatload of sugar and butter, right? As for her bacon grease pastry, I routinely visit parts of the world that use lard in their traditional cooking . . . I mean, it's not like she's lacing her stuff with LSD."

"I'm not suggesting we outlaw guilty pleasures," Lilly clarified. "You and I are adults, and we can make our own informed decisions. But Kaylie's favorite marketing targets are grade schools, and her Three Little Piggies cupcake is deceptive. It looks like an innocent snack, but the thing packs more fat and calories than a double cheeseburger with extra-large fries."

Matt glanced at me. "We aren't selling anything like that, are we?"

"Our portions are standard. We do have decadent pastries but the calories are always posted on our menu, and on our truck, too."

"I said something to Kaylie today," Lilly went on, "caused a big scene in front of Paz's school. I didn't care. I'm on the mayor's Council for Nutrition Awareness now, and I let her know that *and* my feelings about her tactics, *loud and clear*."

Matt's gaze swept across me and Lilly Beth. "So now the Kupcake Kween has a hate on for both the Bobbsey Twins?"

Bobbsey Twins? The remark confused me for a second. But then I realized, sitting side by side, we could have been fraternal twins, if you weren't looking too closely.

For one thing, we were dressed nearly identically this evening—in blue jeans and sleeveless yellow cotton blouses, although mine was a pale polenta and Lilly's more of a lemon curd. We wore our shoulder-length hair in ponytails, too, and from a distance you *could* say the color was dark, even though Lilly's was more of a Spanish roast while mine was closer to Viennese with cinnamon highlights.

True, both of us had complexions on the dusky side, but Lilly's face was nearly a perfect oval while mine was more heart-shaped. Our eyes were different, too: Years ago (*many* of them), Matt once sang about my bright, green "Guinevere" eyes, but Lilly's were much more exotic, it seemed to me, with their liquid dark hue and almond shape.

"Twins . . ." Lilly Beth repeated, glancing at me before winking at Matt. "Is he *trying* to be a bad boy?"

Matt's expression lit up at that. He opened his mouth for a reply, but what he said, I'll never know because his words were swallowed by the sudden surging of Kaylie's fake French menu—

"Fla-*vours* for *vous*! *Chocolat* fooge! *Chocolat* ship . . ."

The volume vibrated our windowpanes and rattled our demitasses. What upset me the most, however, was seeing the reaction of my former mother-in-law.

Through half a century of turbulence and change, Madame had struggled to keep this shop's doors open. She'd sheltered starving artists, sobered up drunken playwrights, and propped up penniless poets. She'd survived a world war and the loss of a beloved husband—the man who's family had birthed this business at the turn of the nineteenth century.

Now she stared with distress at our sidewalk, watching our customers casually leave our café tables to purchase goodies from that preening little vulture.

"Do you want me to go out there and put a stop to this?" Matt asked, beginning to rise.

"No," I said, finding my feet. With a gentle but firm hand, I pressed him back. "Stay."

For nearly two weeks, I had ignored this situation, hoping it would resolve itself, but my conversation with Madame had woken me up to an important aspect of my business partnership with Matteo Allegro.

"This coffeehouse is my responsibility. I'll deal with it."

And her, I silently added. Then I bolted the remains of my espresso and strode toward the door.

THREE

CUTTING the line, I planted myself in front of the Kupcake Kart's service window. "Shut off those speakers."

For more than four decades, my West Village neighborhood—an amalgam of twisting lanes, secluded gardens, quaint bistros, and Federal-style town houses—existed under an umbrella of laws protecting its historical integrity. Generally speaking it was a neon-free zone, a picturesque respite from the city's flash and zoom.

Not tonight.

The kaleidoscopic bulbs encircling Kaylie's truck lit our tranquil café sidewalk with all the subtlety of a pole dancer's stage. Even her front bumper blinked with the glittering LED message: *Squee! I Won!* (This was a reference to the previous year's Vendy Awards, an annual event to honor the street chefs of the city. For that achievement, I couldn't fault her. She took home both the Dessert and Rookie of the Year Cups.)

But the lights were only part of it. Her truck's awful rendition of "La Vie en Rose," punctuated by—"Pea-nut Butt-*tair!* Car-a-mel! Va-nil-*la-la*!"—made me want to dig out my eardrums with a latte spoon.

A bit of jostling occurred inside the truck with my arrival, then Kaylie Crimini's smirking face was in mine. From previous encounters, I put the girl in her late twenties. Tonight, her tight lips and squinty glare more resembled someone entering a bitter and angry middle age. Leaning forward, she gave her head a prissy little shake. Then she made like Marcel Marceau, mutely cupping one ear to indicate she couldn't hear me.

I'd met Kaylie many times in this town. She was a sweetly perfumed, strawberry-glossed shark with a toxic competitive streak. Back in high school, she would have thought herself the most charitable, generous, virtuous person in the entire world—and would have laughed like a hyena when one of her BFFs tripped some awkward, unpopular "weird" kid in the cafeteria.

I, on the other hand, was that quiet "nobody" girl who'd commit social suicide by helping the poor picked-on kid clean up her ruined lunch—while suggesting we hurl the sloppier bits in the general direction of the catty hyenas.

"I *said*, turn that jingle off!"

Now I was resorting to pantomime, slashing my right hand across my throat in the universal signal for *Kill it!* And, yes, I couldn't stop myself from imagining Kaylie's throat in convenient proximity of stainless steel cutlery.

In response to my demand, Kaylie aloofly reached up to adjust the Paris pink paper tiara pinned to her hair, a honey-blond sculpture that resembled a double-dip ice cream cone—or the Mostly Frosting cupcake gracing her sugar-coated menu. The paper tiara was (apparently) her cupcake queen crown. How did I know? It literally read *Kupcake Kween*.

This indifferent act of Kaylie's didn't last, however. The saccharine monarch turned petulant, snapping her fingers at a member of her haughty staff.

A wiry Asian kid with a pink paper hat and Chinese dragon tattoo snaking around his leanly muscled arm glared at me and threw a switch. The jingle ended, bringing down silence like a heavy curtain.

"Can I help you?" Kaylie asked, her pistachio eyes gleaming with superiority. "Perhaps you'd like to sample our new espresso cupcake? We use the very *finest* coffee beans, roasted by Jerry Wang at the Gotham Beanery."

"This parking space is reserved. Move your truck."

Touching a plastic gloved finger to her dimpled chin, she playacted consideration of my demand. "*Nah.* I don't think so. Not when I have *sooo* many customers. Next!" she called to the man behind me.

"No." I said, straight-arming him back. "It's quitting time, Kaylie. I want you and your truck gone. Now."

Before she could answer, a familiar honk startled us all—and I was very glad to hear it.

The Muffin Muse had rolled home. The Blend's boxy food truck was trying to pull into its reserved parking place beside our sidewalk tables, the spot Kaylie had usurped.

From behind the wheel of the diesel-fueled bus, Dante Silva frowned. The shaved-headed, tattooed-armed, fine-art painter was one of the nicest guys you could ever meet—and the *crema* on his espressos was just as sweet as his disposition (as every swooning college coed in the neighborhood could tell you).

Next to Dante sat my Rubenesque goth girl Esther Best (shortened by her grandfather from Bestovasky). A locally renowned slam poetess, Esther was an NYU grad student whose latte art skills were close to national competitive level. I'd promoted her to second assistant manager (partly on the principle that she drew legions of fans to our shop), and she'd proven herself with hard work and bright ideas. More offbeat than Dante, she was far less sweet—a hitch in character that often proved an asset in New York retail.

As horns blared on the wide lanes of Hudson Street, Esther shook a fist. "Get out of our spot!"

Kaylie calmly examined her fingernails. "They're blocking the intersection. That's very dangerous. You'd better tell your people to move along."

Okay, I'm done.

"Listen up, Crimini, unless you want a Three Little Piggies

thousand-dollar repeat-offender summons for playing your jingle while stationary, you'd better move along. Pronto!"

"Don't threaten me—"

"I don't have to threaten," I said, leaning into the precious, rainbow-framed window. "I have a shop full of witnesses to your stupid, childish, *repeated* stunts . . ."

As one of New York's five thousand food-truck vendors, I had received the same consumer affairs paperwork that she had about EPA codes. "So be warned," I said. "The next time I see you in front of my store, I'm not calling 311; I'm walking straight up to the officers of the Sixth Precinct and demanding they send a city tow to confiscate your sorry showboat for *multiple* noise violations."

"You tell her, boss!" Hands on her ample hips, Esther was now standing behind me, providing useful backup (mostly by herding sidewalk customers into our shop).

"Stick it in your demitasse, Cosi," Kaylie shot back. "If your stupid old coffeehouse can't take the heat, then maybe *you'd* better get off the street." The woman's insufferable smirk returned. "See? Your chubby goth barista isn't the only one who can rhyme. So why don't you leave, before you make my customers heave?"

I was about to answer back, but Esther stopped me.

"I got this," she said, stepping forward. (I almost felt sorry for the Kupcake Kween.)

A small gang of spectators closed in. A lean kid in aquamarine spandex stepped out of the pack. I'd seen this young cycling enthusiast in the Blend a few times. He said he practically lived on the Hudson River Greenway, the most heavily used bikeway in the country, with entry points only a few blocks from our Blend.

In a whip-fast move, Cycle Boy pulled out his smart phone camera and hit record. When my "chubby" barista motioned him closer, I knew a worldwide Internet audience was about to be treated to slam poetry, Esther style.

Adjusting her black-framed glasses, she cleared her throat and let it rip—

"Listen up, bouffant brain! Are you listening? *Good!* 'Cause you're not in Kansas. You're in *my* 'hood . . ."

"Woooo!" The crowd cheered.

"Your cupcakes are mealy, your élan is fake, and your infantile jingle gives the world an earache!"

"Uh-ooooh!"

"I may be 'chubby,' yeah, I'm busty, too, and my boyfriend *loves* the way my booty moves . . ."

"Tell her, Esther!"

"You sell the world *pink* with a cheap, plastic smile, but there's no heart in your mart. You got no class, no style. Your frosting, I hear, comes out of a can. And your beans? Sorry, honey, you can't brew worth a dang! So get your buttercream butt *off* my grass, or I'll plant my big black boot in your prissy little—"

Beep! Beeeeeep!

Behind the wheel, Dante had grown impatient and inched our Muffin Muse forward, lightly tapping the Kupcake Kart's rear bumper.

Kaylie instantly shrieked. "He hit us! Did you see that? Did you see! I'm going to call the police, Cosi. The police!"

"Please do," I said. "Advise them to bring a tow truck."

"And don't forget the ER bus," Esther added, tapping her watch, "because in thirty seconds' time, I won't have to rhyme—and you're going to need a boot-ectomy!"

The crowd screamed with laughter.

Inside Kaylie's truck, the young guy with the dragon on his arm glared with pure fury at Esther, then at me. Finally, he tugged Kaylie aside and spoke quietly. Her line of patrons was gone now, most of them gawking and laughing or inside our coffeehouse.

"We'll move," Kaylie declared. Then she bent over the customer counter and lowered her voice. "I've got friends in this town, Cosi—and they know how to back me up. You'll be sorry for messing with me."

"I'll file that information under 'who cares.' Now get lost, Kaylie." Stepping back, I pointed to the empty street ahead of her and channeled my inner NYPD traffic cop. "Okay! Move it! Clear outta here! Now!"

With a clang, Kaylie's window slammed closed, her engine started, and the lumbering truck rolled down the block.

"Chocolate! Oo-la-la . . . Fla-*vours* for *vous . . ."*

As the murmuring crowd melted away, I heard a single pair of hands clapping. Turning, I found Matt standing tall, white teeth grinning through his pirate beard.

"Very impressive. And entertaining, too."

"Yes, admirable job." Madame nodded. She shook her head at the truck's disappearing backside and sniffed, "Gotham Beanery indeed!"

Lilly Beth laughed. "The next time I need that woman exorcised, I'm calling *vous.*"

With a low rumble, our Muffin Muse eased into its berth. Dante cut the engine, which coughed once before blessing us with a wash of exhaust. Esther held her nose. Matt stepped backward. His mother coughed, and Lilly Beth headed back inside the Blend.

"Sorry, guys," Dante said, climbing out of the cab. "I'm still tinkering with the mechanics. I'm sure we'll pass the emissions inspection, though."

"Maybe—if you *bribe* the inspector," Esther cracked.

Dante shook his shaved head and strode into the Blend. "I have some phone calls to make."

Matt frowned at our truck. "It's kind of minimalist, isn't it?"

For once, Matt was putting it mildly. The truck's flat white paint job and stiff block letters identifying the vehicle as the Muffin Muse was not even close to the visual pyrotechnics of Kaylie's Vegas-worthy showboat.

"Don't worry, my boy." Madame winked. "Our *artiste* in residence is giving her a new paint job tomorrow, and when Dante's finished, I'm launching her with a bottle of Laurent-Perrier Grande Siécle!"

"Well, don't whack her too hard, Mother. I'm not sure which will break, the bottle or the truck."

"Oh, pooh. She's a rock. And the interior has been completely refurbished."

"Is that right?" Matt looked over the truck once more. "Okay," he said, turning to me, "how about you show me the inside of our investment?"

"You're willing to keep an open mind?"

"I'm willing to keep listening."

Ten minutes later, we were back on the sidewalk.

"Seems solid," Matt conceded.

"It is."

Madame stepped toward us. "And after tomorrow our Muffin Muse will soon be just as attractive on the outside."

Just then, I noticed Lilly Beth moving through our sidewalk café tables, a Village Blend paper cup in hand.

"Lilly," I called, waving her over, "are you coming to our truck-painting party tomorrow? You should! And bring little Paz. We're serving his favorites."

"I'd love to come, but this is a working weekend for me."

"Something with the mayor's office?"

"No, something else. Remember that high-end spa that I told you about? The one in Hunterdon County?"

"Oh, right. It's pretty out there."

"It is, very pastoral—and the job would be perfect, except that I miss my son. I have to leave Paz with my mother in Jackson Heights, and I can't even call him from the place. The spa has this crazy 'digital detox' rule."

"Digital detox?" Matt laughed. "What is that? Cold turkey for smartphone addicts?"

"Exactly," Lilly said. "No tricknology."

"Tricknology?" He shot me a smile. "Never heard that one before."

"No cells, PDAs, tablets, or laptops allowed," Lilly went on, waving her smartphone with a grin. "Everyone has to surrender them at the front desk until checkout, staff included."

Matt nodded and (predictably) pulled out his own PDA—the very idea of being forced to part with it obviously propelled him into committing to it again. (And, brother, did that sound familiar.)

Lilly glanced at her watch. "I'd better go. I'm heading back to Queens to tuck in Baby Boy. Then I have to catch a commuter bus to Jersey at the crack of dawn."

"Tell Paz I'll save him some Blueberry Pie Bars. And, Lilly—" I surreptitiously tilted my head toward the newly converted Matt. "*Thanks* for stopping by."

"No problem."

Lilly Beth hugged me tight, and with a final wave, she began walking around the side of our big parked truck.

"I like your new friend," Matt said, his gaze still fixed on his text messages.

"I can tell. But don't like her *too much*, okay? That would be weird."

"Weird?" Matt said. "Why?"

"*Because*, Einstein—"

The sudden roar of an engine swallowed my reply. The throaty snarl, like a revving dragster, vibrated loud enough to rattle my being. Then came the squeal of fast-spinning tires.

The next sound I heard was sickeningly familiar—a meaty crunch like the one I'd experienced decades ago (and would never forget) when my pop hit a deer along a dark, country road in Western Pennsylvania.

The grisly smack was followed by Esther Best's bellowing scream.

"Esther! What happened?!"

"Oh, god," she cried, hands clutching head.

My heart raced as I hurried around our parked truck, Matt following. In tandem, we halted.

With one more step, chaos would begin. But for this numbing fragment of time, the planet stopped turning, my limbs went rigid, and my vision tightly narrowed.

The body of my friend, the one who'd laughed with me and held me in a hug, lay crumpled and broken in the middle of the street, the bottom half of her form twisted and twitching.

The scene before me was violent, brutal—yet there was no active brutality to witness. Like a swiftly slicing blade or sudden slash of lightning, whatever had struck here was gone, finished, leaving behind a tableau as disturbing as Picasso's *Guernica*. But this wasn't some still-life depiction of war-torn agonies. This was real.

Struggling to sit, Lilly reached with one arm, as if trying to trying to touch an invisible angel, as if signaling heaven for help.

"Someone hit Lilly Beth!" I shouted, rushing forward as she fell back. "Call 911!"

Four

When I reached my friend, she was lying faceup on the street, still conscious. I dropped to my knees.

"Lilly, can you hear me?"

Her eyes were open and her lips began to move but no sound came out. Then she coughed, foamy blood reddening her lips. "Clare . . ."

"Try not to move."

"I knew it . . ." she said through a moan of pain. "I knew this would happen . . ."

You knew? I stared into her clear, focused eyes. "Did you see the driver coming?"

"No," she said, her voice a rasping wisp. "You don't understand. This had to happen. I deserve this. It's my fault . . ."

"Don't talk," I said.

But Lilly Beth's lips moved again. "My fault . . . my fault . . . my most grievous fault . . ."

The words chilled me. They were not random. Like me, Lilly had been raised a Roman Catholic, and those words invoked the Penitential Rite of the Mass. I could think of only one reason why she'd uttered those words. She wanted Extreme Unction, last rites.

My fast search of the sidewalks yielded no members of the cloth. Desperate to relieve her pain, I began whispering: "Oh my god, I am heartily sorry for having offended Thee . . ."

As I continued, Lilly mouthed the words with me, then her eyelids fluttered, her pupils became unfocused, dulled by pain, and she slipped into merciful unconsciousness. I say merciful because of her ghastly injuries.

Like the canvas of some garish expressionist, her sunny blouse and crisp blue denims were streaked in red—yet I could see no gaping wound, no flowing artery to staunch, only the ghostly draining of her glowing complexion. In the starkness of car headlights, color and warmth seeped out of my friend as if her soul were spilling onto the asphalt.

Traffic idled nearby, its exhaust washing over us, but I didn't care. Pebbles stabbed through my jeans, like little knives, but I didn't move; I just kept on kneeling, kept on praying as I clutched Lilly's bone-cold hand.

About then, my own shakes began, the shudder starting in my hands, moving down my arms and through my entire being. Closing my eyes, I was about to ask for strength when I felt a steadying presence at my shoulder. Looking up, I found the unexpected source—my ex-husband.

Hovering over me, Matt held a tall stack of neatly folded aprons. "To keep her from going into shock," he said.

"Ambulance?" I asked as together we worked to cover Lilly.

"On the way. Don't move her."

"I know. What else?"

"Watch for aspiration. She's on her back. She could choke."

"But if we shouldn't move her—"

"We'll log roll her," he said.

"Log roll?" After decades trekking the wilds of the world, Matt had acquired an Eagle Scout's worth of first aid knowledge. "Tell me how . . ."

Dropping to his knees, he showed me how to stabilize her neck and head. Together we watched and waited. On the sidewalk, Esther frantically barked at passersby—

"We need a doctor! Anyone! How about a nurse?! Come on! I'll take a candy striper, a Girl Scout, a Coney Island lifeguard, for cripes sake!"

Blocks away, a single siren bleated. More howled in reply, and a man in the street started shouting, directing cars toward the curb to give the emergency vehicles room to pass.

With my focus so intense on Lilly Beth, I nearly cried out in surprise when a hand touched my shoulder.

"Let us take care of her, ma'am."

Two navy-shirted members of the fire department's EMS team edged me and Matt out of the way, dropped to the ground beside Lilly, and pulled off the blanket of aprons. Two more arrived with a folding gurney and backboard.

Fists clenched, I continued quietly praying as they attempted to revive her. Another minute passed, and thank god, she finally stirred, opening her eyes.

The paramedics continued their efforts—one starting an IV in Lilly's arm, two more strapping her to the backboard. The trio lifted her onto the waiting gurney and rolled her to the ambulance.

I tried to climb in with Lilly, but the emergency workers shooed me away.

"Can't I go with her? I want to go with her!"

Matt grabbed my arms. "Calm down."

"Let me go."

"Clare, listen to me, your friend is in good hands—and you can't do anything for her at the hospital but pace and wait. If you really want to help Lilly Beth, your chance to do it is over there."

"What are you talking about?"

He pointed to a spot near our sidewalk café tables. Red flashes played across Esther's face. Flanking her were two uniformed police officers.

"Those cops are taking statements," Matt said.

"I know those guys," I said. "They're good customers."

"Come on, let's go over."

I nodded, still feeling numb, until we moved close enough to overhear the cops' pointed questions.

Then my focus came back—*fast.*

Five

"Can't you give me anything more, Ms. Best? You claim you're an eyewitness here."

"It's not a *claim*, it's a fact. I'm an eyewitness, and I told you everything I saw." Esther yanked off her glasses and began frantically rubbing the lenses with the tail of her shirt. "There was a van, no windows. Didn't notice the driver."

She was speaking to Langley, a tall, ruddy-faced officer from the Sixth Precinct. Demetrios, a shorter, swarthier version of his Irish-American partner, was there, too, filling in blanks on an accident report form.

"What about the license number?" Demetrios asked. "Did you see it?"

"Not hardly!" Esther cried. "That idiot was driving like a goth out of Utah!"

On the other side of the street, more navy blue uniforms were either unfurling yellow crime-scene tape or trolling for witnesses. Unfortunately, the bloated crowd had slimmed down faster than a postpartum supermodel. I wasn't surprised.

Accidents birthed excitement and spectacle, but spectating

was easy; getting involved was not—and a statement to the NYPD could lead to depositions, court appearances, and the most irritating of all losses to speed-of-light-moving New Yorkers . . . time.

The Romans had a saying: *Obliti privatorum, publica curate.* Loosely translated, the common good was more important than private matters. But these days, sacrifice with no discernible payoff was an exceedingly rare occurrence.

This unhappy realization made me look with new eyes at my feisty barista. She could very well be the only obliging eyewitness to this crime scene. Langley and Demetrios seemed to have the same thought because the pair began pressing her more zealously for answers. (A reasonable reaction, given the situation. Given what I knew about Esther, however, this was a fairly large mistake.)

"And you didn't notice a thing about the driver?" Langley asked, moving closer.

Esther shifted. "I think I answered that."

"You're sure you can't remember anything on the license plate?" Demetrious pushed, practically in her face. "One letter? One number?"

"Sorry."

"How about the color of the plate? That could tell us what state, at least. Come on, think! New Jersey, New York, Connecticut—"

"Why not Maine or Alaska!" Esther cried. "Toss in all fifty states because I can't tell you that, either!"

For a few seconds, the cops went silent, their expressions defensive—but Esther's hostility had little to do with them. How did I know? Because I knew Esther. Just the other day, she articulated an aspect of her peculiar human condition in an argument with my youngest barista about (of all things) what constituted true love . . .

"It's simple chemistry!" Nancy had claimed between espresso pulls. "Prince Charming comes along. You fall for him. He falls for you. Then you're together *forever.*"

Esther's reply: "Uh, right, Cinderella. Until the divorce."

NANCY: You're too cynical to be in love.

ESTHER: What I am is a realist. One can be in love and a realist. In fact, it's better to be both.

NANCY: I don't know what you're talking about! Aren't you in love with Boris?

ESTHER: Sure, I'm in love with Boris, but I also love him.

NANCY: What's the difference?!

ESTHER: "In love" is a noun—passive. "Loving" is a verb—active. They're distinctive parts of life as well as speech, like the difference between theory and practicum.

NANCY: What-ium?

ESTHER: Practical application. Look, Boris is an assistant baker, right? So he gets up for work at an ungodly hour. I closed here last night and got in way late. Stupid me turned on the bathroom radio without checking the volume. It blasted so loud, it woke him up—and I became so angry at myself for messing up his REM sleep that I yelled at *him* for leaving the volume up when he turned the thing off. He didn't yell back. He knew better. He knew me. Just told me to come to bed so we could cuddle. That's it. That's love. Now do you get it?

NANCY: You're very odd, you know that?

ESTHER: I take that as a compliment . . .

Esther *was* odd. She was also clever, funny, fearless—and relatively easy to understand, if you took the time to know (or love) her.

This hit-and-run had shaken us all up. Emotions were high and Esther was frustrated with herself, angry that she couldn't give these cops more to go on. Those feelings were so overwhelming that they sloshed over her rim and onto anyone in the vicinity.

Unfortunately, neither Langley nor Demetrios was her boyfriend, and I didn't expect them to treat Esther's personality issues as anything more than the raw anger of an uncooperative witness. (Not the best position to be in with men wearing badges and gun belts.)

"You know what, miss?" Demetrios said. "Your attitude isn't very helpful."

"*My* attitude? What about yours!"

"What about mine?"

"We're just doing our job, you know."

"Don't get pissy with me! My attitude didn't run anyone down!"

Langley turned to his partner. "What do you think here? Sounds like she'd rather talk at the precinct."

Oh, god, here it comes . . .

"Yeah, five or six hours in an interview room might calm her down enough to give a simple statement—"

"Excuse me, Officers . . ." I stepped up. "I think I can help."

An awkward silence ensued, which was better than an argument (or a de facto arrest), so at least we were heading in the right direction.

"Do you have a statement, Ms. Cosi?" Langley asked tightly.

"I do, but give me a minute first."

"You need to use the Ladies'?"

"No." I turned to face Esther.

My barista stood stiffer than a cinnamon stick, her folded arms locked into place. There was no way (*no way!*) her memory would be of any help in this state.

I took a deep breath, put a hand on her shoulder, and channeled my Mike—Detective Mike Quinn, probably the best interviewer in the NYPD.

"Esther," I said quietly, "I'd like you to close your eyes."

"Close my eyes!"

"Do it for me, okay . . . and for Lilly Beth."

She sighed but closed them.

"I want you to relax. Got that? *Relax* . . . take a deep breath. Good. Let it out. Very good . . ."

Demetrios and Langley exchanged wary glances, but (thank goodness) gave me some latitude.

"Focus on my voice, Esther. Nothing else. There's nothing to work at here. Just relax. You're just going to play back a few images in your head, that's all. Can you do that for me?"

Esther nodded. "I'll try."

"You saw a van hit Lilly Beth, right?"

"That's right. A van with no windows . . ."

"Now I want you to play back the impact in your mind, as if you were viewing a video recording. Can you see it?

"I see it."

"What color was the van?"

"White . . . sort of . . ."

Sort of, I thought, *what does that mean?* I took a guess. "Was the van dirty?"

"Yes! Definitely. The roof was more gray than white, and there was a lot of dried pigeon crap up there."

"Good, that's good . . ." I noticed Langley and Demetrios scribbling.

"Lots of vans on these streets are commercial vehicles," I reminded her. "Were there any markings on the van's side? Play back the impact. Do you see any company logos, any writing?"

"No logos . . . There *was* something in writing . . . but I couldn't read it!"

"It's okay, Esther, you're doing fine . . . just try to tell me what *color* the letters were."

"Black. They were black and thick and ugly . . . but that doesn't make sense! Why would someone put that on a commercial van?"

"Don't try to think about what makes sense, just play back the image, the point of impact . . . can you see the shape of any of the letters?"

"I think one was a *C* . . . Hey, wait! The letters were spray painted on. The writing was graffiti!"

When she finished describing the markings, Esther opened her eyes to find two *much* happier cops.

Demetrios cleared his throat. He had one more question for her; the most important one: "Ms. Best, if you saw this van again, do you think you could identify it?"

"Yes," Esther said, nodding vigorously. "For sure!"

Demetrios addressed his partner. "I'll get a BOLO out on this description."

"Good," said Langley, and Demetrios dashed off toward his squad car.

"What about you, Ms. Cosi?" Langley asked. "Did you see the vehicle? Any part of the plate?"

"No, I didn't see those things. But I did witness something that I think may help."

"You got a glimpse of the driver?" Langley asked, hopefully.

"No. Like said, I didn't *see* anything. I *heard* it."

Langley cocked his head. "You heard it . . ."

"Yes, the vehicle's engine noise was distinctive. Very loud, like drag racers sound when they gun their hot rods. I heard it when Lilly moved beyond our Muffin Muse truck to step into the street—"

"Go on," Langley said, taking notes.

"I heard tires squeal, too."

Langley nodded. "The driver was probably trying to brake—"

"No," I said firmly. "The squealing tires came after the engine was gunned. That was a few seconds before I heard a thump and Esther's scream."

"What happened next?"

"That's when I saw Lilly Beth, lying there—" I pointed to the spot on the street where I'd been kneeling.

"So you didn't actually *see* this dirty, white windowless van that Ms. Best described, or any other vehicle that seemed to be fleeing the scene?"

"Like I said, my view was blocked, and then my attention was on Lilly Beth."

Demetrios was back now. "Anyone else a witness?" he called loudly.

Across the street, more officers from the Sixth were hunting for pedestrian statements and finding few. One was speaking with a longtime Blend customer, who was shaking his head and shrugging.

"What about you?" Langley asked, pointing his pen at Matt. "See anything?"

Matt immediately tensed. "Our truck blocked my view of the accident, which means it did for all of our customers behind me."

"Okay, did you *hear* anything?"

"Sorry. I was reading text messages. Wasn't paying attention."

Langley noticed Madame, who'd moved to stand rigidly by her son. "Is he right, ma'am? Did the truck block your view?"

Madame's lips pursed. "Yes, young man. I didn't see a thing, either. But I should have!"

I touched Matt's arm. "Your mother needs to calm down."

I could see she was upset; more than that, she was furious, spitting mad. Lilly Beth had been run down like a dog, the cowardly driver speeding away, and it had happened right in front of her. Yet there was nothing she could do to help.

"Settle her at the coffee bar and make her a steamer, okay?" I whispered.

Matt nodded. "Good idea . . ." Gently taking his mother's arm, he tightly addressed the young cops. "Excuse us."

No fan of the police, I knew my ex was relieved to go. Langley let him escape; I was another story. "We'll need you to stick around, Ms. Cosi."

"Fine."

Just then, a dusky-skinned Latino patrolman, one I didn't recognize, approached Langley from behind and gripped the officer's shoulder.

"Bad news," he said. "We got some major myopia on the street tonight."

"C'mon, Perez, nothing?" Langley said.

"No statements?" Demetrios pressed.

"Nothing worth anything," Perez replied. "And, I thought you two should know, the motor heads are here."

Langley frowned. "They called AIS?"

"Yeah, and fair warning. The crash team's Max Buckman and his guys."

Langley sighed, glanced up and down the street.

Demetrios elbowed his partner. "What happened to the luck of the Irish?"

Perez flashed a reassuring grin, one that exposed a gold tooth. "Relax, you two. Street's closed to traffic; cars and pedestrians are rerouted and the accident scene is secured. All by the book. And as first officers on the scene, *you* can take the credit."

"And the blame, too. We're talking Mad Max here—and his Death Race Gang."

"Yeah, good luck with that."

I tapped Langley's shoulder. "Excuse me but what exactly is AIS?" (In my years of friendship with Mike Quinn, I'd gotten used to alphabet soup where the NYPD was concerned, but I drew a blank on those letters.)

"AIS," Langley repeated. "Accident Investigation Squad."

"Oh . . ." A new one for me, but then the NYPD had enough bureaus, units, and squads to police a small Balkan country. "I take it this cop, this *Buckman* . . . he's a hard case?"

Perez grunted a laugh.

"Hard case," Langley repeated. "Now that's a polite way of putting it."

"What do you mean?"

Demetrios exhaled. "The guy's an a-hole, Ms. Cosi. Excuse my French."

"I've heard worse . . ." I told him. (Usually from Matt, *in* French.) "But since I have to deal with this person, can you be a little more specific?"

"Specific?" Langley said. "You need us to define a-hole?"

"Give me something I can use."

Demetrios rubbed the back of his neck. "He's not fond of females."

"In the Biblical sense?"

"No, he'll sleep with them. He just doesn't like them."

The reek of cigar smoke hit us about then. It grew stronger and more noxious until I had a flashback to the exhaust fumes I'd inhaled at tire level while kneeling in the street.

I looked around and finally spotted the tailpipe. The cigar-smoker was a bear of a man standing half in darkness, ironically right beside a police van towing a floodlight unit. He wore plain clothes—black slacks and a blue nylon jacket. The men gathered around him, however, were very much in uniform.

Wheel emblems on their shoulder patches told me they were highway patrol, and they were likely good officers. But at this time of night, their belted leather jackets, motorcycle boots, and military-esque riding breeches gave me the distinct feeling they were plotting to invade Poland.

I turned to Demetrios. "Cigar Guy over there. Is that Buckman?"

"That's him."

Almost immediately, Buckman noticed my gaze on him. He replied in kind, drawing on his stogie as he looked me over. A few moments later, he strode toward us. I firmed up my stance in the shadows of the sidewalk, bracing for the almost palpable force of such a sizeable figure coming at me.

Clearly, this AIS detective was about to become this case's lead investigator. That much I understood. What I didn't yet realize was how quickly "Mad Max" Buckman would become my biggest annoyance—and my best ally.

Six

"Okay, what do you have for me?" Buckman asked, smoldering cigar wagging in his mouth.

Blinking against the tobacco haze, I waited for Langley or Demetrios to answer. Buckman waited, too.

"Ladies!" he finally bellowed. "I asked you a question!"

As I literally flinched, the two young officers exchanged anxious glances. Each had been assuming the other would reply. Now they both blurted out—

"Hit-and-run!"

"That much I know, morons. What else?"

Langley cleared his throat. "A white van, Detective. Possibly the result of a drag race."

Buckman's eyebrow rose at that. So did mine.

Where was Langley getting *the result of a drag race*, for goodness' sake? I hadn't said that! Ready to complain, I opened my mouth, but held my tongue instead. Buckman would get around to me soon enough. No need to embarrass a loyal customer in front of his superior.

"Is that the traffic template under your arm?" Buckman asked, thrusting his hand at Langley. "Give it here."

As Buckman rifled through the template and accident report, I tried to get a handle on him. I gauged his age as fifty, maybe older. He had a hawkish nose, pronounced chin, and smoke gray eyes that stared so intently they appeared to bulge. His dark brows were heavy, his skin craggy from wear, and his hair chopped down to a crew cut.

His was not the fashionable kind of flattop that actors in my neighborhood gel molded into trendy spikes. Buckman's bristles had marine boot camp written all over them, that or the police academy barber. In fact, after one minute in the man's presence, I got the distinct impression that he'd received this cut at the age of twenty and, in thirty years, saw no point in changing it.

His hair color had changed, however. Though his eyebrows were black, Buckman's head had gone salt-and-pepper, save the temple patches, which were completely white. The resulting pattern on both sides of his skull reminded me of a hot rod's detailing.

Maybe cars were too much on my mind that night—or maybe the guy had swapped out his cardiovascular system for internal combustion and that stinky cigar really was a tailpipe.

"A van?" he barked at last, stabbing the clipboard where Langley had written the offending word. "What kind of *van* are we talking about here? A BMW? Some sort of pricey sport-utility vehicle? Got to be, if it was drag racing. This white van crap doesn't make sense."

"But it *wasn't* an SUV!" Esther insisted, stepping forward. "It was an ordinary van. The kind you see on the street every day. Like the vans that deliver groceries or service food trucks."

Buckman's head swung. "You're talking about an express cargo van?"

Esther shrugged. "If that's what you call it, yes."

Buckman squinted. "Who the hell drag races in an express cargo van?"

"I only wrote down what the witness reported," Langley replied. "It was Ms. Cosi here who said it was a drag race."

Here we go. "I'm sorry," I said as gently as I could, "but I didn't claim there was a drag race. I heard one vehicle and the sound of the engine was distinctive, *like* a hot rod drag racing."

For an endless moment, Buckman's gaze looked me up and down. This was a cop evaluation I knew well. The man was assessing my age, race, socioeconomic level, and my use (and value) as a witness, but most of all, my veracity.

Folding my arms, I stared back.

"So you heard a hot rod?" he finally asked.

"I grew up in a factory town. Motor heads on my block were under their hoods daily, and the muscle car engines echoed up through the valleys nightly."

"Okay, Ms. Cosi, tell me more about what you think you heard. Take your time and be as specific as humanly possible."

"The sound was rumbling and very loud," I said. "Much noisier than a normal van. The driver gunned the motor, too, and made the tires squeal just a few seconds before he struck my friend."

At the words "my friend," Buckman blinked. He glanced at the report again then back at me, and I got the distinct impression he was digesting an important fact: The victim in this case was not some anonymous pedestrian to me, but someone I knew well; a woman I cared about.

My ponytail had come loose and, in that moment, my hair scrunchy slipped off my shoulder and fell to the pavement. Stooping to pick it up, I noticed my jeans were streaked with road dirt, my polenta-yellow blouse stained. Tears had dried on my cheeks, and (embarrassingly) my nose was running. As I straightened up, I swiped my face with the tail of my shirt.

A pristine white hanky was suddenly dangling in front of me. With surprise, I realized Buckman was offering it.

"You okay?" His voice was different, the hard edge noticeably blunted.

I nodded, taking the hanky.

"Stay put, Ms. Cosi. I'll be back . . ."

As Buckman moved off the sidewalk, he waved over a

highway patrolman, removed his nylon jacket and gave it over. For the first time, I realized the detective was toting enough hardware to open a small machine shop. Webbed straps crisscrossed his chest like the bandoliers of an outlaw in some spaghetti Western. Instead of bullets, these straps anchored a set of tools—a small hammer, a monkey wrench, and a bevy of devices I couldn't identify.

Our entire side street and two full blocks of Hudson had been sealed off by sector cars parked on either end, but the roadway was not empty. Four plainclothes detectives, wearing the same type of gear as Buckman, had started prowling the pavement.

This, I assumed, was Mad Max Buckman's "Death Race Gang"—though the label was misleading. The bespectacled quartet looked more like professors of engineering than anything else.

With somber intensity, three of the investigators moved their flashlight beams along the street. Every so often, a man would stop, drop to one knee, and mark an area of asphalt with reflective tape. The fourth man—short of stature with a baby face behind wire rims—traveled between each marker, pushing a yellow plastic box on a long handle at the end of which were two small rubber wheels. He reminded me of Joy at age five, playing with her toy lawnmower.

Buckman watched his team work and then called them together. They spoke, they nodded, they pointed. Finally, Buckman left them and headed to our sidewalk post once more.

"You!" He waved his cigar in my direction.

"Me?" I asked.

His gray eyes locked on mine. "Yeah, *you* . . . follow me." As he began to move, he threw a comment to Langley. "The rest of the witnesses can go."

"But Detective . . ." Langley protested, pointing to Esther. "The young lady here. She actually saw the vehicle."

Esther arched an eyebrow. "Young *lady*?"

Buckman halted. "Listen, sonny, what Ms. Best saw was

likely a Chevrolet Express Cargo, either a 1500, 2500, or 3500 version with a model year anywhere between 1996 to 2011. If that sounds helpful to you, then let me add that there are about twenty-nine thousand of these vehicles registered in the Borough of Manhattan alone. I know because half of them were sold by Billy and Ray Klein, off their lot on Northern Boulevard—and I'm not even counting the nearly identical Ford Econolines roaming the five boroughs, not to mention all the little Asian knockoffs."

Esther put a hand on her hip. "Okay, Mr. Car Talk, so maybe I don't know the make and model, but I can still identify this van. There was black graffiti painted on the side, bird poop on the roof, and—"

"And all of that is stated in your report," Buckman said, cutting her off. "We thank you for that, and be assured that your eyewitness account will aid us in tracking down this vehicle. *However* . . . what you saw doesn't begin to tell me the complete truth of what went down here."

"So how do you expect to find that out?"

"With my *ear*-witness," Buckman said, his gaze locking with mine once more. "Ms. Clare Cosi."

Seven

"Follow me."

Without waiting, Buckman strode from the gloom of the sidewalk into the empty street, now an arena of dazzling brightness, thanks to the newly arrived crime-scene floodlights.

As I entered the center spotlight of this eerie play, I felt countless eyes on me. Were they the highway patrol? Buckman's Death Race Gang? Local media? In the face of the tiny suns, I couldn't be sure. All I could make out were vague silhouettes and a murmuring buzz, like a Broadway audience anticipating the curtain lifting.

Buckman moved to the spot on the pavement where I'd cradled Lilly Beth. Tape now marked a crude approximation of a human form. He halted abruptly and turned. I swallowed, bracing myself once more.

"Those sounds you heard interest me, Ms. Cosi."

"So you said."

"I want you to ponder my next question carefully."

"I'll try."

He rubbed his prominent chin. "Do you think maybe

you heard a car fitted with a full intake system and a high-performance exhaust package? There's a lot of that going around. Or could you have heard a real racer, some hot dog with a small block Chevy 454 under the hood? That makes a real distinctive sound . . . you'd know it if you listened to it again. Or is it possible that all you heard was an exhaust popper?"

I blinked. "Sorry, Detective Buckman. I don't speak automotive lingo, not to that extent."

Buckman chewed on the cigar, expended a blue cloud. "Doesn't matter . . . because I really doubt you heard any of those things."

"Okay, what did I hear then?"

"My guess? A piece of crap cargo van with a missing muffler."

"A missing muffler—" *Of course.* Now it seemed obvious. That guttural sound had been so powerful that it reverberated through my body like the muscle cars from my less-than-glamorous youth. That's why I'd assumed it was a racing engine.

"I'm sure you're right," I told him. "So why do you need me out here?"

"Because . . ." Buckman touched his ear with an index finger. "I want to know exactly what you heard—"

"But you solved it. Given Esther's eyewitness account. What I heard must have been a missing muffler—"

"Allow me to finish, honey." A hint of a smile touched his craggy cheeks. "I want to know what you heard and the order in which you heard it. Humor me. The proper sequence is important."

I took a breath. "Okay, I'll do whatever I can to help—and please call me *Clare.*"

"Sure, Clare. You can call me Detective Buckman."

Looking down at the pavement, he began moving in a slow circle. When he was finished, he said, "Tell me, Clare: Do you see any skid marks here? Any rubber on the road?"

I shook my head. "No."

"Yeah, me neither. Just a lot of surface oil . . ."

"I don't understand—"

"Bear with me. We're going to play a round of Highway Houdini."

"Excuse me?"

He moved closer. "Trust me, Clare. Can you do that?"

"I'll try."

"Good. Now first I want you to close your eyes—"

Oh, brother, did this sound familiar. Obviously Buckman was utilizing the same interviewing technique that I'd learned from Mike. But that realization didn't make me any more comfortable.

"I'm sorry," I said, "but can't I do this with my eyes open?"

"You heard the perp's vehicle, right?"

"Right."

"You didn't *see* it."

"No."

"So why do you need those pretty green eyes of yours in order to remember?"

Buckman's bullhorn bark melted into something soothing and coaxing. I shifted in place, preferring the bellow.

"Clare? Do you want to close this case?"

"Yes."

"Then *close your eyes.*"

I exhaled and complied. Within seconds, the buzzing murmur from the darkness seemed to recede. Was I imagining it? Or was my shadow audience falling silent so they could listen, too?

"Relax, okay? Try to empty your mind. Can you do that for me?" Buckman purred, a little too close to my ear. "Forget your worries . . . forget that you're annoyed with me . . ." He chuckled low at that one. "Just let go of all conscious thoughts . . . let them slip away . . ."

Feeling silly, I pretended to give it a go, although I kept watch on this exasperating man through my eyelashes. He went patiently silent for a good two minutes—and eventually I felt my breathing slowing, my limbs relaxing.

"Okay, now, let's drift back to the moments leading up to the accident . . ."

As he spoke, my eyes shut tighter and, amazingly, my mind was able to move backward to those horrifying moments.

"Now I don't want you to analyze or interpret . . . I don't want you to think at all . . . I just want you to tell me what you heard. Just tell me what your ears took in. Let's start with the very first sound you remember . . ."

Slowly, carefully, I repeated the details of the accident in the order I remembered them. Eyes shut tight, I recited events all the way up to Lilly gasping out what might be her final words . . . that she thought she deserved what happened to her.

When I finished, I felt satisfied that I'd provided accurate testimony, and with a deep breath I opened my eyes—only to discover the fact that three highway patrol officers and two crash team detectives had joined Buckman.

As soon as the men saw that I was finished, they broke out in applause. Buckman extended his arm and dipped in a theatrical bow.

"Are you people sick?!" I cried. "Is this horrible event some kind of a joke to you?!"

"On the contrary." Buckman yanked a small digital recorder from his tool belt and played a few of my own words back to me.

"You perfectly described the accident as we pieced it together in our preliminary. You *also* perfectly corroborated your own statement, as given to officers Langley and Demetrios."

He tucked the recorder back into its pocket. "By god, honey, I only wish half the people who witnessed traffic events *saw* as much as you managed to hear. You're the perfect witness for us: sharp, candid, principled. Any jury would love you."

"She's easy on the eyes, too, Max," said one of the detectives. The other men chuckled.

I folded my arms. "Are you being serious?"

Smoke formed a blue halo around Buckman's flattop. "Serious as cancer."

"I'm glad," I said, "because I know that you and your guys are referred to as the Death Race Gang. Somehow I doubt it's because of your killer charm."

"Funny, Clare . . . your *point?*"

"Your people are combing this area with more single-mindedness than gold rush prospectors. What exactly are you looking for? How are you going to use it to bring the driver to justice? And what about that van? How do you plan to locate it?"

"You ask a lot of questions for a witness."

"Well, the victim was my friend—so let's just say I care. Some of my best customers are cops, too, so let's *also* say that asking questions about police cases has become an occupational hobby."

Buckman chewed his cigar. "All right, fine . . . stay close to me then. You still may be able to help us, and you might learn a thing or two."

Eight

Buckman didn't waste any time. Waving over one of his guys, he took possession of that strange yellow tool—the one that reminded me of a toy lawnmower. After aligning its little rubber wheels with the reflective tape on the ground, he flicked a switch on the handle and walked off, moving at a brisk pace.

"You're measuring distance, right?" I asked, hurrying to catch him.

"Precisely. This little number is a Rolatape. It's like a tape measure, but more accurate."

We stopped after twenty feet, in front of the third and fourth members of Buckman's team. Gaunt and intense with thick owlish glasses, the standing man tinkered with a small flying-saucer-like object mounted on a tripod.

"The impact came right about here," Owl Man said without looking up. "The victim was carried, dragged, or thrown the rest of the way. You saw where she ended up."

Buckman chewed his cigar. "Any skid marks around?"

"The brakes were never even tapped. Maybe the laser shots and infrared will show something else, but *lo dudo*."

The stogie in Buckman's mouth wiggled again, and I couldn't stop my mind from sketching his caricature with that cigar as a smoking piston, moving at the behest of the whirring gears in the man's flattop head.

"There are some fresh tire marks back there," the fourth detective offered. Kneeling on the ground, he jerked his bald head in the direction of Canal Street.

"How about the victim's clothes?"

"Secured," said the bald man, "and I counted three sidewalk surveillance cameras along this block. Any one of them might help us out—took down the names and addresses of their businesses."

Owl Man finished adjusting the tripod and grunted, satisfied.

"We're going to need those recordings and the results of this TLS, too," the bald man noted, rising.

(TLS? More alphabet soup . . .) "Excuse me, but what's a—"

"Terrestrial Laser Scanning," Buckman replied, lifting his chin in the direction of the tripod. "We're trying to re-create the accident using 3D scanning technology. Great for convictions. This device cuts through all the crap the slip-and-fall club dishes up in the courtroom."

"What sort of crap are you referring to?"

"Oh, like when a drunk or criminally reckless driver claims an accident was caused by road debris, or a pothole, or poor line of sight, or a defective traffic light, or a flutter from the wings of a butterfly."

"Yeah," Owl Man added. "Or when they give us a song and dance about how their gas pedal stuck, or they tried to brake but the car just skidded anyway."

Buckman nodded. "This scanner, and Bernie here, will limit that sort of bullshit defense—pardon my language."

"Your language is the least of my concerns right now—and thanks for the explanation."

"You're welcome. Let's go."

Buckman took off again. We stopped in front of two long strips of reflective tape on the pavement. Another officer in a nylon jacket was taking pictures with a conventional camera.

"There, Clare. There's your gunning engine and your squealing tires," Buckman said, turning off his Rolatape and hoisting it over his shoulder. I followed his gaze and saw vague black smears on the rutted roadway.

"The sucker slammed on the gas and laid a lot of rubber before the cargo van got up enough gumption to move from this spot. Then the vehicle went from zero to whatever just as fast as the muffler-less hunk of crap could go."

I studied the ground, trying to discern the tea leaves Buckman was using to get this story.

"Do you think this was deliberate?" I asked. "Remember what I told you when my eyes were closed? About what Lilly Beth said before she slipped away. She said she needed forgiveness . . . that she deserved what happened. Maybe someone else agreed . . ."

Buckman rubbed the back of his neck. "I understand what you heard, Clare, but I wouldn't put much stock in what any person says at a moment like that. One time, I pulled this guy out of a burning car. All he could do was cuss out his business partner, and I mean he really cussed the guy out. All the time we waited for the ambulance, all the way to the damn burn unit. I thought they'd just had a fight, you know, something that led up to the wreck, maybe. Turned out the business partner was dead twenty years, and the vic had suffered a brain injury on top of the burns . . ."

"I know what you're saying, but this was different."

"Mentally your friend could have been back in Miss Crabtree's third grade class, where she pinched a candy bar."

I didn't dispute him—not then. This was his job, and he seemed strangely good at it, despite some eccentric behavior.

"How fast was the driver going?" I asked.

"Hard to say. We'll know better after we crunch the numbers and get a report from the hospital about the nature of the victim's injuries. By the way, how well did you know Ms. Tanga?"

"When you talk about my friend, Detective, stick to the present tense—or you're going to piss me off."

For a fleeting moment, a new expression crossed Buckman's face, something between surprise and respect. "Okay, Clare. Deal."

"To answer your question: I've only known Lilly Beth for a few months, but as we started working together, we became pretty fast friends."

"She's in the coffee business, too?"

"No. She used to work as a registered nurse but switched tracks to become a dietician. I hired her for freelance consulting work, advice on cutting the fat and calories on some of my menu items, that sort of thing."

"Does she have other clients?"

"She mentioned a spa in Hunterdon County."

"What does she do for them?"

"Cooking and nutrition classes . . . and she also started working for the mayor's office, a special projects initiative, helping the city's kids eat healthier. She has one of her own, a son . . . his name is Paz . . ."

"Ms. Tanga is a single mother then? There's no husband? No boyfriend?"

A lump formed in my throat and the floodlights blurred. The question made me think of that adorable little boy. Was he going to become an orphan now?

"Ms. Cosi?" Buckman prompted.

"Yes, Lilly is a single mother." I swiped at my eyes. "She lost her husband when she was still pregnant with their son. He was a U.S. Coast Guard paramedic. Benny Tanga was his name. He died in a rescue attempt off the coast of New Jersey. Helicopter crash . . ."

Buckman paused, taking that in. "Tough break."

"I know."

"Current or past boyfriends?"

"She doesn't have one now—none that she's mentioned to me. As far as past relationships, I can't help you there, either. You should speak with Terry Simone. She's a customer of ours—and she's known Lilly much longer than I have. The two met in nursing school."

Buckman scribbled the name. "Where does Ms. Simone work?"

"Beth Israel. I also know Lilly and her son live with Lilly's mother, Amina Salaysay. She owns and runs Amina's Kitchenette in Woodside, Queens. She should be notified."

"It's all right. We'll do that."

"I can't think of anything else to tell you. There must be something more I can help with . . ." I couldn't stop myself from becoming emotional again, but I felt so powerless.

"Take it easy, Clare. You've given us plenty." Buckman paused a moment then suddenly asked—"What cops?"

"Excuse me?"

"You said some of your best customers were cops."

"That's right . . ." I couldn't tell if he was genuinely interested or simply trying to derail my tears with a distraction. Whichever it was didn't matter. I pulled myself together and focused on his question.

"So who are they? Maybe I know these cops."

"Do you know Sergeant Emmanuel Franco?"

"Franco!" Buckman guffawed. "What a goofball. I wouldn't have thought a hump like that would be your type."

"Actually, that 'hump' is more my daughter's type."

"My sympathies," Buckman said, then shook his head as if I'd just told him I'd bought the Brooklyn Bridge on eBay.

"I'm also friendly with Lori Soles and Sue Ellen Bass."

Buckman smirked. "Didn't think you were their type, either."

"What's that supposed to mean?"

"Nothing. I'm kidding." Then Buckman pointed to the Claddagh ring on my finger. "That's not a wedding band."

"No, it's from another cop—but he's more than a friendly customer."

"Okay, now I'm getting something useful. Where is he on the job?"

"He heads his own task force out of the Sixth. His name is Mike Quinn."

"Crazy Quinn?"

Crazy Quinn? That doesn't sound like my Mike. "You must mean some other Quinn."

"Michael Ryan Francis Quinn, right?"

"Yes, but . . . he's far from crazy."

"Believe me, honey, back in the day, the PD knew him as *Crazy Quinn.* A real rogue, that guy."

"Well, that's not the Mike Quinn I know."

"Maybe he got tamer after he got clear of that underwear model wife of his. Nothing like a lying, cheating female to make a man want to take crazy chances—or spit bullets." Buckman paused. "You and Quinn, huh? Well, I guess apples don't fall far from the tree."

"What's that supposed to mean?"

"You said your daughter's friendly with Franco, didn't you?"

"Listen, Detective, we're *way* off topic here, and I'd like to know what's going to happen with Lilly's case. Do you at least have a theory?"

"I'll tell you what I have . . ." He took a final hit on his stogie. "Someone behind the wheel of a white express cargo van, model and license yet to be determined, turned the key and goosed the engine. The driver then came down on the gas pedal, hard enough to spin the wheels, right here . . ." He pointed to the blocked-off section of pavement. "No brakes were ever applied as the vehicle increased speed, proceeding up Hudson and striking your friend, Ms. Lilly Beth Tanga."

Buckman paused at that, tearing the stump from his mouth. With his thumb and forefinger, he squeezed it hard until the tip was cold and whipped the stub forcefully down a nearby sewer grate.

"In other words, Clare, someone turned a simple service vehicle into a deadly weapon."

"You're saying someone hit Lilly, *on purpose?* As in attempted murder?"

"The facts are what I recited to you. A hit-and-run occurred, one of about three hundred in the city this year. Whether it was deliberate, a tragic accident, or the result of drugs or alcohol abuse, I can't tell you, not yet. And no 'theory' is going to interest me, not until all the data accumulated from this crime scene has been fully evaluated."

"When will that happen?"

"Brutally honest? Not until we find the van."

"But what if you don't? It's like hunting a needle in a haystack, you said so yourself."

"We have some solid clues to go on. The graffiti on the side of the truck could be a gang marker. Gang markers are very specific to a place and even a time—"

"So you might know where the van's been, or where it came from. That's good!" I couldn't hide my hope. "That means you'll find it, right?"

"We'll try."

"I want you to do more than try, Detective. And if there's anything else I can do to support you and your team, let me know."

That's when he handed me his card. "My mobile phone number's on there. Call me whenever you like. I mean it. Anytime."

"Thank you."

"You're welcome." He studied me a moment. "You okay then?"

"I will be . . . after you catch this bastard."

With those words, Buckman's dour expression lessened enough to bestow a shining half smile of approval my way. Then he turned and strode off, his substantial silhouette vanishing in the floodlights.

Nine

I wanted Mike. That's all I could think as I numbly moved through the next few hours. I ached for the reassurance in his voice, the strength in his spirit, the affection in his gaze. I wanted him to take me to bed, cover me with his body, and ease me into a deep, forgetful sleep.

But Mike Quinn was scheduled to sleep on another mattress tonight, one with cold, stiff sheets and nightly turndown service. I wouldn't be hearing his voice until I was ready to turn down my own covers.

In the interim, I checked on Lilly.

First I dialed the hospital. Lilly was "in surgery" I was told (and little else), so I phoned Lilly's longtime friend, Terry Simone, who immediately volunteered to contact Lilly's mother as well as Beth Israel. (As an RN on staff, she was likely to excavate more information than I could.)

In the meantime, my own Village Blend still had paying customers—and nonpaying, too, because I'd asked Nancy to deliver coffee to Buckman and his team. Esther was willing to help, but she looked so tired and shaky that I put her in a taxi.

About then, Matt came to my rescue.

After escorting his mother back to her Fifth Avenue digs, he returned to the shop to lend his experienced hands and much-needed vigor. Then I sent Nancy home, and Matt sent me upstairs.

A long shower revived me, and I considered hitting the sack. But the chilly duplex felt too lonely, and my nerves were too raw for sleep. So I stepped into clean jeans, pulled on a long-sleeved T-shirt, and went back downstairs.

MATT had kindled a fire in our shop's brick hearth, and I was glad to see it. The night breeze off the Hudson had grown colder, and the crackling flames warmed my skin and spirit.

When it was time to close, we cleaned and restocked, secured the outdoor tables, and bid the last of our customers good night. Then I locked the entrance, dimmed the lights, and shut our wall of French doors tighter than a Gallic fortress.

Now Matt and I were alone in the coffeehouse, just like the old days. He waved me over to the espresso bar, and I weaved through the tables and chairs of our darkened shop.

Suddenly I couldn't stop appreciating how sturdy the Blend's wood planks felt beneath me, how vivid the flickering firelight appeared, how darkly sweet the shop's beans smelled.

When Death rattles your windows, jams a foot in your door, something cracks you open. Colors seem brighter, angles sharper, noises louder. Quinn attributed this sort of thing to adrenaline. But he was a street-hardened detective. With me it was something more.

As I settled on a stool, Matt slid a cream-colored demitasse across the polished blue marble with an expression so agonized it made me choke up.

Taking a long sip of the *doppio*, I closed my eyes. A heated tear slid down my cold cheek. At nearly the same moment, the caramel-chocolate notes of the espresso double flowed through me like molten lava down an arctic cliff.

Fire and ice, I thought, *summer and winter, day and night, life and death.* The alliance of opposites was an elemental part of human existence. Even a simple cup of coffee was both calming and bracing—*not unlike my relationship with Matt,* I couldn't help musing.

The odd Detective Buckman was an equally apt comparison with his "Highway Houdini" voice, a purr so ironically pushy in its mission to pacify that I could still hear his words echoing through my stressed-out system.

"Relax, Clare . . . relax . . ."

"This thing with Lilly Beth . . ." Matt interrupted.

My eyes shut tighter. "It's horrible."

"I travel in countries where stop signs are treated like suggestions, but I've never seen a pedestrian run down in the street like Lilly was tonight. What a god-awful accident."

I opened my eyes. "Except it wasn't."

"What?"

"He said it wasn't an accident."

"*Who* he? Not that clown with the DIY bandoliers?"

"Buckman's not a clown. The man's so serious, he's almost scary. And he and his Motor Head Mad Scientists think this van-wielding maniac may have meant to hit Lilly."

"How can they tell?"

"When most drivers realize they're hitting a human being, they brake. That's why cops find skid marks somewhere near the point of impact. But the driver who hit Lilly didn't brake. The only skid marks Buckman found were far away—the result of the van's squealing fast start-up."

"So this bastard accelerated, hit Lilly, and kept going?"

"Does that sound like an 'accident' to you?"

"It doesn't make sense, Clare. Who'd want to run over an adorable little Filipina dietician? Unless . . ." Matt fell silent, scratched his furry face. "Maybe she's too adorable."

"What do you mean?"

"I'm thinking jilted boyfriend, angry ex. Didn't your favorite flatfoot say crimes of passion were at the top of his charts?"

"Buckman wondered about that, too, but Lilly has no boyfriend or husband. And last I checked, Quinn's feet have arches. High ones."

"Do I look like a podiatrist?"

"No, but you called him a flatfoot, and his shoes are bigger than yours, so if I were you, I wouldn't bring up Quinn's feet. You know what they say about a man's shoe size."

Matt smirked. "You really want to compare what's in his Oxfords to what's in my boxers?"

"We were talking about *Lilly Beth*."

"Who you claim has no love life whatsoever?" Matt folded his muscular arms. "The way she was flirting with me, I find that hard to believe."

"She was just trying to be persuasive. I asked her to help me sway you to get behind our truck. And as far as Lilly's love life, I spoke to a good friend of hers on the phone earlier. Terry said Lilly's had a couple of boyfriends over the past few years but nothing serious and nothing lately."

"How lately is lately?"

"I don't know. We didn't talk very long. She was anxious to get to the hospital. But, like I said, Lilly never mentioned any relationship troubles to me, or any threats. From what I've seen, she's warm and generous, a loving mother and a beautiful human being—inside and out. I can't imagine who'd think the planet would be a better place with Lilly off it."

Matt exhaled. "The National Pork Producers Council, maybe?"

"What's that supposed to mean?"

"Nothing . . . it's just the way she talked about Kaylie Crimini's Maple-Bacon and Three Little Piggies cupcakes, it had a very Mothers Against Drunk Driving tone to it."

"Well, you're not wrong about her zealousness. She's dedicated herself to reversing the increase of type two diabetes in children, especially among low-income and minority communities."

"Okay, so she's a good mother, a great person—but also a health professional on a mission. And didn't she tell us that she caused a big scene at Paz's grade school earlier today? She publicly argued with that awful Kaylie person, didn't she?"

"Yes, but one argument is hardly a motive for attempted

murder. And you saw Kaylie drive away in that showboat truck of hers. That's why I didn't bring her up as a suspect when speaking with Buckman. Why waste his time? She couldn't have done it . . ." I considered my own assertion and put down my cup. "Unless . . ."

"Unless?"

"Unless she had the van parked somewhere nearby so she could jump into it. Or she put someone else up to it."

"What? Like a hit man?"

"Like a *hit-and-run* man."

I shifted on the stool, getting that prickly feeling of being onto something. "Do you remember the scene Kaylie made in front of our Blend?"

"Of course," Matt replied.

"What if that whole thing was a setup? What if she provoked me on purpose because she wanted a crowd to witness her driving away?"

"That would be pretty shrewd, I guess. But did Kaylie even know that Lilly was inside our shop?"

"Maybe. Maybe not. Given the Kupcake Kween's ongoing feud with us, the goal may have been to run down any customer outside the Blend."

"Why?"

"To send a message."

"What do you mean? Like a mobster? Or a terrorist?"

"Yes!"

Matt stared. "Over *cupcakes and coffee?*"

"Over money and status—as that bouffant brain sees it."

He scratched the back of his head. "Sounds like a stretch."

"Whack-jobs have killed over far less in this town. Talk to Mike sometime, he'll tell you. Anyway, whether it's a good lead or not, I should share it with Detective Buckman . . ." With confident determination, I pulled out my cell—and froze. "What do I say?"

"I don't know. The war against mobile buttercream has had its first casualty?"

Ten

My theory made perfect sense (to me, anyway), but saying it out loud—to someone not familiar with the dark side of Kaylie—well, it did sound ridiculous.

Would Buckman laugh in my face? Or silently humor me?

Oh, who cares, I thought, and dug out his business card. For the first time in hours, I felt a sense of direction, of control. If Highway Houdini wanted to call me an idiot, so be it, as long as he checked out my tip.

Opening my cell, I stopped again. A new message had dropped, direct from Paris.

"Matt, Joy just texted me."

"Joy?"

A message from our daughter carried the same inherent contradictions as a shot of espresso—a rush of warmth followed by the inescapable jolt. *(Is she okay? Why is she writing? Is anything wrong?!)*

Matt immediately pulled out his own PDA—the Lafite of multifunctional devices with every bell and whistle known to Silicon Valley.

The thing had been a gift from his fashionista wife,

Breanne Summour, although "gift" was a euphemism, implying shopping and purchase. As editor-in-chief of trendy *Trend* magazine, the woman got freebies and samples galore. My last birthday gift from her was a gorgeous Fen scarf—with a card that read, *Wear it with style, Bree! Love, Adele.*

"I got the text, too," Matt said.

"Here comes the bride . . ." I read, confused.

"Dum, dum, de dum!" Matt finished and locked eyes with me, his expression a combination of bewilderment and terror. "Clare, I can't believe what I'm reading. Did our daughter just elope?!"

I stared for a moment, processing this.

"She says she sent pictures!" Matt cried.

"Calm down."

"I can't get the attachment open!"

"You're going to sprain your thumbs." I snatched away the man's mobile keyboard, which he was beating on like a Lilliputian bongo drum. "Come on. We'll use my laptop."

"Fine," he said, but he wasn't fine. "So what's the story? She never told *me* a thing! Did *you* have a clue? Did our daughter fall for another line cook? Or get taken in by some backpacking bum? Clare, why didn't you warn me?"

"Will you get a grip? You're overwrought and overreacting. I'm sure she's just kidding around . . ."

Actually, I wasn't so sure.

As our feet clanged their way up the wrought iron steps, I prayed my daughter hadn't done anything rash—like dump her dirty work on me.

Last I heard, Joy and Sergeant Emmanuel Franco were still hot as habaneros for each other. But Franco lived and worked here in New York while Joy was completing her culinary training in France.

After they started seeing each other, I assumed it wouldn't last. Surely one of them would meet a shiny new love interest? Or simply lose interest in the hard work of maintaining a long-distance relationship . . .

But I'd assumed wrong.

The two kept their passions primed via tricknology: e-mails, social networks, camera phone. In the meantime, Joy traveled back to New York when she could; and Franco's overtime pay—not to mention his rudimentary French-speaking abilities, thanks to the Haitian families in his childhood neighborhood—kept him pond-hopping regularly to Paris, the most romantic city on the planet (unfortunately).

Was there a chance that Joy had eloped with Franco? Yes. There was also a chance an earthquake would level New York in the morning, and I hoped neither disaster was in the offing because the last thing I needed (besides a whole lot of broken latte cups) was dealing with my authority-loathing ex-husband once he knew the truth.

Not so very long ago, Sergeant Franco had chained Matt to a metal bar in an NYPD interview room and threatened to have him prosecuted for assault and attempted burglary (another story), all while pressing the most delicate emotional buttons imaginable in the man.

Since then, I had learned to like Franco. I knew the rough interviewing technique he'd used on Matt was SOP for the NYPD. But my ex-husband was another matter, and I dreaded the day he learned his baby girl was cuddling up to a gun-toting, shaved-headed Brooklynite with six-pack abs and a cocky attitude. (Suddenly, a city reduced to rubble wasn't looking so bad.)

Cresting the staircase, we moved across the Blend's second floor, a sprawling living room that boasted more café tables, another fireplace, and a shabby chic collection of French flea market sofas, overstuffed armchairs, and tastefully mismatched lamps.

Something else dwelled here, too. You could almost feel it in the air, the curated artwork, the exposed brick walls . . .

This was where Matt's mother had nourished the bohemians of Greenwich Village for decades—with more than cups of her hot, black French roasts. With her open arms and open heart, Madame had opened this floor to artists of all kinds.

Poets had chanted newly inked verse here. Jazz musicians had tested working compositions. Experimental playwrights had staged read-throughs. Her floor lamps had served as spotlights for impromptu standup; her couches makeshift crashpads for struggling painters who'd lost their apartments—or drunken ones who couldn't find their way back to them.

At the moment, however, this famous floor was empty, the lights dim, the avant-garde ghosts quiet, even though Matt's raving was loud enough to wake the dead.

"I'm betting it was some slick Parisian who schmoozed Joy up when I wasn't looking! And I swear, Clare, over the years I gave our daughter *every* warning I could *think* of about—"

"Guys like you?"

"Exactly!"

Holding my tongue on that well-worn topic, I unlocked my battered office door and fired up my laptop. The e-mail from Joy was as terse as her text message. *Pics attached. Talk to you soon!*

"Hurry it up, will you?"

"Take it easy, Big Daddy . . ."

I downloaded the attachment, unzipped the file. There were about a dozen photos here with captions. A quick scan and I was exhaling with relief. None of them included Franco. In fact, none of them included a *man*. Joy was posing in front of a series of fairy tale castles with her roommate, Yvette—

"Oh, right. Now I remember . . ."

"What?"

"Joy's roommate is the one getting married. Joy mentioned it a few weeks ago. Yvette's family owns an ice cream franchise. They're loaded and they're going all out. Joy is the maid of honor and the two girls spent a long weekend in the Loire Valley scouting a reception site—medieval châteaux cum hotel and catering hall, that sort of thing."

"Oh, god."

"What's the matter? Aren't you relieved?"

"I have to sit down. No. *Lie down*."

Matt stumbled out of the office and collapsed on one of our couches. I took a closer view of the photos.

"You should look at these, Matt. They're very nice!" I called.

He groaned.

I was pleased by how healthy Joy appeared; lovelier than ever with that golden tan on her heart-shaped face and her green eyes laughing in the French country light. She'd traded her bulky chef's whites for a fetching polka-dot sundress and heeled sandals, and from the way she smiled at the camera and tossed her long chestnut hair, I just knew that Franco would be getting these photos, too.

I sighed, feeling that alliance of opposites again: this time, happiness and melancholy. Oh, Joy would make a beautiful bride. But I hoped it wouldn't happen for a few more years because, no matter how old she got, I would always see her standing there with tomboy braids, a missing tooth, and a Hello Kitty backpack.

I knew Matt was feeling it, too—this passing of time—and more keenly than I. So if Joy *did* decide to choose Franco for a groom, then *she* could tell her father.

"I'm going to pass out right here!" Matt threatened.

"You'll get a backache!"

Once more, I considered the on-screen photos. "They must have used Yvette's digital camera for these. Usually, Joy just snaps a single blurry photo with her phone and hits send—"

Snaps a photo with her phone. Oh, my god . . .

"Matt! Did you hear me? She snaps a photo with her phone! Her phone!"

"What?" Matt called. "Who are you phoning?"

"A witness! A *camera phone* witness!"

Eleven

My fingers pounded the keyboard. On my new hunch, I brought up an Internet search engine and looked for "Esther Best" in video. Hundreds of hits immediately came up with that search term—amateur videos of Esther rapping at poetry slams all over the city.

Oh, lord, I thought, how do I narrow it down? I know! Sort by date!

The most recent "Esther Best" video had been uploaded to the Internet less than an hour ago. I hit the tiny thumbnail on the list of search results and found myself viewing a YouTube broadcast recorded right in front of our Blend.

"Bingo!" I cried, and began to watch the familiar scene.

"Listen up, bouffant brain! Are you listening? Good! 'Cause you're not in Kansas. You're in my 'hood . . ."

"Is that Esther I'm hearing?" Matt called. As the crowd cheered, he rose from the dead and wandered back to my office.

"It's Esther," I assured him. "One of her fans shot this video today . . ."

"Your cupcakes are mealy, your élan is fake, and your infantile jingle gives the world an earache!"

"Ouch," Matt said. "She was kind of rough on the Kween, wasn't she?"

"It could have been worse. Kaylie brought up Esther's weight, but Esther refused to go that low."

"What do you mean, 'that low'?"

"Crimini had a nose job over the winter. Esther wouldn't go there."

"I may be 'chubby,' yeah, I'm busty, too, and my boyfriend *loves* the way my booty moves . . ."

"Not exactly Shakespeare."

"I don't know, if she switched to iambic pentameter, I think Esther would make a darn fine Kate."

"What? Like in *Kiss Me Kate, The Taming of the Shrew*?"

"All she needs is a hip-hop Petruchio. I'm thinking Eminem."

"I doubt Boris would be happy about that."

"Your frosting, I hear, comes out of a can. And your beans? Sorry, honey, you can't brew worth a dang! So get your buttercream butt off my grass, or I'll plant my big black boot in your prissy little—"

"Clare, it's past midnight. Why are we looking at this?"

"Because I have a hunch. Be patient and watch."

As Esther ended her rap, the camera drew back to show the entire Kupcake truck. Then it panned around to record the crowd, and that's when I hit the pause key.

"There it is! Look!" I cried.

"What?"

"The van!"

"Where?"

I enlarged the video to full screen. Like a great white, waiting to feed, the cargo van was parked just around the corner from the Blend. I could see the front and part of the side, but I couldn't tell if anyone was behind the wheel. Either the front window was tinted or the evening light had cast one too many shadows.

"Is that the same van, Clare? How can you be sure?"

"I can't. But I can find the kid who shot this video and ask him if he shot any more. He may have been filming something when the accident occurred. And if he was, we may get part of a license plate or a glimpse of the driver. I'll check the kid's YouTube channel to see if he uploaded anything . . ."

"Are you telling me traffic accidents get uploaded to YouTube?"

"All the time."

But in this case, there was nothing.

I noticed the kid's user name, "Homers_HomeBoy," but no first or last name. No website or blog.

"There must be an e-mail address . . ."

I checked around HomeBoy's channel page and found one. But I knew a phone number or address would save Detective Buckman valuable time. So I tried a quick trick I'd learned from Mike. I typed the kid's e-mail address into Google.

"Got you!"

"Got who?"

The Google search results showed all the sites where the kid had included his e-mail address. I hit a link half-way down the page. Up came the kid's digital address again, but this time attached to his profile at the Five Points Arts Collective in downtown Manhattan.

"I know Five Points! Our Dante belongs to that group!"

This was very good luck. The kid's profile wasn't anonymous here. No phone number or address, but his first and last names were displayed: Calvin Hermes.

"Hello, HomeBoy!"

I immediately called my *artista* barista. He answered on the first ring.

"Huruffftt."

"Dante? Is that you?"

"Sorry, boss. I forgot I was wearing a mask."

"Mask? What are you doing, robbing a liquor store?"

"Nadine and I were mixing paint," he explained. "Josh just

got here and we're about to apply the base coat to the truck . . ."

Of course. I had forgotten. Dante had wanted to get a primer on the Muffin Muse before tomorrow's party. "Listen," I said, "I have an important question to ask. Do you know someone named Calvin Hermes?"

"HomeBoy? Sure."

"First thing in the morning, I want you to get in touch with Calvin. Tell him to put together anything he recorded around the Blend tonight and send those digital files to Detective Buckman of the NYPD . . ."

I finished explaining it all to Dante. Then I sent him an e-mail with Buckman's contact information. Finally, I e-mailed Max Buckman directly, telling him to expect digital evidence from Calvin.

I paused, my fingers floating over the keyboard. Should I type up my thoughts on Kaylie Crimini, too?

No, I decided. It was late and Buckman was likely in bed. An e-mail message about a food-truck war might sound like a rant—or half-baked. I needed to explain it calmly, logically, and be ready to answer his questions. So I opted for a request to explain my theory in person, if not face-to-face, then over the phone.

> Please call me or drop by to see me when you have a chance. I have a theory I'd like to run by you.
> Yours sincerely, Clare Cosi.

That sounded sane enough, didn't it?

Hitting send on the e-mail, I took another look at the freeze-frame of video, felt my outrage mounting again. "Look at that thing. That metal monster was just sitting there, waiting for the chance to attack someone from our Blend . . ."

"I hope you're wrong," Matt said, "but I have to admit, what happened out front tonight—I can't shake it off. And I don't like the idea of leaving you here all alone . . ."

"Thanks," I said. "I appreciate it."

"You're the mother of my daughter, Clare. My partner. My friend. You think I'd let anything happen to you?" He smiled then checked his watch. "So where is Big Foot tonight, anyway? On a stakeout or something?"

"Mike's in D.C. for a few days."

"What's he doing in Washington?"

"Consulting with the Feds—at their request. He didn't want to make the trip, said it was pointless, that a simple phone conversation would have sufficed. But his superiors insisted."

"I get it. Politics. Waste of time."

"Mike doesn't like it, either, but it's part of his job—and he loves his job. And since you've brought up politics—"

"I didn't bring it up."

"I have a favor to ask. I need your help schmoozing some Very Important People at our party tomorrow."

Matt frowned. "What party?"

"Dante's going to paint our Muffin Muse truck, and we created an event around it—an Arts in the Street party. We'll have rap artists, live music. The baristas have been distributing flyers . . ."

I handed him one from a stack on my desk. "Isn't it clever? Dante did it."

Matt nodded at the pop art fun of the little advertisement. "So what's he going to put on the truck?"

"It's a surprise. All I know is he's parodying a famous painting."

"As long as coffee's in the composition, I'll be happy."

"That's what I told him—coffee and muffins. Anyway, *Time Out New York* listed it in their events page, and if we're lucky, New York 1 news will send a reporter."

"Sounds like hundreds of people could show."

"Easily."

"So where are you holding this thing? Not in front of our shop?"

"No. Brooklyn."

Matt stiffened. "Where in Brooklyn, Clare."

"Your new warehouse."

"Are you crazy? That warehouse is climate controlled! You can't have a party inside—"

"Take it easy, Blackbeard. Nobody's setting foot inside your bean vault. The party is in the parking lot, and everything's taken care of—the permits, the Porta-Pottys—"

"Porta-Pottys? Oh, man . . ."

"Look, you're worried about money, aren't you? The big monetary investment in our truck? Well, this party could alleviate some of that debt risk. Part of the reason we're holding this event is to win a city grant for the summer."

"A grant?" Matt's annoyed expression suddenly shifted to interested. "Okay, I'm listening . . ."

"It was Esther's idea. She's been working with inner-city kids as part of her NYU practicum. She starts where they are, with their interest in hip-hop and rap, encourages them to write down their stuff. Then she shows them how what they're doing fits into a larger literary movement within the history of poetry. She teaches them some new forms, gets them reading award-winning poets, and shows them where they can go in the public libraries to discover more inspirations for their street poems."

"That sounds laudable, but how the hell does it connect to the coffee business?"

"The Muffin Muse truck travels regularly into parks and pedestrian malls where city kids hang. Esther wants to create a summer poetry program with our truck—a first-step outreach." I turned back to my laptop screen. "I bet you've never seen a Fast-Food Rap, have you?"

"A what?"

I brought up YouTube again and typed Fast-Food Rap into its search engine. Hundreds of results appeared.

"Young people across the country love to rap their fast-food orders. They tape themselves performing the rap and upload the video. It's amazing, listen to this . . ."

I played Matt a few, actually had him laughing. "Clever,"

he said, shaking his head. "I can't believe a hip-hop order at a Taco Bell window has six million views."

"It's a crack in the door. That's what Esther calls it. She wants to build on that nascent level of interest in performance poetry."

"Yes, but how, exactly?"

"We're going to install recording equipment on the truck, beside the ordering window. Kids can try out any sort of rap for our Live Stream. Esther will judge whether it's original and worthy. If it is, they get a free muffin—and she invites them to the next level, a weekly poetry slam right here on the Blend's second floor. By the end of summer, she's confident she'll have a team to take to the National Poetry Slam."

"She's that committed?"

"Oh, yes. Esther is determined to find the kids with real interest and potential. We could help her change lives, Matt."

"All right. You sold me. Who do I have to schmooze?"

"Dominic Chin, for one. He's a city councilman and the odds-on favorite to be our next mayor—"

"I've met Dom. Even better, I like him. Who else?"

"The city's public advocate."

"Aw, crap . . ." Matt closed his eyes, shook his head.

"What's the matter?"

"Tanya Harmon?"

"Yes," I said, "that's her name."

Suddenly, Matt's face took on a stricken, slightly guilty look—one I'd seen far too many times. "Don't tell me. Did you and she . . . ?"

"It was a long time ago, right after our divorce. We met at one of my mother's fund-raisers. As I recall, lots of champagne was involved. 'When I see what I want, I go for it.' She said something along those lines. And that night, it was me."

"Did you part well, at least?"

"I think so. Like I said, lots of champagne was involved."

"Well, do what you can tomorrow," I said, "short of sleeping with her."

"Believe me, that won't be an issue."

"The only issue I can see is political. With Dom there, we have to watch things don't turn ugly."

"Why would they?"

"Tanya's announced she's making a run for the mayor's office, too."

"Then Dom better watch his back."

"They're just politicians. What can they do, short of sniping?"

"Is that it? Who else do I need to impress?"

"Another woman—Helen Bailey-Burke."

Matt scratched his thick beard. "On her, I need more."

"She's in her late forties. Upper East Side. Divorced. Director of special funding for New York Art Trusts. Her approval is key. Make her happy, Matt."

"Hey, making females happy is my specialty."

"I know. My primary problem with you was the plural of the noun: females. As opposed to the singular: wife.

"Bree's not complaining. Speak for yourself."

"I was."

"Okay, enough work for one night." Matt shook his shaggy head and yawned. "I'm wiped."

"Me too." I switched off my computer and locked the office door.

"Uptown feels a world away. Mind if I crash here on a couch?"

"Won't Bree miss you?"

"She's in Milan for the week."

"Well, I really need you schmooze-ready tomorrow, and these couches will destroy your back. Just come upstairs. You'll get a better night's sleep in the spare room."

"Thanks," he said. "I appreciate it."

HAVING Matteo Allegro's larger-than-life presence in my apartment after so long felt a tad awkward, I had to admit, although he didn't appear to feel it. In fact, he acted right at home.

"I'm taking a shower . . ."

"I'll get you some fresh towels."

As Matt headed for the bathroom, I went to the hall closet and was surprised to hear him bring up Quinn again.

"So what did the Feds want with your guy, anyway?"

"I'm not sure exactly. Some U.S. attorney is hot to conduct an epic sting operation—something to do with drug trafficking on the Internet. Mike's OD squad routinely liaises with the DEA, so I guess his name came up as a good man to consult. Anyway, it doesn't matter. Mike's assuming this whole trip is carsmetic."

"Don't you mean cosmetic?"

"*Carsmetic* is a term Mike and his guys use when someone tries to 'grease the wheels' for an ulterior motive. In this case, he says he's being called down there to make life easier for somebody else's operation."

"You lost me."

"If they 'consult' with Mike on what they're doing, they assume he'll feel like he's part of the team instead of an opposing player in some turf war."

"Turf war." Once again, Matt scratched his furry face. "Sounds like your problem—only without the frosting."

"Um . . . Matt?"

"Yeah?"

"Mike has *shaving* stuff in the medicine cabinet. Foaming cream, septic pencil, razor . . ."

Matt grunted once before taking the towels and closing the door.

Did he get the hint? I wondered, heading for the master bedroom. *Maybe razor was too subtle. What I should have said was Weedwacker.*

Twelve

"Hello?" My greeting came out froggy and a bit muffled, thanks to two purring felines dozing under my chin.

"Forget me already?"

"Mike?" I propped myself up—a little too quickly. Java and Frothy slid down, protesting mildly. Detective Lieutenant Mike Quinn joined in with his own complaint.

"What happened to my 'Goodnight Kiss' call?"

"I'm so sorry, Mike . . . I must have passed out . . ."

I glanced at the window, still dark. After I'd left my ex to his shower and (I hoped) his beard trimming, I called Terry Simone, got her voice mail, and asked about Lilly's status. Then I stretched out on the antique four-poster and closed my eyes, whispering prayers for my friend, waiting for the phone to ring.

Clearly, I'd dozed off and Quinn's call had roused me. "I would have phoned earlier, but I didn't know how late your dinner meeting would run. How did it go?"

"Fine. They took me to Georgetown. Nice restaurant. Lousy coffee."

I could imagine Quinn sitting at a linen-covered table in his blue serge suit, the color intensifying the hue of his scalpel-sharp gaze, his dark blond hair in Spartan trim, square-jawed face shaved clean, nodding at the G-men and frowning at his cup.

I smiled. "Who needs coffee when the Feds are footing the bar bill?"

"I was strapped, sweetheart. You know I don't drink when I'm carrying."

"Well, you're un-strapped now, aren't you? Back safe in your hotel room?"

"Close. I'm on the balcony. Nice view of the Potomac. Pretty lights on the dark water . . ."

I heard ice against a glass—not the careless rattle that comes with soda-pop blocks, but the edgy clink-clinking that suggests hard alcohol swirls. *Unusual for Quinn to drink alone,* I thought. *Something must be stressing him.*

"Very romantic view," Mike went on. "I wish you could have gotten away."

"So do I. More than you know . . ." And it hit me*: If I'd gone to D.C., Lilly wouldn't have come to the Blend, or crossed the street just when that metal shark was cruising for a victim . . .*

"Clare? What's wrong?"

I swallowed my tears, told him everything. From my street-food fight with Kaylie to the arrival of the Accident Investigation Squad. That's when he interrupted—

"They sent AIS?"

"Is that unusual?"

"Not if they expect the victim to . . ." His voice trailed off.

"They expect Lilly to *die*, is that what you were going to say?"

"Take it easy. There could be another reason."

"What?"

"It's pointless to speculate."

"Not to me. What aren't you telling me?"

"It's not for me to tell. Who's the lead?"

"A detective named Buckman."

"Mad Max . . ." Mike paused a long moment, as if he needed time to gather up memories—or weigh his words.

"He seems like a good guy," I prompted, "although he's not easy to deal with."

"That's an understatement." Mike paused once more, and then said plainly: "Max has been Mad for a long time."

"Is there a reason? Or is he just eccentric?"

"There's a reason. The story's practically legend in the PD."

"Well, would you mind telling me? It may give me a leg up in dealing with the guy."

"Max Buckman lost a beloved wife to a hit-and-run driver."

"Oh, god . . . How long ago?"

"About fifteen years. At the time, he was a young Bronx precinct detective. Highway patrol handled the crime; didn't gather evidence properly. The driver had a sharp defense attorney. There was no conviction. He walked away."

"Oh, Mike . . ."

"Yeah, you can imagine, right? Buckman and his wife were childhood sweethearts, real soul mates. He lost it. Took a leave from the department for almost a year. But after he . . ."

These pauses were getting to me. "Mike? *What* don't you want to tell me?"

"Let's just say after he 'pulled himself together,' he transferred to highway patrol investigations, dedicated himself to improving their methods, making them better. He earned degrees in applied physics and mechanical engineering, and he brings in new technology all the time, even makes his own stuff. Did you see that tool belt his men wear?"

"The DIY bandoliers?"

Mike chuckled. "Good name for them. He designed those things himself so he and his team wouldn't have to check equipment out. They have what they need at all times, and they can be sure the equipment is in good working condition."

"Funny about the wife."

"What's funny about it?"

"Langley and Demetrios told me that Buckman doesn't like women."

"He liked his soul mate well enough. But after he lost her,

he lost his compass. Made one bad marriage after another. Believe me, I speak from experience. When you're with the wrong woman, you do crazy things."

"Is that how you got the name Crazy Quinn? That's what Buckman told me."

A soft curse followed.

"Mike?"

"That *Bucket-mouth*."

"So it's true?"

"It was a long time ago, Clare. Ancient history."

"It must have been. I mean, I tried telling the man what you're like these days—careful, methodical, in control to a fault. What could you have possibly done to get a handle like 'crazy'?"

"Well, I'm not giving it up tonight, Inspector."

"But—"

"Forget it. Look, given what you went through this evening, you should get some rest. Before I sign off, do you have anything else troubling you about the hit-and-run? Any questions about how Buckman's handling it?"

"He told me everything depends on finding that van."

"It does. The van was the weapon—so to speak. He'll treat it like I used to treat a gun or a knife. The most solid case Buckman can make is to connect the driver to the vehicle and the vehicle to the incident."

"I get it. What I don't get is why there was no muffler on that thing. I mean why would anyone use a vehicle with no muffler for an intentional hit-and-run? Doesn't that strike you as wrong?"

Mike's ice clinked again. "Offhand, I can give you two possibilities. One: The van was in rotten shape when the perp stole it. The muffler fell off, but it was too late to change plans so he or she went ahead with the incident."

"What's two?"

"The perp wanted to call attention to the vehicle. You told me it had graffiti on the side, right? Maybe gang symbols? The driver may have wanted witnesses to see the accident.

With those gang markings on the van, they could be sending a message, telling a rival where the hit was coming from. Was your friend Lilly involved with a gangbanger, Clare? Maybe a drug dealer?"

"No way."

"You'd be surprised how regular these guys can seem at first. How nice, how generous. They have money to throw around. They can buy big-ticket items for single moms and their kids. Isn't it possible, given the brutality of this crime, that Lilly was seeing someone she didn't even know was a dealer or member of a gang?"

"Well, anything's possible. I mean, isn't it possible you could be looking at this crime through your OD squad mirrored shades?"

Mike laughed. "Fair enough, Detective Cosi. But I do see turf wars from time to time. One dealer terrorizes another by going after an innocent girlfriend, a child, a family member."

"I understand—and it's awful to consider. I just don't think that's it."

"Well, if it was a gang hit, the van would have been ditched by now. Probably torched, as well, to destroy any physical evidence, and in that case, I'm sorry to tell you . . ." Mike's voice trailed again. I heard the ice clinking, a bottle pouring. He needed another drink.

"What?" *Just say it!*

"When it comes to using vehicles as deadly weapons, there are plenty of ways people can get away with murder."

I closed my eyes, refusing to accept it—at least in Lilly's case. But the denial took something out of me; the mental effort drained my last reserves.

"I'm sorry, Mike, but I'm done in . . ."

"Of course you are." His voice softened. "I wish I were there."

"So do I."

"Just a few more days. Then we can get back to our sweet routine."

"Sounds like you miss my coffee already."

"I miss everything about you."

"I love hearing that."

"And I love you. Sweet dreams, sweetheart."

After bidding Mike good night, I settled myself under the covers, comforted by the company of my two furry girls, one the color of a medium-roast Arabica bean, the other white as cappuccino foam.

As Java and Frothy tucked themselves close, one on each side, something occurred to me. I'd forgotten to mention that Matt was crashing here. It bothered me now.

I should have told Mike . . .

Given the circumstance, I knew he'd understand. Yawning, I decided there was no harm in waiting. *When he's back in New York, I'll tell him. I'd rather explain it face-to-face, anyway.*

I was about to turn off the light when I heard it—

Rat-tat-a-tat-tat . . .

Slowly, the bedroom door cracked open. "Are you having trouble sleeping?" Matt called. "I saw your light?"

"I was just about to turn it off."

My ex-husband didn't take the hint. He moved farther into the room. I could see his muscular chest was bare, a fluffy white towel wrapped loosely around lean hips.

"I mean, if you *were* having trouble sleeping . . ." Matt smiled. "I could help you relax."

Matteo Allegro's philosophy, in its own way, was stupidly innocent. To him, sex was a simple physical act to be shared with a willing partner—along the lines of bowling or badminton. No harm, no foul.

His marriage was working very well because his new wife understood this character flaw and allowed him a long leash. But I knew Breanne, and I was absolutely certain she equated Matt's dog runs with flings in Rio or beach bunnies in Bali. *Not* rolls in antique four-posters with his New Yorker ex-wife.

But that was beside the point, which was (for me) just as simple and pure: A good man was sleeping alone in a hotel room, two hundred miles away—a good man who trusted me, which is why I flatly informed my ex-husband: "Quinn called. He said: 'Keep your hands to yourself.'"

Matt smile widened. "And what do you say?"

"I say you didn't take my hint."

"About what?"

"The beard." (If anything the shower made it look darker—and curlier.) "I want you presentable for the party tomorrow. What's the story?"

Matt shrugged, folded his arms. "Putting a raw blade to my face every morning has gotten tiresome—and there's something atavistic about it, too."

I stared at his caveman bush. Atavistic was right, but he had it backward. "We're at least six millennia out of the jungle, and three centuries beyond Benjamin Franklin. Can't you get with the program?"

"What do you mean?"

"Go electric."

"Have you ever used an electric razor? They're crap. An hour later, I've got stubble."

"Stubble is in, Casanova. Stubble's been in since Don Johnson posed in a white suit and slip-ons. What you've got now is the call of the wild. I repeat. Go electric."

"Does Quinn shave with an electric razor?"

I sighed. (Matt had a point, but so what.) "No matter how you do it, putting a razor to your cheek is civilizing, isn't it? Wouldn't growing a beard be the thing that's atavistic?"

Matt smirked. "Quinn *doesn't* use electric, either, does he?"

"He doesn't, but—

"Case closed."

"No. *Door* closed!" I pointed. "Your bed is down the hall. I'll see you in the morning."

"Fine. But remember, there are *plenty* of ladies on this planet who'd love to do anything but show me the door. You don't know what you're missing."

"Oh, yes, I do."

Thirteen

"STRAW-BEAR-WEE . . . Lee-*mon* . . . Butt-*tair*-cream . . ."

With a groan, I pulled the bedcovers over my head, but the faux French menu wouldn't stop torturing my eardrums.

"Chocolat . . . Oooh la la—Chocolat!"

I threw off the covers and rolled smack into a hard wall of male flesh. *What in the world?* The bedroom windows were dark, the room dimly lit, but I could see enough to know who was in my bed.

Mike Quinn had a long torso, a powerful set of shoulders, and a number of hard-won scars. I certainly knew his body, but seeing it in bed with me now made no sense.

"Mike? I thought you were in Washington?"

He didn't answer. I gently shook his strong shoulder. "Mike?"

"What is it, sweetheart?"

The groggy voice was certainly Quinn's, but when he turned in bed to face me, he turned *into* someone else—someone with dark bedroom eyes, a Roman nose, and a thick beard.

"Matt!" I cried. "You don't belong here!"

White teeth grinned through his black beard. "Don't I?"

"Oooh la la . . . flavors for *vous!"*

"Boss! You'd better get down here!"

Esther? I could hear her voice rising up from the street outside. Something was wrong. I moved to get out of bed, but Matt's stubborn fingers locked around my wrist.

"Let me go," I told him.

Matt laughed. "Make me."

"Boss!"

"Dammit!" I struck Matt's arm. He released me, and I ran through the room, yanked open the window, and leaned out. But Esther wasn't down there. Nobody was. Just an eerie gray mist that rapidly expanded until even the streetlamps were swallowed, their halogen rings floating golden halos through the inexplicable fog.

"Esther!" I called. "I can't see you! I can't make sense of anything!"

"Clare! Is that you?" This light, musical voice was Lilly Beth's. Pure as birdsong, it floated up on the night air. "I need your help, Clare! Help me! Please . . ."

Lilly Beth's in trouble!

I turned for Matt, but he was gone. My four-poster was empty, and I was alone. Not even Quinn was there to help. I tore through the hall, out the door, and down the exterior stairs that led to the back alley.

"Help! Somebody!"

I moved through the dark, narrow passage between the brick buildings. At the end of the alley stood a door with metal bars. The gate wasn't locked, but I couldn't budge it. I shoved as hard as I could until it swung wide and I tumbled to the sidewalk. The rough concrete scratched my palms and bare legs. As I moved to get up, pebbles stabbed my knees, my hands started bleeding, and I began to cry.

A spotless handkerchief appeared in front of me. A hulking figure held it.

"Detective Buckman? Can you help me?"

Bathed in the searing brilliance of floodlights, Buckman replied, but I couldn't understand him.

"Lilly's lost," I told him. "We can't lose her . . ."

I reached for his handkerchief, but the moment I took it, the man vanished. The fog disappeared, too, and the floods transformed into summer sunshine. Suddenly our sidewalk was filled with café tables crowded with customers.

"Straw-*bear*-wee! Butt-*tair*-cream!"

Kaylie was back. As her rainbow-splashed truck pulled up to our curb, customers rushed forward for coffee and cupcakes.

"Flavors for *vous* . . ."

"Turn it off!" I cried, running to the window. "Turn it off!"

A young Asian man confronted me. He looked wiry and strong. Coiled around his arm was a stylized tattoo, a Chinese dragon that looked as fierce as he did.

Squaring my shoulders, I tried to stand up to him, but he shoved me hard and I stumbled backward, falling again to the ground.

"I'm sorry . . ." Lilly Beth's voice called, this time from somewhere above. "This is my fault, my fault, my most grievous fault . . ."

As I struggled to get up, the young Asian man shouted in another language. With alarm, I realized he wasn't addressing me, but giving orders to the dragon on his arm.

The colorful ink began to move, slithering around his limb until it slipped free, filled out into three dimensions, and inflated like a parade balloon.

Screaming, the crowd scattered as the giant dragon opened its mouth and swallowed Kaylie's Kupcake Kart, Eiffel Tower and all!

Then the monster spied me. Its limbs began to curl and spin, transforming into wheels. Rolling after me, it bellowed but the roar sounded mechanical, like the throaty growl of a muscle car engine.

I rushed blindly into the haze, coughing and choking. My bare feet slapped pavement; I ran and ran but couldn't get away. Glancing behind me, I saw colossal wheels bearing down, moving to crush me.

I screamed in terror—and woke myself up.

Fourteen

A ringing phone roused me again, just after dawn. No faux French menu this time, and no Chinese dragon. When I rolled over, I was relieved to find my bed empty—well, except for Java and Frothy.

"Hello?"

On the line was Nurse Terry Simone. She had news for me about Lilly Beth, good and bad. The good: Our friend was still alive. Lilly had come out of her first surgery okay.

The bad: During post-op, her brain began to swell from a previously undetected head trauma. I tensed as Terry described how the doctors performed a decompressive craniectomy to alleviate the pressure, and then placed her in a medically-induced coma.

"She'll be in that state until the swelling subsides," Terry explained, "which could take hours—or days."

Lilly's life was still in danger, that was clear, but everyone was pulling for her, and that lifted me up. Then Terry's final news sent me spiraling again.

"The neurologist doesn't yet know if the damage to Lilly's spine will result in permanent paralysis . . ."

In other words, Lilly Beth Tanga might never be able to walk again.

I thanked Terry for keeping me in this up-and-down loop, then hung up in a daze. I said prayers for Lilly as I showered, more as I dressed and fed my furry girls.

I ached to hear Mike's voice again, but I knew he had a breakfast meeting scheduled with VIPs, so I gritted my teeth, pulled on low-heeled shoes, and started my workday.

With one last check on my furry ex-husband, still snoring in the guest room, I took the service stairs down to my Village Blend.

"ESTHER, what are you doing here?"

I was surprised to find her sitting at the espresso bar. She wasn't scheduled for an early shift. Tucker and Vickie had opened already—and everybody knew Esther was not a "morning person," which is why mental alarms immediately sounded.

Without a word, she slapped the Saturday edition of the *New York Times* down on the marble countertop, flipped it open to the Metro section, and pointed to a four-column story.

"Is that an article about what happened last night?"

"No," she said. "Our hit-and-run didn't make the papers. Big city, too much news, and nobody died—"

I cringed, thinking, *Not yet.*

"But this article does happen to be about Lilly Beth."

I scanned the headline: *Reading, Writing, Arithmetic: Subtracting Fat and Sugar.* A big color photo showed Kaylie's Kupcake Kart parked in front of a Manhattan public school with a line of tweens queuing up to be served.

"The reporter identifies Lilly Beth as an advisor to the mayor's office," Esther said. "Lilly's quoted many times, and she didn't pull her punches for print. She took a shot at the Unidentified Frying Objects truck for their deep-fried Snickers bars—which aren't bad, by the way. But she saved her worst culinary beat down for Kaylie's Kupcake Kart."

Reading the piece, I was relieved to see that it wasn't completely negative. Lilly praised vendors who offered healthy alternatives, including Veggie Weggie and The Ploughman's Lunch, along with the low-cal, high-fiber offerings from our own Muffin Muse. But she had nothing good to say about Kaylie's fare, citing the excessively high fat in several of the Kween's most popular delectables.

"Empty calories in pretty packages along with sedentary lifestyles are becoming dangerous vehicles for our children," Lilly warned, *"driving them to pediatric diabetes."*

"Check out the part where Lilly Beth urges the City Council to ban food trucks from parking within 150 yards of a school or playground."

I knew plenty of street-food vendors would be angry after seeing that, especially the ice cream trucks. Scanning ahead, I learned Lilly was also pushing the mayor's office to require nutritional information to be posted on all food carts.

The Muffin Muse voluntarily posted the info, but trucks weren't yet obligated the way restaurants were. Most vendors would be upset about the cost and trouble such a rule would impose; and any truck with a menu of excessively high-calorie products was sure to see a drop in business.

"Looks like Lilly gave half the food-truck owners of New York reason to run her over," I said.

"It may look like that, boss," Esther said, "but skip to the last paragraph."

"Here it is: Mr. Ray Grant, owner of Unidentified Frying Objects, maintained that adults have a right to make informed choices about the foods they eat. But he also stressed that he 'never parked in front of schools, or specifically targeted children.' Ms. Kaylie Crimini, owner of the Kupcake Kart, had no comment."

"Had no comment!" Esther rattled the paper. "Which meant a reporter contacted Kaylie about this story. Don't you see? The Kupcake Kween knew this article was coming!"

Esther lowered her voice and leaned close. "It's clear, isn't it? Kaylie learned about this hit piece, hit the roof, and planned a hit of her own—on our Lilly Beth."

I exhaled in frustration. Esther had come to the same conclusion I had. Kaylie did seem the likeliest suspect behind Lilly's hit-and-run. But this article wasn't going to help us prove it to the district attorney's office.

Yes, it solidified my feelings about Kaylie's motives; it even refocused the target as Lilly, instead of just some "random" Blend customer; but it did something else, as well.

"This article gives Kaylie legal cover, Esther, and that's not good news."

"What do you mean?"

"If the police don't find hard evidence connecting Kaylie—or a member of her crew—to last night's crime, then she can point to this piece and claim Lilly had many enemies. Her lawyer can argue that any food-truck vendor might have been fed up enough to take a swipe at her with a service van."

"Okay," Esther said. "But we know different. So what are we going to do about it? We can't just stand by and let that Paris pink poseur get away with running down our friend—and right in front of our shop!"

I checked my watch. Detective Buckman hadn't contacted me yet, but I knew he would. In the meantime, I brought Esther up to speed on what I'd done so far to help—how I'd found that YouTube video and asked Dante to track down the kid who'd shot it.

"If we're lucky, our little Spielberg recorded the hit-and-run, too. By now he would have sent the files to Buckman. When the detective calls, I'll ask him if he's found anything useful in the footage—"

I stopped talking when I saw three men walking through our open French doors. Dante and two guests. The older man I didn't recognize. He wore a summer-weight olive suit and a serious expression. The youngest of the trio, however, was still clad in the same electric green Speedos I'd seen him wearing the night before.

Dante ushered the men to a table near the fireplace and waved me over. The older man in the suit removed a leather bicycle glove and shook my hand with a warm, firm grip.

"My name is John Fairway. I'm a practicing attorney and director of the alternative transportation advocacy group Two Wheels Good. I'm here to represent this young man in both of these capacities."

Tall and slightly gangly, Fairway struck me as mid-thirties, though his lined, sun-dried complexion and silver-blond crew cut gave the impression of his being older. He would have had the outward demeanor of your average lawyer, calm and staid with a conservative suit—except for the rainbow banana helmet dangling from his arm, the Day-Glo orange mini-pack strapped to his back, and the bright yellow bicycle ties around his suit pants.

"And this is Calvin Hermes." Dante gestured to the kid in Speedos. "Calvin is a bicycle messenger for Citywide Quick-Delivery. He shot the YouTube video of Esther you told me about last night."

From his name and uniquely attractive features, I deduced that Calvin Hermes was of Afro-Greek heritage. The kid couldn't have been more than twenty, with a dark complexion and ebony curls that contrasted sharply with wide, light blue eyes as captivating as a young Paul Newman's. Like most bike messengers, Calvin didn't appear to have an ounce of fat on his lean form.

I sensed the kid was nervous, and immediately tried to allay his fears.

"Thank you for coming, Calvin. I hope Dante made it clear that you're not in any trouble and you don't need a lawyer. But I'm glad you and Mr. Fairway are here, because we really need your help."

Calvin visibly relaxed, and Fairway cleared his throat.

"I think I know the reason for this meeting, Ms. Cosi. You want to know if Calvin captured footage of the hit-and-run in front of this coffeehouse last night."

"Dante told you about the incident?"

"He didn't have to. I have a network of cyclists who keep me informed. When one of my people witnesses an injury or fatality caused by a motor vehicle, they forward the data they gather to me electronically, in the form of text messages, photographs, or video recordings."

"And you pass this information on to the authorities." That seemed obvious, but Fairway shook his head.

"No. We don't."

I blinked, certain he'd misunderstood. "What I meant to say was, I'm sure you give this evidence to the police, right?"

"No, Ms. Cosi," the lawyer said. "That's why we're here. The police are the problem."

Fifteen

"Excuse me?" I said. "In a world of rampant corruption, gang violence, terrorism, and drunk drivers, the *police* are the problem?"

"The NYPD has displayed a bias against cyclists and pedestrians—and a cavalier attitude toward reckless driving. What I do is assess data, Ms. Cosi, and then I circulate it to the rest of my group in the form of a 'Wheels Down' alert."

"And what is a Wheels Down alert?"

"Let me explain in a manner you can fully appreciate: One of the goals of Two Wheels Good is to stop reckless drivers. Our members are my eyes and ears. Just last month an anonymous tip from one of my people helped capture a woman who'd fled the scene after running down a child on Queens Boulevard."

"But surely justice would be better served if the authorities had your evidence to help them."

"Certainly, when legally compelled by the NYPD or district attorney's office, we turn over evidence specifically requested. As far as *justice*, however . . ." Fairway's eyes turned flinty. "Most drivers who kill pedestrians in New York City are permitted to leave the scene of the crime without arrest, sometimes with no more than a ticket. It's an unspoken truth that no driver gets charged in a fatal accident unless they violate more than two traffic laws. On top of that, ten to fifteen percent of drivers guilty of vehicular homicide never get prosecuted due to the mistakes of a botched police investigation."

I couldn't argue with Fairway's statistics, mainly because I didn't have any of my own. But I knew studies and statistics could be presented in narrow contexts in order to push agendas. So I never drank the Kool-Aid when an obvious advocate quoted figures. I always assumed there was another side.

On the other hand . . . given Mike's sad tale of Max Buckman's murdered wife, I suspected John Fairway had a pedal to stand on with this one. Even Mike admitted: *"When it comes to using vehicles as deadly weapons, there are lots of ways people can get away with murder."*

"I'm still steamed about that Williamsburg incident," Dante said. "An artist was killed riding his bicycle on a Brooklyn street."

Fairway quickly nodded. "The police failed to gather enough evidence to prosecute the driver, even though he fled the scene. Then the police tried to cover their own stupidity by blaming the cyclist."

"The story's true," Dante assured me, nodding his shaved head. "And when that failed, the NYPD tried giving the victim's family the bureaucratic runaround."

"A good example, Dante," Fairway continued. "Yet for every vehicular homicide that wins the publicity of the Williamsburg incident, ten more are ignored. Two weeks ago, a prominent Manhattan plastic surgeon was run down during an early morning bicycle ride. There were no witnesses and the police have yet to make an arrest."

Fairway leaned across the table. "Even more tragic, this senseless murder was considered so routine it rated very little media coverage on a busy news day. With such public apathy, you can see why the police are seldom interested in the evidence my organization gathers. And in most cases our evidence is inadmissible in criminal court."

"Why is that?"

"Primarily because it's gathered anonymously. My people don't trust the police and they won't cooperate with the authorities."

"Okay then, if you don't pass evidence on to the cops, who *do* you give it to?"

"When enforcement fails, lawsuits are the next best option. We pass our data on to the families of the victim and their lawyers, who pursue justice in civil court."

Fairway slid an unmarked manila folder across the slick marble. "In this case, I'm passing the evidence on to you, Ms. Cosi. I shall be *watching* you to see how it's used."

I ignored the odd Big Brother–esque threat, and opened the folder. Inside I found two blurry photos. The first showed the rear end of a white van. The second image was an enlargement of the first.

"Oh, my god. Esther, look at this!"

The first two numbers on the New York State license plate were clearly legible in the enlargement, though the rest were blocked by evening shadows.

"You claim these photos were taken last night?" I asked excitedly.

"Yes," Fairway said. "Calvin was on scene, taping this lady's performance poetry. He had his smart phone handy when the attempted murder took place—"

"Excuse me?" I interrupted. "You just said 'attempted murder,' which implies you're aware that the driver had a motive. How could you be aware of that? Do you know something about this incident the police don't?"

Fairway shifted uneasily. "You're reading too much into my words, Ms. Cosi. I simply meant that there is no such thing as an 'accident' when a pedestrian or cyclist is run down by an internal combustion engine. In New York City, cars kill more people than guns. Did you know that?"

"I've never thought much about it."

"That's the problem. There are too many uninformed, *unmotivated* members of the public out there. This town had the good sense to ban guns. Why not the automobile?"

I was about to reply when Esther beat me to it—

"That *sounds* very noble," she said, adjusting her black-framed glasses. "But what do *you* get out of all of this advocacy?"

He smiled. "Two Wheels Good dreams of a day when no personal cars or trucks are permitted in Manhattan—and deliveries are made only with special permits. Innocent lives are claimed every day. The authorities are indifferent, so we at Two Wheels Good are sometimes forced to resort to . . . other means."

His words hung in the air for a moment. "Other means?" I echoed. "You're not actually going to argue that your cause puts you above the law?"

"The statistics speak for themselves. We do what we must. What we deem necessary for the greater good."

Esther and I exchanged uneasy glances.

"Hey, listen," she said. "I don't like cars, either. And I hate traffic. I even admire some of your goals. But guess what? I don't like opaque innuendo about 'other means' and 'doing what's necessary' coupled with vague threats like 'we're watching you,' because, frankly, as we know from history, 'above the law' rhetoric can end up with the 'wrong' sort of people being herded into showers that have Zyklon B on tap instead of hot water."

"You have a right to your opinion, Ms. Best."

Fairway's voice had gone cold though his smile never wavered. Rising, he slipped the banana helmet over his bristly blond scalp. Calvin Hermes stood, too, and checked his smart phone for messages.

"You must excuse us. Calvin has work, and I'm expected at a rally in front of the Brooklyn borough president's office. If you need to reach me for any reason, here's my contact information."

Fairway's business card was as odd as he was. No phone

number. No office address. Fairway's name didn't even appear. Just an orange plastic rectangle with an e-mail address under a Two Wheels Good logo—a Victorian-era bicycle with a huge front wheel.

Calvin Hermes took off after that, but Fairway lingered for a moment, surprising Esther by offering his hand.

"I would be remiss, Ms. Best, if I did not add that you are a very talented performance artist. I have been following you with pleasure on the Internet." His gaze slipped for a moment to admire her ample bustier cleavage. Then it moved back up to meet her shocked brown eyes. "It was my personal honor to meet you. I'm sure we'll meet again."

When lawyer and client were gone, Esther let out a freaked-out scream.

Dante smirked. "I can see he won your heart and mind."

She put her hands to her full cheeks and shook her head. "That guy was too *weird*."

"Well, he certainly had the hots for you," Dante noted. "And I thought you liked weird."

"*Artistically* weird, yes. *Socially* weird, check. Not Mr. Smile While I Throw the Constitution Under the Volkswagen Bus weird."

"Esther, focus!" I opened the folder and spread the photos out on the table. "Look closely. Is this the cargo van you saw last night?"

She stared at the pictures for a silent minute. "I'm sorry, Boss," she finally admitted. "I can't be sure. I saw the side of the thing, and I remember the graffiti. That's it. Unlike men's tushes, the rear end of one van looks pretty much like another."

"I think I recognize it," Dante said, leaning across the table.

"You told the police you didn't see anything," I shot back.

"Not last night. But I may have seen this white van before. It looks like Kaylie's service van to me. When she's non-mobile for long periods—like festivals and events—she uses it to replenish her stock."

I knew about the practice of using vans to service food trucks. Bigger vehicles burned a lot of fuel. A service van could keep a large truck replenished for far less money. What I didn't know was that Kaylie had one—a white one.

"I've seen her van come and go a few times while working the Muffin Muse," Dante said. "I don't remember the license number, but the police can find out . . ."

Misreading my troubled expression as one of doubt, he got testy.

"Look, Boss, I know it sounds crazy. I mean, who'd kill over coffee and cupcakes, right? But I really think—"

"Easy, Baldini," Esther interrupted before I could. "We agree with you about Kaylie, but it's not about buttercream turf anymore."

Esther showed Dante the *Times*. After skimming the piece with Lilly's quotes about plans to regulate vendors, he pounded the table and jumped up.

"That's it. I'm going to Kaylie's bakery to find that van—"

I grabbed Dante's tattooed arm. "You know where she bakes her cupcakes?"

"Sure! She rents a kitchen just down the road in Chinatown."

I stood up, too. "Let's *all* go."

Sixteen

We fast-walked the mile from Hudson to Canal Street in Lower Manhattan. The thoroughfares were crammed, of course, as they were every Saturday when hordes of shoppers from all five boroughs, Long Island, New Jersey, and even parts of New England descended on Chinatown.

They came to patronize the Asian food markets, seafood kiosks, vegetable stands, and specialty stores. They stopped by acupuncture clinics, fortune tellers, noodle shops, tea parlors, and the many bakeries that lined the cramped, crowded, serpentine streets between Canal and the Bowery.

In the heart of the action, we were stalled by a rowdy crowd in front of a popular seafood vendor, where the morning sun glinted off the silver scales of smelts and sardines, and lobsters and crabs waved their slate green feelers from ice-packed wooden barrels. On a leaky table, catfish lay exposed, kept fresh and (disturbingly) alive on beds of crushed ice.

Intricately formed hanzi characters were everywhere, on banners, awnings, and street signs, the bold calligraphy set off by scarlet or gold backgrounds. Nothing escaped the Chinese influence, not even the local McDonald's with its façade of ornate columns and a pagoda-like overhang.

Enough English was on display to help tourists, and our resident lady of letters remarked on the amusing collision of Chinese and English that formed the most whimsical "Ching-lish" signs: Happy Panda Trading Company, Very Good Fortune Peking Duck, and The Princely Splendor Furniture and Lighting Company, to name a few.

"But this one has got to be my personal favorite," Esther said, pointing. "I mean, who wouldn't want to get their eyewear from Golden Mandarin Very Finest Optometrist?"

Our progress picked up when we turned down Mott Street, a cramped, crowded, curved boulevard flanked by century-old four-, five-, and six-story buildings. It was so narrow there was not much room for parked cars, and we kept close watch on passing traffic in hopes of spotting Kaylie's service van.

Finally Dante stopped us beyond the bend of Mott Street's gentle curve, in front of the doors to the Church of the Transfiguration. The two-hundred-year-old granite edifice housed a Roman Catholic church; its mass schedule was posted in English and Chinese—three services a day, two in Cantonese.

"The bakery Kaylie rents is on Mosco Street," Dante informed us, "just around the corner."

"Let's go," I said.

We marched down Mosco—more of an alley than a street, descending at a steep angle. Faux-Victorian lamps dotted the tiny wedge of sidewalk, a futile attempt to make this grim urban stretch seem amicable.

The only signage (other than a "no parking" warning) belonged to a little hole-in-the-wall dumpling shop operating behind a curtain of greasy plastic weather strips.

Seeing no white van, we looped the block *three times* (stopping once to nosh on an order of fried dumplings and a fresh, hot carton of chicken lo mein, and twice to gander at knock-off designer purses) before ending up where we started.

I checked my phone messages, but Detective Buckman had yet to contact me. *What now?*

Esther frowned. "Dante, are you sure this is the right street?"

"I'm certain. I came here to work every day for a solid month last year. Look up . . ."

Dante directed our attention to a building rising above Mott. The wall facing us was adorned with a three-story depiction of a beautifully detailed Chinese pagoda sailing across a sea of white clouds. In the distance, above the billowing mist, the torch of the Statue of Liberty, our Beacon of Freedom, gleamed with golden light.

Esther blinked. "Wow," she said with no trace of her typical sarcasm. But the mural was, in my opinion, a true *wow* of a piece.

"You did that all alone?" I asked, giving Dante my *proud mama* smile.

"It's my design," Dante said. "But I brought in two other guys from the Five Points Arts Collective to help me paint—and share the commission."

"Five Points has an art collective?" Esther said. "Now that's downright scary."

Dante titled his shaved head. "Excuse me?"

"Not much for history, are you, Baldini? A hundred and fifty years ago, Five Points—which is just down the block, by the way—was the most violent community in America. There's a whole book written about it. Ever hear of *The Gangs of New York*?"

"I saw the movie," Dante said flatly. "But there's nothing 'violent' about the collective. The only guns we use have paint in them. And as for our work down here, when me and the guys weren't hanging off a scaffold, we were chowing down on pork buns at that little dumpling shop. *That's* how I know Kaylie rents ovens on Mosco. The dumpling shop sits right across from the entrance to her kitchen. I saw her coming and going."

"Show me where, exactly," I said.

Dante pointed to a green archway beside a steel door painted black. Neither the archway nor the door displayed any kind of sign or business name.

"Through that unmarked archway is a steep flight of stairs. The bakery is on the second floor. Dominic Chin told me the family who owns that kitchen makes the very best egg custard tarts in the city."

"You know Councilman Chin?" I asked, surprised.

"Sure. He's one of the sponsors for Five Points. He and his fiancée. I hear she's a doctor on staff at Columbia University Medical Center, some kind of plastic surgeon. They're a real power couple, those two."

"Ugh," said Esther.

"Yeah, I know," Dante replied. "Despite the obviously shallow aspects of swanning around the bon ton—and the fact that he's a politician—Dom's a pretty cool guy."

"Dom?" Esther pushed up her black glasses. "My, aren't we making first-name friends in very high places. Especially if that dude becomes mayor like everyone says he will. A girl's gonna go far if she marries you."

Her tone was dripping with irony, but Dante answered straight. "I'm a working artist. Any girl who marries me better be ready to eat a lot of hole-in-the-wall pork buns."

Marries, I thought, *egg tarts* . . .

"That's it!" I cried.

Esther blinked. "What's it?"

"Huddle up," I told them. "I have an idea that will get us into that kitchen—a plan that will let us ask as many questions as we want about Kaylie, her van, and the people who drive it."

"Sweet! Spill it!"

"Yeah!"

I quickly laid out my scheme.

"Fine," Esther said after I finished. "I'll pretend to be Dante's fiancée. But I'm going to be one disappointed bride. I expected to marry *up*."

"Wow," Dante replied. "I can already feel Esther's unconditional love wafting over me."

"Come on," I wheedled. "It's a solid cover story. You two are the happy couple who want to serve Chinese pastries at your wedding. I'm the proud mother of the bride, ready to write a big fat check. Of course they'll talk to us!"

"Maybe if you speak Cantonese," Dante said. "It's a family-owned kitchen in Chinatown. That means the family doesn't hail from Kansas, you follow?"

"Too bad they aren't from Kansas," Esther said. "We could call Nancy down to translate."

"Look, you two, we're New Yorkers, in the *food-service* industry, the language barrier is an obstacle we live to overcome."

"Okay, I'll do it," Esther said. "On one condition. I want one of those knockoff Coach bags we saw around the corner—and a Buddhist ceremony. It's my dream wedding, and I *am* the bride."

Dante stroked his chin. "I don't know. Mom would be heartbroken if I didn't have a Catholic wedding."

"Do we need to rehearse?" I asked, a little worried.

Dante and Esther exchanged glances then shrugged.

"I'm good," Dante said.

"Me too," Esther affirmed before slipping me a crafty little smile. "After you, Mother Dear . . ."

Seventeen

"Okay, here we go . . ."

With a deep breath, I led Esther and Dante through the unmarked archway and up the steep staircase. As we climbed, the clang of metal pots and trays grew louder, then the buttery, nutty smell of baking pastry hit us, and I knew Dante's intelligence had been spot-on.

At the top of the landing, I expected to find a locked door with a buzzer to ring, but the long, narrow L-shaped kitchen sprawled right up to the staircase with commercial-sized stainless steel refrigerators and a sink deep enough to float a tugboat.

I heard voices speaking in Cantonese. The sound came from around the corner, and I assumed the mixers, pantry, and ovens were located there. I also reasoned, given the open nature of the space, that this kitchen ran 24/7.

Sweet scents wafted over us, and I recognized the source. Dozens of Chinese almond cookies were cooling on a stainless steel table. These weren't your average egg-washed hockey pucks brought to your table after a quickie restaurant meal. These weren't even the more delicate almond rounds that were essentially an Asian cousin to the French sable or Scottish shortbread. These almond cookies were über crispy, baked so amazingly thin they were practically caramelized into nut brittle.

Beside those fragrant treats, I recognized a tray of bite-sized walnut cookies (*Hup Toh Sow* in Cantonese). Baked beautifully golden, they looked as crunchy as biscotti, like little nuts themselves, which was likely how they got their name since traditional Chinese walnut cookies didn't actually contain walnuts. I sniffed the air, curious whether this bakery actually went the old-school route or added the advertised ingredient. (After all, a walnut cookie without walnuts, though traditional, would be difficult to explain to many Western-thinking customers.)

Continuing to check out the baked goods, I swooned at the site of warm, fresh coconut tarts. They looked like fancy macaroons, all dressed up in their formal pastry shells for a night on the town (or in my mouth, thank you very much) with a bright red cherry literally on top.

Finally, I felt a rush of relief when I spied a pair of baker's carts next to the wall. Each rack was stacked with trays of colorfully frosted cupcakes that looked a lot like Kaylie's product line, all ready for loading onto her giant truck—or that elusive white service van.

Not far from those racks sat a gangly teen in a denim skirt and a purple tee embroidered with a glittery pink kitten. Nose buried in a textbook, she wiggled a pencil between two pink-tipped fingers. A fall of dark hair obscured her face, so she hadn't noticed our arrival.

I moved forward. "Excuse me . . ."

The teen looked up, blinking at us from behind knockoff Vera Wang glasses. When she spied Dante Silva, her jaw quite literally dropped.

"Hello, ma'am. May I help you?" The girl was addressing me, but her gaze stayed glued to my *artista* barista.

Dante took it in stride, tossing her a friendly little wink. She blinked, thunderstruck, and dropped her pencil.

"The coed magnet strikes again," Esther cracked before I gently elbowed her into silence.

Our boy's appeal could work to our advantage here. It certainly did at our coffeehouse. On a daily basis, Dante served a smile, a wink, and a warm cuppa welcome to the female student bodies of NYU.

So, okay, the boyfriend experience lasted only as long as the espresso pull, but that was an Italian barista, a guy who served you like a boyfriend, even if he wasn't—about as traditional in my culture as serving up Chinese walnut cookies without the walnuts.

Clearing my throat, I stepped closer to the girl. "Yes, you *can* help me. My daughter and her groom are planning their wedding, and they want to serve egg custard tarts."

The girl nodded excitedly. "Oh, sure! Let me get my—"

"You want custard? You came to right place!" The plus-sized woman in a white chef's jacket barreled around the corner. Her sleeves were rolled up, her meaty, flour-speckled arms outspread in greeting, her jovial smile expansive.

"Mrs. Ping make the best. Ask anyone in Chinatown. And custard very lucky for wedding. Very, very fortunate."

"Are you Mrs. Ping?" I asked.

"I am Mrs. Li," she clarified. "Mrs. Ping was my *yeh-yeh* . . . grandmother. I am the youngest woman of her most distinguished line of bakers."

The teen cleared her throat, loudly.

Her grandmother folded her arms. "Yes. The youngest woman who is *not* a lazy student who refuses to study."

The teen rolled her eyes, but Mrs. Li was not moved.

"Go now. Bring custard for our guests. Then you get back to homework."

The teenager retrieved her fallen pencil, gathered up her work, and scurried around the corner. Mrs. Li turned back to us.

"Where were we?"

I smiled. "You were telling us about Mrs. Ping?"

"Yes, Mrs. Ping was very young when she worked at Jimmy's Kitchen."

"Jimmy's Kitchen in Hong Kong?" I asked, impressed.

Jimmy's was one of the first restaurants to bring Western cuisine to what was then a British colony. Why did I know this? Two words—Matteo Allegro.

Well over a decade ago, he'd called me from a Hong Kong hotel room. After three hard weeks trekking Indonesia for the best cherries in Sumatra, he was craving Western food. On a layover in HK, an old friend treated him to dinner at Jimmy's.

There was escargot to start, soft and succulent, with a perfect balance of garlic and parsley. Then came the tenderloin with goose liver, a fusion of beef and fried *foie gras* that was crunchy on the outside and buttery on the inside. For dessert, steamed ginger pudding with hot custard sauce. As I recall, our entire conversation consisted of the flavors, textures, and aromas of that meal. It bordered on phone sex. (I thought it best not to mention that part.)

"You must be proud to have such a grandmother," I said, keeping it simple—while wondering if I could get that custard sauce recipe.

Mrs. Li nodded once more. "Yes, Mrs. Ping's cakes, pies, and custard were the very best. One day Mr. Ping tasted her custard and he liked it very much. They married and came to America, where they had big family." She nodded sagely, adding, "So you see, egg custard truly is lucky for weddings. Very, very fortunate."

The teenage girl returned, carrying a tray with six tarts, each nestled on a bed of waxed paper, along with three foam cups containing slightly sweetened oolong tea. She placed the tray on the folding table and departed with a final, longing gaze at Dante.

Mrs. Li put her hands together and smiled. "Please taste."

When it came to eating, you never had to ask Dante twice. His first bite consisted of half the tart, which he devoured with unabashed yummy sounds.

Esther, proud of her pickiness, bit tentatively into hers, and a moment of rare silence followed as our typically talkative wordsmith slipped into a food trance.

I picked up the pastry and quietly considered it. Still warm, just as tarts are traditionally served in Hong Kong, the custard was sunny yellow and unblemished; there was no dark caramelization on the top (like the very similar yet different Portuguese version).

My first bite revealed a buttery crust—tender, crisp, and flaky. With only a hint of sweetness, the pastry complemented rather than upstaged the silky eggy-ness of the custard. Like a classic Hong Kong egg custard tart, I detected no nutmeg or other spices, nothing to take away from the purity of the experience. Before I realized it, I'd consumed the entire thing.

"Wonderful," I declared. "The crust is flaky without being dry. The custard is creamy—velvety smooth as mousse—yet baked enough to hold its shape. So humble yet so elegant! I'm very impressed!"

Mrs. Li's smile broadened even more, if that was possible.

"Mother is right," Esther said. "And since I'm planning a traditional Buddhist ceremony, I think these would look spectacular on my dowry tray."

Dante, who was already on his third tart, nearly gagged. "Dowry tray? Who said anything about a dowry?"

Esther faced the grinning baker. "You *do* know about dowry trays, don't you, Mrs. Li?"

"Of course!" she replied. "A lovely tradition. The groom presents you with two candles. Each of you will light one during the ritual as a symbol of the union between your two families."

"That sounds easy," Dante said.

"The groom must also provide trays with incense to burn, and more trays containing wine and rare tea," Mrs. Li began counting with her pudgy fingers. "And to eat there are trays bearing fruits, meats, grain or rice, and sweet cakes, too. And finally there is a tray of fine jewelry."

"Sadly, I have to keep costs low, so I'm only going to have

six dowry trays." Esther hiked her thumb in Dante's direction. "Let's face it, there's no shaking jewelry out of this loser."

Dante frowned. "Hey, I'm no loser. If you want, we can have seven trays, or even *eight*."

Mrs. Li suddenly paled, as if those gasping catfish at the seafood monger fell into a fresh vat of her sweetest moon cake filling.

Esther exploded. "Zip it, Baldini! Do you want to curse our union before it even starts? In Buddhist tradition it's either six trays, or nine trays. Seven and eight are unlucky."

Mrs. Li's expression turned grave. "You must respect tradition, Baldini. Seven is bad. Very bad."

Okay, I thought, *we've really sold this nice lady on the bride and groom act. Time to steer the conversation in the direction of a certain Kupcake Kween.*

"I see you bake cupcakes, too," I said, gesturing to the fully loaded bakery carts. "Those goodies look delicious. Are they spoken for?"

"No, no, not my work," Mrs. Li explained. "They are baked by another; she is not from our family. She pays to share our kitchen. Something my grandson arranged."

"Your grandson? Is he a friend of hers then? Or more of a boyfriend?" I lowered my voice, giving Mrs. Li a look that said, you can confide in me, mother to grandmother. *Let's dish!*

"They met last year," Mrs. Li replied, taking the bait. "Jeffrey owns a restaurant truck called the Dragon Fire. Very good food. The Kaylie girl owns one that sells sweets. Now they are sweet on each other!" She laughed with gusto. "And now she shares our kitchen. Maybe they will get married like you two young ones, maybe not. We will see!"

"What a romantic story," I replied. "So romantic that I really do think we should add cupcakes to the menu. Is this girl coming here today? Was that her van we saw out front? You know, I'm pretty sure I noticed a police officer giving that van a parking ticket? Did you see it, Esther?"

"Oh, yes! Tickets are a pain in the bumper, aren't they?"

"Maybe we should call her driver," I suggested.

"No, no! Not her van!" Mrs. Li interrupted, waving her arm. "Her van is broken, in the shop. The girl cursed about it this morning . . ."

I glanced at Esther and Dante. They looked as stunned as I felt. The van was in the shop? That was too much of a coincidence! Did Kaylie actually think she could get the thing repaired and repainted? Remove all evidence of the hit-and-run? Well, it wouldn't work. We were on to her!

"You buy cupcakes, she will deliver, no problem," Mrs. Li continued to assure me. "I have another grandson. He is my youngest. He works for Jeffrey and also for the girl. Billy always makes deliveries on time— Ah! Here he is now! He will tell you . . ."

"*Yeh-yeh!* What is going on here?! Why are you talking to these people?"

The furious voice came from behind us, startling Mrs. Li and cutting off my next query. I turned to find my nightmare had come true. I stood face-to-face with Mrs. Li's youngest grandson—and he was one angry dragon.

Eighteen

CLAD in black, Billy Li sneered at me and my baristas. His muscles rippled under tight Speedos. The only bit of color on him, from his ebony topknot to the dark Nikes on his feet, was a bloodred splash of lettering across his formfitting tank—a logo for his cousin's Dragon Fire truck.

This was the boy with the dragon tattoo, the one I'd seen last night on Kaylie's Kupcake Kart, the one who'd heard me threaten police action.

Sure, dozens of witnesses had seen Billy and Kaylie drive away from our coffeehouse. But had they really gone? Or had Billy slipped out of that food truck, circled the block, and gotten behind the wheel of the white cargo van parked at our corner? Had Mrs. Li's Dragon Boy run down Lilly Beth Tanga?

In this *High Noon* moment, I should have been yelling in fury. Instead, Billy was the one shaking his angry fist, his expression as twisted as the creature snaking around his sinewy arm.

"Why are you here?!" he shouted. "To spy? To sabotage our business?" Suddenly, the kid rushed me.

"No, no!" I heard Mrs. Li cry.

Dante leaped between us, shoving me out of the way. Then he straight-armed Billy, pressing the flat of his strong artist's hand against the boy's narrow chest. "Back off," he warned.

A martial arts sweep knocked Dante's hand aside and Billy punched forward, aiming to connect with Dante's chin. Esther yelled out as Dante reared back, and Billy missed his target.

Cursing, the boy raised his fists to strike again.

Now Esther jumped in, pummeling his Dragon Fire logo. "Leave my fiancé alone!"

Billy froze, clearly distracted by Esther's bouncing bustier. She wasn't doing much damage—but she *was* confusing the heck out of our opponent, giving Mrs. Li enough time to sweep in.

Employing a martial arts technique known only to elderly Chinese *yeh-yehs*, she gripped her grandson's earlobe between two fingers and tugged hard. Dragon Boy yelped like a startled puppy, and the fire went out of him.

Using her prodigious weight advantage, Mrs. Li hauled her helpless grandson to the other side of the kitchen.

Esther and I took the opportunity to beat a hasty exit—no easy task, since we were forced to push a protesting Dante down the stairs in front of us. Sputtering and cursing the three of us blew through the green archway and onto the sidewalk.

"Why did you pull me off?" Dante cried. "That's the bastard who ran over Lilly Beth! He deserves a beat down!"

"It's not our job to beat anyone down," I said. "We're not above the law. We *tell the police* what we found out here. Got that?"

"But he must—"

"We tell the police," I repeated, trying to cut through Dante's adrenaline-fueled fury. "Listen to me: There's a difference between working to see justice done and exacting your own."

"Yeah, Baldini, calm down," Esther said then yanked his arm. "I'll help. Come with me . . ." She pulled him across the street, through a curtain of hanging plastic weather strips, and into his favorite hole-in-the-wall dumpling shop. "Eat some pork buns."

"That kid was ready to tear our boss apart!" Dante cried, pointing back across the street. "How is eating pork buns going to help?!"

"Eating pork buns always helps."

"Lower your voices," I scolded.

The little dumpling shop was packed with customers. Okay, so most of them were speaking Cantonese, stuffing their faces, and ignoring us, but the last thing we needed here was a scene. Still, I wanted Dante to know—

"I did appreciate your help. Thank you for jumping in."

Esther pouted. "And what am I, re-steamed milk?"

"Thank you, too, Esther. You were very brave, the way you busted in."

Dante snorted. "Busted or *busty*?"

"What's that supposed to mean?" Esther snapped.

"It means the shock and awe that you inflict doesn't come from your fists."

"Stop bickering, you two, or I'll cancel your wedding."

"No problem, *Mother*," Esther shot back with a sigh. "Alas, what kind of a ceremony could we have had anyway? No cupcakes, no egg tarts—and a bad-luck number of dowry trays."

That's when I noticed the activity across the street. I nudged my team. That mysterious black door next to the green archway had slid open to reveal an elevator shaft. Inside was a primitive freight car, little more than a metal cage.

Dragon Boy emerged with another youth. Each pushed a wheeled cupcake rack. A moment later, a third man stepped into the light.

"What is that third guy carrying?" I whispered.

The man was older than the others and much bigger. Good thing, too, because he was carrying bulging black bags, one over each shoulder. Each sack looked as large as a sailor's kit.

"You're right, Boss, that's weird. What could be in those black bags?"

"Well, they're not restaurant supplies. Those come in neat

boxes, and you certainly wouldn't carry fruits or vegetables in polyester bags."

"They're big enough to be body bags," Esther noted uneasily.

Dante frowned. "Let's follow."

"From a distance," I insisted. "We don't need any more violence."

"But what if—"

"No buts, Dante. I may not be your *yeh-yeh*, but I'm still your boss."

"Come on, before they get away!" Esther cried. Pushing through the hanging weather strips, she raced off, heels clicking on the pavement as she ran down Mosco.

Dante glanced at me. "Women who wear bustiers should never, *ever* run."

We caught up with our bouncing barista at the end of the block. Cautiously, all three of us peered around the corner. There was no sign of Kaylie's van—but I finally got a look at the Dragon Fire food truck.

Bright red with gold trim, the vehicle's elaborate artwork depicted a coiled dragon, its fiery breath providing the heat beneath a giant wok.

"Cool design," Esther whispered as we watched the big black bags being loaded into the truck. Next, Billy and his helper rolled Kaylie's cupcake racks up a steel ramp and into the belly of the beast.

"Wonder what's on today's menu?" As Esther craned her neck, I heard a man loudly curse.

"Son of a bitch!"

For a split-second I thought we'd been spotted. But the shout came from the other side of Mulberry, near Columbus Park.

"Who the hell did this?!" The raging man circled his sleek BMW. Every window had been slapped with dozens of neon orange stickers bearing the *Two Wheels Good* bicycle logo.

The man clawed at the stickers, trying to pull them free, but the glue wouldn't budge. The most he could manage was to shred some of the orange paper with the edge of his key.

"What's going on?" I wondered aloud.

"Dude's Beemer is parked illegally, in the middle of a designated bicycle lane," Dante explained. "Guess he just expected a ticket. Looks like Fairway's people thought he deserved more than that."

"Yeah, and Big Brother is still watching," Esther said, pointing. "Or should I say Big Sister? Check her out."

Frizzy blonde hair in a ponytail, athletic body clad in silver sports bra and bicycle shorts, a pink sweatband around her forehead, Warrior Barbie sat astride a sleek chrome racing bike in the middle of a narrow stretch of Columbus Park. The girl was tittering with undisguised glee as she used her smart phone camera to capture the reaction of BMW guy.

"Whatever means necessary," Dante said, echoing Fairway's refrain.

I could tell he was impressed. Esther was, too. And I understood their frustration with scofflaws. There were enough of them in this town—men and women who thought they could get around the rules and regulations that the rest of us lived by because they could afford to pay the traffic tickets or their lawyers or do whatever it took to game the system.

It angered me, too. But it wasn't an excuse for committing crime—because that's what this was: vandalism. And as I considered Warrior Barbie's gratification from this guy's grief, I couldn't help wondering how she'd feel if she learned he'd parked there because his little girl went missing, or his elderly mother had suffered a heart attack.

And how far would Fairway's people go? If someone did something more serious than this (at least in their eyes), would they consider more extreme illegal acts justified? A necessary means to accomplish their "better ends"?

Just then, a diesel engine rumbled. The *Dragon Fire* truck was pulling away from the curb. We watched it lumber down Mulberry.

I checked my watch. "We have time."

"Time for what, Boss?" Esther asked.

"I'll tell you on the way. Taxi!"

Nineteen

"FOLLOW that food truck!"

"Huh?" Our newly minted citizen cabbie (Mr. Jun Hon, according to his hack license) turned in his seat for clarification, his lined brow wrinkling even more. "Where you going, lady?"

"You see that truck ahead of us? The one with the dragon breathing fire under a giant wok? Well, wherever it goes, I want you to follow."

Sitting at my left in the cab's backseat, Esther pushed up her glasses. "Geez, Boss, if you needed a nosh, we could have gone back for pork buns."

"We're not following the *wok*," I said. "We're following what's on it."

"The cupcakes?" said Dante, at my right.

Sitting in the middle, I shook my head. "The black bags."

OUR odyssey began as we rolled down Mulberry—the section that paralleled Columbus Park.

Esther was right about the area's history. Over a century

ago, this placid green space was the historical site of Five Points, one of the most dangerous slums in the country, until New York's leaders became fed up with their violent turf wars and swept it away, replacing it with this park.

The "Columbus" name was meant as a tribute to the community's Italian population back when it had been Italian. The influx of Asian immigrants (up to and including our cabbie, Mr. Hon) eventually reduced little Italy to its current few blocks of restaurants, cafés, and souvenir shops. The only thing named Five Points these days was a restaurant in Noho and Dante's favorite arts collective, housed in a converted firehouse nearby.

At the intersection with Bayard, our taxi hung a right and practically came to a standstill. It took us nearly fifteen minutes to negotiate the relatively short distance from here to Mott to Canal.

"Alas," Esther sighed, "the drawback of 'four wheels' in Chinatown."

The roadway was so narrow that the five- and six-story brick structures—most of them cramped tenements dating back to the nineteenth century—felt like towering hulks. Delivery trucks and cargo vans were the biggest issue. Drivers pulled over and bailed out, sometimes with their motors running, to unload boxes, barrels, and bins.

We rolled by more Chinese take-out joints, hair salons, dry cleaners, green-grocers, two aromatic herb stores, and a very popular acupuncture clinic.

"Pin It!" Esther cried.

Dante rolled his eyes, and I pointed out another site: a striking, pagoda-like building housing a jewelry store and a bakery on its ground floor. "Mike once told me this address used to be the headquarters of a notorious Chinatown gang."

"On Leong Tong," our driver informed us.

According to Mr. Hon, this "Chinese Merchants Association" was now simply an alliance of Chinatown businessmen, but for nearly one hundred years—and as late as the 1990s—On Leong Tong leaders were running protection rackets out of this building with a street gang known as the Ghost Shadows.

"Nice name," Esther said.

"Maybe," our driver said. "But methods—not so nice."

Dante pointed out they had nothing on the Italians. I couldn't argue. Just a few blocks away, in what was left of Little Italy, sat a café where the Genovese family had a "social club" and bookmaking operation, until the Mafia-busting Rudy Giuliani put an end to the party.

Before he'd run for mayor (or president, for that matter). Giuliani had been a U.S. attorney, wielding the RICO law like a sledgehammer to bust up the Five Families with charges of extortion, labor racketeering, and murder for hire. His efforts resulted in four thousand convictions and only a handful of reversals.

"It must have felt good—bringing down guys that bad," I said.

"Ha!" barked Mr. Hon.

"You don't agree?"

"How good you feel when bad guys put a price on your head?"

"I don't know," I said. "It never happened to me."

"Hold up," Dante interrupted. "You're telling me that Giuliani had mob contracts put out on him?"

The cabbie and I both nodded.

"How much?" Dante asked.

"First contract, eight-hundred thou," said Mr. Hon. "Second contract, four-hundred thou."

"That doesn't sound like a lot," Esther replied.

"A lot for scumbag! Rudy G one lucky lawyer."

At last, we escaped the congestion and gloom of those former tenement streets. Turning onto Bowery, we felt the world open up again as the blocked light gave way to sun and sky. This six-lane boulevard offered vast space between buildings and boasted many newer ones—Confucius Plaza being a shining example.

The modern skyscraper was the first federally subsidized

project to create affordable housing for the Chinatown population, most of whom had been jammed into those cramped tenements back on Mott, Bayard, and Mulberry.

"Confucius Plaza over there, see?" our driver proudly pointed. "We have medical office, public school, day-care center, seven hundred apartments. But you know what people visit most?"

"I'll bite," said Esther.

"Statue of Confucius." He pointed again as we rolled by the fifteen foot bronze sculpture.

I smiled. "I take it you're a fan of the philosopher, Mr. Hon?"

"Confucius rock star in Chinese culture. Master Kong's teachings written down in *Lun Yu*. I read every page. Better than *Harry Potter*." He laughed.

"I haven't read the *Lun Yu*," I conceded, "but I've heard enough to know he was a very wise man." (During the age of Chinese feudalism, when intrigue and vice were rampant, Confucius—aka Master Kong—urged feudal leaders to live by higher ethical and moral standards.) "We could use him now, I think."

"Lady, don't know why you follow big, fat dragon wok. But you right about that. Yes, you right about that."

BEFORE long, we were moving faster and turning onto a thoroughfare that ran parallel to the East River and below the FDR, an expressway that skirted the length of Manhattan's east side. The heavy traffic moved quickly here, and I soon realized our destination: South Street Seaport.

The Seaport complex covered twelve blocks and featured some of the oldest architecture in Lower Manhattan. At the heart of this property was Pier 17, a rebuilt dock holding a modern glass shopping pavilion that offered gorgeous views of the fast-flowing East River and that beloved neo-Gothic span of suspended steel wires known as the Brooklyn Bridge. There was a maritime museum, a marine life conservation lab, and the largest privately owned fleet of historic ships in the country, including a fully-rigged cargo ship circa 1885.

On this balmy, sunny day, tourists and locals packed the area, milling between Pier 17 and the preserved cobblestones of Fulton, a street featuring more shops and restaurants.

According to Esther, the area's history embraced the likes of white-maned poet Walt Whitman, who'd described the port as a forest of masts, and author Herman Melville, who'd taken a job as a customs inspector after penning *Moby Dick*, one of the greatest novels of all time, which hadn't earned him a penny.

"Thar she blows!" Esther pointed. "Kaylie's truck!"

The rainbow-colored Kupcake Kart was here, all right, Eiffel Tower and all. Kaylie had beached her psychedelic whale by a curb across from Pier 17, and a line of customers were eagerly scarfing down the Kween's decadent menu.

"Good location," Dante said.

"In more ways than one," I noted.

Esther understood. "May the Great Buttercream Spirit in the Sky keep her far, far away from us!"

"And Brooklyn," I added. "Today especially."

We were all feeling pretty relieved to find her—and triumphant about our recon. In our minds, tracking the dragon truck here was absolute verification that Kaylie's white service van was off the street, which strongly implied her van was the very one used in last night's brutal hit-and-run.

I could almost hear Mike Quinn in my head. *"Nice work, Cosi. You nailed motive, opportunity, and even the weapon."*

But my soaring spirits fell as I watched the Dragon Fire truck roll right by Kaylie's Kart.

"Hey! Where are you going?" Esther cried.

"What you mean? I follow truck!" Mr. Hon replied.

"No, not you!"

"Keep going, sir," I urged our driver.

Mr. Hon followed the dragon as it blew by Kaylie and most of the milling tourists. But I held out hope—Jeffrey Li's mobile dragon didn't leave the area completely. At nearby John Street, it hung a right, made another turn, and pulled up next to a Fast Park lot near the middle of the block.

"Stop, Mr. Hon!" I cried. "Don't get too close!"

The cabbie double-parked, and we waited.

"Lady, you getting out?"

"Not yet. Keep the meter running, please."

"Okay. Your dime."

"Actually, it's looking like quite a few dimes," Esther said, pointing to the taxi's mounting meter.

Luckily, we didn't have to wait long. Out of the Dragon Fire truck came the same big guy we'd seen back in Chinatown. As he stepped onto the sidewalk, Dante wailed.

"Oh, man! If that Dragon truck drops off those cupcakes here and not with Kaylie, how can we be sure her white service van is out of commission?"

"We can't," I said. "We'll just have to wait this out . . ."

All four of us (Mr. Hon included), blinked and stared, watching to see what would be next to come out of the metal beast.

"Look!" Esther cried.

The big man on the sidewalk was being handed something—and not cupcakes. I recognized one of those two big black bags we'd seen him lugging on Mosco. He hoisted it over his shoulder and carried it a few car lengths. Then he quickly hung a left, disappearing into an alley.

"Now where is he going?" I murmured.

"You want to go down alley?" the cabbie asked, sounding just as intrigued. He began to shift the taxi into drive, but I stopped him.

"Stay parked, Mr. Hon. We don't want to spook the guy."

"I'll see what's up." Dante popped the door. With all my strength, I dragged him back.

"Billy Li is on that truck!" I reminded him. "If he recognizes you walking by, there's sure to be a fight!"

"I don't care," Dante snapped. "I told you I can take that kid."

"No, Dante! I mean it!"

"Then why are we here?" he demanded. "We can't see a thing. We don't know what's happening."

Come on, Clare, think of something!

"Mr. Hon, do you have a map?" I asked.

"Map! What you need map for? You have Mr. Hon."

"I know. But for now, I need a big, paper map. *Any* paper map—"

"No paper. GPS."

"I have a subway map in my bag," Esther said. "Will that help?"

"Perfect!"

As I unfolded the thing, Dante frowned. "Boss, what are you doing?"

"Sit tight." I said and began to climb over him, but he grabbed my arm.

"I really think you should let me go."

"I don't want there to be any violence, Dante, and my number one *artista* should be using his hands for painting not punching." I squeezed his shoulder. "I'll handle it my way."

Twenty

Holding the giant paper rectangle in front of me, I strolled along the sidewalk, mixing with the crowd as I moved passed the idling Dragon Fire. At the entrance to the alley, I turned around and peered into the gloomy light, careful to keep the map hanging like a screen between me and Billy Li.

Inside that narrow passage, I saw two men quietly talking. I recognized the big one from the Dragon Fire truck. The older, smaller Chinese man was not someone I'd seen before. Both stood in front of an open door. Neither was speaking English.

The location appeared to be the back end of a shop, although I couldn't be sure. But there were two things I was sure of: (1) The black bag was gone. And (2) the big guy had dropped it off inside that doorway.

If only I could hear what they're saying . . .

I risked a few more steps closer, into the alley itself, and picked up a farewell of some kind, along with these words, which were spoken so loudly they reverberated with clarity off the high brick walls—

"Hah go láihbaai! Hah go láihbaai!"

Immediately, the big man turned and began striding toward me.

Better move it, Clare . . .

I sprinted from the spot, rushing passed the Dragon Fire truck. Unfortunately, Billy Li was looking out the front window. My map was still up, but my speed made me a tad obvious.

"Hey, you!" Billy called. "You with the map!"

Billy had recognized my bottom half, but I refused to turn. Instead, I rushed across the street, directing the kid's attention away from the cab. Then I ducked around the corner, out of his sight, and prayed the others on the truck wouldn't allow the kid to waste time following (and possibly pummeling) little old me.

Thankfully, I heard two males shouting in Cantonese (an argument?), then the revving of a diesel engine. With a deep breath, I peeked back around the corner, saw that Billy was gone and his dragon ride lumbering down the block.

With relief, I hurried back to Mr. Hon's cab, stuck my head in the window.

"What's up, Boss?" Esther cried.

"What did you see?" Dante demanded.

"Nothing incriminating," I told them, "but I have a strong hunch."

With almost fatherly concern, Mr. Hon frowned. "Lady, you, okay? You need help?"

"Actually, I do. May I trouble you with a question?"

"Trouble? No trouble. Ask!"

"Can you translate this for me. I'm pretty sure it's Cantonese: *Hah go láihbaai! Hah go láihbaai!*"

"Easy," Mr. Hon said. "It mean: 'Next week! Next week!'"

Next week, I thought. *In other words, these deliveries were a common occurrence. Excellent!*

"Are you getting in?" Dante asked, popping the door again.

"In a few minutes," I said. "Sit tight, okay? I'll be right back!"

I jogged down the sidewalk, passing the alley this time and moving all the way to the next corner. I hung a left and made a note of the storefronts, all lined up in a row: a florist on the corner, then an optometrist's office, a women's shoe store, and right next to it—a small shop decked out with tourist bait: New York T-shirts and tote bags, tiny Statues of Liberty, Yankee hats, and bobblehead dolls.

This is it . . . My gut was sure. The Dragon Fire truck had delivered that black bag to this little shop's back door.

I took a deep breath, tried to appear as casual as possible, and strolled through the shop's entrance. Space was tight, every inch packed with shirts, posters, and more souvenirs. *Where are they?* A women's shoe store sat right next door. If what I suspected was true, then I'd have to ask.

"May I help you, ma'am?"

"Yes," I told the store clerk. "At least, I think so. The woman next door, in the shoe store? She said you sell a private line of products . . ."

A few minutes later, booty in hand, I climbed over Dante and once again settled into Mr. Hon's backseat.

"So?" Esther asked. "What was in that big black bag?!"

"I didn't eyewitness what came out of the thing. But I did talk my way into a back room, where I saw a similar black bag folded in a corner, and on the shelves around it, I saw a number of very interesting items—one of which you asked for when we were back in Chinatown."

"Excuse me? What did I ask for?" Esther stared, perplexed.

In answer, I handed her a white plastic sack.

"What's in the bag?" she asked.

"Kaylie is—if I have anything to say about it."

Esther opened the sack. "My knockoff Coach purse!"

"A bargain's a bargain, Esther, and dowry trays or not, one day you will make an unforgettable bride."

"Great," Dante said, throwing up his hands, "but what about the cupcakes? By now, we've lost the Dragon Fire truck."

"You know what? I have a hunch about that, too . . ."

I asked Mr. Hon to loop the corner and drive us right back to the heart of the South Street Seaport. Sure enough, between Pier 17 and Fulton's cobblestones, we saw Jeffrey Li's mobile dragon parked right behind the Kupcake Kween.

"Looks like the truck made its delivery of knockoff bags and then backtracked . . ."

We all watched as Billy Li transferred Kaylie's cupcakes from his cousin's truck to hers.

"That's it," I said, feeling triumphant once more. "We got her!"

All I had to do was explain our findings to Detective Buckman, and Lilly's hit-and-run would be solved.

"Where to now?" Esther asked.

"Back to the Blend," I said. Then I thanked the very kind gentleman driving us, promising him a very nice tip—while promising my baristas two very strong shots. We were going to need them. Dante had a truck to paint. Esther had a grant director to impress. And we all had a long day ahead.

"We're done here, Mr. Hon," I said. "Please take us uptown."

"We follow another truck?"

"Only if it's on the FDR."

Minutes later, while on that expressway, I heard my cell phone's ringtone go off. Apparently, while I was sampling egg custard tarts and chasing down a distributor of knockoff handbags, Max Buckman had stopped by my Village Blend. He'd waited ten minutes before calling me.

"I'll be right there!" I promised Buckman from Mr. Hon's backseat. "A quarter of an hour tops. Stay put!"

"Clare, I'm already gone. I'm on my way uptown right now. There's been a development in Ms. Tanga's case. I'll track you down again."

"No wait! You have to hear this . . ."

I told him about Two Wheels Good and how I'd obtained an image of the van's license plate (two numbers of it, anyway), as well as my very strong suspicion that Kaylie Crimini and/or a member of her truck crew (most likely Billy Li) were the perpetrators behind the hit-and-run of Lilly Beth Tanga.

"I understand," Buckman replied neutrally. "Hold on to that photo, and we'll talk more about it, I promise you. Be patient. I'll be in touch soon."

I closed my cell phone and collapsed back against the cab seat, relieved the detective had the info he needed. At that point in my day, I was absolutely certain that within twenty-four hours Billy or Kaylie (or both) would be taken into custody by the NYPD.

I never would have presumed, not in a thousand guesses, that the person to be taken into custody—by even higher authorities—would be me.

Twenty-one

True to his word, Buckman caught up with me a few hours later, and I didn't recognize him—at least, not right away.

Our truck-painting party was in full swing, with a temporary stage playing host to a rotating lineup of live bands, rap artists, and street poets. Young and old were enjoying the day; kids were playing, balloons bobbing, while Dante and his two arts-collective worker bees, Nadine and Josh, diligently painted our Muffin Muse, a curious audience looking on.

I was busy helping with the refreshments when Buckman caught me by surprise. He looked very different from the night before. For one thing, his stinky cigar was gone. For another, he'd lost his do-it-yourself bandoliers, the ones that dangled tools off his torso like a walking Home Depot.

Twenty pounds of Knight of the Road gear had been replaced with casual khaki pants and an open-necked pastel polo that displayed somewhat hairy arms. He'd shaved close and slicked his bristly flattop into a style that actually looked approachable—more average Joe than boot-camp marine. In fact, the only indication that Buckman was on duty were the cuffs, badge, gun, and holster affixed to his belt.

"You're out of uniform, Detective."

"It's casual Saturday."

"Isn't that casual *Friday*?"

"Maybe for you. I work six days a week."

"Then allow me to feed you. You must be hungry?"

"*Nah.* Not much. But I like the coffee I'm smelling . . ."

"That's our new blonde."

"Oh, really? What's *her* name?"

"Blonde *roast.* It's a nutty little number with a sweet and sassy note of honey-drizzled blackberry. She's a real kick, too—mainly because she's a lighter roast so there's slightly more caffeine left in the bean. But there's an even better reason men tell me they enjoy drinking her in."

"What's that?"

"She's far less trouble than a real blonde."

That cracked a smile out of him.

"I insist you try a selection of our mini-muffins, too. They're complimentary today. But for you, they're free."

"Okay, I'll bite. But make it all to go, okay? We need to talk, and we can't do it here."

"Why not?"

"Because I have something to show you. We'll do it in my car."

"Excuse me, Buckman? Do *what* exactly?"

"You'll see."

"But can't you just—"

"Don't argue, Cosi. Come now or I'll have to lock you up for your own protection."

My own protection? That shut my mouth. Not that his remark intimidated me. Mad Max didn't scare me in the least, but his implication that I was in danger did get my attention.

BUCKMAN led me through the buzzing crowd and toward the property's chain-link fence.

The location of our party was the parking lot of Matteo's new warehouse in Red Hook, a "residustrial" neighborhood on a peninsula of west Brooklyn. Mixed zoning allowed light industry to share the landscape with rickety row houses, packed with new immigrants and young urban pioneers, some of whom had opened trendy dive bars and quirky eateries.

I'd already commended Matt for purchasing land here. While gentrification had pumped up property values in surrounding neighborhoods, this hardscrabble area had real potential for development, yet property costs were still reasonable—and we were close enough to New York Bay for a splendid view of sparkling blue.

I also liked this location because it benefitted our Muffin Muse. Nearby, the famous Red Hook ball fields hosted local soccer teams every Sunday. The event attracted some of the best ethnic food trucks in the city, so serious foodies flocked to this area every week.

That's part of the reason we were getting such wonderful press attention for our party. Saturday was a slow news day anyway, and we had several angles going other than a culinary one: an original piece of art was being painted before the public by members of the Five Points Arts Collective; Esther and her budding young street poets were performing their latest work; and (the topper) we had two (count 'em, two!) mayoral candidates glad-handing potential voters, City Councilman Dominic Chin and Public Advocate Tanya Harmon.

The crowd was thick—three hundred, at least—but Buckman was big, cutting through the sea of bodies like a battleship. I followed in his wake, across the concrete toward the eight-foot chain-link gate festooned with balloons.

We crossed the street to his double-parked car, and with one look, I nearly dropped the snacks I was carrying.

"*This* belongs to you?"

"You're proud of your blonde. Well, this is my baby." Buckman's smile was back and even bigger. "A 1971 Pontiac GTO, which in my humble opinion was *the* classic muscle car of the 1970s. We're talking wire-mesh grilles, headlamps that glow like the eyes of a jungle cat—and look at those dual scoops on the hood."

"Fetching color. Is that cherry red?"

My response wasn't the one Buckman had been hoping for.

"'And what is under that hood, Detective Buckman?' is the question you *should* have asked. Then I would have said, 'Why it's a 335 horsepower HO engine, Ms. Cosi. The top power plant of its day. This little gem can pop zero to sixty in under six seconds.'"

He paused, waiting for my reaction.

"I can speak some Italian, French, and even a bit of Spanish. But I don't speak automotive."

Buckman laughed—and gave a short wave. The hand gesture wasn't for me. Glancing over my shoulder, I gawked at the arrival of a big police motorcycle with an equally big highway patrol officer astride its seat.

"Is that cop here to keep an eye on your car?"

"Actually, he's here to keep an eye on you. Get in and I'll explain."

But he didn't explain. Not right away. Mr. "Nah, Not Much" ripped into my mini-muffins, which he washed down with prodigious gulps of my steaming hot blonde.

"These are good," he garbled, mouth full.

"'And what *kind* of muffins are these, Ms. Cosi?' is the question you *should* have asked, Buckman. Then I would have said, 'Why, low-fat Strawberry Shortcake, Detective. As well as Nutella-Swirled Banana, Cherry Cheesecake, Blue Velvet, and Forbidden Chocolate . . . '"

Then I shared the fact that Lilly Beth was a key contributor to his present pleasure. At that, his eyes lit up.

"Take that Blue Velvet muffin you nearly swallowed whole. The color was inspired by the bluish purple *ube* cake that Lilly's Filipina mother bakes using an exotic purple yam.

"And the muffin you're enjoying now is our Forbidden Chocolate. Lilly Beth based that recipe on a combination of Filipino favorites—the puto rice muffin and chamborado, a chocolate rice pudding nearly every Pinoy kid grows up eating for breakfast. For extra nutrition, she found us a supplier of forbidden rice flour."

"Forbidden?" Buckman managed between bites. "Sounds dark."

"It is, literally. Forbidden rice is black. But the 'forbidden' name actually comes from feudal times. The farmers reserved it as a tribute payment to emperors who ruled out of Beijing's Forbidden City, which meant peasants were forbidden to eat it."

"I get it. Like the part of my paycheck that's forbidden for me to spend because it's reserved for Uncle Sam."

"Never thought of it that way . . . but since we're speaking about the dark side of food . . ."

I handed him the photos that attorney John Fairway gave me, and began to tick off my reasons for suspecting Kaylie Crimini of attempted murder: (1) the threat she'd made to me before the accident; (2) the argument she'd had with Lilly earlier that same day; and (3) the *New York Times* article in which Lilly Beth publicly criticized Kaylie and announced her endorsement of regulations that could hurt the Kween's marketing routine.

Finally, I recounted my trip to Chinatown, stressing the part about how Kaylie's service van turned up missing less than twelve hours after the hit-and-run. "It's all too much of a 'co-inky-dink,' as my barista Nancy would say."

When I finally stopped talking, Buckman blew out air. Then he set his cup on the dashboard. "I'm sorry, Clare, but if you're going to act like a detective, then you're going to have to swallow crow, just like we do."

"What does that mean?"

"It means, you're wrong. Missing or not, Kaylie's van did not hit Lilly Beth."

"How can you be sure?"

"Remember that development I mentioned to you on the phone? Well, we recovered the real van. Traffic found it parked on Thompson, near New York University. My guys are still going over it, and we're in the process of retrieving surveillance camera footage for the surrounding blocks."

I let out a breath—a severely disappointed one. "The van doesn't belong to Kaylie?"

"The van is registered to a Mr. Shun Xi, a fruit vendor on Canal. I had a talk with him this morning. We went over the details of his stolen vehicle report and he comes up roses."

"What did you find inside the van?"

"Multiple fingerprints. My guys are pulling them off the steering wheel, the window, the door handles, the rearview mirrors. Some belong to Mr. Xi, of course, but he was solid enough to give over his prints so we could match them out."

Buckman wiped his mouth with a napkin, brushed crumbs off his polo shirt. "The driver wasn't careful. We found a wineglass on the seat. Good stuff, too."

"You found alcohol?"

"I meant the glass. Quality. Real crystal. Like that gift registry crap they sell to rich stiffs on Fifth Avenue. I have someone tracing it now."

"I see. Waterford only interests you if it's a hood ornament?"

Buckman ignored my quip, reached into the backseat. When he turned around again, he held a laptop computer. "I hate to do this to you, Clare, but you need to watch this. It's not pretty, but it is important."

He opened the computer and placed it in my lap.

"What is this?"

"A surveillance video taken from the Hudson Antiques near your coffeehouse. They have lots of security cameras."

Buckman hit play and the cursor began to spin. "It's twelve seconds long. The footage is going to run twice. First at normal speed, then in slow motion."

In black and white and shot from the second floor, the camera looked down at the street. Hudson's asphalt was all grays and blacks, with the van suddenly streaking through the murk like a great white shark.

I was surprised to see *two* people in the vehicle's path, not just Lilly Beth. The van clearly swerved, missing a man in plaid shorts before striking Lilly, dragging her out of the frame.

"God," I choked.

"Watch it again," Buckman insisted.

It was worse in slow motion, like some catastrophe that you're sure you can stop, but you can't. Buckman's grim narration didn't help. Then he suddenly punched the pause key.

"Nobody mentioned this guy, and I wish we could find him." He was pointing to the man in plaid shorts.

"I've seen him in the Blend a few times. I'll keep an eye out for him. Get me a screenshot of this, and I can have my baristas look for him, too."

"Good. Now watch." He restarted the video. "You see how the driver swerves to avoid the guy in the plaid shorts, then gets back on track and points the van directly at Lilly Beth."

This time I looked away before the van hit my friend. Once was enough.

"What you saw just now tells me something you haven't considered. It could easily have been you who stepped around your food truck and into the street. At that angle, the van driver may not have been able to tell the difference between you and Lilly."

"I don't understand."

"You've got your hunch. Here's mine. I think you were the target. I think the driver saw you earlier in the day, noted what you looked like, what you were wearing, and waited for a chance to kill you. I also think this driver isn't finished. He, or she, is going to try again."

Twenty-two

Buckman closed the laptop. "Do you understand, Clare? You could be in danger."

"I don't believe it."

"You need more reasons?"

"Please."

"Here are *my* facts: (1) You and Lilly are about the same height, have similar hair color and attractive builds. At the time of the hit-and-run, you were both wearing jeans and yellow blouses. (2) The incident occurred in front of your coffeehouse, where you work every day. Lilly could have been run down at a lot of locations, easier ones than Hudson Street on a busy Friday night. This driver could have run her down near her home in Queens, where she takes her son to school every morning and picks him up every afternoon. Lilly's mother even told me she jogs nearly every day on the streets of Jackson Heights—"

"You spoke to her mother?"

"At the hospital."

"How is she doing?"

"Okay, considering what she's going through. You know, I was expecting a waterfall as soon as I started to grill her.

Don't get me wrong. That's just how it is after an accident. People are wrapped up in their own grief; they can't think of anything else. But not Lilly's mother, Mrs. Salaysay. As soon as we met, she treated me the same way you did."

I drew a blank.

"She asked after me—wanted to know if I was hungry. Did I want to eat something? She had this box full of goodies beside her. Kept dishing out treats to the people at the ICU. Crazy stuff. Plantains and yam chips, or some damn thing . . ."

"She had a *balikbayan* box—"

Buckman blinked. "Looked like a regular box to me. Corrugated, about yea big—"

"A *balikbayan* box is tradition. Filipinos are generous by nature, with their families and friends, even with strangers. When they travel abroad, they gather gifts from that foreign place—trinkets, edible treats, toys for children. They pack the little gifts into those big boxes and ship them home. That's how it started, anyway, as a homecoming gift."

"So it's a Christmas-all-the-time kind of thing."

I nodded. "Lilly's mom runs a small eatery in Queens, and lots of people in the community know and love her. These days, *balikbayan* boxes go both ways. She probably has boxes shipped to her all the time. The tradition itself is called *pasalubong*."

"Sounds like pass-it-along." Buckman smiled. "Nice. I like it."

"You would like Lilly, too. I mean . . . I hope you get the chance to like her . . ."

"I like her already," Buckman said with a softness in his voice that surprised me. "I spent some time at her bedside," he explained. "I was hoping she'd wake up, that I could talk to her. But there were complications. Another surgery. Brain surgery."

"I heard."

Buckman rubbed his prominent chin, glanced away. "Why does a woman look so small in a hospital? Is it because the beds are so big? Or because she's just fading away . . ."

As his voice trailed off, I wondered if he was talking about

Lilly, or flashing back to his late wife—the first one, the soul mate who'd died at the hands of a hit-and-run driver. Did Mrs. Buckman linger in a hospital bed? Did Max watch helplessly while the love of his life slowly slipped away from him? I wanted to ask, but it wasn't appropriate—and the last thing Quinn would want was for me to betray his confidence.

"Lilly's not fading," I said instead. "She's too gutsy for that. She won't give up, Max. She's a fighter."

He turned back to me. "I got that impression from the article in the paper."

I stared the man down. "I want you to know something about that article, about the way she came off. Lilly's seen the hardships and heartbreak that pediatric diabetes can cause, especially in poor communities. If the article makes her sound strident, a little too John Fairway, that's just a measure of her passion."

"Nice speech, Cosi. But we're on a detour. I'm asking why this incident went down in front of your coffeehouse, and I'm concluding it was because of you."

He reached into the glove compartment, brought out a narrow notebook and a pen.

"Let's do this by the book, shall we? Have you noticed any suspicious people hanging around your place of business? Your home?"

"They're one in the same. And I run a coffeehouse, so I have lots of people 'hanging around.' You might also define 'suspicious,' and bear in mind we're talking about New York."

"Okay, anyone following you? Phone calls late at night? Hang-ups? Threatening letters or e-mails?"

"Nothing! The only thorn in my side is Kaylie Crimini."

Buckman nodded. "We covered her."

I swallowed the last of my coffee. "So you'll get statements from her and her crew?"

Buckman nodded again.

Great, I thought. "And you'll get fingerprints from Kaylie and her staff to check against what you've found in the van, right?"

"As long as their prints are in our database."

"What if they aren't? Can't you bring them in, get their prints that way?"

Buckman massaged his eyes. "That won't be my first order of business, no."

I bristled at that. "Why not?"

"Because my theory that you were the target has no hard evidence to back it up—not yet anyway; that's what I'm looking for. Meanwhile, that *New York Times* piece quoting Lilly gave half the food-truck drivers in the city a reason to go after her. Any half-wit lawyer could stop me from compelling Kaylie and her staff to give me fingerprints by showing a dozen other food vendors as angry as Kaylie about Lilly's statements and proposals. Others may have argued with her publicly, too, even made threats."

"Listen, I know the *Times* piece gives cover to Kaylie. But don't you find it suspicious that this whole thing seems to center around Chinatown? Kaylie rents a kitchen down there. Vans and trucks are constantly loading and unloading with their motors running. I saw it myself today. She could have snatched that van easily, or a member of her staff could have done it for her—I'd bet my new coffee truck on the boy with the dragon tattoo. I even saw that kid involved with some black market activity today. Nothing I can prove, but . . ."

"Are you arriving at a point?"

"Yes. Your team is lifting fingerprints, right? So why don't we save some time here and cut through the legal red tape. Let's say I happened to collect something that had Kaylie's fingerprints on them or, even better, a *very suspicious* member of her staff—prints that were legally captured in a public place and freely given?"

The idea lit up Buckman again. Like a lot of cops, he was half in love with getting around the law—as long as it got the bad guy.

"Tell you what . . . my team would be compelled to check any fingerprints that you provided against the ones we find in the van. And if one of those prints should happen to prove a match, then we'd get a warrant and enough proof to arrest the SOB."

"Good, and I know someone who can help . . ." I pulled out my phone and sent a quick text message to my daughter's boyfriend. Sergeant Emmanuel Franco was the youngest member of Quinn's OD squad, and he'd happily backed me in the past.

Seeing my frantically moving thumbs, Buckman shot me a warning look.

"Just so we're clear, I have a philosophy. Pushing too hard, too fast, usually ends in a crash. I like results, but this isn't some Crazy Quinn stunt you're planning, is it?"

"I don't know. Define 'Crazy Quinn stunt.'"

Buckman waved me off. "There are too many to recount."

"Tell me one."

"I don't know if I should."

"For heaven's sake, why not?"

"For one thing, it's a bad example for you—"

"Bad *example*? What, am I in grade school?"

He folded his big arms, pointed a thick finger. "What you are, Clare Cosi, is a latent vigilante."

"Certainly not."

"I checked up on you. Over the past few years, you've done an awful lot of testifying for the prosecution."

"I'm a fixture of the West Village, Buckman. I'm the 'Coffee Lady.' People come to me with information. I see things, hear things . . . sometimes what I see and hear helps an official investigation. That's all."

"Pull the other one."

I exhaled. "Look, if someone I know is harmed or in trouble, it drives me a little crazy—maybe just like 'Crazy' Quinn. Maybe that's why we're together. But I'm no John Fairway. I share my information with the police. I don't think I'm above the law, and as much I'd like to exact my own punishment against scumbag criminals like the one who ran down Lilly, I have principles. I know the difference between vengeance and justice."

"You sure do like speeches."

"You're the one who accused me of—"

"Take it easy, Clare. I'm not accusing. I'm *recognizing*." His lips quirked in a little smile. "Let's just say it takes one to know one."

It takes one to know one? What did he mean by— I froze, the realization hitting me. *The year off . . . Buckman was talking about his leave of absence from the NYPD.*

He must have done something during that year—from his own admission—something akin to what I do. Was it a private investigation? A stakeout of the driver who escaped punishment for killing his wife? Did Buckman watch the man until he found a reason to put him in jail?

The way Buckman was looking at me now, like he had a secret, like we were two of a kind—I knew I was right. And I strongly suspected Mike knew the truth, too. That was probably the reason he'd been so careful on the phone, telling Buckman's story in the vaguest of terms.

"As far as the Crazy Quinn stuff," Buckman continued, "I like Mike. The fact is, I owe him, and I don't want you to get the wrong impression of your guy."

"Oh, come on. One story . . ." *Spill it, Bucket-mouth, you're dying to tell me.*

Buckman shrugged. "You twisted my arm."

He retrieved his coffee cup from the dash and drained it. "So here's your Mike Quinn, three months *maybe* on the narcotics squad, and he's stuck doing the grunt work: scooping up street sellers, interrupting trade, stop and frisk. That sort of crap.

"One reason he can't move to bigger stuff is because he won't skell up—grow the hair, the beard, wear crap clothes, behave like a dirtbag drug buyer. He was still trying to make that underwear model wife of his happy and she wouldn't allow it."

"That I believe."

"One day Mike's on the street. He collars this guy just out of the joint who's looking to take up his old crack-dealing ways. The scumbag's got a jacket as long as Trump's tax return and he's facing twenty more years mandatory time if he's convicted again. Well, Mike figures he'll turn the guy, get him to wear a wire when he goes in to talk to one of the biggest independent suppliers in the Bronx, a thug who's familiar with the perp and seems willing to do business with him.

"Only on the day Mr. Parole Violator is supposed to get wired and go to the meet, he pulls a Jimmy Hoffa." Buckman gestured with his hands. "The dude is gone. Most cops would pack it in at that point, but not Crazy Quinn. He wires up and goes in himself, all alone, *as is*, police-academy haircut and all. He's even wearing his badge."

"You're kidding?"

"*Now* you see? Crazy Quinn. What he did was suicide, and everybody knew it—including the dealer. But Mike is so ballsy and so convincing that the dealer actually buys his off-the-cuff story that he's a bad cop ready to facilitate smuggling in exchange for bribes!"

Buckman laughed, relishing the memory. "For three months Quinn takes bag money from this dealer. All the while he's learning the dealer's routes, his connections, even the names of cops who really were on the take.

"When the hammer finally came down, fifty guys were taken off the street. The kingpin decided to shoot it out and was killed—good thing for Mike, because the dealer would have reached out from prison to get revenge."

I cringed at the thought of Mike taking a chance like that. But he didn't have to prove himself anymore. He was a necktie guy now, off the street, for the most part, behind a desk, safe.

"Wait for it." Buckman laughed. "Because this story gets better. One of the deputy mayors, a total political animal, hears about the busts and comes up to the precinct to glad-hand. Wants to meet Mike personally and find out how he did it. Crazy Quinn could have been vague, mumbled something about solid police work and that crap. But no, Mike tells the DM the truth, the whole truth, and nothing but the truth."

"What's wrong with that?"

"It's wrong because this guy knew *zero* about police work. He comes out of the meet, calls the police commissioner, and 'suggests' Mike be investigated by Internal Affairs for corruption because he admitted to accepting bribes in the line of duty!"

"What did the commissioner do?"

"For once, 'politics' worked out for the good guy. The commish had a strong bond with the mayor—and he couldn't stand that DM. Out of spite, he did the exact opposite of the man's 'suggestion,' and kicked Mike upstairs. Bigger job. More responsibility. Mike passed his sergeant's exam the following year, and the rest is an NYPD success story."

"Then maybe Quinn wasn't so crazy after all."

"You've got a point. Only now I hear Mike's big rep is finally giving him blowback. Uncle Sam has been watching—and now they want him."

"What's that supposed to mean?"

"In a short window of time, Mike brought down an illegal Internet pharmacy and then exposed a rotten apple high up inside the NYPD. An ambitious U.S. attorney took notice, singled out Mike to be part of a special team based in D.C."

"Excuse me? You're saying Mike got a job offer from the Justice Department?"

"Sorry to give you the bad news. Powerful people got that way for a reason. When they make you an offer, they don't expect to be refused."

No, I thought, *there is no way Mike is considering a move to Washington.* With firmness I told Buckman, "You got it wrong."

"A little birdie I know in D.C. says otherwise."

Oh, that tone was insufferable. I'd grown to like Mad Max, but I could see how trying he could be—and irritatingly persuasive. He actually drove me to rethink my last phone conversation with Mike. He hadn't mentioned a job offer last night. But something wasn't right with him, either. He was stressing. And he was drinking, which wasn't like him.

"You're wrong, Detective," I said—though not as firm this

time. "Mike wouldn't leave his guys on the OD squad. He put the whole team together. It took him years . . ."

And what about me? I silently added. *Would Mike expect me to move with him? He knows how much the Village Blend means to me, not to mention my relationship with Madame, my family of baristas, the century-old legacy I mean to pass to my daughter . . .*

Buckman didn't reply. He was staring straight ahead, through the windshield, at the empty street. His attention had strayed back to Lilly's case, or more likely, from what I knew after being with Quinn, a part of his brain had never stopped thinking about it.

"I just can't figure out that wineglass," he muttered. "What was it doing on the front seat? Was hitting Lilly Beth something to celebrate?"

"Are you okay, Detective?"

"Sharp as a tune-up." Buckman said, suddenly back to business. "And I want you to stay that way, too, which is why I'll be giving Mike Quinn a call."

"Excuse me?"

"You're his main squeeze, right?"

I nodded.

"I'm sure he's mentioned what happens on the street. How drug dealers sometimes go after a rival's girlfriend or family member."

"No. You're not saying—"

"It's another possibility. The driver of that van could easily have been some friend or relative of a scumbag that Quinn put away. So watch your back. Officer Gifford will be outside until the party's over. If anyone threatens you in any way, let him know."

"I will."

"I don't have the manpower to assign you a private bodyguard. Gifford's off duty after the party, so go home and stay there. Will you do that for me?"

"I'll try."

"Do more than try, Cosi. I do not want the next hit-and-run I investigate to be yours."

Twenty-three

Buckman threw me a short wave and pulled out, his GTO engine revving with the power of a Formula One on the starting line. When he was gone, I glanced across the street at Officer Gifford, still astride his motorcycle. The burly cop noticed my gaze and smiled behind dark glasses.

Turning, I discovered Matt leaning against the warehouse fence, the harsh bite of industrial chain-links softened by our hand-painted party balloons, some shaped like muffins, others coffee cups—courtesy of Josh Fowler, Dante's Five Points friend.

"So, what did Bozo want?" Matt asked.

"How long have you been standing there?"

"Too long."

I shrugged. "Detective Buckman was just giving me an update. I'll fill you in later."

"You know that car he's driving is worth a quarter of a million dollars? How does a supposedly honest cop afford something like that?"

"Buckman's a motor head, Matt, with a degree in MechE. I'm sure he bought it used in the seventies when it wasn't worth spit."

"Here's another question." Matt unfolded his arms and pointed. "Why is that Chopper Cop sitting across the street from my warehouse?"

"Security for our party." (That was true.) "With two city officials here—both about to run for mayor—it makes sense, doesn't it?"

Matt grunted suspiciously. "Seems to me Dominic Chin and Tanya Harmon brought their own entourages, security included."

I could have said more, but the truth was too complicated to explain with three hundred guests in our parking lot. Besides, that sticky issue—the part where Buckman believed Quinn's work may have put my life in danger—would have sent Matt over the moon. And I needed him here in Brooklyn. So I changed the subject.

"Did I mention how good you look today?"

He blinked. "No . . ."

"Well, you do! Good enough for Helen Bailey-Burke to eat . . ."

I wasn't fibbing this time. My Esther needed Helen's approval to get us that grant money for the Muffin Muse. Matt could be a big help schmoozing her up. Thankfully, he looked tanned and rested, but best of all, he'd done as I'd asked and spent the morning hacking through jungles of facial hair. Like Michelangelo sculpting David, Matt had come away from the mirror with a masterpiece. Unfortunately, the neat, perfectly shaped goatee was a little too sexy.

"That's the problem," Matt said. "Maybe you failed to notice, but Helen arrived *with* wannabe mayor Tanya Harmon."

"I noticed. But then Helen is well connected. She raises money for a lot of causes, including political ones. I'm sure Tanya wants Helen in her pocket—if she's not there already."

"Well, here's the problem. Remember that little story I told you about me and Ms. Harmon?"

"Let's see . . . after one of your mother's fund-raisers, you and our city's current public advocate had a night of too much champagne. Is that about right?"

"Yes, and today I learned the champagne didn't affect her memory."

"Excuse me?"

"She wants an encore."

"You're kidding? She made a pass?"

"To put it mildly. First the woman dropped every suggestive double entendre she could think of, and when that failed to grab my attention, Tanya grabbed something else of mine. And right in front of *Mother*."

I bit my cheek to keep from laughing. "Take it easy, okay? Your mother is a bohemian at heart. And she knows your history. I'm sure she took the display in stride."

"Well, I didn't! Tanya doesn't even care that I'm married now."

I raised an eyebrow. "Being married never seemed to hamper you before."

"This is different. And I'll be frank: Tanya's a man-eater. She treats her employees like servants and her constituency like they work for her. Do you know what a woman that awful is like in bed?"

Matt fell silent. The statement was rhetorical, and I should have minded my own business, but the snoop in me was already on overdrive.

"Don't stop there," I said. "You've got me curious."

He sighed, glanced around, and lowered his voice. "You know me, Clare. I like to have fun in bed, but it's got to be a mutual thing. Spending a night as Tanya Harmon's lover was on par with being her waiter. The woman snapped her fingers and expected to get what she wanted, *when* she wanted it. And if you didn't deliver, a tongue lashing ensued—and not the good kind."

"Okay, I get it." I checked my watch. "The woman hasn't been here long, and she probably won't stay long, either. Just try to avoid her . . ."

"What do you think I've been doing? Thank goodness Dominic Chin is here. I've been hanging around him near the Five Points group at the truck. Tanya won't go near the guy—" Matt shuddered. "He's like a cross to her vampire."

"Come on. She can't be that bad."

While Matt assured me she was, I pulled out my cell phone and checked for new text messages. With relief, I saw Franco had responded to my request for help:

No problem, Coffee Lady. In transit to Red Hook now . . .

"I've got to hand it to you, Clare," Matt was saying. "How did you manage to lure the city's two biggest political rivals to your muffin mixer?"

"It just happened that way. I didn't plan it."

"Well, that's why there are so many reporters and photographers here. They're waiting for the fireworks."

"I dearly hope there won't be any. This isn't about politics. It's about art."

"Everything is about politics, which is why I came looking for you. Esther's been schmoozing Helen Bailey-Burke just fine. Mother is there for backup. But Esther's due on stage any minute, and Mother wants you to take over, stand beside Helen and answer any questions she might have about Esther's plans for your truck."

Matt pointed. "They're over by—"

I grabbed his hand and dragged my unwilling business partner along.

"You're coming with me," I said, "even if you have to face Countess Dracula. You have a *stake* in our success, too."

Matt groaned, but I wasn't sure why. It was either my lame joke or the thought of Tanya Harmon sucking the life right out of him.

"THERE you are, Matteo! Wherever did you disappear to?"

I'd seen our public advocate on television and expected the woman to be much smaller. In person, there was nothing diminutive about her. Alpine tall, with a lush figure, the blond Valkyrie's determination was as large as her stature, which is why Matt and I didn't get within ten feet of Esther and Helen Bailey-Burke.

Like a raptor streaking toward her prey, Tanya stepped out of the crowd to head us off. Matt told me Tanya's modeling days were long over, but to my mind, the ice-princess was still catwalking the runway.

"That's so like you, Matt! Here we were having a marvelous time, and you just scurry off!"

Tanya's eager eyes were bright under makeup more suitable for a late-night rendezvous than a family-friendly afternoon bash. Her clothing choice, a shocking pink couture suit, made me fear for the redecoration plan of Gracie Mansion should she actually become our next mayor.

"Duty called, but I'm back," Matt replied.

Though my ex wore a strained smile, at least his facial muscles functioned. Tanya's expression—well, there wasn't much of one, actually. Her eyes moved in their sockets, but not much else, and I feared the worst: Botox addiction.

"So, Matt, you were telling me that your wife is out of town. The way you two travel, I'll bet you don't sleep together more than a few weeks every year. That's got to be *hard*, especially on a man like you . . ."

Oh, god. She did not just say that. But she did, and now she was moving her hand, reaching for Matt's— *Oh, no, lady. Not on my watch.*

"Hello!" I said, stepping forcefully between them. I grabbed her wayward hand. "I'm Clare Cosi, Matt's business partner. I'm also his ex-wife and mother to his grown daughter. I'm so glad you could come to our party."

"Ah, the little woman . . ." Tanya gave my hand a quick politician's pump. "So nice to meet you. I hope I can count on your vote."

"Yes, well . . ." *(Not in this liftetime.)* "I am glad you could come today—" I began to tell her, but Tanya's attention was gone.

"I'm going to a soiree later," she informed Matt, "and I

heard amazing things about this fusion restaurant in Chinatown. It's right near my acupuncture clinic—"

I threw a loaded look at Matt. *Botox? Acupuncture? Is this woman in love with needles, or what?*

"So, Matt?" she prompted. "Want to share an early nosh?"

His glance at me was desperate: *Can I please tell her to go to hell? Please?!*

No!

Fine! "I'll, uh, get back to you on that, Ms. Harmon . . ."

Undeterred, the Terrible Tanya took another tack—

"Wait, what am I thinking? You're an *importer*, so this will be right up your alley. I'm going to the Atlantic-Pacific Trade Commission Ball tonight at the Pierre Hotel. Join my group, Matt! You can do a little glad-handing, make some connections. Raise your profile." She frowned at me and lowered her voice. "This is all so low-rent. You're above this . . ."

Matt shifted uncomfortably. "Well, I . . ."

"He can't," I said, moving between them again. "He's *busy*."

I'm quite certain Frozen Face would have raised an eyebrow at me, if she could have. In lieu of working muscles, she simply glared down as if I were an annoying little pest-bug. "Excuse me?"

"Our daughter is working in Paris right now. She's calling us tonight, and Matt doesn't want to miss Joy."

"Oh, I assure you, dear, if Matt comes with me tonight, he won't miss joy. I'll see to that!" Tanya laughed, her gaze still fixed on my ex. "So, we're on? Tonight at the Pierre? The APTC ball. I'll *expect* you."

Matt could see I wanted to get to Esther, but I was unwilling to abandon him. He cleared his throat and tried to get us both out of this: "Tanya, don't you want to shake a few hands? Greet the people? They could be your constituents, someday."

"This bunch? Why bother? I don't see any deep pockets. That's why I'm sticking close to Helen. You're a big boy, aren't you? You should know elections are won with dollars, not handshakes. And the big money is at the ball tonight." She lowered her voice. "And speaking of dollars. I have quite a lot of pull with Helen. If you want this grant, you might reconsider my invitation . . ."

I stared in disbelief, flashing for a moment on Buckman's warning about people in power. To my surprise, Matteo didn't appear fazed by the ugly proposition. In fact, the threat changed his gaze from long-suffering to cold as finished steel.

"Matt," I whispered, "you don't have to—"

He squeezed my arm. "Go to Esther. She needs you. I'll take care of this."

Twenty-Four

"At its core, literature is about the sharing of experience . . ."

From behind a standing microphone, Esther addressed the audience. With her onstage was a group of inner-city children, trying their darndest to keep from fidgeting.

Smiling, Esther pushed up her black-framed glasses. "Here's what I teach my kids: The subject of our poetry might be a flash of awareness, affection, even anger. It might be an epic story that retells years of pain and struggle. Whatever the form, if the poem shares a unique human experience, then it can help us better understand ourselves, our neighbors, even our enemies . . ."

The crowd had been restless when Esther first started, but with her last moving words, most of the packed parking lot fell as silent as a church.

"We may live in a world of divides, but there are bridges, too; and poetry is one of them. The best poetry does more than reach across; it helps us reach each other."

"You go, Esther!" called out a fan. The crowd lightly clapped.

"With tools of language and imagery, we poets sharpen up our musings. Then we pull back the bow, open our mouths, and *let fly*, seeking to pierce the hard human shell of our audience . . ."

Hard human shell is right, I thought with a glance at the brittle brunette to my left.

Our typically cynical Esther was showing us a whole new side of herself today—one of rare eloquence and sincere passion. Yet the director of special funding for the New York Art Trusts appeared unmoved.

Maybe Helen Bailey-Burke was in the habit of withholding approval, an occupational hazard from her profession as a high-powered fund-raiser. Or maybe she was just (to borrow a phrase from Allen Ginsberg's generation) *uptight*.

Unlike her big, brassy friend Tanya (a harridan of the first order), petite Helen impressed me as a woman of patrician beauty and aristocratic grace. Just like Tanya, however, she'd come to our neighborhood block party impeccably overdressed.

Her off-white skirt rippled with knife-sharp pleats, and the sienna highlights in her cocoa-colored French twist precisely matched the piping of her tailored Fen jacket and the shiny polish on her pedicured toes. A string of black Tahitian pearls with diamond rondelles dripped from her neck, and the marquis-cut ruby on her right hand was at least the size of two Kona peaberries.

In contrast, Madame was a portrait of Hepburn simplicity. Her silver pageboy loosely framed her gently wrinkled features, which carried only a hint of silver-blue eye shadow and a light pink gloss. Under an open silk shirt the color of today's crystalline blue sky, she wore comfortable Kabuki slacks and a colorful tee emblazoned with Roy Lichtenstein pop art. Even her jewelry was whimsical: a chunky street-fair necklace of rough-cut amethyst and a wristwatch of neon plastic.

She now stood on one side of Helen while I stood on the other. Where my ex-husband was standing, I had no idea.

After Tanya's shocking proposition, Matt had taken her

forcefully by the elbow (a move the pink-suited Valkyrie actually appeared to enjoy) and led her somewhere private. Exactly what he was saying (or doing) to Tanya Harmon, I had no idea, but my blood was still on the boil at her arrogance.

"Okay!" Esther cried, bringing up the energy on stage. "My youngest group is up first. For today, they've written in the haiku form, which is three lines with each line carrying a set number of syllables: five, seven, and five. The subject of their poems is something we've all come here today to sample—*food*!"

Esther waved at the audio-video crew, where her boyfriend Boris, aka Russian rap artist B.B. Gunn, flipped a switch. An urban beat flowed from the speakers. The crowd responded with an excited buzzing.

"Here we go!" Esther cried. "Tag-Team Haiku, do your *thang . . .*"

As Esther backed away, the children formed a half circle and began to clap with the beat. The first poet, an African-American girl, stepped up.

Gooey, toasty melt
Feeding me with all her heart
Mommy makes grilled cheese.

After blowing a kiss to her mother, she turned and held out her hand. A light-skinned boy with Asian features slapped it and recited:

Uptown and downtown,
China, Mid-East, Italy,
Melting pots—best soup!

He turned and slapped the hand of a Latino girl, who said:

Piling it higher,
The city, like my sandwich.
Is sky the limit?"

She slapped the hand of a Korean-American boy, who jumped high, kicked out, and chanted:

Crack it then hack it.
Open wide and attack it.
What is eating you?

He pumped his fist in the air then slapped the hand of an auburn-haired girl. With an Irish lilt, she softly declared:

Roll with it, New York.
Everything inside us knows
Heroes fill us up . . .

When the kids finished, the crowd went crazy, cheering and applauding. Then Esther was back on stage, introducing the next group. A little older, a little harder edged, they performed free-form poetry as rap.

The subject was food again, but each poem was vastly different. One was funny: a Chinese-American girl's failed attempt to make her mom's fried rice. Another was sad: an African-American boy's difficult memories triggered by a sweet potato pie, his dad's favorite, served at the man's funeral. Another was angry: a Latino girl's fury over her "hot *dog* of a boyfriend" buying another girl a Nathan's footlong. Yet another pulsed with love: a Pakistani boy's appreciation for his grandmother's "spice for life" cooking.

Madame was so moved by Esther's work that she brushed away a tear, and when the show was over and our "big-bootied" barista joined us again, she hugged Esther's ample form and kissed her on both full cheeks.

"Thank you, my dear, dear girl! Thank you for keeping alive the legacy of my Village Blend! Along with Dante, Gardner, and Tucker, you are bringing our link to the arts into a new century—" Her voice caught. "I only wish I could be there with you through the next four decades. I could not be more pleased, or proud."

Esther was tearing up now, and I was close to waterworks. Glancing to my left, I saw the reaction of Helen Bailey-Burke.

There was no smile, no warmth, no generosity of spirit. Just a lackluster monotone: "Thank you so much."

"You're welcome!" Esther exclaimed with a grin. Then she pointed. "Ma'am, do you see those buildings in the distance? Those are the Red Hook projects. Now, I can't take a kid from there and talk to him about literary movements—how the Augustans of the eighteenth century share similarities with the Postmodernist of the twentieth. Yeah, right! I might as well speak to the kid in Martian!"

Esther laughed. "But with your grant this summer, what I *can* do is listen to him imitate his latest rap-star hero, ask him to make up some rap of his own, write down the lyrics, and help him start to find his voice as a poet and writer.

"I'll teach that child that he's part of an ancient tradition—a time when poems were once transmitted orally from performer to performer. He'll learn how to measure a poem in feet and meter, how his favorite rappers use rhythm, rhyme, repetition, and kennings—just as William Shakespeare did—to facilitate memorization and recall . . ."

I wanted to applaud Esther right then and there. And if I were Mrs. Bailey-Burke, considering her for grant approval, I would have been peppering her with questions. But Helen continued to listen without comment.

"Esther is quite a popular street poet, herself," Madame pointed out.

"Is that right?" Helen asked.

"Yes, ma'am," Esther said. "I am popular. But in the scheme of things, I'm nothing special. You see, this grant is not for me. It's for the undiscovered poets out there in our city—the next Nikki Giovanni or Pedro Pietri. After working with these kids, I now know that my most profound work on this earth isn't going to be what I rap, but how I rap open the door to a new world of ideas, of literature, of potential for our inner-city kids . . ."

"I see," Helen blandly replied.

God, I wanted to shake the woman! Months ago, five independent advisors had reviewed Esther's written application and highly recommended the grant be awarded. Unfortunately, Helen had the sole power to deny it.

New York City Art Trusts facilitated financial awards to worthy programs, but they were not a public group. Their funds came from private donors, and very generous donors (like Helen) were assigned "director of special funding" status.

Helen had set up the endowment in memory of her deceased daughter, Meredith. She reviewed each grant personally. Regardless of what the advisors recommended, she insisted on playing the Roman empress, giving each applicant her final thumbs-up or -down.

With Helen's next question, I knew how that thumb was wavering, and it had nothing to do with the worthiness of Esther's program.

"Whatever is Dominic Chin doing here?" Helen intoned. "This is awfully far from his Manhattan district, isn't it?"

"Councilman Chin is a big supporter of the Five Points Arts Collective," I quickly explained, "and they've been very helpful to us with the truck painting and decorations. They invited him. But he has nothing to do with Esther's work or her plan for inner-city summer outreach."

Maybe if I point out the obvious?

"I noticed you arrived today with our public advocate, Tanya Harmon . . ."

Helen waved a hand, as if my bringing up her own political leanings (not to mention conflict of interests) was of no significance when it came to evaluating a grant objectively.

"Tanya and I were in the same sorority, that's all there is to it." Then she huffed, as if I'd imposed upon her in some manner. "*Really . . .*"

I hoped I was wrong about Helen, but I doubted it. Maybe it was the way she continually exhaled with inappropriate impatience or lifted that too-perfectly sculpted chin. But I got the distinct impression the East Side socialite looked down her razor-straight nose at everyone—not just Esther, me, those kids, or even Madame, but the entire peninsula of Red Hook, Brooklyn.

Madame exchanged a glance with me, an unhappy one. Was she displeased with what I'd said? Or with Helen's behavior? Maybe Matt was right, after all. From the arts to academics, politics to food, it seemed everything came down to a turf war.

I'd better step away before I say something I'll regret . . .

Excusing myself, I moved toward the parking lot entrance, hoping I'd run into Matt, and that's when I heard it—

"Chocolat ship . . . Straw-*bear*-wee . . . Butt-*tair*-cream . . ."

Speakers blaring, the Kupcake Kart was back to torture us.

Twenty-Five

For this afternoon's surprise appearance, Kaylie Crimini had added something special to her psychedelic sugar bus. Her mock Eiffel Tower was trailing a fluttering banner with the words *Kupcake Kween*, just so we didn't forget.

As the vehicle rumbled closer, heads turned to watch the Kween's kaleidoscopic cart roll to a stop across the street from our front gate. Inside of a minute, Kaylie was clanging open her window and customers were lining up. *(Traitors.)*

"Fla-*vours* for *vous*! *Chocolat* fooge! *Chocolat* ship . . ."

Kaylie's odious jingle actually began to drown out the melodic tones of Four on the Floor, a jazz quartet headed by our Blend's musician-barista Gardner Evans.

"Boss!" A livid Esther appeared at my shoulder. "Are you seeing this? Kaylie is out to ruin us!"

"It's okay," I said.

"Okay!" Esther cried. "How can it be okay?! The last time we saw Moby Crumb, she was raking in the cash at the Seaport. Now, what could have prompted her to change venues? Trashing our party, that's what! Her obnoxious jingle will ruin everything!"

"Kaylie's not going to ruin anything—*or* run over anyone. Not today." I pointed. "Look . . ."

With easy precision, the giant Officer Gifford, in full highway patrol regalia, dismounted from his motorcycle and ambled to Kaylie's window. A few words were exchanged, then Gifford made a sharp hand gesture—as if he were flipping off a radio in mid-air.

Five seconds later, Kaylie's speakers went silent.

Behind her black-framed glasses, Esther's brown eyes widened. "Oh, I like that dude . . ."

"Yeah, me too."

"Who invited him?"

"Our friend Detective Buckman. But I'm on the lookout right now for someone else: Joy's boyfriend. So if you see him—"

"Franco!" Esther waved through the crowd. "There he is!"

I turned and joined the welcoming chorus. "Franco! Over here!"

WEARING a white tank and dark blue sweatpants, Sergeant Emmanuel Franco had come to our party directly from a workout. His scalp looked freshly shaved, his muscles newly pumped, but the dead giveaway was the scent on his fresh-scrubbed skin—the unmistakable smell of Irish Spring, the soap of choice for Mike Quinn, if not his entire OD squad.

Mr. Clean grinned broadly at my enthusiastic greeting. "Wow, Coffee Lady, I haven't had a reception like this since I brought donuts to the working girls along Eighth Avenue."

Esther smirked. "So the Boss and I remind you of *working girls?*"

"*Girls* is a catchall term, you understand," Franco replied. "Some of them were trannies."

"Gee, that silver tongue sure knows how to flatter a woman."

"Just curious," I asked. "Why the donuts?"

Franco shrugged. "One of the ladies iced on bad heroin.

Your man Quinn wanted answers. Girls eat together and they gossip." He paused to let out a put-upon sigh. "A cop's work is never done."

"I'm glad to hear you say that. How do you feel about a little unpaid overtime?"

"I'm civic minded."

I explained the situation and pointed out Kaylie's truck.

To his credit, Franco didn't grill me with questions or lecture me on police procedure, primarily because, at this point in our relationship, he knew me—and my nosy ways.

"Give me a few minutes to check things out, Coffee Lady, and I'll be back."

Ten minutes later, Franco was true to his word. After observing Kaylie's Kart, he came back with a plan—and a half-dozen cupcakes.

"I hope you bought those for cover," I said.

"For cover and a snack." He tucked into one. "Oh, man, these Maple-Bacon Buttercreams are as good as they look!"

I folded my arms. "You know she whips bacon grease into her batter."

"Really? *Awesome*."

"Let's get back to the business at hand, shall we?"

"More like *on* hand," said Franco, shoving the rest of the cupcake into his mouth. "Getting fingerprints off that kid with the dragon tattoo will be a trip to Coney Island. All I need are a couple of props and your professional opinion."

"What about?"

"Kaylie's coffee. I'll need to chat up dragon boy about it. Is the stuff any good?"

Oh, lord. How do I answer without sounding like a shrew . . .

"Kaylie's beans are roasted by Jimmy Wang, a pro out of Portland who just opened a shop in Chelsea. I'm sure they're excellent, but beans are just the beginning of a great cupping experience, and Kaylie isn't there yet. I suspect her equipment isn't kept clean enough, and her crew keeps a pot around too long, so it's buyers beware of getting anything close to a fresh cup."

"Whoa, slow down, Coffee Lady. You know what? Change of plan. I'll talk up the dude's tats instead."

"His tattoos?"

Franco nodded. "Good tip to remember: You can always make a felon your friend if you compliment his body art."

"I'll make a note of it."

"You saw it, right? The guy's got a whole lizard on his arm. He probably gave it a *name*."

"What about these props you need?"

"A small thermos and a plain paper bag big enough to hold it."

"I have lots of paper bags," I assured him. "What I don't have is a thermos small enough to . . . Wait! Dante has a small thermos! He's using it for his coconut water . . ."

I led Franco through the still-growing crowd, to the party's main attraction.

Formerly plain, even a bit drab, our Muffin Muse truck now sparkled like a golden nugget in the afternoon sun. The night before, Dante and his Five Points protégés—the lean, purple-haired Josh Fowler and the strategically pierced, spiky-haired Nadine Wells—had primed the exterior with a coat of golden brown enamel. At the moment, its flanks were covered with white stencils and miles of masking tape, but I had high hopes for the big unveiling.

Behind a crowd-control perimeter of yellow rope, Dante and his two helpers were reloading spray guns and preparing brushes for the detail work. Franco and I ducked under the rope and crossed the sprawling canvas tarp splattered with enough color to stretch a Jackson Pollock knockoff.

Dante was more than happy to give up his thermos. "Keep it," he told us, brandishing his paint gun like it was a semiautomatic. "It's worth losing a lousy thermos to nail that punk, Billy Li."

Franco looked the thermos over, opened the cap, and sniffed.

"Yummy . . . smells like a Mounds bar." He turned to me. "But I'll need to clean it, inside and out."

"There's soap and a sink in the truck," I said.

We stepped inside the Muffin Muse, and Franco quickly scanned our equipment-packed interior. Turning, his broad shoulders brushed a cabinet.

"Whoa . . . I've seen roomier digs at Rikers."

"This is not a prison cell; it's a small kitchen—and it's much less claustrophobic when our big side window is up. It's shut now because of the painting . . ."

I showed him the sink, gave him towels and a paper bag. Franco rinsed out the thermos and wiped every inch of the exterior with a towel. Then used his handkerchief to lift the thermos and slipped both into the paper bag.

"You're going to an awful lot of trouble, aren't you? Why don't you just buy coffee and a cupcake from Billy and use the cup for your fingerprints?"

Franco gave me a patient half smile. "You want a tutorial, Coffee Lady? Fingerprints 101?"

"Sure. Why not."

"There are three kinds of fingerprints. The first is plastic—like if Dragon Boy shoves his thumb into the icing and then hands over my cupcake. I *might* get an imprint in 3D."

I frowned. "There's no guarantee he'll do that—or that you won't eat the cupcake first."

"Exactly. Then there's latent prints you get off paper and cardboard, what the lab coats call 'absorbent surfaces.' They're invisible, which means the techno-geeks will have to give the cup a chemical fuming, then wait six hours to know if they got a print, or a partial, or most likely just a smear."

"So I guess my coffee cup idea was . . ."

"Less than stellar. Good thing you texted little old me. See, what you want are clean, visible prints created by perspiration or body oil. All you need is a little powder to make them pop. You get those kinds of prints off a smooth, nonabsorbent surface like glass or metal—or this thermos."

I nodded, grateful. "So what's your big plan?"

"I give the guy Dante's thermos, chat him up while he fills it with stale Jerry Wang coffee. I hold up my bag like so—" Franco lifted the sack, gripping it by its rolled-up edges. "Dragon Tattoo dumps the thermos into the bag, and *voila*, I have a perfect set of the dude's prints."

And Matt thinks you're a mook. "You're amazing, Franco."

"Be sure to tell you daughter that, will you? Early and often."

"That's the trouble—I don't talk to her often enough. I did get some photos from her, taken in the Loire Valley—"

"So did I." He smiled, the wistful boy-crush in his gaze. "They're in my wallet."

I knew it . . . I knew she'd sent him the photos, too!

"Well, thanks again, Franco. Just be careful, okay? I saw it myself. Billy Li can be dangerous."

"So can I."

I didn't dispute it.

Tucking the bag under his arm, he sauntered to the truck's back door. "As soon as I have the prints, I'll take them to Buckman's team at AIS." He paused. "If anybody asks, it was you who got these prints. I'm just the delivery boy. Got it?"

"Believe me, I'm getting to know Max Buckman. Nobody will ask."

As I watched Franco depart, I couldn't help feeling a sense of relief. Billy's prints would soon be in police custody. And if Billy's didn't match what Buckman's team found on that van—or the wineglass that was curiously sitting on the front seat—Sergeant Fingerprints would help me out again.

We'd go for Kaylie's next, then more members of her staff, ruling each one out until we found the driver.

Humming to our party's live music, I straightened up the kitchen, finally feeling that things were back under control . . . until I heard the agitated tone in Madame's voice—

"Have you seen Clare Cosi? I *must* speak with her *at once*!"

"Just a minute, ma'am. I think she's in the truck . . ."

Twenty-six

"Ms. Cosi? Are you there?" Josh Fowler stepped into the truck's small kitchen. "Mrs. Dubois is looking for you."

"Thanks, I heard . . ."

As I moved to follow the lean young artist with the purple hair and sideburns, I noticed something for the first time. His paint-flecked tee, emblazoned with the words "A for Anarchy," displayed a bright orange button bearing the logo for Two Wheels Good.

"Josh, hold up." I pointed. "Where did you get that button? Is John Fairway here?"

"I don't know if he's here, but I got the button from that woman—"

We were outside now, and Josh pointed to a knot of people near our refreshment tables. I recognized the woman immediately—frizzy blond hair, silver bike shorts, pink sweatband. This was the Two Wheels Good activist, the one I'd seen in Chinatown. She was moving aggressively through our parking lot, passing out buttons and pamphlets. She didn't appear to be doing anything threatening . . . *yet.*

"Is anything wrong, Ms. Cosi?"

Gee, where to start?

"Clare!" Madame cried, charging me like the java Joan of Arc. "We must talk!"

My groan was barely audible, but Josh heard me.

"What is it?" he asked. "Maybe I can help."

Nice kid. I patted his shoulder. "Thanks, Josh. I appreciate it. I'll get back to you."

"That woman!" Madame wailed. "That *awful* woman!"

"Which one?" I asked. *Helen? Tanya? Kaylie? Warrior Barbie? Or is there someone I missed?*

"The woman to whom I am referring is that *so-called* grant director!"

"Helen Bailey-Burke?" I said, and noticed Josh stop in his tracks. He'd been moving to rejoin Dante and Nadine. Now he turned to openly stare at us.

Madame hooked my arm and guided me toward the rear of the truck, where we had a bit more privacy. We stopped next to the chain-link fence on the far perimeter of Matt's warehouse. On the other side of the fence, a dead-end road ran straight to New York Bay, a choppy, sparkling plane of blue now scenting the breezy air with the fresh tang of sea salt.

"What happened?" I asked.

Madame's forehead crinkled in distress. "She's turning Esther down. She's rejecting the grant."

"I'm sorry to hear that, but I'm not surprised."

"What you should be is *outraged*. There were five independent advisors who highly recommended approval."

"I know."

"And do you know how I'd characterize the reasons that woman gave me for turning Esther down?"

I shook my head.

"Bullshit!"

I'd been squinting in the sunlight; now my eyes widened. Madame rarely cursed. And when she did, it never went beyond the mild French merde. Her curse seemed to lift on the wind and bob (like our custom-shaped party balloons) before breaking to pieces.

"According to Helen Burke," Madame furiously explained, "our Esther did not have the right 'polish' or 'presence' to join her 'exclusive group' of awardees for her memorial grant. Well, I've been around the block, and I know how to read code!"

"You're saying the woman wasn't judging Esther's work?"

"She was not. Helen Burke was judging Esther on how she would *look* in photo ops beside her, with a caption attached to her grant. She was judging Esther on how she'd be viewed when shown off at cocktail parties—be they corporate, political, or networking shindigs masquerading as charity dinners."

Fists on lean hips, Madame appeared ready for battle.

"I've met far too many Helen Burke's in this town, Clare. So-called patrons of the arts who judge with a ridiculously superficial yardstick how poets and painters, writers and artists 'should' speak, act, think, and dress—just like they do, of course! Well, I gave her a piece of my mind, I can tell you."

"You did?" I bit my cheek to keep from grinning.

"Oh, I stayed civil—even though I dearly wanted to kick that cow in the rump and be done with her. Our party was 'low-rent' she said. This area 'unsavory.' What a complete moron! Here's a woman who has no understanding of our cultural history, who thinks Greenwich Village was always filled with trendy bistros and expensive boutiques, that the heart of bohemia is found in a chic shoe store and a cupcake shop!"

I'd never seen my former mother-in-law so angry. I was witnessing a rare thing: *Madame Unleashed!*

"That odious woman had the *nerve* to tell me she'd come here expecting a 'classier act' given Esther's attachment to our Village Blend, and that's when I *educated* her."

"I see . . ." I finally stopped biting my cheek. The grin just had to come out. "And what did you say?"

"I informed Her Highness of High Heels that Greenwich Village—not to mention Soho, Noho, and Tribeca—may have undergone facelifts in recent years, but for over half a century, they were not 'classy' parts of town. The Village was a place you went because the rent was cheap! It was dangerous and dirty and filled with drunks and drug addicts, but it was also filled with brilliant oddballs: young artists and poets, musicians and painters, comedians and playwrights, none of whom could afford designer sandals, spa memberships, teeth whitening, and nose jobs!"

"Touché!"

"Then I set the woman straight. Art isn't about what's *pretty*. It's about what's *true* and what's *real*. Being an artist is about finding your voice and vision—just as Esther described it. And you don't find truth through cosmetic surgery. You find it through authenticity."

"Beautiful!"

"I'll tell you something else, Clare, that awful woman did one good thing today. She made me realize that this food-truck idea of yours and Esther's is much more than a business investment. Esther was right when she talked about poetry reaching across divides."

I couldn't nod my head fast enough. "Didn't you urge me to take chances, cross boundaries? Didn't you say, 'If you don't dare, you don't survive'?"

"Indeed I did, but I was so busy lecturing you, I failed to heed my own advice. Esther has restarted my engine. I will rise to her challenge and travel across divides with her, across these bridges to support tomorrow's young artists and writers where they live now!"

Clearly, Madame was ready for a Washington Square soapbox, and I was delighted to see her so fired up, but I had to point out—

"We're going to have to deal with one ugly truth today. Esther's been badly let down. How is she taking the disappointment?"

"Our girl doesn't know yet. My conversation with Helen was private, and I *do not* want Esther told."

"Is that realistic? She's going to find out soon enough."

"The formal rejection will come in the mail next week. But I'll have things in hand before that . . ."

"What things?" I asked, seeing the impish flash in her blue-violet gaze. "What are you cooking up?"

"I know why Esther didn't come to me for help with arts funding. She wanted to do this on her own, and she *did*. The grant was technically approved. So I am going to take her written application and that videotape Boris made of her young performance poets and find her another donor. My Otto will help, of course . . ."

Otto was Madame's beau—a "younger" man in his early seventies, and a gallery owner. He'd been supportive of the Village Blend for some time. Although he'd been unable to attend our Red Hook party, I had no doubt he'd join Madame in making Esther's summer poetry outreach a pet project.

"Bailey-Burke may be brilliant at raising money, but she knows nothing about where real art comes from." Madame waved her hand. "She needs to learn a little more about those gemstones she likes to wear. They may have been sold out of a Tiffany display case, but each was created by years of pressure and dug out of a dark mine."

A single pair of hands began to clap. Turning, we found Josh Fowler eavesdropping.

"Ma'am, you are so right!" Before we could respond, he added, "Helen's a snob. She always was."

"You know her?" I asked surprised.

"I was best friends with her daughter, Meredith."

"The one who died?"

"Yes. I was hoping Esther would get one of those grants. That's why I told her about it. I wanted at least one of my friends to get some of Meredith's money."

"You mean her mother's money, don't you?" I said. "The endowment came from her donation. That's why she was given director's status."

"Helen Bailey-Burke is pretending the money was hers. But it didn't cost her a penny. Meredith's grandfather put that money in trust for Meredith when she was born. She was supposed to get it on her twenty-first birthday. What she got instead was a death sentence at eighteen."

My heart nearly stopped at his wording. "A death sentence. My god, Josh, how did the girl die?"

"You don't know?"

I shook my head.

"Her mother killed her."

Twenty-seven

"Helen Bailey-Burke killed her own daughter?" I asked in shock. "Why isn't she in prison?"

"Believe me, Ms. Cosi," said Josh, "if it were up to me, she would be."

Madame and I exchanged confused glances. Then Josh explained his statement. Like a lot of young people, this budding young painter saw things in melodramatic terms, and the story, while awful, was more tragic than criminal.

It seemed Meredith Burke was a lot like Esther—arty, quirky, intelligent, funny. She was also on the Rubenesque side of femininity, with facial features that were strong and full of character—as opposed to delicate and runway ready.

"Meredith's mother and father divorced when she was little," Josh explained, "and Meredith resembled her dad. I think that was the biggest issue between her and her mother. Meredith took after her father in so many way, not just looks, that Helen never stopped wanting to change her . . ."

"Change her into someone more like herself?" I assumed.

"Exactly." Josh folded and unfolded his arms. His frustration was almost palpable. "She bribed Meredith. Pushed her into getting this done and that done. Small stuff at first, but then Helen's plastic surgeon offered this three-in-one thing. Dramatic stuff in one day. Helen told Meredith that if she went through the three-in-one, she'd release a big chunk of money from her trust fund. And we both really wanted that money . . ."

"Why did you want the money, dear?" Madame asked curiously. "Did you want to travel together, something like that?"

Josh shook his head. "Meredith and I had been drawing a series of comic books for years. They were her ideas and her words—but my art. We did it together, and we wanted to publish them."

I was already dreading the end of this story. "What happened, Josh? How did Meredith die?"

"Something went wrong after her cosmetic surgery. They said it wasn't the doctor's fault. Whatever happened was part of the risk anyone takes when they have surgery done—and that's why I'll never stop blaming her mother. Helen may not have shoved Meredith off a cliff, but she sure as hell led her to the edge and bribed her to jump."

The idea of Helen pushing her child to have herself redone made me sick to my stomach—but also grateful. Madame exchanged glances with me. I knew we were having the same thought.

Thank goodness that woman walked away from our Esther.

I'd grown as protective of my baristas as Madame had of me. And the last thing I'd want is for Esther to have someone as toxic as Helen Bailey-Burke making her doubt herself.

The irony didn't escape me: Before this discovery, I'd been incensed over Helen's rejection. Now I was grateful for it. Even my octogenarian employer came away with an inspiring new quest. But life was funny that way. Blessings in disguise were never recognizable—until they were. Like a dark night that gradually lightens until suddenly you realize its day.

I was just getting to feel positive about *this* day when the sound of bickering voices drew my attention. Two women nearby were arguing, and their conflict was escalating fast.

"Not *you* again . . ."

The first voice belonged to (surprise, surprise) our favorite person, mother of the year Helen Bailey-Burke. Her tone was thick with disdain.

"Let's not do this, Helen. I deliberately came late, expecting you'd be gone . . ."

The second voice was one I didn't recognize. The argument was taking place along the dead-end street. Helen had left our party and was walking toward her parked car when she confronted a statuesque redhead who had just arrived.

Madame gripped by arm the moment she spotted them. "That beautiful redhead—I recognize her from a *New York Now* feature. That's Dr. Gwen Fischer, Councilman Chin's fiancée."

Oh, no. Here we go . . .

Matt had warned me to watch out for fireworks at our party. With two rival politicos present, he was sure there'd be an explosion. Well, he turned out to be wrong and right. The ugly scene didn't occur between the principals but between members of their camps.

Chin's fiancée wore light summer slacks, a sleeveless blouse, and an expression of extreme patience—a challenge in the face of Helen's raw anger.

"Is it the *guilt*, Dr. Fischer?" Helen asked. "Is that why you don't want to see me?"

Dr. Fischer ignored the question and tried to step around Helen. But the petite socialite blocked her path

"*Answer* the question," Helen demanded.

"I have nothing to say because I had nothing to do with what happened—"

"I don't want your excuses!" Helen cried, her tone growing hysterical.

Despite their remote location, the fringes of our crowd took notice of the loud squabble. They'd moved toward the fence to observe. At least one freelance photographer was among them.

Dr. Fischer noticed the audience and lowered her voice. So did Helen.

The two continued arguing until Dr. Fischer uttered a final comment. Whatever it was made Helen's cheeks flush nearly the color of Josh Fowler's hair.

Helen's response wasn't in words. Despite the audience (or maybe because of it), she lifted her hand and swung with furious force at Gwen Fischer's cheek.

Like a gunshot, the sound of the slap reverberated in the dead-end street, off the row houses and chain-link fence. Dr. Fischer reeled back as her cheek reddened.

Helen took a step forward, and I was sure she was going to strike again.

Cameras were snapping now. More people were moving to see what they were missing.

I have to do something . . .

Rushing toward the front gate, I noticed Matt near our refreshment tables, sipping coffee. He hadn't noticed the altercation, and I didn't have time to explain.

"The fireworks have started, Matt. Unlock the warehouse. I'll meet you there."

Matt didn't ask questions. He tossed the cup and took off. I was through the gate five seconds later. By the time I reached Dr. Fischer, Helen Bailey-Burke had climbed into a black sedan and slammed the door.

Mortified, the doctor stood there as Helen drove away. With the people gawking, she seemed unsure what to do or where to go. I took the woman's shaking arm.

"Come with me, Dr. Fischer. I'll take you somewhere private."

Twenty-eight

We were in Matt's warehouse now, the loading dock area, a windowless concrete space with a high ceiling and harsh fluorescent lights. But at least it was cool after the heat of the afternoon, and I soon felt chilly in my thin V-neck tee.

"This is a terrible way to meet, but I'm Clare Cosi from the Village Blend. I sent my business partner to find Dominic for you. I'm sure they'll be here shortly."

"Thank you so much," she said, offering her hand. "I'm Gwen Fischer, and I'm sorry I caused a scene at your party."

"I'm sure it wasn't your fault."

"Yes, it was. I shouldn't have said what I said."

Gwen pulled out a compact to check the damage. Her green eyes clouded when she noticed the red handprint on her cheek had inflamed the freckles across her nose. She shook her head.

"Helen caused an equally pleasant scene when we met at Gracie Mansion, but at least she didn't slug me in front of the mayor. But then . . ." She threw me a self-deprecating look. "I hear His Honor loves a good catfight."

We both laughed, and soon Dr. Fischer was chatting amicably as she repaired her makeup.

"So you ran into Helen at the mayor's office?" I pressed.

"The mayor's birthday party," Gwen replied. "It was so humiliating. She accosted me right after the Dancing Mayors act."

"Dancing Mayors?"

"A dozen Rockettes wearing rubber masks of His Honor and kicking it to 'New York, New York,'" Gwen shook her head. "Come to think of it, that dance number may have been more embarrassing than my run in with Mrs. Bailey-Burke."

"What's Helen's problem with you?" I asked plainly.

"Her problem is with my late ex-husband, not me." Gwen combed her scarlet pageboy. "Frankly, I think the woman is unhinged. That's why I shouldn't have provoked her. Now I feel terrible."

"It couldn't have been that bad."

"It was shameful. Helen's daughter died a few years back after Harry performed surgery on her. I'm not in practice with him. I never was—or wanted to be. My plastic surgery work is research oriented, up at Columbia. So I told Helen: if she wanted someone to blame for her daughter's death, she should look in the mirror. I told her if I were a parent, I never would have coerced my child into having three cosmetic procedures that she never wanted in the first place."

The door opened, and Matt ushered City Councilman Dominic Chin into our warehouse. Chin's face was strained, tense, and he didn't relax until he saw that Dr. Fischer was okay. Their embrace was long and lingering, and Matt and I gave them their space. I needed a moment with Matt, anyway.

"Where did you go with Tanya?"

Matt raised an eyebrow. "Jealous?"

"Curious."

"I brought Tanya here, actually."

"You two didn't—"

Matt shook his head. "Tanya thought there'd be an encore here. I played it that way, long enough to keep her away from Helen Bailey-Burke. I wanted Esther to have a fair shot at her presentation."

I hated to tell Matt that it didn't matter, but I supposed he'd figured that out by now. "So how did you finally lose the woman?"

"When the time was right I reminded Tanya that my wife was an influential magazine editor who could ruin Tanya's career with a single exposé, which she would do if she found out we'd been intimate. Then I showed Tanya to the door."

"Bravo."

"People like Tanya enjoy threatening. They're not always prepared to be threatened right back—but then I learned to deal with people like her from the best."

"Your mother?"

"Of course."

"Excuse me, Ms. Cosi? I wanted to thank you."

Dominic Chin's hand found mine. "Gwen told me what you did, and we both appreciate it. And thanks to you and Matt for letting us stay here until the press drifts away. And by the way, your coffee is phenomenal."

Councilman Chin's summer sports coat had been flung over one shoulder, the sleeves on his white shirt rolled up. Dominic was half-Chinese, half-Italian—a product of the proximity of Little Italy and Chinatown. His district loved him. He had a foot in both worlds and an appetite for both as well, having famously grown up on one grandmother's biscotti and another one's moon cakes.

A spot of bright orange on the man's shirt caught my eye—another Two Wheels Good button. *Warrior Barbie sure gets around.*

"This coffee warehouse is pretty phenomenal, too." He sniffed the air. "I don't smell coffee, though."

"Green beans have an earthy, grassy smell," I told him. "Beans don't smell like the coffee you drink until we roast them, and we don't do that here."

I pointed to the button pinned to the councilman's shirt. "Two Wheels Good, right? Do you know John Fairway?"

"Sure, I work with John on occasion. He's been pushing me to create bike lanes in my district, but the streets are so narrow we'd have to shut half of them down completely to comply with his wishes."

"I got the impression that is *exactly* his wish. To stop all motor vehicle traffic."

Chin shrugged. "He says some pretty extreme things."

"What about Fairway's tactics?"

I told Chin about how Fairway's group withheld information from the police, the curious way they collected their data, and the group members' extreme reaction when they felt their rights as bicyclists had been violated—all of which I could verify from my experiences that morning.

The councilman's expression went stony. "John is critical of the police. But he's right to be disturbed about the slipshod way hit-and-runs are often investigated. The truth is, it's just too easy for a careless driver to kill someone and get away with it."

I told Chin about Lilly Beth, and I mentioned how effectively Buckman and his team gathered clues.

"Maybe the police are changing their ways, but there are still too many hit-and-runs," Chin replied. "Just the week before last, Gwen's ex was killed by a hit-and-run driver on his Sunday morning bike run. There were no witnesses and no arrests. Maybe it would have been better if Fairway's people had been there. The driver might have been caught."

"Dom," Gwen Fischer called from the door. "I think the coast is clear."

Chin nodded. "Yeah, I think we'd better go. We've worn out our welcome."

"Not at all," I protested.

Dr. Fischer approached me. "Aren't you guys part of Deputy Mayor Levin's food-truck wedding reception next Friday? They listed the trucks on a little card in their invitation. It was adorable, so different and fun."

"We'll be there."

"Great. We can talk more then."

Dr. Fischer gave me a quick hug. Dominic Chin thanked me again. Then Matt opened the door and the earnest city councilman and his bright fiancée melted into the crowd.

"Did you hear that?" I called to Matt. "Two weeks ago, Dr. Fischer's ex-husband was the victim of a hit-and-run, just like Lilly."

Matt nodded. "It's a big city, isn't it? There must be accidents like that all the time."

"That's exactly what John Fairway would say. And isn't it interesting that both of those accidents happened to people in the sphere of political power? People who'd be noticed by City Hall?"

Twenty-nine

Thirty minutes later, the party was winding down. The crowd in the parking lot had thinned to maybe one hundred guests. Even Kaylie had moved to a more lucrative location.

Most of us were circling the Muffin Muse, where Josh and Dante had replaced the rope with a curtain to hide their masterpiece until its unveiling.

"I'm so happy Otto bought us a bottle of Laurent-Perrier Grand Siècle!" Madame announced.

Matt perked up. "Champagne? We're going to celebrate?"

"To christen our new baby, my dear boy. Our ship must be launched with style."

"At one hundred bucks a bottle, that's pricey style," Matt griped.

I nudged my ex. "I didn't hear you complain about cost when you thought we were drinking it."

Madame insisted on getting so close to the action we were nose to nose with the curtain when it dropped moments later.

The reveal was greeted by cheers and whoops. Finally laughter and applause erupted as the audience absorbed the image and got the joke.

Dante's work was beautiful, stunningly detailed, impressive in size and scope, even witty and playfully imaginative. But when I saw it, I almost threw up. Madame's reaction mirrored my own, and I heard Matt's groan.

Dante, Josh, and Nadine had created a spoof on Andrew Wyeth's realist masterpiece *Christina's World*. The original depicted a young woman lying at the base of a low hill, legs curled. Propped up by her arms, she seemed to be gazing across the hill's tawny grass at a distant farmhouse.

This spoof was rendered in the same style as Wyeth's, but Dante had replaced the grassy hill with coffee beans. In place of the farm, he'd painted our Village Blend with a muffin and demitasse of steaming espresso floating above it. The human figure wore denims and a T-shirt instead of a farm dress, her dark hair bundled in a neat, modern ponytail.

I looked away. A too-similar image had been burned into my mind the night before—Lilly Beth, legs crushed, struggling to rise.

Madame gripped my arm. "Does Dante know anything about the original painting?"

As a student of art history, I understood Madame's question, though I couldn't answer it. Certainly, Dante had seen Wyeth's original, which was on permanent display at New York's Museum of Modern Art. But did he know that the model for the painting—a woman named Christina Olson—only seemed to be lounging in the field while gazing at the farmhouse? In reality, Christina was *crawling* toward her home. The real Christina was a victim of polio, paralyzed from the waist down—just as Lilly Beth was likely to be, according to her doctors.

I lowered my gaze and rubbed my forehead. *Oh, god, this is awful. I'll never be able to look at this painting without thinking of the night Lilly was hit. Can things get any worse?*

The sharp crack of the first gunshot reverberated off the surrounding buildings. Someone screamed as a muffin balloon burst over our gate.

By the time the second shot exploded, most people were

ducking, and more than a few seasoned urbanites were already hugging the ground. I remained standing—because the noises didn't make sense. The sound of the shots came from one direction, the actual bullets from another.

Why? What in heaven's name is going on?

I listened for a third shot, but when it came, I was in no position to judge from which direction. My ex realized I was still standing and dragged me to the ground, covering me with his body.

Madame was already on the ground beside me, and our eyes met. I didn't see fright reflected there, or even alarm. Only anger and determination. I clenched my jaw and I took my strength from her example.

A loud, commanding voice followed a long silence—Officer Gifford, ordering everyone to stay put and demanding to know if anyone had been harmed. Then, weapon drawn, the Highway Patrolman guarded the gate as police sirens announced the approach of reinforcements.

Thirty

Miraculously, no one had been hurt and no real damage done—except perhaps to the Blend's image, though it was too soon to know for sure.

Police from the Red Hook precinct took over the investigation. After I had a very long talk with Sergeant Fidel Ortiz, during which I mentioned both Kaylie and Detective Buckman, I felt a tap on my shoulder.

"I'm clocking overtime now, Ms. Cosi," Officer Gifford said. "My boss told me to take you somewhere, anywhere but here."

"My employer and I are taking her car to Beth Israel Hospital. We have someone we'd like to visit."

Gifford nodded. "You'll have a motorcycle escort."

While Madame and I waited for Otto's driver to bring the car, I stifled a yawn. It had been a long, hard, dangerous day, and I could not wait to see it end.

When we arrived at the hospital, we found Lilly Beth's condition unchanged. She was still unconscious, her family sitting vigil. For a little over an hour, Madame and I visited with Lilly's mother, son, and a small gaggle of relatives before heading home. I was glad to get there—and surprised by what I found.

With every step up the Blend's service staircase, a new aroma enveloped me. Sweet garlic. Earthy cumin. The tangy brightness of simmering tomatoes. And under it all, a savory scent of sizzling pork, ambrosia to almost anyone with Italian blood.

Clearly someone was cooking *inside* my apartment.

With a killer supposedly stalking me and shots fired, I should have been alarmed. But I doubted an assassin would prepare me a last meal. And, anyway, the identity of the kitchen bandit was no mystery. My sense memory exposed the culprit almost instantly.

Carnitas—Spanish for "little meats"—were a Matteo Allegro specialty from the early years of our marriage. Braised, tender, and succulent, the pork chunks had been a budget-friendly buddy to this struggling young mother.

Insanely easy to prepare, one pot yielded the basics for a week's worth of mouthwatering meals. Inside a corn tortilla with chopped onion, fresh salsa, and aromatic cilantro, they made a delicious little taco. Fried up with Matt's special black beans and a scoop of rice, they became a burrito filling.

Our daughter's all-time favorite way to eat them was in my special Taco Cups, one of my most popular *In the Kitchen with Clare* recipes. (Essentially tasty little mini-quiches with quartered flour tortillas as crusts and fillings of leftover taco meat.)

But that wasn't all.

For a culinary trip down memory lane, one bite of *carnitas* with fresh spinach and banana peppers on a crusty Italian roll would take me back to one of the best street foods in Rome, a *porchetta* sandwich, with the juicy, warm pork cut fresh for you at a market stall. It was one of the first meals Matt and I ever shared together.

In those early years, we wouldn't even let the *carnitas* pot stickings (what my beloved chef daughter called *"au fond")* go to waste. After deglazing with red wine, I'd add a can of San Marzano tomatoes (sweet, plump imports from the volcanic slopes of Italy), oregano, and scalded onions. Thirty quick minutes later, I had an unctuously rich pasta gravy that tasted like my nonna's six-hour Sunday dinner sauce.

What I was smelling now—not just the batch of *carnitas* but also that supernaturally satisfying pasta sauce—made me wonder how long Matt planned on staying around.

I unlocked the front door and found him in my cozy, exposed-brick kitchen, sampling the deglazing wine from a long-stemmed crystal goblet.

"Matt, what are you doing? Who's going to eat all of this food?"

"You are. You're not leaving this building until Big Foot is back—and neither am I."

Matt's tone was grim and so was his expression, completely out of character for my *devil-may-care-but-I-sure-as-hell-don't* ex-husband.

"Did the police call?" *That has to be it.* "They found out something about the shooting? The shooter? Please tell me they have someone in custody—or are at least tracking a good lead."

"It's not that. It's something else. Something that involves me. But you have to let me explain it . . ."

I flashed on a very young Joy in that moment. Whenever I caught her in the act of being naughty, that's when she most resembled Matt. Guilt wasn't exhibited by our darling daughter as much as petulance at being caught. Her father was wearing that look now.

"Matt, what have you done?"

He ignored the question, asked me to sit, then put down a bowl and mounded it with spaghetti dressed in that succulent red sauce.

"Eat first."

"But—"

He placed a fork in my hand and tucked a napkin under my chin.

"What am I? Three?"

"Just eat."

He didn't have to tell me again. While I twirled the pasta around my tines, he poured the wine. Then he drained his own glass and poured a second. Or was he on his third?

I tasted the pasta and sauce—tangy, aromatic, rich with umami—and began to devour it.

Matt sat down across from me. "While you were at the hospital, I talked to the detective in charge of the Brooklyn shooting. They still haven't recovered bullets or even bullet fragments, and they've stopped looking."

"Oh, come on. Not a clue who fired?" I said, mouth half-full.

"For starters, that whole cupcakes-versus-muffins turf war stuff didn't fly with Sergeant Ortiz. Maybe he listened politely while you 'explained' it"—Matt made little quote marks in the air—"but Ortiz was practically laughing it off when I talked to him."

"So who were they shooting at?"

"Nobody. Detective Ortiz believes they were stray bullets, the result of local squabbles. There are housing projects not far from my warehouse, and Red Hook has a notorious history of gang violence. He says shootings like that are common enough in the area."

"But I told his officers what Buckman said, that someone out there might be trying to kill me. Didn't Ortiz call Buckman to verify?"

"They talked," Matt said with a nod, "but in the end Buckman didn't convince Ortiz that the two crimes were connected. Ortiz believes if you have a stalker, his MO is vehicular homicide, not gunplay."

I set aside my empty bowl, took another hit of wine. "From the guilty look on your face, you have a theory. What is it?"

"I think your friend Buckman is right, Clare. Someone is out to kill you, and I know who it is."

"You *know*?" I stared. "How long have you been holding out on me?"

"I haven't been holding out on you," he insisted. "I started to put two and two together after the shooting this afternoon. That's why I called Ortiz for an update."

"Well, if this is another one of your jilted party girls, tell her to go stalk your wife—"

"It's more serious than that . . ." Matt said. "It involves . . . it's hard to explain. There's a lot to the story."

"*Tell* me. Cut to the chase."

"Okay. When I was in Brazil, I took a meeting with one of the biggest drug lords in the country, and now he wants you dead."

THIRTY-ONE

THE wineglass slipped from my hand and rolled across the table, leaving a bloodred trail.

"A Brazilian drug lord wants me dead?! Me? An innocent little Greenwich Village shop manager? Why?"

"I told you, it's complicated."

I held my head. "Explain, Matt. Tell me *everything*. And dial it way back. Start at the beginning."

Matt took the chair across from me, and then took a breath—

"It all started with coffee."

"Coffee?"

He nodded. "I ran into Nino Duarte on a layover in São Paulo. Nino is an old *carioca* pal from my crazy days in Rio—"

"I remember Nino. You introduced us once."

"Nino invited me to Terra Perfeita, his coffee farm."

"In the Golden Valley, right?"

The Golden Valley, better known as Carmo de Minas, was obscenely fertile. Farms in that valley produced bananas, mangoes, limes, lettuce, and tomatoes, and higher up, about a million coffee plants clung to a thousand miles of rolling hills. I knew all about Brazil's Carmo de Minas. Everyone in the trade did—which was why Matt's next statement came as a surprise.

"Nino's farm is not in the Golden Valley, Clare. It's located between São Paulo and Rio de Janeiro, in the Paraíba Valley. That's actually where the coffee industry began in Brazil."

"That I didn't know."

Matt nodded. "Those plantations were prosperous once. But they've been abandoned for decades."

"Because?"

He glanced at his empty glass. "After two centuries of overfarming, most people believed the soil was played out, but Nino thought they were wrong, and his gamble paid off. Turns out the soil is amazing. *Terra roxa*—'purple dirt,' the old Portuguese plantation owners used to call it. Nino said it was the unique properties of the soil that helped him create, in his words, 'the best cup Brazil ever produced.'"

Matt finally gave in to temptation and reached for the wine. I blocked his hand. "Listen to me. This is life or death—according to you, *my* life or death. I need to understand what you're telling me, which means I need you to be *sober* and in control. Now tell me more about Nino."

Matt nodded, set the bottle aside. "I was dubious about his boast, but I went to see his farm anyway. He calls his yellow bourbon Terra Perfeita Dourada—'Nuggets of Gold from the Perfect Land.' It's a mouthful, and for my money Nino should have called it Ambrosia, because this stuff really is the nectar of the gods."

"Come on, Matt."

"No, no, I'm not exaggerating. Nino was right, Clare. It is the best cup ever produced in Brazil."

"Do you have a sample?"

"Now you're talking . . ." Matt rose from the table. "The green beans arrived at the warehouse about an hour before your party—and a couple of days ahead of schedule, thank God. I couldn't wait to see your reaction, so I used our small-batch sampler in the basement to roast a pound . . ."

Matt returned to the table with a French press. He prepared the beans, allowing me to smell the gold-flecked grounds before covering them with water, just off the boil.

The aroma was, I had to admit, astounding. Beyond mere nutty or earthy—there was a sweetness to these ground beans that was so powerful I could almost feel it on my tongue.

"Smell it, Clare! This coffee is going to win Brazil's Cup of Excellence. And when it does, we're going to rake it in, because I practically cornered the market."

I tensed. Matt's unbridled enthusiasm brought me to a new level of wary skepticism.

The Cup of Excellence was an extremely strict worldwide competition, crowning the very best coffees produced in a specific country for a given year. It was an imprimatur of coffee excellence, and winning the coveted cup raised the profile of the producer to an international level—and sometimes even the roasters who scored the beans for distribution.

Brazil had the most competitive producers in the world, and its Cup of Excellence was one of the most difficult to win. Matt's claim that *his* sourced coffee would win it was akin to a Hollywood producer bragging that he was going to win the Oscar for Best Picture of the Year—no matter how good the film, there were bound to be others up there with you that were just as good. It was always a crapshoot.

"I bought as much of the micro-lot as Nino would sell me," Matt continued. "The rest is going to auction, *after* the awards are judged and the price goes through the roof."

"And you paid *how much* for this privilege?"

"About three times the going rate for Brazil premium. Nino needed quick cash to pay last year's bills, so I got a real bargain. It looks like a lot of money on paper, but when Terra Perfeita Dourada hits auction, it will sell for eight or ten times the amount I paid—"

"*If*, Matt. *If* it wins, places, or shows in the Cup of Excellence!"

"It'll win." Matt poured, careful to keep the sediment out of our cups. "It damn well better win."

"What's that supposed to mean?"

"I'd already gone through my budget for this year's harvest—and then some—before I paid Nino a visit. I had to take an additional line of credit from a bank in Zurich to make the purchase."

"You went into debt on a *bet*! What were you thinking?! We're not running a casino! Putting all your borrowed money on this stuff winning the Cup of Excellence is unbelievably risky—"

"As risky as borrowing cash to buy a *food truck*?"

And that's when I understood. That was why Matt had been so upset about my food-truck investment. We were both crossing our fingers over gambles that might—or might not—pay off.

"Matt, I know your brokerage business is separate from the Blend, and you have every right to keep risks like that to yourself, but I wish you would have told me about this sooner."

"Why?"

"Because we're more than business partners. We're friends. And if you're in a jam, I might be able to help you out of it."

Matt appeared skeptical.

I sighed. "You should at least give me a chance to try."

"Okay. Then start by trying this coffee. It really is ambrosia. One sip and you'll forget your troubles."

Matt slid a cup across the table, and I brought the warm liquid to my nose and inhaled. The smell was complex and tantalizing. Bright, clean, and sweet, so sweet the scent practically compelled me to taste it, so I did. Then I sipped again. And again—

"My God . . ."

I stared into space, unseeing. Then I actually closed my eyes. I didn't want my sense of sight to get in the way. "It's so smooth . . . balanced on all levels . . . yet the spectrum of flavors is mind-blowing." I sipped again. "There's a kick here, too. Holy cow, it's so heavily caffeinated it goes down like crack!"

Matt grimaced. "Ouch."

"Ouch is right—you still haven't told me about this drug dealer?"

"You wanted me to start at the beginning, didn't you?" Matt tapped his cup. "So tell me what you taste."

I licked my lips. "First the brightness. A berry . . . there are notes of cocoa, of course, but it's a light note like a Belgian-style milk chocolate. And I can taste a caramel sweetness, but it's more than just sugars caramelizing in the roasting process . . . this is a toasty, buttery caramel, like a shortbread, rolling around the mouth with complexity . . ."

"I taste blueberry," said Matt, "some raisin . . . but mostly cherry . . ."

"More like cherry *Lambic*."

"You're right. It's like a deep, almost fermented dimension to the fruitiness." Matt took another long sip and a wistful expression crossed his face. "*Ciliegie sotto spirito . . .*"

"The spirit of cherries," I translated with a nod, and I knew the taste was bringing him back, as well—to that special Italian spring when we met and those sweet red orbs soaking in grappa and sugar.

"With that shortbread note, it's almost like a fresh-baked slice of cherry pie, isn't it?"

I nodded. "Cherry pie with a splash of my grandmother's *liquori casalinghi*."

Matt smiled. "Like that cherry liqueur you made for me one summer from your nonna's recipe."

"I haven't made that in years," I said, suddenly needing to. "How is this bean processed? Semi-dry?"

"Water pulped. Then sun dried."

"Spot on, Claire. That explains the complexity, all those wild flavors, yet so clear and clean." I sipped again. "The profile's changing . . ." Which wasn't unique—most quality coffees revealed new flavors as they cooled.

Matt nodded. "The cherry is mellowing into a subtler flavor, like an—"

"Apple," I said. "I'm getting a slight note of exotic vanilla, too, and with that sweet-buttery profile, it almost tastes like a—"

"Caramel apple."

I met Matt's gaze. He was right about this coffee, even though in the roasting he went too far—an all-too common occurrence for my lack-of-impulse-control ex. He'd given the green beans a long, lusty lip-lock of heat, when a much more careful kiss would have gotten him to a higher plane of ecstasy.

"Next time," I advised, "you should go a little lighter on the roast."

Matt shrugged. "You're the expert."

I paused to finish my cup. "Okay. The coffee is superb."

"Thank you."

"But you still haven't explained—"

"The processing?"

"No, Matt. The other part. The Brazilian-drug-lord part. Tell me how this coffee is going to get me *killed*."

He nodded, refilled both our cups. "You said it yourself. This coffee goes down like crack. Well, you were closer to the truth than you knew."

"You're scaring me."

Matt rubbed the back of his neck. "I never talk about the places I go and the things I see."

"Yes, you do."

"Okay, but mostly I tell you about the good times. In reality, some of the best coffee is cultivated in the worst geopolitical regions on the planet. Wars, murder, terrorism, revolution . . . you name it, I've seen it, heard about it, or witnessed the aftermath . . ."

Matt liked to think of me as naïve, but I was as familiar as he with the infamous history of brown gold. And I respected his efforts. In fact, I couldn't help flashing on his mother's remark earlier this afternoon—about the hard work of digging gemstones out of the darkest mines.

"When we were married, I didn't want to scare you so I kept my mouth shut about the worst of it. Then not talking about it got to be a habit, and habits are hard to shake."

"I know you've been in some bad situations."

"And bad places, too . . . Lately, Brazil has become one of those places . . ." Matt pushed his cup of ambrosia aside, reached for the wine. This time I didn't stop him. "Don't get me wrong. I still love Rio, and the Brazilian people are warm and good-hearted. But something's gone very wrong in that country, and things are deteriorating fast."

Matt poured a heady glass. "There are more than fifty thousand murders a year in the urban areas, and because of the economic gap between rich and poor, the violence is escalating. Jobless and hopeless, lots of young Brazilians are turning to a new form of crack cocaine. The *traficantes* get rich dealing it; the rest use it and die young . . . Too young."

"And you met with one of these *traficantes*? Why, Matt, what were you thinking?"

"I was ambushed."

"How?"

"Have you ever heard of *oxidado*?"

"No. Is it Spanish?"

"Portuguese. It means *rust*, and this drug is so toxic it really does rot your body. It's like crack 2.0, too. Smoke it once and you're hooked. The Brazilian police claim *oxidado* kills three in ten addicts within a year of regular use. It's gotten so bad that a chunk of São Paulo's ghetto was known as *Cracolândia*—Crack Land—until the cops drove the junkies into the streets with tear gas and clubs . . ."

Matt's tale brought back my worst memories of New York City during the days of crack cocaine. "With that kind of rampant drug abuse, you get all of kinds delightful consequences. Muggings, burglaries, robberies, turf wars, gang shootings . . ."

Matt nodded. "I'm pretty careful when I visit Brazil these days. I have no desire to run afoul of *oxidado* dealers or their violent, desperate customers. So imagine my surprise when Nino invited me to breakfast one morning to meet a very special guest."

He paused for a long moment, as if he'd forgotten the rest of the story—or desperately wanted to.

"Matt, tell me. Who did Nino want you to meet?"

"The biggest cocaine *traficante* in São Paulo."

THIRTY-TWO

I closed my eyes again, but for a very different reason. I no longer cared about heightening my other senses. I simply didn't want to see what was coming.

"You took a meeting with a drug lord over your morning coffee?"

"Not willingly."

I opened my eyes. "Does this drug lord work for Nino Duarte, or does your friend work for him?"

"I don't know exactly how Nino got involved with him. My best guess is loan-sharking. Nino probably needed money to develop his land—this man has plenty of it. The dude calls himself O Negociante, and he kept things pretty formal during our meeting."

Matt's eyes glazed as his focus melted into memory. "I'll never forget this guy. Neck as thick as his head. Lots of gold teeth, scars, and prison tattoos. A smile wider than a killer shark."

"What did he want?"

"What do you think? He made me an offer I had to refuse, and I did refuse. But until my flight lifted off from São

Paulo's Guarulhos International nine hours later, I wasn't sure I was going to make it out of Brazil alive. Once I was in the air, I thought the whole thing was over. But after shots were fired this afternoon, I got to thinking that maybe it isn't over after all."

"O Negociante wanted you to smuggle drugs, right?"

"Right." Matt nodded. "Two shipments a month of *oxidado*. I was supposed to traffic this new Brazilian crack into New York City. He knew I'd been shipping through customs for decades and was seen as a legitimate importer, so he expected me to be given a pass—or provide money to bribe whoever I needed to."

"My god . . ."

"This guy really did his homework, Clare. He said he'd been informed that I was financially stretched, and he could make my money problems go away forever. And just to show he was a swell guy, he would pick up the tab for Nino's coffee in exchange for my immediate cooperation."

"What did you tell him?"

"The truth. First I told him I wasn't interested—that my financial problems were seasonal and would vanish soon. But that tack failed, and he really began to pressure me, so I said . . ."

Matt paused, and I tensed. He was suddenly wearing that bad-boy pout again.

"What did you say?"

"I said that it would be too dangerous for me to go into business with him because . . ."

"Because?" I prompted.

"Because my business partner, the manager of the Village Blend, was romantically involved with a high-profile narcotics cop in New York City."

I wanted to yell. I wanted to scream. I wanted to hurl my favorite cast-iron skillet at my ex-husband's thick skull. Instead I just clutched my head and nearly bounced it off the table.

"So you used *me* as your excuse, because of my relationship with Mike Quinn! And now you think O Negociante has put out a contract on my life?"

"I had to think on my feet."

"Think on your feet! Matt, take note: there are no brains in your feet!"

"Let's not overreact, Clare."

"Overreact? Someone took a shot at me today! But that's not the worst and you know it. Lilly Beth is lying in a coma because Buckman was right! Some murder-for-hire scumbag thought she was me! And you say *I'm* overreacting?"

"I'm going to make this right," Matt promised. "I'll do everything I can to help Lilly. And you know I won't let anything happen to you—"

"Drug smugglers? *Madre santa!* In Brazil of all places . . ." I buried my head in my arms again. "And for years I was agonized about your trips to Colombia."

"Colombia is so last century," Matt said with a dismissive wave. "With pressure on in Bogota, Brazil has become a safe haven for the next generation of cocaine growers and traffickers. And business is booming. There's a new Medellín Cartel growing in Brazil's Amazon jungle."

"And one of these Amazonian drug lords wants me *morte.*"

I shook my head. Mr. Hon was right. Now I knew how Rudy Giuliani felt. But when gangsters put out contracts on him, New York's esteemed former mayor had trained bodyguards watching his back.

"Matt, what am I going to do? I'm not a government official! I don't have a security detail! I have an espresso machine!"

"You share a bed with an NYPD lieutenant who's an expert in drug trafficking and has friends in the Justice Department. Big Foot will fix things when he gets home."

"I should call Mike right now." I lifted my head and lunged for the phone.

Matt blocked me. "No. We'll both tell Quinn when he gets back here. Face it, the guy's going to have a *reaction* to this story. Don't you want to be in the same room with him when he does?"

"I do, but I'm not sure you should."

"Why not?"

"Because when Mike hears this story, he's going to fold you in half and crumple you into a ball."

"Fine! Let him—as long as it's *after* we both know you're safe."

An hour ago I couldn't wait to crawl into bed. Now my flesh was crawling.

I felt so helpless, like a sitting duck a l'orange.

I rose from the table, began pulling out ingredients. Maybe it was my emotions. Maybe the super-crack coffee. Or maybe just the knowledge that some Pablo Escobar–wannabe had put a contract out on me. Whatever it was, I had to move around!

"What are you doing?" Matt asked.

"I'm going to make my special Oatmeal Cookie Muffins. Quinn loves them, and I've got enough bad news to dump on him. The least I can do is bake for the man, but the first stage is a long soak."

Matt groaned. He looked as though he wanted to soak his head. I would have obliged him, but I didn't have enough buttermilk—and the container was too small.

Done. Now what?

Looking with pity on my pathetic ex, I tapped his shoulder. "You said there's a bag of those golden nuggets in the basement?"

Cheek against the table, he murmured: "A hundred-and-fifty-pound bag, just waiting to be roasted."

"Great. I'm wide wake. I'm going to fire up the Probat."

Matt's spirits lifted, along with his head. "I'll go with you."

THE Village Blend's roasting room was in its basement, an expansive space with stone walls and thick rafters. For a coffee lover, the aromas down here were psychotropic. For the Allegro family, they were legacy.

Generations of roasting had gone on in this chilly

underground, and Matt and I wanted it to keep going on for generations to come. Tonight was just one more little turn of the drum batch roaster. At least, that's what I thought it would be.

While Matt moved to hit the starter button on our shiny red Probat, I examined Matt's magic beans.

The bag itself was jute, with "Terra Perfeita" stamped in faded black ink beside the tiny hole Matt had cut to extract a few cherries. I used the razor cutter to open the bag from the top. With a scoop, I began transferring the green beans to an empty plastic holding container. About one quarter of the way down, I looked at the beans and gasped.

Matt, who was turning up the Probat's gas, called out, "You're impressed, right?"

"Oh, I'm impressed." In fact, I was wide-eyed.

"Do you see how the cherries look like little golden nuggets?"

"I see nuggets, all right."

"How about defects? Are there any rocks, twigs?"

"Yeah. I see rocks. Lots and lots of big white rocks wrapped in cellophane bundles—the kind that get you six figures on the street!"

"Clare, what are you talking ab—"

He finally saw them, the flat white bricks mingled with those golden beans. His face turned as purple as I imagined *terra roxa* to be, and his lips moved like a Chinatown catfish gasping for air.

Finally Matt blew his top, and the coffee-scented rafters rattled with the sound of curses, mostly—but not exclusively—in Portuguese.

"Is that what I think it is?" I asked numbly. *Really? How many shocks can a person be expected to absorb in a single evening?*

Matt tossed one of the plastic-wrapped squares on the floor and pierced it with a stab from the box cutter. He had to really dig in, as there were layers upon layers of wrappings. When finally reached the dull yellow paste, the smell that rose from the pierced plastic was noxious, almost like kerosene.

"It's *oxidado*," Matt said grimly. "The petroleum stink comes from the way the drug is processed."

"I'm calling Quinn right now," I said, making for the stairs.

"Wait!" Matt seized my arm. "I thought of a bright side."

"This I've got to hear."

"Maybe this is a test—you know, like a test charge?"

"A what?"

"When you check into a hotel, you give them your credit card, and they do a 'test charge' of a couple of bucks to make sure the card is valid. I'm thinking this might be a test."

He said it with such hope, I wanted to believe him.

"Before we tell anyone, we need to know how bad this situation is, don't we?"

"How could it be worse?"

"Don't ask."

I took his face in my hands. "I'm asking."

Matt's eyes locked on mine. "I have *fifteen* more bags of this stuff at the warehouse. Every single one of them could be laced with crack cocaine."

THIRTY-THREE

MATT and I streaked through the night in a fully-loaded silver BMW. The car belonged to Matt's wife, Breanne, so he insisted on driving. Besides the speed limit, my ex was breaking at least one other traffic law—he was talking over his cell while operating a motor vehicle.

Most of Matt's extremely agitated conversation with his coffee-farming friend in Brazil was conducted in pidgin Portuguese, and since I was only hearing Matt's side of it, I couldn't follow.

Matt cursed and slammed the smart phone into the soft leather upholstery. The device bounced and hit the ceiling. I caught it before the phone shattered against the dashboard.

"What did Nino say?"

"He claims he had nothing to do with it. Nino blamed O Negociante for everything!" Matt pounded the steering wheel. Once, twice—

I touched his arm. "Calm down. You're going to blow a gasket."

Matt wiped away the sweat on his brow. "Look, if we opened the only dirty bag—if the others in my warehouse are clean—I can dump the crack we found in the East River. Nobody will be the wiser, and Quinn never has to know."

"Somebody will be the wiser," I countered. "O Negociante, for one. And maybe the driver of the car that's been following us since we crossed the Brooklyn Bridge."

"What!"

"Don't turn your head. You can see it in the rearview mirror. That black car—"

"The Chevy Impala? Okay, I see it. Let me speed up a little. If he tries to pace us, we could be in trouble . . ."

Matt pushed the gas pedal until the BMW purred like a housebroken cheetah. The Impala sped up, too.

Not a good sign.

Matt tried weaving around a slow-moving Ford. The Impala did, too. After a minute or so, Matt cursed and slowed again. So did our Chevy stalker.

"The Atlantic Avenue exit is next," Matt said. "I'll shake him there."

"But the ramp is here *now*! You don't have time to cut across two lanes of traahhh—"

Matt swerved at high speed, cutting off the SUV in the next lane. Brakes slammed, tires squealed, horns blared—and the pasta I'd consumed for dinner threatened to make a reappearance.

Our BMW shot down the exit ramp at twice the legal speed, and we hit busy Atlantic Avenue just as the traffic light flipped to green—a miraculous piece of good luck since we never could have stopped before the intersection.

"The Impala's still coming," I told him, white knuckles gripping my shoulder harness.

"Fine. Let's see how this SOB likes the old double-back."

"The old wha—ahhhh!"

Without braking, Matt cut across the opposite lane of traffic and turned into a fast-food parking lot. I nearly bounced off the passenger-side window before the safety harness righted me again.

The place was an all-night burger joint. A red Kia was

stopped at the intercom, blocking the road, so Matt twisted the wheel. We bumped onto a low curb and off again, taking out a bush as we passed the little red car.

Bree's BMW mirror on my side shattered against a steel menu display. Matt shifted gears again, and we burst out of the parking lot.

Tires streaming smoke and rubber, the BMW screamed back onto Atlantic. But this time we zoomed in the opposite direction, leaving the Impala stuck in the wrong lane. Before I knew it, we were on the expressway again.

Needing fresh air, I cracked my passenger-side window. Howling night wind filled the compartment. I heard a triumphant snort and turned to see Matt's white teeth gleaming in the dashboard lights.

"Maybe we should have confronted the driver," I said. "Maybe this whole mystery could have been solved."

"Yeah, right. And maybe the driver had a gun, Clare, and a bullet with your name on it."

My jaws clenched, and I didn't speak again until we rolled to a stop in front of the warehouse gate minutes later. The engine still running, Matt popped the door. "I'll open the gate."

The memory of gunshots in the afternoon, coupled with the late hour and the moonless night, cast a sinister pall over everything. The mixed-zoning neighborhood no longer seemed bohemian friendly. Industrial buildings loomed like giants, and the windows on the surrounding houses were dim. Even the bodega at the corner was lightless, and there was not a soul on the sidewalk.

Matt unlocked the chain-link gate and tore away ribbons of yellow police tape that crisscrossed the entrance. He eased the BMW into the parking lot, cut the engine, and closed the gate.

As we approached the main door, a motion detector activated security lights, bathing Matt and I in a bleached halogen glow. That light made us targets, so Matt hastily punched in the code on the keypad and killed them.

Clutching his key, Matt input another code. When the little red light blinked to green, he inserted the key, twisted it, and pushed the heavy steel door inward.

The code had triggered fluorescent lights embedded in the high ceiling, so the windowless loading dock was now awash in sterile light.

Stepping inside, I smelled fresh paint, and I knew why. For the past few months, this area had served double duty: loading dock by day, depot for the Blend's coffee truck at night. Our newly painted Muffin Muse was parked here now, gleaming in the harsh brilliance.

Out of habit, Matt checked the digital gauges monitoring temperature and humidity. Grunting his satisfaction, he extracted a second key and unlocked a pair of double doors. A gust of cool, dry air chilled my skin as we entered the coffee storage area.

The sacks of Terra Perfeita Dourada were stacked just inside the entrance, still resting on the wooden pallet on which they'd been delivered. Matt, clutching an iron carting hook, tore into the nearest jute sack with the sharp edge. It didn't take long to locate the drugs.

Desperate now, Matt dropped to his knees and ripped into a second bag, then a third. All were laced with packets of *oxidado.* Matt staggered to his feet, stepped back. The metal hook fell from his limp hand to clang loudly on the concrete floor.

I reached into my handbag.

Matt hung his head. "If the police or the DEA find out about this, we're ruined. I mean *ruined.* The Feds will seize the warehouse, probably the Blend, too." He paused, rubbed the back of his neck. "Call Mike Quinn," he said. "Tell him everything."

The phone already in my hand, I hit speed dial.

"Hey, sweetheart," Mike answered in a sleepy voice. "It's almost midnight. Are you checking up on me?"

"Mike," I said in a shaky voice. "I need your help. Like I've never needed anyone's help before . . ."

"Clare, what's wrong." He was wide awake now.

"Matt found drugs. Cocaine. In a shipment of coffee."

"Where are you now?"

"With Matt, at the warehouse, in Brooklyn. Mike, there's a lot of crack . . ."

A loud crash boomed from the loading dock, followed by the sound of running boots on the concrete floor.

Matt grabbed the carting hook and whirled to face the double doors as a strident voice boomed.

"DEA. DEA. We're coming in. We have a warrant."

"Mike!"

"I heard, Clare. Do what they say and you won't get hurt. I'll get you out of this."

The double doors burst open. I saw beetle-blue body armor with DEA stenciled across torsos, guns aimed at my heart. Then blinding bright light struck my eyes and I saw stars.

"Get on the ground, now! NOW!" This time, the voice belonged to a woman. "Down and drop the phone."

I wanted to hear Mike's voice one last time, but I remembered his final instructions and released the phone.

"Facedown on the ground!" she cried and I dropped.

Beside me, I heard another voice. My ex cursing.

"Matt, *listen* to me. Don't say a word to them. No matter what they say to you—and they're going to say *terrible* things—ask for a lawyer then bite your tongue. No matter what they tell you, be strong, and just—"

"Shut up!" the woman commanded. I felt rough hands cuffing my wrists.

Over all the chaos, a monotone voice droned. "You are under arrest. You have the right to remain silent. Anything you say can and will be used against you in a court of law . . ."

THIRTY-FOUR

THEY separated us immediately.

I heard Matt cry out in protest before a pair of DEA agents shoved me into the back of a van. Then it was a long, lonely ride to a faceless building under the High Line. I got only a brief glimpse of my surroundings before I was hustled through a glass door, pushed onto an elevator, and deposited in a dark, windowless cube.

I'd seen other interrogation rooms, and this one was no different—soundproofing, three walls, a trick mirror, a couple of chairs and a table. And like the last time I was in a place like this, I was handcuffed to a stationary object; in this case, a metal chair.

I knew what the agents were planning. Mike Quinn was one of the toughest, smartest interrogators in the New York Police Department, and I'd shared enough pillow talk with him to know how he thought, and how he worked.

Mike walked into an interview room like a lawyer going into the first day of trial—or (apparently) a Brazilian drug lord trying to turn a coffee broker. He learned almost everything he could about his suspect, including what he or she cared about most in the world—and especially what would hurt them the most.

If he didn't know, Mike grilled his suspect until he discovered it. Once revealed, he hammered that idea until the suspect broke. Then he used the suspect's statements against him (or her). Whether they were truth or lies, any statements had the potential to give police and attorneys exactly what they needed to charge and convict.

That's what was in store for me.

I closed my eyes, mentally preparing myself for it. The absolute smartest thing I could do now was ask for a lawyer and clam up.

They will not break me, I vowed. *Whatever they try, I won't say a word . . .*

I glanced at my empty wrist, forgetting that the agents had taken all of my personal possessions, including my watch, even the Claddagh ring Mike had given me. I imagined them going through my purse, my wallet, the pictures I carried around. Photos of my daughter, my cats, of Mike . . .

The door opened, jerking me back from that dark place to this one.

"Oh, no," said a woman's voice. "Did they leave you sitting in the dark?"

Yeah, lady, like it was an accident.

Suddenly the room was flooded with fluorescent lights. I blinked against the glare, my eyes tearing. When my vision cleared, I saw white blond hair, pale water-blue eyes, a mannish jacket, and billowing slacks the color of burnt coals.

The woman slapped a manila folder on the table between us and sat down. "So," she said, linking her hands.

I let the word hang in the air.

"Can I get you anything—"

"A *lawyer,*" I said, loud and clear. "I want a lawyer."

"A glass of water? How about a soft drink? We have a machine."

I said nothing.

"All right, Clare . . . May I call you Clare?"

Call me anything you like, but call a lawyer first, was my unspoken reply.

"That's a beautiful name, by the way . . ."

Shut up.

"My name is Virginia Blanco, I'm a special agent with the Drug Enforcement Administration." She leaned across the table. "I think we both know why you're here, Clare. But maybe this is all a mistake. Maybe we can clear it up right here, right now."

Sure, Virginia. And pigs fly . . .

Special Agent Blanco opened the folder, flipped through the pages. I avoided the temptation to peek.

"So you manage a coffeehouse?"

My lips remained firmly pressed together.

"You know, Clare, if you're not going to speak with me, I might as well go back to the other interrogation room. Your husband"—*Ex-husband!*—"is spinning some pretty amazing tales in there. And those stories are about you, Clare. They're all about you."

Matt's not talking. I know he's not. You're allowed to lie in here, and you're lying now . . .

"Of course, you don't have to speak with me if you don't want to. We can just sit here in silence—"

Great idea. So shut up, already.

"Or I can tell a few stories of my own." Special Agent Blanco closed the folder again. "When I was training for this job, my psychology instructor taught us that the mousy, quiet ones were the toughest to crack, pardon the pun."

Special Agent Blanco studied her fingernail. "Like the little old lady who sells crystal meth to school kids. Or a seemingly innocent coffeehouse manager who smuggles Brazilian crack."

Not true. I'm not guilty of anything! I was dying to shout the truth, scream it. But I bit my cheek instead.

Frowning, Blanco leaned across the table, so close I could smell her shampoo. "I can break you, Clare Cosi. And I will."

Oh, yeah, honey? Bring it on.

"My instructor was right about one thing," Blanco continued. "You meek, quiet ones are stone-cold monsters."

Yeah, that's me. Godzilla with an apron.

"A sociopath, he'd call you."

I'm a lady, so I can't call you what I'd like to call you . . .

"A sociopath has no empathy. They don't care who they hurt. Friends. Lovers. Their own children."

Blanco tapped the folder with her index finger. "By the way, did you know your daughter, Joy, visited Marseilles last week? A city known for heroin smuggling? Are you using your daughter to establish another drug route, Clare?"

Leave my daughter out of this, you b—

"Only a sociopath would use their own daughter to commit a felony. Only a sociopath would wrap a good cop like Michael Francis Quinn around her finger, blind him to the fact that he's actually sleeping with a drug dealer."

Shut up!

"You quiet ones are patient, I'll give you that. How long were you planning this operation, Clare? The timeline is amazing. First you divorce your first husband, separate for over a decade. Then suddenly you're back, living above the coffeehouse, your ex-husband a part of the business. Was that the plan all along?"

There's no plan. There's only my life and the choices I've made. If I had a plan, *I never would have gotten pregnant when I was nineteen!*

"I admire you, Clare. You're smarter than most. Did you wrap your ex-husband around your finger, too? Or is Mr. Allegro a willing accomplice?"

The gods couldn't twist Matt around their fingers. What hope did I have of reining the man in?

"And Mike Quinn? Besides turning the guy into a patsy and burning his career at the NYPD, what do you have planned for the detective? Corruption? Murder?" Blanco leaned forward again. "You don't really love the guy, do you? You can't. A sociopath isn't capable of love."

I love him. I've loved him for a long time . . .

"Is that the point of that sappy 'friendship ring' instead of a real diamond? Does Mike have cold feet, or is it you, Clare?"

You don't understand. Sometimes love isn't enough. I don't want to make another mistake.

"If you really do love Mike Quinn, then answer one question. Why did your ex-husband spend the night with you while Mike was out of town?"

Oh, god . . .

"Still silent? I guess I'll have to put the same question to Detective Quinn, and see how he replies."

Oh, god . . . oh, god . . . My face felt hot and my heart began to race. *I didn't tell Mike. I was so tired after Lilly's hit-and-run . . . half-awake . . . I forgot. I didn't think it would matter. And now . . .*

A lump swelled in my throat. I tried to swallow, felt hot tears. I pretended not to notice as the first drop trickled down my cheek. Through a watery blur I saw Virginia Blanco's smug smile, and began to sob.

She broke me . . . The woman broke me . . .

I heard the door open. A portly man with a receding hairline stuck his head into the room. "Lieutenant Quinn is here," he said.

Blanco noticed my sharp gasp, and her smile went from obnoxious to insufferable. "That was fast," she told the man. "My god, that poor cop must have a real Jones for this one . . ."

Grabbing the file, Blanco left the room. But she didn't close the door this time. I was certain she'd left it open on purpose, so I could hear the terrible things they were going to tell Mike.

But if that was the plan, it backfired, because the DEA agents hardly had a chance to speak. It was Michael Quinn who dominated the conversation, and *them.*

What I was about to hear, for the first time in my life, was Michael Ryan Francis Quinn *Unleashed.*

THIRTY-FIVE

"YOU'RE holding my people," Mike began in a dead-cold tone. "I want to see them *now*."

"Your people?" Blanco snapped back. "What are you trying to—"

"My people, you *moron*! My *assets* in your wonk-assed administration parlance. Matteo Allegro and Clare Cosi are *mine*. They work for *me*!" He was a lion now, absolutely roaring. "When you grabbed them up, you jeopardized *everything*!"

"How can that be?" It was a man's voice this time.

"Dig the graft out of your ears, Special Agent Weiss, and *listen*. When you blundered into that warehouse, you may have jinxed a sting operation that took thousands of man hours to set up!"

"What?" Weiss responded. "We were never informed of that!"

"You didn't inform anybody on my squad before you pulled your asinine raid, either!"

"We dotted our i's and crossed our t's," Blanco replied. "The paperwork will cross your desk on Monday. So listen up, Quinn, if you think we're going to release—"

A trilling phone interrupted Special Agent Blanco. In the ensuing silence I imagined all three of them staring at the thing.

"The call is for *you*, Weiss," Mike said smugly.

It trilled again.

"I think you'd better answer it."

"Special Agent Darryl Weiss speaking . . ."

A long silence ensued, followed by a couple of respectful "yes, sirs" and "thank you, sirs" followed by a crisp "good night." Then Special Agent Weiss hung up.

"So . . ." Mike said.

"Who called?" Blanco asked, voice tense. "Was it the director?"

"No," said Weiss. "Higher up."

"What do you mean, higher up?" Blanco demanded. "How high?"

"That call came from God."

Dead silence ensued.

God? I thought. *Who was God? Certainly not the real God. The real God didn't call DEA agents in the dead of night.*

When Special Agent Weiss spoke again, his tone was conciliatory, almost apologetic. "What can we do to fix this, Lieutenant Quinn?"

"I want your people out of Allegro's warehouse ASAP," Mike replied. "If my targets think the DEA is sniffing around, they'll turn tail and run—and if that happens, I'm coming back here with a machete to collect *heads*."

"What else?"

"I want any and all phone taps you have on my people gone, instantly. Surveillance by your agents is over. I don't care what you do with them—take them to Central Park and put them on a merry-go-round, but get them the hell *off* this case *tonight*!"

"Consider it done."

"Good. Now send this woman to fetch Clare Cosi."

"Fetch?" Blanco spat back. "Who do you think you—"

"Do as the man says, Virginia."

A frowning Special Agent Virginia Blanco refused to meet

my gaze as she unlocked my cuffs. I ignored her, too. Rubbing my sore wrists, I rose on unsteady legs.

I should have felt liberated, like a great weight had been lifted. I had been rescued, after all. But as bad as this experience had been, I knew things could get much worse. So far, I'd only sparred with the Drug Enforcement Administration.

Now I had to face Crazy Quinn.

THE kitchen clock read 4:23 AM when Matt, Quinn, and I arrived at the apartment above the Blend. Out of habit, or perhaps necessity, I began to prepare a pot of coffee.

"No," Mike said, taking the pot right out of my hand and setting it aside. "Sit down, Clare. I have things to say. You, too, Allegro."

I dried my hands and sat at the table. Matt sunk into a chair across from me, hair disheveled, an angry bruise below his left eye. (He didn't say how he got it, and I didn't ask. Rough interrogation was possible. But, knowing Matt, it would have to be *resisting arrest.*)

Not a word had been spoken by any of us during our brief, tense drive from the DEA's headquarters on Tenth Avenue to my apartment above the Blend.

By now, "Crazy Quinn" was gone, but he'd been replaced by another stranger. This Quinn was inaccessible, but not in the taciturn way I'd seen him act in the past. This Quinn was brooding and, I feared, simmering with unspent rage.

I studied Mike's stony face, tried to meet his gaze, but the man was someplace else. So I took a breath, let it out, and told myself to hang in there and stay tough. Mike and I hadn't been together in days, and this was hardly the reunion I'd anticipated, but things could have gone far worse tonight for me and Matt.

"Listen up, Allegro," Quinn snapped, leaning across the table. "You're not out of the woods yet. Not even close. You could still lose your warehouse, your business, and do hard time in a federal penitentiary—"

Matt pounded the table. "But *we're* the victims here."

"You're the victims? Oh, great. So we're going with the plea of choice for nine out of ten hotel heiresses caught with the wrong white powder in their compacts, otherwise known as the 'that's not my cocaine' defense?"

"But it's not!"

"Shut up and listen. I'll hear your side of the story later, after we all get some sleep. But before we can close our eyes, I have to lay down a few rules. Obey them, or we're all going to face some pretty ugly consequences for what went down tonight."

The chair creaked as Matt leaned back again.

"As of this moment you both work for me. You're assets, informants, snitches. You will cooperate with the NYPD in all matters pertaining to this investigation. Is that understood?"

I couldn't nod fast enough, but Matt was, as usual, resisting.

"What do you mean, cooperate?" he griped.

"I mean you will do *everything* I tell you to do," Quinn said. "In my absence, you will do everything *my squad* tells you to do. You will talk to these drug dealers when they contact you. You will pretend to play along. You will meet with them if I deem it necessary, and wear a wire at that meeting."

"Didn't you catch that article in the *Wall Street Journal*?" Matt replied. "The one about how tight neckties cut off oxygen to the brain?"

"And if you *don't* want to cooperate with *me*, I can give you back to Weiss and Blanco and you can deal with them."

Matt slumped in his chair. "My lifelong ambition is finally fulfilled. I've become a rat for the NYPD."

"I don't require that you like it, Allegro. But for all our sakes, you have to do it."

Matt nodded, at last admitted, "I know."

"Later today, I'll meet with my squad and dole out new assignments. Everybody under me, and I mean every *body*, is going to be on this case. We'll obtain warrants to tap your business and personal phones, and set up surveillance at the warehouse and here at the Blend. Everything should be in place by noon."

"Geez, you work fast," Matt said.

"I have to," Quinn said, "and do you know why? Because we have maybe one week to clear this up. In ten lousy days *max* my deal with the powers that be will expire. If we don't have a decent lead by then, you'll end up in custody, and I'll likely be swept up for internal review."

For the first time that night, I felt Mike's ice blue gaze fix on me. "You're part of this, too, Clare. Buckman called me about the hit-and-run. The DEA told me about the shots fired—by the way, that's why they moved in on you two so fast. They saw Brooklyn locals on the case and they didn't want to lose the collar. Either way, your life is in danger, so until this is over, Sergeant Emmanuel Franco will be a member of the Blend staff."

Matt groaned. "Oh, man . . . not *him*."

"Train Franco, Clare, make him look convincing as a barista—"

"I can't turn an amateur into a barista overnight. The training process takes three months minimum!"

"Do your best. If the barista thing doesn't work, make him your dishwasher, or have him mop the floor. I don't care. But Franco has got to look like he belongs there. And not just sitting at a table. Franco goes wherever you go, on duty and off. He's your shadow and your shield. Don't make a move without him."

"Come on, Quinn," Matt complained again, "why the mook?"

"One reason, Allegro. To annoy *you*."

"That's it!" Matt jumped to his feet. "I'm going home."

"You're not going anywhere. Those smugglers are going to contact you. Not Clare. And not me. I don't want you partying in the Hamptons or clubbing in Soho when the call comes down. I want you close and ready."

"The three of us are going to the mattresses together?" Matt said. "Like in *The Godfather*?!"

"Look on the bright side," I said, remembering those *carnitas*. "At least we have enough food."

"Fine," Matt said. "So where do I sleep?"

"There's a bed in the guest room," Quinn said. "But then, you already know that."

THIRTY-SIX

WHEN Matt disappeared, silence fell. For a long and terrible minute, Quinn and I sat together, sharing nothing. Finally, I spoke.

"So . . . how was your trip?"

Mike gave me an unreadable stare. Then he rose from the table, loosened his tie, and uttered one word—

"Bedtime."

Taking my hand, he led me upstairs.

The master bedroom was dark, save the murky gray light seeping through the half-closed curtains. Quinn didn't bother turning on the lamp or turning back the covers, just collapsed into the four-poster, pulling me with him. I tucked into his arms, inhaled his strength.

"Thank you," I whispered on the exhale.

"You can thank me when this nightmare's over."

"You got me out of that interrogation room, which was loads of fun, by the way. I'll stick by my very big *thank you*, if you don't mind."

Shifting on the mattress, I rubbed my sore wrists and realized they weren't the only casualties. My upper arms were bruised, too.

"Oh, man. What did they do to me?"

Mike examined the darkening welts, softly cursed. "After they cuffed you, your feet didn't touch the floor, did they?"

"Not much. Everything happened so fast. My wrists were locked behind my back, they hoisted me by my upper arms and half carried, half dragged me all the way to the van in the parking lot. Why do they do that? Does it save time? Or just start the softening-up process for the interview?"

"Both."

"Well, it sucks . . ."

His probing touches were tender, but they still hurt. "Ouch."

"I'm sorry, Clare." His voice remained clipped, careful, and a little bit chilly. The coldness upset me, but I had to hang in there. I had to wait . . .

Mike Quinn had been willing to wait for me. That's why he'd given me the Claddagh ring instead of a diamond. He didn't want to rush me, to scare me. He cared enough to put aside what he wanted. Now it was my turn to do that for him.

I cleared my throat. "So are you going to tell me how you accomplished what you did tonight?"

"It started with phone calls—lots of them."

"That's an explanation?"

"For now."

"At least tell me one thing."

"What?"

"Who in the world is *God*?"

Mike paused. "That's an existential question, Cosi. I don't think I'm qualified to answer."

"You're being cute?"

"I'll tell you soon. Not tonight."

"Technically, it's morning." I gestured to the window where the sun was transmuting our bedroom light from desolate gray to the palest of yellows. The dawn was staking its ancient claim, warming the night-shrouded earth, cooking away the dark.

"How about you answer me a question," Quinn said.

"If it's about Matteo, I promise you that he spent the night in the guest room. I was going to mention it during our conversation, but—

"*Did you miss me?* That's my question."

I looked into his eyes. *Yes, I missed you*, I wanted to say. *And I'm still missing you . . .*

All night, Quinn's gaze had been glassy as a frigid arctic pond. Silently, I moved my hand to his cheek, now rough with stubble, and held it there. Before my eyes, the ice began to thaw. In the privacy of our room, Mike's frozen mask finally melted away and he came back to me . . .

"Ask me again," I whispered.

His eyes were shimmering now, warm blue pools in the golden light. "Did you miss me, Clare?"

My answer wasn't in words.

Thirty-Seven

"Oooh . . . *Figaro! Figaro! Figaro!*"

I rubbed my eyes. The late morning sun was strong through the partially closed drapes. My bedside clock informed me it was 11:52 AM, and my ears told me Matt was in the shower.

"Oooh . . . la-la-la! La-la-la! La-la-laaaaa!"

My head was aching, my arms black-and-blue, my wrists raw, and when I rolled over, I ran smack into a wall of naked muscle. For a moment, I thought I was dreaming again. But no, this time Mike Quinn really was here—and he was pissed.

"Ah, che bel vivere, che bel piacere!"

"Is that your asshole ex-husband caterwauling?"

"Yes," I said with a yawn. "He's singing Rossini, and I think it's a message for us . . ."

"For us?" Mike groused. "What's the message?"

"The aria he's singing is from *Barber of Seville*," I informed him. "The *barber* part's for me. The opera's libretto is for you . . ."

"I don't speak Italian."

"Pronto a far tutto!" Matt crooned. *"La notte e il giorno! Vita più nobile, no, non si da!"*

"Ready to do everything," I translated. "Night and day. A more noble life is not to be had."

"That's his message for me?" said Mike.

"I'm fairly sure he's being sarcastic."

"Aaaah . . . Figaro! Figaro! Figaro! A te fortuna non mancherà!"

"Ah, Figaro," I translated. "You'll never lack for luck."

Mike groaned, and I knew exactly what he was thinking: *This is going to be one long week.*

With a resigned sigh, I spooned in closer and rested my cheek against his broad back. He felt sturdy and warm and good—but then Mike was good, and good for me in so many ways . . . So why was that awful moment from last night's interrogation still bothering me?

"You don't really love the guy, do you?. . . Is that the point of that sappy 'friendship ring' instead of a real diamond? Does Mike have cold feet, or is it you, Clare?"

It was me. I knew that. But my reluctance to accept a diamond from Mike had nothing to do with not loving him. I loved the man with all my heart.

Then why haven't I said yes to more with him?

The answer wasn't simple. Though I didn't doubt Mike's love, I did doubt something . . . mainly the future—and all the things that might happen between us, painful things that could lead to the decline of our relationship, things I'd experienced with Matt and had no desire to relive. *How can I risk another commitment before God, when there's a chance it could all fall to pieces?*

Softly, a different voice seemed to answer . . .

"In times like these, Clare, failing to take a risk is the biggest risk of all . . ."

The words were Madame's, advising me on the difficulties of running a business. But love was a difficult business, too, and as I lay in bed next to Mike, I began to wonder: *Is playing it safe with him creating another kind of risk? Could delaying our union lead to the end of it?*

The very idea caused me far more pain than the purple welts on my arms.

Almost of its own accord, one of those arms now curled around Mike's long, powerful form. Needing to be closer, I pressed my lips against his neck, brushed my fingers lower, and heard his thrilling intake of breath. Thirty seconds later, he was rolling to face me.

We'd made some very sweet love before drifting off earlier, and I hadn't bothered to get up for a nightshirt, which meant the only stitch currently covering my curves belonged to a thin section of bedsheet.

Utterly naked, I looked into Mike's eyes and silently promised: *When this whole thing is over, I'm going to tell you how I feel. I may be worried, doubtful, even a little bit scared, but I don't want to risk losing you. Not after you've risked everything for me . . .*

In the hazy light of the half-closed curtains, Mike gazed at my secret smile and slowly his expression changed from pleasantly aroused to intensely ravenous.

"Oooh . . . la-la-la, la-la-la, la-la-laaaaa!"

It was enough to render us both deaf—at least, for the next twenty minutes.

"YEAH, Sully, find Franco. This is his assignment for the foreseeable future. We can brief him later about our meeting at 1PP . . . No, not 24/7. He's with Clare only when I'm not, and he's got to appear as a barista . . . *uh-huh.* Just get him here. One hour. I'll fill in the blanks . . ."

"Shower's free," I called, returning to the master bedroom in my terrycloth robe. (Mike had one, too. It usually hung on the bathroom door. Now it appeared to be missing.)

With a nod to me, Mike wound up his call with Sullivan, his right-hand man on the OD squad—although, technically, it wasn't a squad. It was a special NYPD task force with a more official-sounding moniker.

A few years back, an epidemic of deaths from prescription drug overdoses alarmed the mayor's office. The police commissioner was asked to find a solution. The OD squad was it. Mike got tapped to take it over and remade it completely, bringing in his own people, aggressively pursuing leads, and shaping it into one of the most effective teams in the NYPD.

A few of Mike's cases carried high profiles, so I wasn't all that surprised he'd caught the attention (if not admiration) of VIPs in the U.S. Justice Department. I hadn't enjoyed Mike's time away, but I had to admit, I was grateful they'd brought him to Washington when they did. Who knew whether last night's phone calls would have had the same impact without that trip?

"So," I said, "are you calling God this morning, too?"

Mike smiled. "It's Sunday. God's busy."

"I talk to him all the time, you know? *Especially* on Sunday. So if there's anything else you need?"

He pulled me over, touched my cheek. "I need you to be careful."

"Well, if shots ring out again, I certainly plan to duck."

Mike was no longer smiling. "I need to tell you something, Clare. A secret."

"Oh?"

"Last night in the kitchen with Allegro, I lied. Your life is not in danger. If I thought it really was, I'd be bundling you off to some safe house in Tennessee."

"Well, could you make it Memphis? I hear they have good coffee in Memphis."

"Listen to me. It's important. If these dealers wanted you dead, you wouldn't be standing here now."

"What about the hit-and-run?"

Mike shook his head. "Murderers for hire are paid to get the job done. If some assassin planned to run you over and failed, he would have remedied his mistake the next morning, before the drug lord found out. And I guarantee he would have used a more reliable method than a van with no muffler."

"What about the gunshots?"

"Those weren't meant for you."

"How can you be sure?"

"Because drug dealers assassinate at close range, almost without exception. And there are other reasons. I talked at length with Sergeant Ortiz. You were standing in front of a large truck yesterday. If an assassin was aiming for you, our CSU would have picked up bullets or fragments in or around that truck. Yet they found nothing. To top that off, witnesses said they heard shots coming from behind the truck while the balloons popped were in front of it."

"That was my impression, too. The sound of the shots didn't match their supposed trajectory. So what was it?"

"Maybe a coincidence. Maybe stray shots from the projects at the exact time the balloons popped for some other reason."

"You told me when it comes to investigating cases, there are no coincidences."

"I did. And maybe there really was something deliberate behind yesterday's incident. Whatever it was, it was not an attempt on your life. But, listen, here's where the secret comes in: I want Allegro to think your life is in danger. If he does, he'll stick around. And it's vital that he doesn't flake out on me or disappear on the squad. He has to continue to cooperate or we'll lose any chance we have of getting a lead on the dealers on this end. The ones who were supposed to pick up and distribute that new Brazilian crack."

"Okay, I get it. I'm not a sitting duck a l'orange, after all. So what's Franco for then? Show?"

"Franco's there to back you up if the dealers approach you. Despite what I said last night, I think it's highly likely they will want to talk with you, Clare."

"Talk with me! Me? Why on earth?"

"If this drug lord wanted you dead, you would be. The only reason you aren't is the same reason those DEA agents tried to break you last night—you're a way to get to me. This new crack involves new people, brand-new networks. That's why they were hot to set up Allegro. They're going to want their own corrupt cops in their pockets, too, which makes you the opposite of a target. It makes you an asset."

"But I'm *your* asset."

"They don't know that . . . and Franco's there so you won't be afraid or wonder what to say and do. We'll go over all of it. I've seen you in action, sweetheart. You like to take down bad guys, just like me. In fact, you're the main reason I was able to sell my story to Justice Department brass."

"Me again?"

"It's all on the record. You were instrumental in the case that caught their attention."

"You mean when I helped you take down that creep's Internet pharmacy?"

Mike nodded. "You weren't just our primary witness then, Cosi. You're the primary reason Allegro is not on his way to a federal penitentiary now."

I closed my eyes. "This is a lot to digest, Mike. I need coffee. Bad."

He pulled me close, pressed his lips to my forehead. "I'll see you downstairs."

THIRTY-EIGHT

"CLARE, I have a problem . . ."

I was taking two-dozen Oatmeal Cookie Muffins out of the oven when Matt marched into the kitchen wrapped in Quinn's missing bathrobe. (Mystery solved.)

"My thing doesn't work anymore!"

"Your what?" *Geez, was Tanya rougher on him than I thought?*

"My smart phone! Those fascists at the DEA must have fouled it up."

"Matt, don't you remember? You bounced 'your thing' off the ceiling in Bree's BMW. You broke it yourself when we were evading those drug dealers."

"What's that about dealers?"

Now Quinn was sauntering in, freshly showered, his short light brown hair still damp. He'd donned slate gray slacks, a white dress shirt, and a silver-blue tie that brought out the cobalt of his irises. What drew my attention, however, were the items on his belt. I recognized the usual signs of his profession—a gold shield and a pair of handcuffs. But I noticed a few other things, too, an extra magazine of ammo, OC spray (aka pepper spray), and a pouch for a multifunctional tool, which I knew included a serious-looking knife. The man was packing for war, which didn't exactly cheer me.

"You saw the dealers following you?" Quinn asked, hanging his shoulder holster off the back of a kitchen chair.

"They were," I said, "until Matt made some clever moves and shook them."

"What make of car?" Quinn asked.

"Chevy Impala," Matt said. "Late model. Black."

Quinn's lips quirked. "Seventy percent of federal law enforcement drives late model Chevy Impalas, black."

"You mean I shook the DEA?"

"Not for long, apparently." Quinn touched my shoulder, kissed my head. "Something smells wonderful."

I smiled. "Cinnamon, brown sugar, raisins, and buttermilk-soaked oats, all baked up for you in a nice, warm muffin . . ." I gestured to the cooling treats.

"Mmmm . . . I love those. They smell just like my mom's oatmeal cookies."

"That's the idea." He reached for one, but I directed him to the chair. "Those are for your squad meeting. I have another favorite for breakfast."

Matt leaned against the counter. "I don't get it, Quinn. I mean, I've been thinking this through. You work with some of these DEA people, right? Why didn't you get some kind of tip about last night's raid?"

"Simple," he said, sitting back. "They knew I was involved with Clare. The last thing they would have done is inform me or my squad. And by the way, Blanco's claim was a load of crap. No 'paperwork' was going to cross my desk. Those agents planned to take me down along with you and Clare, once they broke you in the interview. That was the plan, anyway."

"So you really are in it with us." Matt said, smirk finally gone.

"We're a team now, Allegro. The three of us. We sink or swim together."

"Then answer me something. Do you know how they

found out about the drugs? I mean, I didn't even know until last night."

"They didn't tell me, but it's highly likely some asset tipped them—an informant, just like you two, only in that drug lord's circle. The Justice Department . . . that is the NSA, CIA, DEA—"

"All the 'As'," said Matt. "We get it."

"They have informants all over the world. The tip came in and they watched you. I'm sure they would have kept watching you to see where those drugs went. Who picked them up—and where and how they intended to distribute them."

"And that's what you want to know?"

"That's what God wants to know. And we're going to find out for him."

"Who is God, anyway?" Matt asked.

I froze, hoping to hear . . .

"That's a very personal question. A spiritual matter, really. Not something I can answer for you . . ."

Before Matt could snap back, I pointed to Quinn's face. "Mike, you have something on your jawline . . ." *(Like a half-dozen tiny dots of scarlet-speckled white tissue.)* "What happened?"

"Well, it seems *somebody* used all of my Barbasol, which left me with trying to get a lather out of my Irish Spring. And my razor was dull as hell . . ." He glared at Matt, whose hacked-away black beard, courtesy of Quinn's shaving kit, was presently reduced to a slight morning stubble.

"Maybe you should keep more than one disposable around," said Matt. "Even a second can of shaving cream. I mean, I realize on a public servant's salary, things are tight, but you might consider an occasional backup."

"Allegro, do me a favor today?"

"What?"

"Resist arrest."

"Come on, guys. Don't fight. Eat!"

With that, I set down a napkin-lined basket of my fresh-baked Blueberry Muffin Tops—my healthier and much more convenient alternative to pancakes.

(While flapjacks were fab, they were time-consuming to cook, only a few at a time on a stovetop griddle with a spatula-wielder forced to stand by and flip. My muffin tops, on the other hand, could be dropped on a sheet pan and baked all at once.)

The batter was your basic quick bread, plus the slight tanginess of a good quality yogurt. For the fat, I chose healthy canola oil. For flavor, I found the tartness of lemon zest was a must—though I balanced its smart mouth with a sweet kiss of vanilla.

An affectionate hug of ovenly heat seduced my plump farmer's market blueberries to relax inside their little cake pillows. Some of them, I was delighted to see, became so overwhelmed that they oozed their sweet bluey goodness into the crumb.

With my two-dozen cakelets all baked and cooled, breakfast was ready. Well, almost. Using my still-sore wrist, I finished the pastries with a back-and-forth dusting of powdered sugar. Then I brought three empty cups to the table and filled them with the bright, nutty flavor of my fresh-brewed Morning Sunshine Blend. (Okay, so it was early afternoon, but we all needed the caffeine hit from the light roast.)

The men dug in and for a few minutes I enjoyed blissful silence—save the chewing of warm little blueberry cakes, slurping of hot coffee, and occasional guttural male noises of gustatory pleasure.

"So what *are* your plans today?" Quinn finally asked Matt.

"Oh, some partying in the Hamptons. Then clubbing in Soho."

At Quinn's dead-cold stare, Matt shrugged. "Or not. I have work. Clients in Japan and Germany are expecting updates on shipments, and I have to reply to e-mails and messages."

"How are you going to do that without a working PDA?" I asked.

"I'll have to use your computer later, okay? Tomorrow I'll buy a new smart phone."

"What about your address book?"

"I use the Cloud for backup."

"The what?" I asked. *First Quinn's talking to God, now Matt's getting data from the heavens?*

"The Cloud is a backup service, Clare. It saves computer data. I'll download my files from their server later and—"

Quinn cut him off. "Before you do any of that, you're coming downtown with me."

"I am?"

"Yes, I want you to debrief with my squad and some people above my pay grade down at 1PP."

The smirk was back. "What's that you're saying, Quinn? Something about PP? You have to use the John?"

"*One Police Plaza* is where the NYPD has its headquarters. And I'd lose the smart mouth. Not every gold shield has the extreme patience that I do."

"Yes, Matt . . ." *(I know you can't stand authority, but . . .)* "Please remember. The majority of these men are heavily armed."

"And, by the way, I need things at my apartment—change of clothes, toiletries, my personal shaving kit."

"Believe me, Allegro, we *all* want you to have your personal shaving kit."

"So I'll just run up there first—"

"You're not running anywhere alone. Not for the foreseeable future. I'll send Sully with you."

"Who?"

"Finbar Sullivan, one of my men."

"I do not need some Irish cop to babysit me while I go uptown and back."

"It's either him or Franco."

"Fine." He stood up, theatrically rewrapped Quinn's bathrobe, and headed for the kitchen door. "Send the leprechaun."

Quinn threw me a look, grabbed another muffin top, and opened his phone. Between bites, I heard him instruct Sully to bodyguard Matt to Sutton Place then straight to 1PP. "And I know you, Sully, do not let this operator sweet talk you."

He hung up, exhaled, and took a long hit of coffee. "I

swear, Clare, if those two end up in a Soho bar drinking imported beer, *this* unhappy leprechaun will be going after more than their lucky charms."

Note to self, I thought, watching Quinn stew. *Work on recipe for Irish Coffee Muffins . . . double the whiskey.*

"I take it you don't need me down at 1PP?" I said.

"No. All I want you to do, Clare, is resume your normal routine. What's your schedule this week?"

"I'm here in the Blend for most of it. Wednesday I go out with the Muffin Muse to the Dragon Boat exhibition. Friday we have a food-truck wedding reception in Central Park."

"That's fine." Quinn checked his watch. "Franco should be here any minute. Remember, he'll be with you wherever you go. Just make sure he looks like he belongs."

"I know. Barista 101. Crash course. I only hope all the shots in our future come from my espresso machine."

THIRTY-NINE

AFTER thirty minutes of uneven tamps and poor extractions, sampling espressos that were too flat, too sour, too bitter, or too weak, I watched the muscle-bound Franco attempt another delicate pull.

This time my undercover barista tamped the coffee evenly. I had high hopes for a nice, syrupy stream and a competent shot—until he mis-attached the portafilter and the grounds that didn't hit Franco ended up on the floor.

"Whoa! My bad!"

"Don't sweat it, honey," Tucker called from the register. "I've been pulling espressos since the cows came home, and I made that same mistake last week."

Tucker Burton had never dropped a portafilter in his life. My lanky, floppy-haired actor-cum-assistant-manager was an exceptional barista. His attempt to save Franco's pride was just another example of his big heart and team spirit.

"I'll get the broom," Nancy sang, flipping a wheat-colored braid.

With patience Tucker had been watching my quest for the impossible—cramming three months of barista training into one afternoon. But the portafilter drop had been the last straw. Grabbing my elbow, he pulled me aside.

"CC, I'm sure you had high hopes this boy would be some kind of espresso idiot savant. But as far as his barista skills go, he's more of an—"

"Stop right there, because we need a good shot right now, one that has nothing to do with espresso. And Franco's our man. He's here to watch our backs after that shooting in Brooklyn yesterday." *(A Quinn-worthy statement, misleading but necessary.)*

"But the customers! I can't believe you're going to let him—"

"Take it easy. I have no intention of letting Franco pull espressos for customers. I simply want him to be familiar with the process. Be able to act the part."

"Listen, honey, my directorial skills have been honed on and off-Broadway. Were Franco a competent thespian, I might be able to help him at least look competent behind our machine. But he's a police detective, not an actor."

"I have news for you, Tuck. Good detectives are *great* actors." Quinn's performance with the DEA deserved a Golden Globe nomination.

I felt a heavy arm on my shoulder and I was suddenly jerked into a three-way huddle.

"So what are we going to do with me now?" Franco asked.

"How about the register?" Tuck suggested, sinking slightly under the weight of Franco's limb. "He's a cop. I *think* we can trust him not to steal."

"What a vote of confidence," Franco said.

I'd already considered the register. "I don't think that will work."

"Agreed," Franco said. "Here's me, worrying about correct change or else the John Doe in front of me gives me grief—which means I'm not watching for guys I should be watching for. And, sorry, Coffee Lady, burying me behind your over-complicated coffeemaker won't be any better. It'll cut off my line of sight."

"I only wanted you to understand what we do here," I explained.

"I get it," Franco said, squeezing his arms a little tighter around us so we'd get the point. "Now it's time to try something *new*."

"I'm good with something new," Tuck quickly agreed.

"Fine," I said, "but what?"

"Ahem, *people*," Nancy called to us in an exaggerated whisper. "I have a solution."

Our youngest barista gestured to me and Tuck. "You two, come here . . ."

Franco released us so quickly from his powerful half-time huddle, we practically stumbled toward Nancy. She stared at Franco.

"Do me a favor. Go to the men's room."

"What?"

"Just do it," said Nance, "I'll have a solution by the time you come back."

Franco shrugged and headed for the back. As he did, Nancy quietly directed me and Tuck to watch a table at the other end of the coffeehouse. A Sunday afternoon gathering of single women suddenly stopped talking. As Franco passed by them, they froze, their gazes tracking my undercover barista like searchlights on a fugitive.

"The boyfriend experience," Tucker whispered. "Franco can bus, wipe tables, and *flirt* with customers."

I tensed, thinking of that Three Stooges huddle. "I'm not sending him out there raw. He's going to need a crash course in coffeehouse etiquette. Tuck, can you talk to him about the right touch with—"

"Wrong guy," Tuck said, chucking his thumb to a table on the sidewalk, where his boyfriend Punch had his nose in *Variety*. "If you want an expert in charming coeds, you better ask Dante . . ."

"What are you three whispering about?" Franco asked a minute later.

We all jumped.

"We have a new assignment for you," I replied. "And I think you're going to enjoy this aspect of the job."

But when I explained it, his response was a bemused smirk. "Just what are you selling here, Coffee Lady?"

"Java and a smile," I insisted. "In the Italian tradition, a barista is outgoing, friendly, personable. He or she strives to give each customer a positive, uplifting experience. Take our Dante, for instance. He's charming and friendly, but he's *especially* friendly toward our female clientele."

"Wink, wink. Nudge, nudge," Nancy quipped.

"Dante makes eye contact," I continued, "he engages them in conversation. In a very special way, he makes them feel like more than just a customer. We call this 'the boyfriend experience.'"

"Using me as a boy toy? I feel so violated."

"Chill, Sergeant," Tuck said. "There are no lap dances in this coffeehouse."

"I can certainly do the first part," Franco said seriously. "I used to bus tables at a gin mill when I was a kid—"

"Child labor in a tavern?" Tuck said, horrified. "Is that legal?"

"No. But the tips were great."

"Well, at least you have *some* food service experience," Tuck conceded. "Let's set you up . . ."

Minutes after Tuck and Franco wandered off, I noticed a familiar couple sitting at a table near the French doors.

John Fairway, the attorney from Two Wheels Good, loosened his tie while casually scanning an e-reader, a half-empty latte at his elbow. Beside the lawyer, Warrior Barbie had curled into a chair, her long legs tucked under her. The lithe young woman had traded silver bike pants and sports bra for pastel blue, and her frizzy blond hair had been freed from its ponytail. She appeared to be watching me between sips of bottled water.

Now what are they doing here? I was about to approach the pair and fish when Dante burst through the door and strode up to me.

"We're being punk'd on Twitter!" Dante declared, waving his iPad. "Check it out."

His Twitter account was already up on the screen. The hashtag search was "urban violence," the tweeter someone named *KittyKatKlubette*, and in one short tweet this person had fired a broadside at our newly minted food truck.

Shots fired near Muffin Muse. Bad scene. Keep clear.
Gansta rap and mealy muffins do not mix.

"Why do I think Kaylie's behind this?" I said.

"Because she probably is," Dante replied.

"Is there an e-mail publicly linked to that account?" I asked.

"There should be . . ."

Dante found it, and I told him to try my little *gotcha* trick. We plugged the e-mail into Google to search for other references to that address. We got a hit on a cartoon site that featured a glittery pink kitten.

The pink cat was the clue I needed. And when we found a small photo attached to a fan profile, we hit pay dirt. KittyKatKlubette was none other than Mrs. Li's pretty young granddaughter, the teen in the Chinatown bakery who'd been so smitten with Dante.

"Kaylie or Billy must have put her up to it," Dante said, "or they're using her account."

"Either way, that connection to Kaylie is enough for me."

"So what do we do?"

"Nothing yet," I said. "But we're going to stop Kaylie. I promise you . . ." I already had the ammo, and I was more than ready to pull the trigger. I just needed the right opportunity.

Tuck tapped my shoulder. "Our boy's on the job," he declared. "And you'll be pleased to know Franco is exceptionally talented at balancing a full tray of dirty latte cups on his shoulder."

We watched Franco clear one table and move to the next. He worked with efficiency, but when it came time to flirting, the boy came off a little *too* friendly.

Coming upon a young woman intensely reading, he brashly interrupted her to convey a joke. It didn't exactly work like a charm. She nodded nervously then packed up her things and fled.

Dante saw the problem immediately. "Franco's flirting like

a boroughs guy. Manhattan women require a different touch. Don't worry, boss. I'll set him straight."

"Hey, boss!" Nancy dangled our store phone in her hand. "Detective Buckman wants to speak to you. He said something about Sunday dinner . . ."

I took the call in my upstairs office.

"I was just about to call you," I said. "What's this about dinner?"

"Time for another meal of crow," he replied, deep voice rumbling like his GTO engine.

Great. "You're talking about Billy Li's fingerprints, right?"

"Yeah, Cosi. Sorry to break the bad news, but the prints you sent over don't match any of the prints we found in the van. And don't bother trying for Kaylie's, or anyone else on her crew, because my guys checked them out and none of them were involved in Lilly's assault."

"And you know this how?"

"Two Sunday mornings ago, Kaylie, her truck, and her entire crew boarded the ferry to Governors Island where they spent the day selling cupcakes to the spectators at the Five Boroughs Little League Soccer Playoffs."

"I don't understand. Why is Kaylie free and clear because of somewhere she was two weeks ago?"

"The van that struck Lilly was involved in another hit-and-run after Kaylie and her staff boarded that ferry to Governors Island. Her boyfriend, Jeffrey Li, along with his truck and staff, were on the same ferry. Now it's possible a stolen van used in one hit-and-run was abandoned by the perp and later stolen by a second perp for a subsequent attack, but we very much doubt it."

I did, too, and the news could not have been worse.

From the start I'd been convinced that Kaylie or her cow-orker Billy Li was responsible for Lilly's injuries. Now that Buckman proved me wrong, I had no clues, no motive, no suspects—and about a million questions, none of which this motor head detective was willing to answer.

"I'll talk to you again soon. Take care."

* * *

AFTER ending the call, I descended the stairs now happy that John Fairway and Warrior Barbie were in my coffeehouse.

This is good timing, I thought. *I can press them about what they know on this other hit-and-run.*

But when I reached the main floor, their table was empty. Fairway and Barbie were gone.

With an exhale of frustration, I returned to work behind the counter, where Dante, Tuck, and Nancy were now gathered in a knot.

"What's going on?" I asked.

Tuck grinned. "Our little boy is all *growed* up."

A burst of feminine laughter floated through the air. Tucker pointed, and I searched the crowded floor to find Franco chatting up those single ladies who'd admired him earlier. My undercover barista appeared relaxed, natural, friendly, and personable—in short, a perfect example of the boyfriend experience.

"Amazing . . ." I turned to Dante. "How did you do it?"

He shrugged. "I told him flirting with women was no different than pouring them coffee. Too hot, you'll burn them. Too cold, they'll dump you. But serve it up with *just* the right balance of warmth and stimulation and, brother, they'll be back for more."

I patted Dante's shoulder, happy he'd steered Franco in the right direction. At the same time, I couldn't help wondering about Max Buckman's.

What lead is he following? What does he know?

I had some educated guesses about the identity of that other hit-and-run victim, but I'd have to wait for the detective to contact me again before I could be sure.

I sighed, giving it up—for now.

With Franco squared away, Quinn preparing for a drug sting, and Mad Max hot on the trail of our killer driver, it was time I refocused my energies on the coffee business.

Forty

As the week progressed, Mike Quinn continually reminded me to keep things looking normal. I did my level best—although it was hard to relax into routine when your next customer might be a Brazilian drug runner.

Still, Monday and Tuesday went without a hitch: no shots fired, no DEA raids, nobody run over. I did, however, face one daunting challenge, and it had nothing to do with the workplace or the crime wave.

My biggest problem was domestic.

Quinn and Matt continued to squabble over just about everything from bathroom time, to second helpings at dinner, to the last slice of my special "Melt-and-Mix" Double-Chocolate Espresso-Glazed Loaf Cake. *(Really, I would have melted and mixed two if I'd known they were going to eat the entire thing in one day.)*

Then came Wednesday, and for the first time since our truck-painting party I was out in public—the middle of Flushing Meadows Park to be precise—where criminal smugglers could chat me up at any moment.

As scheduled, I'd come to Queens with our Muffin Muse

to participate in the Dragon Boat Festival, aka Duanwu Jie, a yearly event held in China and in Chinese communities around the world. New York's was typically held in August, but today's late spring event was an exhibition for visiting diplomats and was very well attended.

Cheers and drumbeats now echoed across the park's Meadow Lake, where dragon-prowed rowboats shot across the water. Along the shore, spectators watched from a forest of colorful tents with fluttering banners emblazoned with team logos.

At sunset, Chinese lanterns would be lit for martial arts demonstrations, live music, and Esther's kids reading Chinese poetry—capped by a fireworks display at nine.

Our Muffin Muse truck now sat in a grassy field next to the lake, alongside a half circle of food trucks featuring a United Nations of taste: Korean barbecue, Mexican tacos, Salvadoran papusas, and Asian shaved ice. I'd already snagged a half dozen of their frozen yogurt bites with exotic flavors like mango, green tea, and lychee.

Unfortunately, Kaylie's Kupcake Kart was also here, just twenty feet away from us, and the Kween had been glaring at me for the past two hours.

After that snarky tweet on Sunday, even more appeared on Twitter under the hashtag #DragonBoat, and I was convinced Kaylie had another prank up her buttercream-stained sleeves—specifically for this event—which is why I'd enlisted Franco to help me end her sugarcoated reign of terror once and for all.

"Anything suspicious?" I asked.

Franco grunted. "Not yet, but I'm pretty sure Billy Li recognized me from the day I snagged his prints. Perps are like elephants. Chat up their tats and they never forget."

"Maybe Billy will have second thoughts about trying something, now that he knows we're watching."

"I doubt it," Franco replied. "Not with that blonde in the paper crown giving you the fish-eye. By the way, if she sends over cupcakes, I would advise you not to eat them."

"Kaylie would love to poison me. In her mind, this is some kind of turf war. But there's plenty of business to go around. It doesn't have to be this way."

Franco shrugged. "Then convince Kaylie. That's how I did things when I was working anti-gang. We couldn't lock up all the gangbangers. Sometimes I had to negotiate."

I smiled, patting him on his big shoulder. "*Now* you're sounding like a member of the family . . ." Madame's family, for sure.

Nancy Kelly's angry cry interrupted us. "Holy smokin' rockets! Dante's talking to *another* girl."

My youngest barista's mad crush on Dante was ongoing—though, by now, we'd discouraged her from pursuing a workplace romance. She tossed her head, clearly miffed.

"That's the fifth girl in an hour to hit on him."

Dante, who'd been placing muffin- and coffee-cup-shaped balloons around our truck, had been garnering attention, but I didn't think he was the attraction.

"It's not Dante this time, Nancy. Those girls were asking him about the hand-painted balloons that Josh Fowler created. I've had a dozen people ask me how much they cost. I'm thinking we should sell them."

"Well, that chick is only *pretending* to look at the balloons," Nancy insisted. "I can tell. It's a sneaky excuse to press Dante's flesh."

Franco folded his arms. "You know, Nance, there's more than one sexy bald guy aboard this truck."

"Oh, please." She rolled her eyes. "Everyone knows you're taken. You're so into Joy it's scary." Then her scowl melted into a dreamy smile. "But it is *soooo* romantic, though . . ."

Another batch of customers arrived, many of them directly from the office, and boy did they crave caffeine. They nearly cleaned us out of Blueberry Pie Bars, too. The Asian-American crowd seemed more impressed with Lilly's Forbidden Chocolate Muffins and Black Bean Brownies.

During a lull, an older man appeared at our window, his wrinkled face animated with good cheer.

"Map lady! Good to see you again!"

"Mr. Hon! I see you're not driving your cab tonight."

"And you're not chasing dragon trucks!" Mr. Hon laughed.

"No truck chasing," I said. "But I'll tell you a secret. I am still chasing the boy with the dragon tattoo. See, he's over there in the cupcake truck, and I'm sure he's up to no good."

Mr. Hon frowned, shook his head. "When boy is headed for trouble, he need to be put on right path. Right path important. Like this festival today. Duanwu Jie, all about staying on right path."

"Do you know anyone competing in the dragon boat races, today?"

"Yes, yes . . ." Hon nodded. "Two cousins, three nieces, one nephew. We all meet later, watch fireworks and eat *zongzi*." He smiled.

I didn't want Mr. Hon to leave empty-handed, so I poured him a free coffee and gifted him one of Lilly's special Black Bean Brownies. Munching happily, he sauntered off.

"Hey, boss, look who's here," Dante called. "Mother of the year—that's what Josh calls her."

He gestured to a knot of formally dressed men making their way toward our food-truck area. These were the visiting dignitaries from China, I realized, and plenty of local politicians were gathered around them for photo ops. But Dante was pointing out the only woman among them—Helen Bailey-Burke.

I had no desire to see Mrs. Bailey-Burke again, not after she so coldly rejected Esther's grant proposal and then publicly slapped gentle doctor Gwen Fischer. I had no love for her sidekick, either, sorority sister Tanya Harmon.

But where was Tanya (and her naughty hand)? Not here. Not today. It appeared Helen had now attached herself to a new politician, handsome African-American state assemblyman Wilson Seacliffe.

A former college tennis star turned history professor, Seacliffe was also a mayor wannabe. Like Dominic Chin and Tanya Harmon, he'd just announced his bid to live in Gracie Mansion.

As the VIPs drew closer, I confirmed my passing observations about Helen. She wasn't just infatuated with Seacliffe. She was wearing his campaign button.

Looks like the sorority sisters had a falling out. But why did Helen dump Tanya? And why now? My next thought was spoken out loud. "I wonder what happened . . ."

"Yeah, me too," Franco growled suspiciously.

"Are you reading my mind?"

"Only if you're thinking about Billy Li, because he's missing."

"What?"

"He disappeared inside the truck while you were talking to that little old man, and I haven't seen him since. I think maybe Billy slipped out the back."

I scanned the area. "This is bad, Franco. I know he's up to something. We can't lose sight of—"

"There he is!" Franco cried. "He ducked inside the tent with the dragon logo."

I blinked. "They *all* have dragon logos!"

"The black tent—"

The first bang was loud enough to shock the birds out of the trees, scary enough to cause panic—especially after a bobbing muffin balloon popped right beside my head. People ducked, many hugged the grass. But I didn't panic, and in fact I'd lied when I told Mike if shots rang out I'd duck, because when Franco jumped through the service window to chase down Billy, I was right behind him.

I landed in the grass and started running just as the second blast echoed across Meadow Lake. No balloons exploded this time, because Billy Li's plan had been interrupted.

Fleeing a determined Franco, the boy with the dragon tattoo burst out of the tent, clutching what looked like a long tube. Legs pumping, he raced toward the parking lot, knocking people out of the way.

Billy was fast, and he had a great head start. With so much distance to cover, there appeared to be no way Franco could catch him. I despaired—until a familiar figure stepped into the Billy's path. *Mr. Hon!*

The elderly taxi driver didn't have a chance. Billy was about to slam right into him. "Out of the way, old maahhh—"

Billy's shout transformed into a howl as the "old man" upended him with two swift, expertly executed martial arts moves. The boy's legs danced in the air before he landed on his back in the grass.

Oof!

By the time Franco and I reached them, the wind had been knocked out of Billy, and Hon kept him pinned to the ground with his foot.

"You looking for this boy, Map Lady?"

"Where did you learn that stuff, pops?" Franco asked.

"Shaolin kung fu," Mr. Hon replied. "Long time now. Black belt."

"But you're such a little guy—"

"Little guy, big guy." He shrugged. "Size not matter. Victor knows how to turn enemy's strength against him."

Franco scooped up Billy's plastic tube and examined it. "Looks like a homemade super slingshot. Pretty cool. And what's this?" Franco yanked a plastic bag out of Billy's belt pack. I expected drugs, but I was wrong.

"It's ice."

I couldn't believe it. "Little icicles . . ."

"Clever," Franco said with a fellow bad-boy smile. "Pop a balloon with an ice spike and a sling shot. Add some bang, bang noise and distracted crowds think shots were fired. Cops come and there are no bullets or pellets because by then the evidence melted."

I stood over Billy Li until his gaze met mine. "Kaylie put you up to this, didn't she? You pulled this same stunt at our party?"

He nodded twice.

"Where did the sound effects come from?"

"Speakers," Billy gasped, "inside the tent."

I glanced at Franco, who gripped his phone, ready to summon the park police and have Billy carted off to Rikers. But I met his eyes, shook my head. I shifted my gaze to Mr. Hon, who removed his foot from Billy's chest, waiting for me to state my piece.

As the boy sat up, moaning, I cleared my throat.

Okay. Here goes . . .

"Listen up now, Billy. I know all about the black market knockoff business you're involved in—and I *could* turn you over to this nice police detective right now. Or . . . you, me, and Kaylie could work something out today. Something that will put an end to our stupid turf war for good. What do you say?"

Billy glanced at Franco, then at Mr. Hon. Finally, he rubbed the back of his neck, shook his head and shrugged.

"Okay, Coffee Lady. Talk."

Forty-one

I was feeling pretty good the next day. It's not often you get to make offers that can't be refused—but Billy Li and Kaylie Crimini accepted my "egg-tart truce," and our turf war was over for good.

I would sell Mrs. Li's delicious egg custard tarts and, with Madame's help, find her many more vendors uptown, as long as Billy agreed to abandon his part in the knockoff-designer-handbag business and make extra money delivering his grandmother's pastries instead.

We also agreed that Kaylie would (literally) steer her truck clear of the Village Blend if I would start selling a few of her most popular cupcakes. (Franco convinced me Maple Bacon had to be one of them.)

In return, Kaylie agreed to drop her current coffee supplier and sell mine, after a few lessons on how to properly prepare and serve it. (Freshly brewed, thank you very much.)

One problem solved. A few more to go, and at least one of them involved coffee—Matt's coffee.

Our Muffin Muse was scheduled to join a select group of food trucks the following evening to help cater an elaborate

Central Park wedding. The bride and groom were longtime Village Blend customers, and earlier in the week I had served them a sample of a very special coffee that I called Ambrosia.

This was, of course, Matt's special Brazilian "crack" coffee, and I asked if they'd like to share this superb find with their wedding guests. They flipped for it, readily agreeing to pay the exorbitant price. (They were loaded, *natch.*) This development landed me in the basement roasting room for much of Thursday.

As sunset came, I crested the service staircase and headed toward the front. Franco immediately moved to check in with me.

"Everything copacetic, Coffee Lady?"

"You tell me."

He smiled. All was well, he assured me, still no sign of drug dealers or shots—other than singles, doubles, and triples.

Business always picked up during my roasting sessions. The rich, sweet aroma of caramelizing beans acted as an aromatic siren to every caffeine-deprived mariner within smell-range. Consequently, our sidewalk tables were packed, our main floor busy, our counter hopping, and my wonderful Tucker running it all like a perfectly tuned muscle car engine.

Like an audio cue to that very thought, the roaring *vroom* of a vintage GTO prompted half my coffeehouse to search the street.

After the *bang-bang* of Brooklyn gunplay and that lovely interview with the DEA agent from hell, the sound of Mad Max's Buckmobile actually lifted my spirits.

The glint of cherry red steel and bright silver chrome rolled parallel to our sidewalk. The door popped open, and Buckman emerged. Out of uniform again, he sauntered into the Blend, and I waved him over.

The AIS detective greeted me tersely, glanced around, and stressed one word: "Privacy."

I nodded, fixed us drinks, and led him up our wrought iron spiral staircase to our much quieter second floor lounge. We sat near a large open window, where the evening breeze entwined the aroma of my freshly roasted Ambrosia with the soft buzz of voices from the coffeehouse below.

"I didn't know whether to look for you here or in a federal lockup," Buckman quipped as he sunk into a comfy easy chair. I took the chair opposite.

"I take it you spoke with Quinn?"

"I never reveal my sources. Well, hardly ever. The point is, Cosi, I'm glad you're okay." He took a test sip of his Americano, then downed a satisfying swallow. "What did you do to get out of a DEA sweep, anyway? Sweet-talk them?"

"Yeah, I sweet-talked them, Max. And then Quinn sweet-talked them. I think their ears are still ringing from his tender tone."

Buckman laughed. "No muffins?"

"No muffins."

"But you finally met 'Crazy Quinn'?"

"More like Quinn *Unleashed*."

"I take it you're an asset now? You don't slip the grip of the Feds without some kind of deal."

"No comment."

"Keep it to yourself then, because I came here to tell you something."

I leaned forward. "There's a development in Lilly's case? You got another lead?"

Buckman bumped his cup against mine. "Here's to coincidences that aren't." After another long swallow, he sat back and crossed his legs.

"The van that struck Lilly Beth—remember I told you it was involved in another hit-and-run two weeks ago?"

"I remember."

"Well, it was brutal and the victim was a big-shot doctor—"

That grabbed my attention, and I tossed back an educated guess: "Was the man a plastic surgeon, by any chance? I don't know the guy's last name, but I'm pretty sure you're talking about a doctor named Harry who was once married to Gwen Fischer, Councilman Chin's fiancée."

Buckman's leg slipped from his knee. "Man, you are good. No wonder Quinn wants you as his asset."

"It's no big deal. I just heard about his death at our party on Saturday. How many physicians could have been run over in the past two weeks, right? What was the victim's full name anyway?"

"Dr. Harry Land, he operated the Better You Cosmetic Surgery Center on Seventy-Fifth Street and Broadway."

"If the van committed hit-and-runs on both Dr. Land and Lilly Beth, I assume you're looking for a connection?"

"My first thought, too, Inspector. Only trouble is, it didn't pan out."

Buckman was eyeing me closely now, and I could guess why. He was angling to use me as *his* asset. That's why he was sharing all this. He certainly didn't need my opinion of his theories. He had plenty of colleagues for that.

"Tell me more," I said.

"We know Lilly worked as a nurse before becoming a dietician. But she didn't work for this plastic surgeon. According to the Better You employment records, no one named Tanga ever worked there."

"I take it you checked into Lilly Beth's employment history anyway?"

A shadow crossed Buckman's weary face. "According to all the records and databases available to me, the last nursing job Lilly Beth held was the graveyard shift at Beth Israel Hospital, and she quit that job six years ago."

"Well, Lilly told me herself that she left nursing three years ago. She got her degree, took on freelance consulting work, and then started working with the mayor's office."

"What we have here, Cosi, is a black hole in Lilly Beth Tanga's life. One that needs to be filled," Buckman said. He tapped the coffee cup with his finger. "I have a strong hunch there's a connection between Lilly and this Dr. Land. The driver of that white van wanted them both dead. Why? I want to *know*. And since Lilly's employment records don't show us a connection, I'm thinking the relationship might have been purely personal."

"A love affair?"

Buckman nodded. "This doctor was married during those

missing years of Lilly's life, so it would have been an extramarital affair on his part. But from what I've been able to determine, it's not so farfetched. This Dr. Land was popular with the ladies, and he had a lot of very prominent female clients who went for his healing hands, if you know what I mean."

"Was Public Advocate Tanya Harmon one of those special clients?"

"Now how did you know *that*?" Buckman asked, astonished again.

"Another educated guess. I met her at my party. She appeared addicted to Botox—and a close friend of hers used Dr. Land for her daughter's surgeries, so . . ." I shrugged.

"Well, you're good at hunches, Cosi. Tanya Harmon was on Land's patient list. Whether she was in his little black book, too, we don't know yet."

I didn't know, either, but it *was* an intriguing notion, and one I hadn't considered before. Could Tanya have killed Dr. Land in some kind of jealous rage? After a relationship had gone sour?

I wasn't sure an ambitious man-eater like Tanya was capable of such feelings, but she may have had another motive. Could she have been doing a favor for her well-heeled political-donor friend Helen Bailey-Burke? Those two had been tight for years—until lately, anyway—and Helen had been openly hostile with Dr. Land's ex-wife, Gwen. She'd actually slapped the woman in public, so she must have been even more upset with Dr. Land over the death of her daughter, Meredith. But why would either of them have gone after Lilly? That didn't make sense.

"With Dr. Land dead and Lilly unconscious, I can't ask either one if they were lovers," Buckman said. "But whatever their connection, we have to find it."

"You said we." *(There it is.)* "I take it you want me in on this?"

Buckman locked eyes with me. "I've spent time at the hospital—"

"A lot of time, I've heard."

"And I've talked to Lilly Beth's mother, Amina Salaysay.

Nice lady, but every time I try to question the woman about her daughter's past, she claims she knows nothing."

He leaned forward again. "I know she's holding back something. Maybe Mrs. Salaysay is ashamed of something her daughter did. Or maybe it wasn't kosher, something outside the law, and she's afraid to share it with the police. Whatever it is, I have to know, so . . ."

"So?"

"So I'm thinking a woman's touch might work on Lilly's mother, not another cop, but someone she knows and trusts already. I'm thinking you could talk to Mrs. Salaysay."

Buckman paused to rub his eyes, and I flashed back to a man from my old neighborhood, a widower who worked on his vintage Cadillac daily after his wife died. By the end of that first summer, the car was a showpiece. My nonna used to say it was sad, that he focused on his car because he didn't have a woman in his life any longer, a real human being to lavish his attention on.

It seemed to me, Buckman was that man.

But who was Lilly Beth to him? A stand-in for the wife who'd been run down? A new pet project? Or something more?

Seeing the tortured expression on Buckman's face, I wasn't so sure the answer mattered. Not now, anyway. So despite my own problems—and I was up to my assets in them—I agreed to help Buckman, the way he'd helped me. The way he was trying to help Lilly Beth.

"I'll do it . . ." I said and squeezed Max's hand. "I'll reach out to Mrs. Salaysay tomorrow morning, have a talk with her, and pass along everything I learn."

A bit of Buckman's weariness seemed to lift with my reply. I asked him a few more questions and we discussed Lilly's condition. The news was good. Her vitals were strong and the doctors were more hopeful than ever.

Finally, Buckman drained his cup and stood.

"See you soon, Cosi. Thanks for the coffee."

Forty-two

"MIKE?" Hearing a noise, I lifted my head off the pillow.

"Don't bother with the lamp, Clare. I can see . . ."

The image of the man I loved moving toward me in a silver pool of shimmering moonlight might have been romantic, even magical, if he hadn't been peeling off a shoulder holster—and I hadn't been waiting to talk with him about a brutal hit-and-run.

I rubbed my eyes, trying to wake up. "Did you see the carnitas burrito I left for you?"

"Zapped it in the microwave. It was good, thanks."

As I propped myself up, Quinn wrapped his holster straps around his weapon, set it on the dresser, then removed his extra ammo clip, gold badge, knife, and pepper spray.

"So . . ." I said, suppressing a yawn. "How is Matt holding up?"

The edge of the bed depressed as Quinn's solid form sunk down. He unlaced his shoes. "Considering everything he's going through, I'd say your ex-husband is doing okay . . ."

I really felt for Matt this week. While Quinn had stopped the DEA from totally trashing his warehouse (and my coffeehouse), the agents who'd arrested us had ripped open and dumped out the entire shipment of Ambrosia beans, crushing a percentage in the process.

Luckily, most of the lot was salvageable. For days now—when Matt wasn't answering an endless list of questions for Quinn's squad, NYPD brass, and a select group of federal officers—he was in Red Hook with bodyguards, determinedly shoveling up those exquisite beans and preserving them in plastic containers.

"I'm no fan of Allegro's, you understand," Quinn added, "but under this kind of pressure, plenty of guys would have broken down by now."

"Matt's made of tough stuff," I said. "He's spent a lot of time in the Third World, seen a lot of harsh things."

"I know . . ." Quinn pulled off his tie, unbuttoned his shirt. "I haven't been to the countries he has, but I've been to plenty of those places . . . dark places. You know what I mean?"

"I do . . . and I think Max has, too."

"Max Buckman?"

"He stopped by tonight."

"Oh?"

I shifted on the mattress, making room for Mike's broad shoulders. As he stretched out under the covers, he exhaled a familiar little note: the "Quinn Hymn to Being Horizontal," that's how I always thought of it.

"Come here . . ."

He didn't have to ask twice. I tucked into him, resting my head on his solid chest. His sigh this time was one of deep pleasure. I felt it, too. Then his callused fingers began drawing sweet little circles on the bare skin of my upper arm.

I closed my eyes and sighed. Ben Franklin had nothing on the electrifying charges Mike Quinn's lightest touches sent through me, but I couldn't shake my worries. So I took a deep breath and explained—

"The reason Buckman stopped by . . . he needed a favor."

The delicious caressing stopped. "I hope it involves coffee and muffins."

"A little more than that . . ." I cleared my throat. "He asked me to talk to Lilly Beth's mother. She won't talk to the police, and he thinks I can help fill in some blanks in her life."

"Mmmm . . ." (This noise I recognized, too—it wasn't happy.)

"Early tomorrow, I'm going to Queens."

"Franco goes with you, Clare. That's not an option."

"Don't worry. He's driving us."

"You and Buckman?"

"Me and Matt's mother. Lilly's mom might feel more comfortable with Madame there."

"I hope you're able to help, but remember, it's Buckman's case."

"That's what's troubling me."

"What do you mean?"

"He's trying to make a connection between a hit-and-run that killed a plastic surgeon and one that killed Lilly. But it seems to me Max might have a motive beyond simply solving a case."

"And what would that be?"

"Add it up. He came to see me on a Sunday night, clearly obsessed about having every year of Lilly's life accounted for. I think, on some level, he's still chasing that driver who killed his wife, the one he couldn't put away."

"No," Quinn said without hesitation. "That's not it."

"How can you say that so definitively?"

"Because, Clare . . ." Quinn hesitated then plowed forward. "Max Buckman did put away the man who killed his wife."

"What?" I sat up, brushed back my hair. "How?"

"I shouldn't really share this—"

"Tell me!"

Quinn blew out air. "I'll have to start with the incident . . . the one that killed Sara. An insurance broker got crocked at a Second Avenue bar, hopped the curb, struck Max's wife with his SUV, and drove away. Sara Buckman had massive internal injuries, head trauma, the works. Max fell apart after it happened. She lay in the hospital two weeks before the docs told him she wouldn't wake up. He kept hoping, praying—until he put her in the ground."

"God, that's awful . . ."

"Six weeks after her death, Max went back to work, found out how badly things were handled during the on-site investigation. The driver wasn't found in time for a breathalyzer test to matter. He hired a top attorney and with spotty evidence, the prick walked."

"And that's when Max went after him?"

"Yeah. He'd been saving up to build a dream house for his wife. He didn't need that money anymore, so he took a leave from the PD, moved into an apartment in Jersey near the guy's brokerage firm."

"What did he do? Wait for him to drive drunk again?"

"No. He wanted more than a simple DUI. This man's firm was worth millions. He had clients across the whole tristate area, and in his year of investigation, Max uncovered an interesting hitch. Every third policy this guy wrote was a fraud. He'd sign up clients and pocket their money instead of passing it on to the insurance companies. Then he'd hand them phony policies not worth the paper they were printed on. Max built the case. The prick was doing this in three states, which made it interstate commerce fraud."

"So he went to the Feds with it?"

"Yeah, when he was ready, Max called in the FBI, and the Feds did the dirty work. The man was sentenced to twenty-five years."

"And he called me a vigilante."

"Is that right?" Quinn said, tone clearly amused. "Well, Buckman's entitled to his opinion. To me, you're a concerned citizen, maybe a little more *curious* than your average taxpayer, but you're a good woman, Clare, with a good heart."

"He said we were two of a kind."

"Then you might as well include me and make it three. We all want to get the bad guy. We want to see justice done."

"Let me ask you something," I said. "How did you know

all this? I mean, Bucket-mouth talks a lot, but I can't see him sharing all that with just anyone."

"I know the story because while he was on leave, Buckman needed help on occasion—running background checks, getting addys off license plates, that sort of thing."

"And you risked your career to help?"

"Me and a few other friends—on and off the force. We were Max's Mice, quiet little fact finders."

"You had a code name? Like a comic book?"

"Max was hurting. We were motivated."

I stared off into the moonlit room. "If Buckman resolved the issue of justice for his wife's killer, then what's driving him so hard with Lilly? Transference? Is he looking at Lilly in that hospital bed and seeing Sara?"

"No, Clare. He's aware that Lilly is not his wife."

"But it's the best explanation. A man can't fall in love with a woman he doesn't know."

"Take it from me. He knows her."

"No he—"

"He knows Lilly Beth Tanga because he's investigated her. By now, Max has talked to her mother, her son, her family and coworkers. He's talked to friends in several circles. He knows things about her that her own family doesn't. He's seen photos of her, heard stories of her—"

"And he sits by her hospital bed, every night, putting it all together as he gazes at her face?"

"Yes."

"So what happens when Lilly wakes up? Everyone's confident now that she'll survive this, but what's she going to make of this odd man who's fallen for her?"

"That's one I can't answer. And neither can you." Mike tapped his chest. "Lie down, Clare, please. Give it a rest for a few hours. I know I need to."

"I'll try . . ." I reclined in the bed again, tucked in close. "By the way, we're officially out of carnitas."

"Good, because if I eat another burrito, I'll grow a sombrero."

"I'll have Franco take me shopping after we visit Lilly's mother. How does chicken sound for the weekend? Roasted whole with a crispy, golden skin and moist, juicy meat flavored with rosemary and lime?"

"Oh, man, that sounds great." Mike's callused fingers found their way back to my bare arm.

"And my Fully-Loaded Colcannon . . ." (It was one of Mike's favorites.) "Red potatoes, cabbage, and onions like your Irish mama used to make, but sautéed up in olive oil and rendered bacon drippings, with my little Italian kiss of garlic and a big old American-style topping of gooey melted cheddar and smoky crumbled bacon . . ."

"My mouth is starting to water . . ."

"Then I'll bake you up my light-as-air Cappuccino Chiffon Cake. But instead of mascarpone, I'll do a Whipped Cream Frosting. A forkful of that cake should fill your mouth with the most delicate flavors then dissolve on your tongue as if you've bitten into a cloud from heaven. Maybe I'll add white chocolate ganache for an extra layer of decadence. I'll spread it warm, just under that fluffy mound of rich dairy cream that's whipped until it—"

"Stop!" Quinn moaned. "I can't take anymore! Sweetheart, your food porn is driving me crazy—and, by the way, you don't have to cook for me. You have a lot on your plate. We can always order take-out."

"You know I like to cook. It's my oasis. It comforts me. And it's something in my life I can actually control. But mostly I like the sounds you make when you eat my food."

"Funny . . . I like the sounds you make, too."

"Oh? When is that?"

His caressing hand shifted its position by a few inches, and I got the idea.

Reveling in the moonlight at last, I let Mike's skillful fingers play my body until it veritably hummed with pleasure. Then I turned in his arms and covered his mouth with mine. Finally, our lips were moving again, but for this oasis we didn't need words.

Forty-three

The next morning, Madame and I nursed cups of my Breakfast Blend as Franco guided our sedan through Manhattan's shadowy canyons of glass and steel. The AM rush was slow-going, but we soon hit the Williamsburg Bridge, and the world opened up to a dome of brilliant blue.

Crossing the East River's sparkling chop, our speed picked up and Franco relaxed enough to make his daily query. "So, Coffee Lady, what was it this morning?"

"The shaving cream *again*," I said, brushing a bit of lint off my charcoal gray dress slacks. I'd worn stacked heels, too, and because of the bruises on my upper arms, I chose a shimmery pearl blouse with bell sleeves that fell past the elbows.

Before I'd selected this outfit, however, I'd woken up to Matt loudly complaining. Apparently, his personal shaving kit included a canister of French beard-softening cream, a gift from Bree, which retailed at $55.00 a pop. In a few short days, the full can was close to empty.

"You've been helping yourself to my imported products!" Matt wailed at Quinn.

Peace would not be ours until I inserted myself between the men (a regular occurrence this difficult week).

Quinn acted innocent, but I knew what that little quirk on one side of his mouth meant. *It's called payback, Allegro. Go sing an aria about it.*

Franco snorted upon hearing today's terrible-threesome tale, then he steered us off the bridge and onto the Brooklyn-Queens Expressway.

That's when Madame piped up. "You know, Clare, I've always heard that ménage à trois is quite a challenge to pull off successfully."

I literally choked on my coffee. "No, no! You misunderstand. Mike Quinn and I are not, repeat *not* in a ménage à trois with your son."

"Of course you are. Matteo informed me earlier this week. Oh, he claimed Bree is redoing their Sutton Place apartment, but I know she's out of town—and when the cat's way . . ." She gave a little *oh-so-French* shrug.

"I can't believe you'd think I'd to such a thing!"

"Calm down, dear. Ménage à trois simply means household for three. Clearly, you three are sharing the duplex, aren't you? And your meals . . ."

"And a bathroom," Franco noted from the front.

Madame fluffed her silver pageboy and waved a dismissive hand. "Whatever else you're sharing really is entirely your business."

"You know what my grandmother always said?" Franco called.

"What's that, dear?" Madame asked, leaning forward.

"Two roosters and one hen gets you no eggs—and a whole lot of trouble."

They laughed, and I frowned. "We have eggs, Franco. But I did promise Mike a chicken dinner. On our way back, we're going grocery shopping."

"Yes, Mother," Franco sang.

Madame hid behind her coffee cup, but I could see she was still laughing.

Gritting my teeth, I endured—but I swore it wouldn't be for long, because if those drug dealers didn't contact Matt soon, I was going to fly down to Rio and whack O Negociante myself.

WHEN we finally exited the expressway, Franco swung the car into the neighborhood of Jackson Heights, a polyglot section of Queens with Hispanic immigrants to the east and newly minted Irish Americans to the west. From the aromatics alone, I knew we'd landed between them, in Little India.

The spicy smells of curry, coriander, and turmeric mingled with the savory scent of Tandoori chicken and the toasty smell of baking flatbreads. (One sniff and I was feeling the pain of skipping breakfast.)

We rolled by sidewalk carts grilling lamb kabobs, green markets showing off long beans, and stores with Taj Mahal façades hawking saris, gold bracelets, and Bollywood music.

Turning onto Roosevelt, we progressed beneath the elevated section of the Number 7 line, aka the "International Express." Like an amusement park roller coaster, the 7's rattling tracks were wide open. No concrete barriers muffled the subway cars, and they roared overhead like a succession of mechanical dragons.

Continuing on, we entered Woodside, the neighborhood Lilly Beth called home, and the aromas here were very different. This part of Roosevelt was the "Little Manila" of the borough. According to Lilly, this community had the highest concentration of Filipinos on the entire Eastern seaboard.

Pinoy restaurants and bakeshops dominated the area, along with Filipino-owned businesses and stores. The amount of air cargo and freight carriers on these blocks was what puzzled me most, until I saw the term Lilly had taught me, right on the signs: *We ship Balikbayan Boxes.*

"Oh, that smells wonderful!" Madame exclaimed.

The aromas hitting us now were unique to this very block. I recognized Amina Salaysay's special pork bun filling first, then the chocolate from a *champorado*, and finally—

"Brioche," I told Madame, who'd been enjoying the scent of a yeast-raised dough, rich in butter and eggs, baking to perfection.

Madame was delighted but puzzled. "A French bakery here?"

"No. You're smelling the Filipino version of *ensaymada*, which starts with a brioche dough. We'll sample some inside . . ."

I called Franco's attention to the big glass widow of Amina's Kitchenette, and he pulled the car over. The little twenty-four-hour eatery occupied the first floor of a multistory building with a travel agency on one side and a beauty shop on the other.

"Hot *puto*?" Franco read on the awning. He turned in his seat. "You've got to be kidding me."

"It's not what you think," I assured him. "In the Philippines *puto* is a steamed rice muffin."

"Glad to hear that," Franco said, "because in the Hispanic world, selling 'hot *puto*' would earn you a visit from the vice squad."

With that, Franco opened our door and wished us luck.

"Sure you don't want me to come with you, Coffee Lady?" he asked.

"Thanks, but I understand Lilly's mom is reluctant to discuss certain things in front of the police."

Well aware of that sentiment, especially in immigrant neighborhoods, Franco nodded and climbed back into his car. Then Madame and I strode inside.

Forty-Four

Like her daughter, Mrs. Amina Salaysay was a petite, attractive woman with a dusky complexion and exotic, almond-shaped eyes. She was heavier than her daughter and threads of gray generously salted her dark cap of hair, but she had that same die-hard immigrant energy of Lilly's and the same openhearted warmth.

After we greeted her, she invited us to sit down for a visit. The restaurant was cheerful with sunny yellow walls, colorful photos of the Philippine Islands, and mounted curio cabinets with figurines and souvenirs, including little toy "jeepneys"—the name Pinoys gave to former U.S. military jeeps they now painted in wild colors and used for public transport on the islands.

Lilly's adorable son, Paz, waved hello, then went back to his warm bowl of chocolate rice pudding—that common Pinoy breakfast known as *champorado.*

Filipino cuisine was a unique combination of East-meets-West, and Amina Salaysay's menu reflected the country's melting pot of influences from Spanish to Chinese to American. From my last visit, I knew she owned and ran this kitchenette on a twenty-four-hour schedule.

Even with Lilly Beth in the hospital, she came by once in the morning and once at night to prepare her specialties, including those steamed buns filled with spicy-sweet pork called *siopao* and her amazing *ensymada*.

Many tables were occupied for breakfast, the buzz in the air a combination of English and Tagalog. One of her waitstaff served us coffee and a basket of those fresh-baked brioche buns we'd smelled on the street.

Madame sampled hers with great interest. The egg bread was light and tender, the top generously buttered, but also deliciously gooey from an ample addition of melted cheddar cheese along with a light sprinkling of sugar. This unique way of serving the rich, raised pastry reflected the heart of Lilly's native cuisine—

"It's sweet and savory," Madame cooed, "quite a unique combination and absolutely delightful."

We continued talking and snacking with Lilly's mother until finally I stated plainly, "We're here to pay our respects, Mrs. Salaysay, but we're also concerned about finding the person who put Lilly Beth in the hospital."

"Yes," Madame chimed in. "And to do that, we need as much information as we can get about your daughter's past."

"Lilly is a good girl," said Amina, looking suddenly unhappy.

"We know," I assured her. "But we're looking for any connection she may have had to a doctor named Land, a plastic surgeon? Did she ever work for him?"

Mrs. Salaysay touched the gold cross at her neck. "Lilly's always been a good girl, a hard worker. But with our extra expenses . . ."

She looked distressed, and I got the same feeling Buckman did. *She knows something she's afraid to share.*

"Lilly tried to help me, you understand?" Mrs. Salaysay went on. "Because of the extra payment. Now this . . . I'll be honest. I don't know what's going to happen to all of us. How we're going to *pay*."

Madame and I exchanged glances.

"Pay?" I said. "Do you mean pay the hospital bills?"

Mrs. Salaysay sighed. "That is our burden now, too. We have insurance, but that nice police man—"

"Detective Buckman?"

"Yes, he warned me. Lilly's therapy bills may become difficult. And we have the extra payment every month. My concern is only for my daughter. If we lose this place, it will break my heart—but Lilly comes first."

Extra payment? I glanced at Madame again. *What does that mean?*

We went around again, but she wouldn't explain and we weren't getting anywhere. Well, that was all right, because I had one last card to play: Lilly's computer.

Buckman may have searched her computer files and e-mails for a link to Dr. Land, or evidence of a threat. That seemed very basic to me, and I was nearly convinced he'd done it by now.

On the other hand, Lilly's mother might have been protective of her privacy, and the computer sat in her house. She may have denied him access and he may have been reluctant to strong-arm her with a warrant.

Was I Buckman's last resort before he had to play hardball with a woman he clearly didn't want to offend? *Maybe.* Which was why I gave it a shot . . .

"Mrs. Salaysay," I said, "the day Lilly Beth was hit, she was going to send me a few recipes. Would you mind if I checked her computer? Once I get those files, I can authorize a new freelance payment."

Amina Salaysay nodded and checked her watch.

"I must get Paz to school, then I must go to the hospital. I speak with Lilly's doctors every day."

"I understand."

"But I do want to help you . . ." She thought a moment, then seemed to decide something. She reached into her pocket and took a key off a ring. "This is my house key. Go in and find Lilly's computer in her bedroom. Take what you need from it and lock up. Then leave the key here with my girl at the register."

As we said good-bye to her and Paz, we passed our gifts to them: a Transformer toy for the little boy, and for Lilly's mom, two pounds of freshly roasted Kona.

"We'll continue to pray for Lilly," I assured them both.

She thanked us and Paz did, too. He seemed pleased with his toy and excited to tell us something special.

"The beans," said the little boy, tugging with determination on the bell sleeve of my blouse.

"Beans?" I asked, petting his soft head.

He pointed to the coffee beans. "If you're praying for my mom, then you can put beans in her jar. *Opo?* She'd like that."

I looked to Mrs. Salaysay, who just smiled and shrugged.

Dismissing the cryptic comment as one of those awkward moments in our cultural divide, we politely said good-bye and slipped out the door.

FRANCO drove us the ten blocks to Mrs. Salaysay's two-story row house. The place was modest, well kept, and quiet. We found Lilly's computer laptop on a desk in her apricot-painted bedroom. While I turned on the device, Madame moved about the room, looking at framed photos and knick-knacks.

Getting into her computer was easy, and I started with general searches of her documents using keywords like *Land*, *Dr. Land*, and just plain *Harry*.

That didn't work, so I tried going to Lilly's document library, and re-sorted everything by date. But the oldest folder wasn't old enough.

"There's nothing here that goes back far enough! Nothing that can give us a clue about the black hole in Lilly's life—"

"Clare . . ." Madame's voice was sharp. "You need to see this."

Still focused on the screen, I didn't bother looking up. "What?"

Madame was behind me somewhere, and I suddenly heard the sound of a sliding door being forced all the way open. I spun in the swivel chair to see what she was up to—and gasped.

The right side of Lilly's closet held neatly hung clothes with shoes lined up beneath. But the other half held a stack of shelves. And on those shelves were jars. Some jars were large, some small. In their past lives they'd held pickles and peppers and all kinds of sauces, but the colorful contents had been emptied out and replaced with a solid wall of black.

"What in the world?" I moved to examine this bizarre find.

"These jars are filled with coffee beans." Madame opened a lid to show me.

"Every jar is labeled. January, February, March . . ."

"Do you remember what Lilly's little boy told you?" Madame asked.

I nodded, recalling Paz's words: "If you're praying for my mom, then you can put beans in her jar . . ."

"So the beans are prayers," Madame said. "But what is Lilly praying for?"

"How far back do these dates go?" I wondered.

We went through them all, lining up the jars, and soon realized the label dates coincided with that black hole in Lilly's life—all the way up to the time she was struck by the van.

That's when it came back to me. The night Lilly was nearly killed, she tried to tell me something before losing consciousness.

What did she say? Think . . .

"Clare? What's wrong?"

"Give me a moment," I told Madame.

Sitting on the edge of Lilly's bed, I closed my eyes. With a deep breath, I summoned back those painful images from just one week ago.

In my mind, Lilly was lying on the street again, her body broken, twisted, twitching. Then I ran to my friend, dropped to my knees, saw she was still conscious . . .

"I knew it . . . I knew this would happen . . ."

"Did you see the driver coming?"

"No. You don't understand. This had to happen. I deserve this. It's my fault. . . my fault . . . my most grievous fault . . ."

"Clare? What is it?"

My body was shaking, one fist crumpling Lilly's coverlet. "She wasn't asking for Last Rites. I know that now."

"I don't understand?"

"When a Catholic confesses her sins to her priest, she receives penance in the form of prayers. The priest instructs her to recite Hail Marys and Our Fathers, or full rosaries—"

"And rosaries are prayer beads!"

"Yes, they're a way to count and keep track. A way to add it all up."

"But we know that already, don't we?" Madame said. "Paz told us these beans represent prayers."

"More than prayers. They're *penance*."

"Penance for what? What did Lilly do?"

"Help me find the first jar . . ." I scrambled, looking. "When did this begin?"

Madame found it, picked it up, and we both noticed something buried at the bottom—a small, white square.

"Look, there's something inside!"

Together, we dumped the dark beans onto Lilly's pretty coverlet, pulled out the folded square of white. My hands were still shaking, and Madame took the paper from me, unfolded it, and slipped on her reading glasses.

"These are medical records," she said, scanning the document. "They involve an eighteen-year-old girl . . . the comments are about her vital signs . . ."

"What's the name of the patient?"

"Oh, my," Madame whispered. "Clare, I know this girl. And so do you . . ."

I searched the top of the form for the patient's name. Madame was right. The patient was the daughter of Helen Bailey-Burke and the best friend of Josh Fowler.

"But Meredith Burke is dead," I pointed out.

"Then why is Lilly keeping these records?" Madame asked.

"That's what I want to know."

Forty-five

On the drive back to Manhattan, I phoned Lilly's longtime nurse friend, Terry Simone. Taking a chance, I simply asked her to drop by the Blend to talk. She agreed to a one o'clock meeting.

I considered calling Buckman, but decided to wait. Terry could provide answers on what I'd found, and those answers could save the man a great deal of investigative time. So I refocused my mind on work and tried to ignore the clock.

During a lull, I noticed Matt sitting alone in the corner, an empty demitasse in front of him, his gaze fixed on the smart screen of his brand new "thing."

I pulled two doubles and crossed to his table. Matt accepted the fresh cup, leaned back in his chair, and took a satisfying hit.

"Thanks."

"How's it going?" I sat down opposite, took a sip for myself.

"The Red Hook warehouse mess is cleaned up," he said. "Now all I have to do is sell Nino's beans." He shook his head, looking defeated. "Maybe once *this* mess is over . . ."

"Well, I'm not waiting to sell those beans. I'm taking a stack of your business cards with me tonight. We're serving Ambrosia to the public for the first time, and—"

"That's what you're calling it?"

"Don't you like the name?"

"I do—and I appreciate your trying, Clare, but you're no broker. Fifty pounds for a wedding reception is a drop in the bucket."

"A *sterling silver* bucket," I pointed out. "Lots of wealthy alphas will be there tonight, Matt. Chefs, journalists, owners of restaurant chains. It's the perfect showcase for the perfect cup."

"And the Cup of Excellence?"

"There's always next year. I mean, face facts, you're not hot to travel back to Rio anytime soon, are you?"

"You have a point."

"Give it a chance. Ambrosia is superb. It can sell itself."

He took another espresso hit, ran his gaze over my shimmery pearl blouse. "You look nice today."

"Listen, I hate to mention this. But your mother thinks you and me and Mike are . . ." I could hardly bring myself to say it.

"Are *what*?"

"Are in a ménage à trois."

He waved his hand. "She's jerking your chain."

"No, she really thinks—"

"Mother knows what's going on, Clare, I told her everything."

I was surprised, but Matt was firm. "That mother of mine's been through hell and back, you know that. She survived a war, buried more than one man she loved, even dealt with drug dealers in her day—and kicked their asses. I knew she could handle the truth. Besides, she's still the owner of this business, and she has a right to know what's happening in it."

"Does she have an opinion about how things will turn out?"

"She's an optimistic person at heart. And she thinks your

Quinn will take care of us, keep us safe. She thinks a lot of him."

"So do I. And, by the way, he thinks a lot of you."

"Really?"

"He told me so last night."

"I don't know, Clare. I don't know if I'm worthy of that." He ran a hand over his face. "I never set out to hurt you. It's the last thing I wanted. I hope you'll remember that when this is over." He shook his head. "You're never going to forgive me."

"Matt, take it easy." I reached out, squeezed his hand. "None of this was your fault. It was a scumbag outlaw who tried to ruin us."

"Maybe so, but it was my business decision that put the whole thing in motion, and now it's you who's going to have to make the sacrifices. I never meant for it to happen, Clare. Never. Please remember that. Will you do that for me?"

"Matt, *what* are you talking about? I don't like the look in your eyes . . ."

My mind began casting about for logical answers. My ex was spending a lot of time with Mike Quinn, giving statements, working out strategy. *That must be it.* Quinn told Matt something that he didn't want him to share with me. *A sacrifice I had to make . . .*

"Matt, what are you and Quinn keeping from me?"

"Clare! Oh, Clare!"

Terry Simone couldn't have approached our table at a worse time. The second Matt saw me distracted, he excused himself and fled.

"You wanted to talk?" Terry asked. Slight and energetic with short-cropped yellow hair, she was already wearing pale blue nurse's scrubs for her shift.

Gritting my teeth, I forced myself to shift gears. "Sit down, Terry . . ."

I motioned to Nancy to bring us coffees. Then I started my interrogation.

"I was wondering," I began lightly, "have you spoken with that policeman who hangs around Lilly's hospital bed?"

"Detective Buckman?" said Terry, her voice pitched far too high. "Oh, no, no . . . not since the first time we talked."

"That's funny. I mean, you work right there at Beth Israel, and Buckman's there an awful lot. I thought you would have gotten to know one another."

Terry's shook her head so forcefully I thought she'd lose an earring. "I mean, I saw him last night, but I was on duty and too busy to chat."

"Then Buckman didn't ask you about Lilly's life? He didn't press you to tell him about those lost years of employment as a nurse—after Lilly quit the graveyard shift at Beth Israel and before she earned her registered dieticians degree?"

"Lilly was just going to school, that's all."

"So she wasn't working for plastic surgeon Dr. Harry Land?"

Terry's nervous ticks stilled, but she didn't say a word, only continued to shake her head.

Thus far, none of these denials surprised me. After all, if Buckman had gotten the whole story from Terry, he never would have come to me . . .

"Well, never mind that," I said. "I need your help with something else."

Terry seemed relieved to change the subject. "Sure, anything."

I pulled out the papers I'd found folded up in Lilly's jar, placed them flat on the café table marble, and attempted to press out the years of crinkles.

"I'm not a medical person, you understand? But these sure do look like important records to me. There are a lot of terms here I don't understand. Could you tell me what they mean?"

Terry's hands settled on the paper, and she skimmed the first few lines, blinked in surprise when she saw the patient's name. "What is this?"

"You tell me," I said. "I found these in Lilly's apartment. What was she doing with Meredith Burke's medical records?"

Terry pushed the papers back at me. "I don't know what you're trying to find out here, Clare. But I promise you, Lilly Beth did nothing wrong. She tried to save that poor girl. It was the doctor's fault. And because of Lilly's arrangement with Land—"

"What kind of arrangement? Were they having a love affair?"

"No! Lilly was working off the books for the man at his private surgery center, that's all. She needed cash to pay for school, for Paz, and to help with her mother's money troubles—"

"So Lilly was Meredith's nurse?"

Terry frowned and looked away. This was a terrible crossroads for her, and I could see her struggling with her moral compass. *Which way should I go here? Am I about to help my friend or hurt her?*

I knew how Quinn would handle Terry. By now he would have seen her emotional button—the thing that mattered most to her. Ironically, I had the same button, and I knew what I had to say.

"Terry, listen carefully to me. Detective Buckman isn't interested in punishing Lilly. It's clear whatever she did involving Meredith Burke's young death has been eating her up inside. Lilly convinced herself that she should be punished in some way for it—but so did the driver who'd nearly killed her. *Nearly* is the key word. When Lilly gets out of her hospital bed, that hit-and-run driver may be waiting to strike her down again. Only this time that driver won't be running until he or she is sure Lilly's corpse is left behind."

Terry blanched at my brutal picture, but I had to make her understand.

"To find the driver who hit Lilly, the truth has to come out . . ."

Terry closed her eyes. For almost a full minute, she hung her head, and I got the distinct impression she was praying. Whatever she was doing, however, I knew more babbling from me wasn't going to help, so I simply sat, waiting for her to make her decision.

Finally, she lifted her head. "Okay," Terry said quietly. "I'll tell you everything I know . . ."

According to Terry, Dr. Harry Land had performed three procedures on Meredith at the same time, what he called his three-in-one. During recovery at the surgery center, the girl seemed anxious and frightened. She complained of lightheadedness, shortness of breath.

The anesthesiologist was already gone for the day. As the nurse on duty, Lilly notified Dr. Land of the change in Meredith's vital signs, but he dismissed her fears. He was busy giving a Botox treatment to another patient and didn't want to take the time to cross the hall and check Meredith's vital signs for himself.

"I can't believe Dr. Land wasn't concerned," I said.

"Believe it," Terry assured me. "When Meredith checked in, she was already suffering from nervous anxiety. The girl had a history of emotional issues, and she'd been prescribed valium by another doctor. Post-op, Meredith was eating and drinking normally, so Dr. Land thought she was just fine and ordered her discharged, even though the vitals Lilly took showed indications of a problem. It wasn't until the next day that Lilly learned the poor girl had died."

"What happened?"

Terry explained how Meredith had acquired a blood clot during surgery. "That can happen, and it's nobody's fault. Where Dr. Land erred was in attributing symptoms of a blood clot to *anxiety*. Sure Meredith had a history of it, but he wasn't careful enough. If he'd acted properly, been more vigilant, Meredith could have been treated for the clot before it went to her lungs, and her life might have been saved."

Terry drained her cup. "When Lilly went back and double-checked Meredith's records, she found they'd been re-created, right down to her handwriting and the little *L* she used to end her entries. Dr. Land struck all evidence of shortness of breath, and he normalized the vital signs. Lilly knew it was a lie. She found the original records in the trash."

"Why did Lilly keep these papers?" I asked.

"She wanted to do the right thing and confess, but Dr. Land convinced her the facts would ruin them both, professionally and financially. Lilly did absolutely nothing wrong—until she let Dr. Land convince her to disappear, bought her and Paz a little vacation visiting family in Makati. There was no record of her employment, only several other nurses he'd hired on a revolving basis through a service. He said it would be easy. But it wasn't easy, because of Helen Bailey-Burke . . ."

According to Terry, during the malpractice suit, Helen insisted "some Spanish or Filipino nurse" had discharged her daughter, though she couldn't recall the nurse's name or even be sure of the woman's national heritage. Dr. Land lied and claimed he'd discharged Meredith himself.

In the end, Helen lost her suit. The jury concluded that Dr. Land had acted appropriately, but only because they didn't have all the facts and evidence. Helen Bailey-Burke knew Dr. Land had lied and covered his error, and she hired private detectives to hunt for Lilly.

"I talked to three in the space of four months!" Terry said.

"You claimed you knew nothing?"

"I was trying to protect my friend."

I understood that motivation, but I wasn't so sure Lilly had benefitted from it. She was lying in a hospital now, and she might never walk again.

"The only reason Lilly took that awful off-the-books job was to boost her salary fast. She was trying to help her mother. And she did, for a while."

It when then I recalled the term that Lilly's mother kept using, an "extra payment." I asked Terry if she knew what it meant.

"You've been to her restaurant, right? Amina's Kitchenette in Woodside?"

"Yes, it's adorable."

"Well Amina's been there for close to two decades, built up a loyal clientele. They're practically family to each other."

"Believe me, I can relate to that."

"Well, for years that woman had a handshake agreement with the old landlord, this Filipino guy who owned a lot of property along Roosevelt Avenue. When he died a few years ago, his young widow took over, and that one really knows how to work the rent regulation system. She'll slap a coat of paint in the hall of her buildings and raise the rent to cover the cost of 'major renovations.' Or buy new garbage cans and raise the rent again for 'external improvements.' You've lived in this city long enough, Clare. You know the type."

I did indeed. Madame owned the town house we now sat in, but I'd seen far too many businesses in the neighborhoods around us build loyal customers at one location, only to find themselves at the mercy of a greedy landlord.

I felt for Lilly's mother, but as awful as her new landlady sounded, there was nothing I could do about her. On the other hand, there was one lady I could do something about—Helen Bailey-Burke.

"She's obsessed with getting justice for her daughter," Terry insisted. "She has the money to do it, too."

But did she have the criminal mind to go even farther than justice? Did Helen exact vengeance by killing Dr. Land and attempting to kill Lilly? Or did someone else drive that van? Was this an instance of murder for hire? Would the murderer try to kill Lilly again?

"Sorry . . ." Terry glanced at her watch. "I have to go. I'm working the three-to-eleven."

I appreciated Terry's help and told her so. Now I had plenty of answers. I just had to let Buckman know what they were. So I pulled out my phone and began to dial . . .

It seemed to me that Dr. Land had protected his career. Terry had protected her friend. Lilly had protected her mother and son. But no one had protected an eighteen-year-old girl named Meredith Burke—and somebody out there cared deeply about that.

Whether it was the girl's mother or someone else, Buckman would have to find evidence to prove it. I wasn't thrilled about giving Max these incriminating papers, but this wasn't a kid with a slingshot. This was life and death.

At least I could be sure of one thing: Mad Max would do everything he could to protect Lilly Beth Tanga, and that was good enough for me.

Forty-six

The Driver took a sip from the cup, glanced around the coffeehouse. No one was looking. This was going to work. It truly was going to work . . .

Calm down. Just wait. Watch and wait.

At tonight's reception in Central Park, victim and patsy would be together again. The Driver expected to be there, too. All the plans were drawn up—and the payoff would be huge.

The Driver felt confident, yet a spider of apprehension began to creep its way in . . .

The wineglass didn't work. What if something else goes wrong?

This next deadly outing was inevitable, ingenious. But what if . . .

No. No! No changing lanes!

The wheels are in motion for a greater good. No matter who has to die, there is no turning back . . .

Forty-seven

"I still can't get over it," Nancy said, eyelids batting. "Franco in formal wear."

"I know," I said. "He looks good enough to stand on tonight's wedding cake."

"What about *your daughter's* wedding cake?" Nancy cooed.

"I'm not sure of that yet, Nance. I was thinking of snapping a photo and sending it to her, but I don't want to give her ideas. I'm conflicted."

"Well, Franco's not," Esther told me flatly.

"What do you mean?"

"He asked Josh Fowler to snap a pic from his cell phone when he was putting up balloons. He already sent it to Joy."

Nancy nodded. "By now, she's probably got it on her Facebook page!"

I sighed. *The world was moving way too fast . . .*

Franco had been the one to suggest this change in his cover. In my low heels, sheer stockings, and little black dress, I was overseeing two service stations, and he wanted to move with me, blending in with the wedding guests wherever I went.

The reception was taking place on a southwest section of Central Park. An enormous white tent hosted VIP guests with flowing champagne and a raw bar stretching from one end to the other. Outside those canvas walls, strings of lights wrapped tree trunks and formed a glowing canopy over a corridor of food trucks gathered to help feed the well-heeled crowd.

Our Muffin Muse sat among a select group of street vendors: Schnitzel & Things, Korilla BBQ, Solber Pupusas, Patty's Taco, and Wooly's *(amazing)* shaved and flavored ice.

For two hours I'd been moving between our truck crew outside the big tent and Tucker Burton, who was serving Ambrosia and a smile to the guests inside—right next to the multi-tiered cherry-vanilla wedding cake.

At the moment, I was checking on our truck's activity. We'd set up serving tables in front of the Muffin Muse to present pretty slices of our café-inspired groom's cakes: Espresso-Glazed Double Chocolate, Orange-Vanilla Creamsicle, and Nutella-Swirled Pound, all lined up on colorful plastic plates for guests to help themselves. We had Caramel Latte Cupcakes, too. They were tucked inside custom-designed paper holders that looked like tiny coffee mugs, complete with little handles.

Thanks to Josh, we were once again displaying hand-painted balloons, this time in the shapes of the bride's and groom's faces—kissing, of course.

Esther and Nancy were in charge of the cake service. Dante was stationed inside the truck, pulling espresso drinks to order.

"Don't forget, ladies," Dante called after hearing their Franco-in-formal-wear discussion. "The man is *packing* under that black jacket."

"Oh, it's *so* James Bond," Nancy said.

"Bond?" Esther smirked. "More like a bowling pin in a rental tux."

Nancy frowned. "He doesn't look like a super-hot super-spy to you?"

"Only if his code name is Double-O Twelve Pin."

"Oh, Esther, I understand . . ." Nancy gave out a romantic sigh. "You only have eyes for Boris!"

"I realize this is a wedding," Esther told the girl, "but *please* keep your sap level under control. With all this cake around, you could send me into sugar shock."

Okay, I thought. *Everything's perfectly normal here.*

Stepping away from my truck crew, I checked in with our very own well-dressed bowling pin, keeping watch a few yards away.

"Hear anything yet?" I asked.

Franco gave a little headshake. *"Nada."*

Shortly before the reception began, Franco informed me that the dealers on the New York end of O Negotiante's network finally made first contact with Matt. A text message had warned him to be ready for a meeting late tonight.

Instructions to come.

"Why didn't they just send all the information!" I'd asked in frustration.

"Bad guys want every advantage, Coffee Lady. Until we know the venue, we can't set up surveillance or security. They have the upper hand."

"Oh, that's comforting."

"Relax. Your man Quinn's done this before—like a hundred times or two."

"Yes, I know. But for me it's the *first . . ."*

Now, standing among the mingling guests, Franco threw me a pathetic little smile. "Hey, the meeting may not even go down tonight."

"Nice try," I said. "But you don't believe that. Why should I?"

Under his black dinner jacket, Franco's big shoulders shrugged. "Just trying to ease your mind."

It was a lovely idea, but short of chugging a bottle of Dom Perignon and passing out cold, I didn't see how that was going to happen.

I was about to head inside the tent again, when a felt a hard tap on my shoulder. I turned to find Max Buckman looming over me. He wasn't in khakis tonight, or DIY bandoliers. He wore an honest-to-goodness Quinn-type detective suit—smoke gray jacket and slacks, white shirt, silver tie. Quite fetching, actually.

"Got it?"

I nodded. "Follow me."

I led the detective into the rear of our truck, pulled Meredith Burke's medical records out of my bag, and handed them over. Max thanked me. But when he turned to go, I grabbed his arm.

"Not so fast," I said. "Tell me what's happening."

On the phone earlier, I'd spilled everything I'd discovered. Now he folded his arms and gazed down at me. "You did good, Cosi. What more do you need to know?"

"Are you going to arrest Helen Bailey-Burke?"

Buckman shifted on his feet. "My team's in high gear off what you found, I can tell you that. We're putting a case together against her. Twenty-four hours, *maybe*, we should be ready to name her as a person of interest."

"She's here tonight. Can't you pick her up now?"

"You should know better than that. The woman will lawyer up with the best. We have to do it right, check any alibis. We may even have to surveil her."

"Why?"

"Think it through. It's possible she hired someone to do her dirty work. If that's the case, we'll need to establish a connection, payments—or promises. Otherwise, all we'll get is the driver and she'll go free."

Payments. Or promises. That put my mind in motion . . .

Promises had certainly been made between Public Advocate Tanya Harmon and Helen. Were they only political?

"And remember that plaid shorts guy?" Buckman continued. "One of your baristas recognized him at your coffeehouse a short time ago, sent him our way. Apparently, he stops by your Village Blend on Friday evenings."

I felt a chill, realizing that Lilly was hit almost *exactly* one week ago. "Did this man see the driver?"

"Yes, and he confirmed it was a woman. He said what struck him about her was her expression. She seemed so determined to hit Lilly that her face seemed frozen, like a mask. Her expression never changed."

A mask? "Like too much Botox, maybe?"

"Don't know. We're sitting him down with a sketch artist now."

"A woman was driving with a determined look," I repeated. "That sounds like Helen, doesn't it?"

Buckman seemed reluctant to confirm this. Something was troubling him with that conclusion. "Just steer clear of her," he warned. "The woman's either a killer or she's hired one. And keep your wits about you tonight—"

"I push caffeine. I'm probably the most awake person you'll ever meet."

"Stay that way. You remember that wineglass we found?"

"The one on the front seat of the white van?"

"Yeah. Guess where we traced it?"

"Uh, let me see. Waterford County, Ireland?"

"Gracie Mansion."

"You're kidding? Our mayor's residence!"

Buckman nodded and he didn't look happy. "The last time anyone used that glass was during a birthday bash for His Honor."

"Did you get any usable prints?" (Thanks to Franco, my Fingerprint 101 instructor, I knew it wasn't as easy as it looked.)

"The prints on the wineglass were smudged, barely readable, but there was something telling in the lab report. We picked up a residue from a plastic food storage bag."

Buckman and I both stared at each other on that one.

"You're telling me that someone took a glass from the mayor's birthday party, dropped it in a plastic bag for safekeeping, and then removed it from the bag and set it on the front seat of a stolen van used in a deadly hit-and-run?"

Buckman nodded.

"Frame job."

"Obviously. And a bad one."

Now I understood why Buckman wanted me to stay alert. The guest list at this party was nearly the same as the one at the mayor's birthday bash.

"It sounds like Helen, or someone close to her, tried to frame someone else. Is that right?"

"That's what it looks like. 'But can we can prove it, Detective Buckman?' That's the question you *should* be asking, Ms. Cosi."

Forty-eight

As Buckman departed, I felt gobsmacked.

I thought this party would be a diversion for me, but Max's revelation made me look at everyone with new eyes—*suspicious* eyes—because it was very likely that Helen Bailey-Burke had tried to frame someone at this party for murder.

But who? And why? And—as Buckman pointed out—how do we prove it?

I moved through the food-truck area and back inside the tent. Since coffee was my business, I joined Tuck at the Ambrosia station, but I was actually casting about for "persons of interest."

Amid the black dinner jackets and designer gowns, the mayoral wannabes were working the crowd—Tanya Harmon, Wilson Seacliffe, and Dominic Chin. Members of Five Points were scattered about, including purple-haired Josh Fowler, who'd once again done up our custom-made balloons.

Two Wheels Good was here, as well, and I noticed John Fairway looking my way more than once this evening. Why? Dominic Chin was a friend of his. Did Dom tell John about my concerns with his organization?

Something else of note: Fairway had come with Warrior Barbie on his arm. She's cleaned up quite nicely and donned a slinky dress—metallic silver, of course, just like her biking outfit. And I'd noticed she'd been talking quite intensely with Tanya Harmon. What was that about? Were they friends? Or were they both politicking?

On the coffee end, Tucker had everything under control. Our Ambrosia was flowing freely. And Matt would be happy because the compliments from guests were stellar. A celebrity restaurateur took Matt's card from Tucker as did the mayor's personal chef and the owner of a high-end hotel chain.

I soon found out that two of Ambrosia's biggest fans had sent these connections our way: Councilman Chin and his fiancée, Dr. Gwen Fischer.

"This coffee is outstanding," Dr. Fischer said, her smile genuine. "All those flavor profiles together, it's almost magical."

"Ambrosia describes this cup perfectly," Dom agreed, arm wrapped around Gwen's trim waist. "It's a light roast, right?"

"Right," I said. "Coffee lovers usually enjoy that bit of extra caffeine."

Gwen took another sip and closed her green eyes to savor the taste. "You know what? This stuff almost makes up for my absolutely crappy day. One that started in a coffeehouse, by the way."

"I hope it wasn't mine."

Gwen shook her red head, curled a sweep of her pageboy behind an ear. "A little hole in the wall near Columbia. I was checking messages on my smart phone, so I hung my purse over the back of the chair and someone snatched it."

"That's terrible."

"It gets worse." Gwen said. "My Volvo was parked outside, the keys were in the purse, so the creep snatched my car, too."

I felt for her. "I hope you have insurance."

"Plenty. But according to Dom's mother, bad luck comes in threes, so I should be waiting for one last shoe to drop."

"No way," Dom said. "Tomorrow's got to be better, right?

Despite her harrowing story, Gwen laughed through its telling. "So now you know why I'm here," she concluded. "To drown my sorrows in Ambrosia . . . and raw oysters. They have a lovely selection from the Pacific Northwest."

"Are you both foodies?"

"I love to eat," Gwen said, "but Dom's the cook. He really did grow up on one grandmother's biscotti and another's moon cakes—and learned to make both." She touched her fiancé's arm. "I actually fell for him back in college over a dish of his Chitalian Lo Mein. We parted ways for grad school, med for me, law for him—and I stupidly married the wrong guy. But I found my right guy again."

"That's very romantic—but you stumped me on Chitalian Lo Mein. What in the world is that?"

"It's just lo mein made with Italian spaghetti," Dom said. "But it has to start with my Chinglish marinade."

"Tell her your secret," Gwen insisted.

"Well, you have to understand, my Chinese grandmother makes a great marinade with Shaoxing cooking wine. But it's not so easy to get Shaoxing outside of New York or LA, so I figured out a pretty good substitute: white rice vinegar and grape juice."

"He should have been a chemist," Gwen quipped.

"I should have been a *chef*," Dom countered.

Dom's Chinese cooking reference made me realize: "You two weren't at the Dragon Boat exhibition. That was a pretty major photo-op for the mayoral candidates."

Gwen squeezed Don's hand. "I'm afraid it was my fault he wasn't there. I had a Smile Train fund-raising event that night, and Dom didn't want to disappoint me . . ."

The Smile Train was such a worthy charity. I spoke to them a little more and discovered Gwen donated her plastic surgery skills to the cause.

I recalled what Dante had said about these two. He called them a "power couple," and that might be true. But it seemed to me they were using their powers for good, and I found myself sincerely hoping Dom would fight hard in the election and become our next mayor.

Suddenly, I noticed Gwen tensing. Her animated good cheer stopped, her face frozen into an unreadable mask. I quickly learned the reason. Helen Bailey-Burke had entered the tent.

Helen was alone tonight, pressing the flesh with members of the city hall staff. Dom tactfully shifted position, trying to shield Gwen from Helen.

"I hope that woman doesn't come near me," I murmured.

Gwen heard me. "Is she suing you, too?"

Suing me, too? "Helen is suing you? Why?"

Dom cleared his throat.

"Oh, sorry . . ." Gwen shook her head, embarrassed. Her face had finally relaxed. "I shouldn't have said anything."

But she did say something, and I recalled that terrible slap Helen had given her at our Red Hook truck-painting party. I needed to question Gwen privately. She clearly wanted to let off steam, and if I could get her away from Dominic, I was sure she would spill something useful.

A call on Dr. Fischer's smart phone interrupted us. Gwen stepped away to talk and returned a minute later looking very distressed.

"Dom's mother was right. Bad things do come in threes," she said.

"What's the problem?" Dom asked.

"I just got a call from the lab. There's been some kind of fire. My research may have been damaged. I have to go."

"I'll drive you," Dom offered.

"That's silly. You're due to make a toast soon. I'll catch a cab on Central Park West."

After another hug from Gwen, she hurried out of the tent. Concerned, Dom watched her go.

"I'd better get to work." He shared a smile. "A little more hand-shaking couldn't hurt . . ."

The mention of a hand reminded me of Dante, and ten

minutes later, I was heading back out to the Muffin Muse to lend him mine.

The sound of muted music and laughter carried on the evening breeze. But as I emerged from the tent, the tranquility of the evening was shattered by the roar of a speeding car—and not Max's GTO.

West Drive ran through the entire western edge of Central Park, and right past Sheep's Meadow and the white wedding tent. The four-lane road was closed to traffic on weekends, and cars had also been banned from the roadway during the wedding.

But somehow a car had gotten onto that road. It raced along at twice the legal speed until it hopped the sidewalk and struck one of the guests from the wedding party. The victim, a woman in a formal gown, was tossed by the impact.

As the car disappeared around the bend, the victim sprawled on the pavement. Amid a chorus of screams and shouts, I raced to the poor woman's side—and recognized her immediately.

Helen Bailey-Burke was gasping out her last breaths. She was also conscious and aware that her life was slipping away.

"It was Fischer, I saw her," Helen gasped, foamy blood bubbling on her lips. "She aimed for me. I couldn't get away. It was Fischer who did this to me. Gwen Fischer . . ."

Helen's rasping voice faded after that. She was too weak to talk. An elderly man in evening clothes knelt beside her and performed CPR. The concerned crowd gathered around them.

Finally Helen closed her eyes and slipped away. A shocked, shroud-like silence descended over all of us, until the only sound we heard was the mournful wail of the approaching ambulance.

Forty-nine

Dante loaded a final stack of folding chairs onto the Muffin Muse and paused for a big gulp of coconut water.

"Everything's loaded," he said, rubbing the sweat from his neck.

"Sorry you had to do that alone. I sent Franco to talk to the investigating officer, but I thought he would have been back by now."

My gaze shifted to the cluster of police cruisers and uniformed officers still working the crime scene on West Drive. Twilight had turned to night, and flashing emergency lights strobed the trees.

"I hope Franco is helping the cops find the real killer," Dante replied. "There's no way Gwen Fischer ran Helen down. The police are wrong."

"But I heard Helen's accusation with my own ears, and others heard it, too. Her dying testimony will be tough to refute."

Dante shook his head. "I still don't buy it."

"You know Helen was harassing Gwen, with a lawsuit and with physical violence? Those are strong motives for murder."

"But Gwen is a Smile Train fund-raiser, boss!" Dante cried. "I've talked to her a million times. She and Dom are two of the nicest people I've ever known."

"Look, I don't believe Gwen is guilty, either, Dante. I was just following the policemen's logic."

The misery etched on Dante's face was mirrored on my own. Without Helen Bailey-Burke as a suspect, Buckman and I were back to zero. We thought she was the culprit, and her motive was her daughter Meredith's death by malpractice.

Buckman and I were wrong about Helen, but I was still convinced Meredith's death was the key to everything, despite what happened tonight.

"Here's Franco," Dante said, and we both rushed him.

"Have the cops figured out their mistake and released Gwen?" Dante asked.

Franco frowned. "Sorry, kid. The detective in charge is convinced Gwen Fischer is the killer, and he can prove it."

"Helen's accusation?"

"That, and a whole lot more," Franco replied. "The detective knows the killer slipped around the police barricade at Seventy-Seventh Street about ten minutes before the murder, because there's an eyewitness."

"Who?"

"A uniformed officer from Traffic IDed the car and the driver, which he described as a female redhead wearing a scarf and sunglasses. The woman flashed a VIP wedding pin, so the dumb-ass waved her through without even talking to her."

"Did they find the car?" I asked.

"It was abandoned on Central Park South, near the Pond. Detectives are going through it now."

"Great! Maybe they'll find fingerprints that will exonerate Gwen."

"Sorry, Coffee Lady. It's her car. A 2011 Volvo 360, registered to Dr. Gwen Fischer."

Dante cursed. "Poor Dom must be going nuts."

"This *has* to be a frame-up," I said. "Gwen told me her car was stolen earlier in the day."

"She told the detective that, too. He's actually using her stolen-car story to build a case for premeditated murder."

"Oh, no . . ."

"When they scooped her up, Gwen couldn't account for her movements," Franco continued. "She told the detective she'd gotten a call about a fire at her lab, and left the park to hail a cab."

"That's right, and I was standing beside her when that call came in!"

"Only there was no fire. Maybe Gwen got pranked; they can probably trace that call if it's real. But the detective is so convinced Gwen is lying that he's not going to look too hard for evidence that clears her."

"We need to help her."

"I hate to burst your balloon, but the case looked open and shut to me," Franco said. "It was the doctor. In the park. With a car."

Burst your balloon . . . that's it!

"The balloons!" I cried. "The custom-made balloons! There's your *Clue*."

Franco leaned into Dante ear. "She's lost it."

"Don't you see? Josh made the balloons. And Josh was good friends with Meredith Burke, though he didn't much care for her mother, Helen."

Dante snorted. "You got that right. Josh sued Helen last year. The case is still moving through the courts."

"Sued? For what?"

"He and Meredith worked on a comic together. She wrote, he drew. It was Meredith's autobiography, real emo stuff. After Meredith died, Josh wanted the comic to be published, but the artwork was in Helen's possession and she refused to give it back."

"I still don't see the connection to balloons," Franco said.

"You saw the balloons Josh created for this wedding," I told him. "They looked just like the bride and groom, right? Well, what if Josh could make masks, too—"

"Josh does make masks," Dante interrupted. "He made a

dozen masks that looked just like the mayor for the guy's birthday party. The Rockettes performed a dance number wearing them. Josh said the show was kind of creepy."

"Josh was there? At Gracie Mansion?"

Dante nodded. "Judge Fowler was on the guest list. Josh sat with his family."

"His father is a *judge*? But I thought Josh was some kind of working-class kid from Five Points."

"No way," Dante replied. "Josh lives on the East Side. He went to the same private school that Meredith attended. He's got a Vacheron watch that probably cost more than Gwen's Volvo."

"Let's get back to the masks," I said. "How are they made? Where are they molded?"

Dante shrugged. "At Five Points. All Josh needs are a couple of photographs and he can make a mask of anyone. He has 3D computer graphics software and a digital sculpting program that pretty much does the work. Josh has a molding machine, too. He's like a one-man factory."

My mind raced. Josh cared for his friend Meredith, maybe too much. He blamed Helen and the plastic surgeon for her death—maybe he blamed everyone involved, including Meredith's nurse, Lilly Beth.

Josh probably resented Gwen Fischer because she was once married to the man who killed his friend, so why not frame her? And that's why he stole the glass from the Gracie Mansion dinner. It was probably Gwen's glass, with her fingerprints all over it. He was hoping to frame Gwen for Lilly Beth and the surgeon, but he preserved the glass improperly and the prints got smudged.

So Josh tried again, this time killing Helen with Gwen's stolen car, so there wouldn't be any doubt about the killer's identity in the minds of the police.

"Is Josh still around?" I asked. "I saw him here earlier."

"He dropped by the Muse around seven to say good-bye," Dante said. "Said he was leaving early because he had things to do."

Like commit murder and frame an innocent woman?

"Do you think he's at Five Points?"

Dante shrugged. "Maybe. He hangs out there a lot."

"I need to ask Josh some questions. Can you give him a call?"

Dante used his iPhone, but he had to leave a message. Josh was unavailable.

"Maybe this is better—"

A double ringtone interrupted me. My own cell was singing. So was Franco's. My call was from Mike Quinn.

"Clare, I just wanted you to know the meeting is going down."

"When? Where?"

"Nine thirty. The rendezvous is a restaurant in Chinatown. The squad's there now, setting things up. Sully and his team are inside a surveillance van on Mulberry Street, near Columbus Park. They'll listen in on Matt's meeting with the drug dealers, make sure nothing goes south."

"I want to be there," I said.

"That's not a good idea," he warned.

"This isn't a debate. I'm on my way."

"Fine. Have Franco drive you. But do what Sully says. This has to go down right. It's our only chance to get clear of this mess."

I closed the phone and faced Dante. "Franco and I have to go. Another emergency."

"Anything I can do?" Dante asked.

"I want you to go to Five Points. If Josh is there, keep him there until you hear from me. If he's not, go through his computer, his locker. Everything."

Dante scratched his head. "What am I looking for?"

"Proof that Josh made a mask of Gwen," I said. "Proof that he's a murderer."

Fifty

THERE was only one van parked along Mulberry Street at Columbus Park. Blue-black and windowless, it seemed empty. I went around to the back, slapped my hand against the doors, and they opened.

"Get in." Finbar Sullivan said as he pulled me inside. A man in a tailored suit shut the door behind us.

The van's interior was dim, stuffy, and stank of ozone. A small fan tried to circulate air, but it was hopeless.

Beside Sully's familiar carrot-top, a young Asian cop gave me a nod. I recognized him, too, but the third man I didn't know. Hunched over a computer console, tapping keys and frantically whispering into a headset, the stranger was too preoccupied to notice my arrival.

"So where the hell is Franco?" Sully asked.

"He drove me here. Now he's looking for parking."

"In Chinatown? Good luck with that." Sully gave me a hard look. "And what are you doing here, Clare?"

"I had to come." Bent in a half crouch, I bumped my head against the ceiling light. "Matt is my business partner, the father of my child."

Sully's expression softened, and he slid a folding chair my way.

"Please, tell me what's going on," I said, sitting.

"We were ready to go when the call came down," Sully began. "Lucky for us, Detective Hong has intimate knowledge of the area and was familiar with the restaurant in question. Have you met Charlie?"

"We've met," I replied, reaching for his hand. "You were Franco's partner once, right?"

Hong smiled. "Who do you think recommended me for Chinatown recon?"

"Lou, here," Sully hiked a thumb at the man behind the keyboard. "He's establishing contact with his partner, who's on Pell Street with a parabolic aimed at the chophouse."

"Parabolic? Is that like a wire?"

"More like radar. Think of it as a wire without a wire," Sully said. "We'll be able to hear the conversation, provided the meet takes place inside the restaurant."

"So if the smugglers drag Matt into a back room, he'll be out of range?"

Sully waved my fears aside. "No worries. We have an undercover couple. A man and woman. They're going to wander into the joint before Allegro arrives and order a meal. They'll listen, observe, and make sure nothing goes wrong."

"What if the smugglers try to take Matt for a drive?"

"We'll follow," Detective Hong answered. "Lieutenant Quinn is sitting at the end of Pell in an unmarked chase car, and another detective's waiting on Mott. Nobody leaves this street without a tail on them."

I understood what these men were saying, but there was no denying it. I was incredibly anxious. No matter how much Mike and Sully and Charlie Hong insisted Matt would be safe, I found it a difficult to believe.

"Visuals are up," Lou said, gesturing to the console's panoramic screen.

The Hop Sing Chophouse was close to a dive. The entire dining room was visible behind a picture window, with red vinyl booths along the walls, Formica tables in the center. Faded bamboo prints with Asian landscapes decorated the walls, and a pot with plastic flowers squatted in a corner. Business was poor; only one booth was occupied.

"The food's always great in Chinatown," Sully told Hong, "so why are the restaurants so shabby?"

"I could say it's to ward off fussy shamrocks like you, but that's not why," Hong replied. "Truth is, my people don't trust fancy digs. They figure if a restaurant is spending money on décor, they're probably skimping on the food."

I could hardly follow what they were saying. *Why aren't they as worried as I am!*

Sully glanced at me, seemed concerned about my emotional state. "Hey, Clare, you know it's too bad you didn't bring any of those oatmeal muffins from the other day."

"What?" *First Chinese food, now muffins?*

"Yeah, they were a big hit at One PP. You know I even saw Popeye munching one—"

"The police commissioner?"

"He was actually smiling as he ate—well, his lips curled a tiny fraction, anyway. For him, that's a full-blown grin."

"Here's the audio," Lou said. Voices speaking Cantonese filled the cargo bay. We were listening in on the diners.

"And here comes our undercover tourists," Sully announced.

Both Asian, the plainclothes cops pretended to read the posted menu, then they entered the chophouse. The waiter seated them and brought tea.

"We're in," said a woman's whispered voice.

"That's not the parabolic," Sully told me. "Our undercover cops are wired so we can talk to them if we need to."

"Okay, everybody, it's show time!" Hong announced.

Matt appeared on screen, casually dressed, no jacket. He lingered in front of the chophouse, then pushed through the door. The same waiter who greeted the undercover cops intercepted Matt and led him to a table in the back, beside the plastic jungle.

Matt had hardly settled when a man emerged from the kitchen and sat down across from him. As big and as brawny as Matt, he had small eyes and pockmarked features. A heavy moustache as black as India ink draped over his thin lips.

Matt looked up from the menu, smirking. "So, what's good tonight? I'm leaning toward the Lobster Cantonese."

"Where is the woman? Where is your partner?" Moustache Man said.

Matt set the menu aside. "I told you I didn't want her here—"

"And we told you this meeting is pointless without her."

"Look." Matt leaned across the table. "We don't need some woman around when we talk business. We can hash this out, mano-a-mano."

Moustache Man set his elbows on the table, stared at Matt over linked hands. "I'm afraid that is impossible."

I faced Sully. Even inside the gloomy van, he couldn't hide his guilty expression.

"They wanted me at the meeting, too?" *I can't believe they kept this from me!* "Why wasn't I told? Was it Mike's idea to keep me out of the loop?"

"Not just Mike. Your ex-husband didn't want you to go, either. They're trying protect you, Clare—"

"But who's protecting Matt? How could you let him go it alone? They might kill him!"

"Matt's a big boy. He's been in tense situations all over the world. He said he could bluff them," Sully replied.

"Something's wrong," Lou cautioned, eyes on the screen.

Moustache Man was speaking in a low voice edged with menace. "It is now ten minutes to ten, Mr. Allegro. If your woman does not arrive by ten o'clock, I will get up and walk out of here. There will be no second chances after that. No further negotiations. Angry men on two continents will be forced to . . ."

A crowd sauntered past the restaurant, interfering with the parabolic.

"Listen to what that man is saying!" I cried. "It's me they want, not Matt. In their eyes, *I'm* the asset. This meeting is going to fall apart unless I show my face."

I jumped to my feet—and banged my head on the low ceiling. Ignoring the stars in front of my eyes, I pushed the doors open.

"Clare!" Sully grabbed my arm. "What do I tell Mike?!"

"Tell him I'm pulling a *Crazy Quinn*!"

Then I broke away and hit the pavement running.

Fifty-one

I'D been sweating inside the surveillance truck. Now the cool night air, or my stark fear, had me shivering.

I dashed up Mosco, the skirt of my black dress flaring, knowing that Sully probably thought I was crazy. Why would a woman risk her neck for an ex-husband?

But Matt was more than that to me, so much more. He and I had met and married at a young age. We'd spent more than two decades loving and resenting each other, arguing and bolstering each other, raising a daughter and running a business. Somewhere amid the fighting and forgiving, the favors and failures, we became family—and you don't stand by and watch family go down in flames!

As I turned down Pell Street, I nearly flattened an actual tourist. I slowed long enough to catch my breath, and the cell phone rang. I slipped the bag off my shoulder. It was Dante. I had to take it!

"Did you find Josh?"

"No sign of him. But Josh was definitely here before the party, long enough to totally wipe his computer."

"All the files?"

"All the *everything*. The computer's a blank. He even erased the software programs for the injection molds and fabricators. Josh took his personal stuff, too. He's not coming back."

I closed my eyes. "God in heaven, help me."

"Boss?"

"In heaven . . ." Of course! You can't erase your sins when the truth lives up above—in the Cloud.

"Dante, listen! Do the computers at Five Points routinely upload data to another source? Can you check to see if you're data is backed up in something like the Cloud?"

"Maybe. Nadine would know."

"Call her, get her down there. If there is a system, download the data. Restore Josh's computer."

I closed the phone, took a deep breath. Then I entered the Hop Sing Chophouse and boldly crossed the dining room to Matt's table.

The undercover officers couldn't mask their surprise, but their reactions were nothing compared with Matt's. He watched me sit down beside him with wide, then baffled, then absolutely horrified eyes.

Yeah, I know what you're thinking, but get used to it, Matt. You're not in this alone. Not as long as I'm around.

I reached deep for a persona and came up with a tough, cocky personality who'd been my shadow all week long. Locking eyes with Moustache Man, I channeled Sergeant Franco.

"So?" I said with clipped annoyance. "You wanted to see me."

Just visible beneath his facial hair, the corners of the man's mouth morphed into a suspicious frown. We stared in silence for a long, slow beat.

"Talk, or I'm out of here, and you're out your *oxidado*," I said, my gaze unwavering.

Another beat, and Moustache Man rose. "Come with me."

During the run up to this meeting, Mike had instructed Matt and I to cooperate with these people, to pretend to go along with their plans and agree to their terms. But I soon regretted my decision to follow Moustache Man when he bypassed the busy kitchen, pointing to a flight of wooden stairs to the basement.

I knew Sully and his crew would lose track of us if we went into that pit. Moustache Man must have sensed my reticence, because he reached under his oversized Izod shirt and pulled out a very large *gun*.

"Downstairs," he commanded.

Matt shot me a look that was easy to interprete: *Do you finally get it, Clare? That's why I didn't want you here. If something bad happens now, it happens to us both, and Joy is an orphan!*

His message sent and received, Matt pushed by me and went down the stairs. I followed, with Moustache Man bringing up the rear.

The basement was long and narrow, with naked bulbs screwed into the ceiling to illuminate the scene. A few dozen sagging cardboard boxes were stacked against crumbling brick walls, beside dented cans of cooking oil.

"Straight ahead," Moustache grunted. When Matt didn't move fast enough, our captor jabbed the gun barrel into his kidney.

"Watch where you're pointing that thing or I'll make you eat it," Matt growled.

Moustache Man's face flushed, and his lips curled to reveal a missing tooth. *This is it, he's going to pull the trigger.*

I thrust myself between the angry men—a position I'd found myself occupying for much of this past week!

"Enough of this macho crap," I said with all the forcefulness I could muster. "Let's talk. Right here—"

"No. Someone else will do the talking," Moustache replied.

A few more steps and the basement came to an end, but our journey did not, because an irregular hole had been cut into the ancient brick wall. Through that hole a long, narrow tunnel faded into shadows. I nearly yelped as a cat-sized critter darted across the tunnel floor.

Rats!!!!

Moustache hit a switch, and bare bulbs running along the roof of the underground passage sprang to feeble life. The tunnel smelled of wet earth, mildew, and even nastier things.

Matt took my arm and led the way. Again Moustache brought up the rear.

I tried to gauge the distance by counting footsteps, but there were so many twists and turns, noxious drips to dodge, puddles to jump, and rodents to avoid that I soon gave up. I knew we were far from Pell Street by now, in a place where Mike and his squad could never, ever put a tail on us.

The tunnel ended inside a dim underground garage empty of cars, save for a windowless van parked in the middle of the oil-stained concrete.

Moustache Man kick-slid a dented aluminum trash can toward us.

"Everything goes in there," he commanded. "Wallets. Money. Phones. Watches. Jewelry. All of it."

"So our journey to the center of the earth is all about a friggin' armed robbery?" Matt groused. "Why didn't you save time and mug us in the restaurant?"

"I'll take your keys," Moustache said, beefy hand outstretched.

We handed them over, and the gunman made us face the wall. The sound of more footsteps emerging from the shadows followed: two people, I guessed.

The pat down was gentle but thorough—and a little humiliating. Moustache Man didn't give a reason for this harsh treatment, but I knew his people were looking for wires, recorders, a GPS device, or any kind of tracer.

"Keep your hands off my junk," Matt warned.

The body search ended—and then rough hands seized me from behind. I struggled, but everything went dark as a blindfold was tied over my eyes. Handcuffs followed, and the cold steel bruised my already sore wrists.

Matt cursed a blue streak, until I heard a smack.

"Matt?" I cried, just as I was hauled off my feet (yet again!)

and tossed into the back of the waiting van. Matt bounced off the floor beside me. Doors slammed, the engine roared, and the irony didn't escape me: Except for the rodents, there wasn't a whole lot of difference between being kidnapped by a couple of drug runners and being arrested by the DEA.

"Are you okay?" I whispered.

"Just peachy," came Matt's terse reply.

"No talking," Moustache Man warned as the truck lurched into motion.

BLINDFOLDED, rolling around on the floor of the bumpy cargo bay, I tried to gauge where we were going. I feared our destination was the Red Hook warehouse, where these men expected to retrieve *oxidado* already confiscated by the Feds.

I had no illusions about our fate once Moustache Man discovered the drugs were missing.

But Mike sent cops to watch the warehouse, I reminded myself. *They would see us arrive, step in for a rescue—unless they'd been pulled away to participate in the chophouse surveillance, in which case they were probably scratching their heads and wondering where we were.*

In too short a time the van rolled onto a bridge—this I knew from the distinctive hiss of the wheels on the roadway. We had to be crossing either the Manhattan or Brooklyn Bridge because there wasn't enough time to reach any other span—which meant we were probably on our way to Brooklyn and the warehouse. By the time we hit the Brooklyn-Queens Expressway, I was certain Matt and I were doomed.

I didn't know how long the van was actually on the BQE, only that we ran into a traffic snag when we exited. As we idled, the van's interior began to heat up, so either Moustache or the driver cracked the window.

Cool air washed over me, along with a series of familiar smells—coriander, turmeric, curry: the basics spices of Indian cuisine.

We certainly weren't in Red Hook, where the aromas were very different. Had we gone north to Queens instead of south to Brooklyn?

Moments later, the rattling roar of an elevated train passing overhead rocked the van. The sound seemed too loud to be anything but the exposed tracks of the Number 7 line.

That theory was reinforced by the sweet, yeasty smell of brioche and a hint of chocolate—like the *champorado* I had smelled that morning. But it was a sweet, tangy, distinctive, and very familiar aroma that finally convinced me. I had to be smelling Amina Salaysay's special pork bun filling!

I knew where we were! On Roosevelt Avenue, near Amina's Kitchenette, in Little Manila.

A sudden turn sent me rolling into Matt. The van bumped onto a curb and braked. The horn blared three times, followed by the rumble of a garage door. I smelled motor oil and old rubber as we rolled into the garage.

The engine was cut, and the doors opened. I sat up and someone ripped away the blindfold. Blinking against the sudden brightness, I didn't resist as the handcuffs were removed and I was lifted out of the van.

When my vision finally cleared, I glanced at the youth in front of me. Short, stocky, with black hair and dark eyes, he was definitely Pinoy. If I had any doubts, they vanished when I saw *Balikbayan Boy* emblazoned across the front of his red T-shirt.

Fifty-two

BALIKBAYAN Boy led us to a small, windowless kitchenette with white walls and a faded hardwood floor. He sat us down at the table, then headed back to the garage. Moustache Man was nowhere to be seen.

"God, Matt," I groaned when I saw his swollen eye.

"I'm fine," he replied in an angry hiss. "But what were you thinking when you came to that restaurant?"

"I was thinking of you—"

Muted cheers interrupted me. The noise leaked through the walls, or maybe from above. It sounded like a party.

"At least someone is enjoying their weekend," Matt grumbled.

We both heard the first strains of a familiar pop tune.

"Peelings . . . Nothing more than . . . Peelings . . . Trying to poor-get . . ."

"Karaoke?"

Matt blinked. "What does she mean by 'peelings?'"

"The singer sounds Filipino," I said. "Lilly Beth told me they sometimes switch their *Ps* and *Fs*."

I was also dying to tell Matt that our location was no mystery. Despite the blindfold, I knew where we were. But I feared someone might be listening to us, so I kept that fact to myself.

"You know what? Puck this," Matt said angrily. "I'm tired of waiting—"

Another door opened and Moustache returned. This time he was armed with a tall, tinted bottle and three shot glasses. He set them on the table and departed without a word. He left the door ajar, and we heard more party noises.

Matt reached for the bottle. "Lambanog. No wonder they're so happy."

"That's arrak . . . Coconut wine, right?"

Matt nodded.

"In vino veritas . . ."

"Here's the truth. This stuff is ninety proof and packs a wallop." Matt glanced at the label a second time. "And it's bubble-gum flavored?"

He set the bottle down when we heard high heels clicking on hardwood. A stunning brunette sauntered through the door. Petite, she flaunted her fabulous shape with a flimsy yellow sundress that set off her perfect, bronzed complexion. Her ensemble was completed by fetish-style dominatrix shoes and little else.

Without introduction, she sat across from us, crossed her silky-smooth legs, and batted her heavily made-up eyes. (Okay, most of her looked real, but those lashes had to be fake.)

"So, how did you like our test charge?" she asked, her leg bouncing up and down on her knee.

Test charge? Matt and I glanced at each another in surprise. *Didn't we have this conversation in the roasting room last Saturday?*

"I didn't like it," Matt replied. "I turned down O Negociante's offer."

"My cousin doesn't take no for an answer. He's pushy that way."

"So you're Brazilian?" I assumed.

"Half." She snapped her darkly polished fingers. "The rich half."

"Who are you? What's your name?"

She leaned forward, pursed her lips. "I'm a successful businesswoman. I own real estate, a delivery service, a few bars, the party house upstairs, and the girls who work there. It's a humble beginning, but I'm looking to branch out."

I was willing to bet Dragon Lady's real estate holdings included the building leased to Amina's Kitchenette. I couldn't believe it. I was sitting across the table from Mrs. Salaysay's greedy, gouging landlady!

Dragon Lady poured three shots. "A drink, then we talk."

Without waiting for an invitation, I snatched a shot glass and downed its contents in a single gulp. The lambanog was smooth, and reminiscent of vodka, though I could have done without the bubble gum aftertaste. When the ninety proof part began its slow burn, I nearly gagged.

I covered the urge to cough by slamming the glass down on the table.

"Okay, let's talk," I said, tossing my hair. "And FYI, sister. You're negotiating with me."

Dragon Lady's eyes went wide. "Wow, pretty tough. And this one?" she gestured at Matt.

"He's just an amusement, as long as it suits me."

"I heard there's another one at home. Things are pretty hot in the hot coffee business, eh?"

Dragon Lady downed her own glass and flipped her shoulder-length hair. "Oh, I like you. What's that crazy name of yours again?"

"*Cosi*. And if you like me, you'll like my connections even better. I have lots of little mice doing my dirty work, some on the inside at One Police Plaza. The police commissioner himself even likes my muffins!"

Matt choked on his lambanog.

I took a break, channeled more Franco. This time I was the one leaning across the table. "You listen up, honey. I don't appreciate your lowlife cousin using my shipping connections. Not without adequate compensation."

"You'll be compensated," Dragon Lady said. "And if we

make a long-term shipment deal, you'll get rich, too. But we need to complete our test charge first."

"What?" I said, a little slow on the uptake. (Matt was right, lambanog really did pack a wallop.)

"I want that *oxi*, girl!"

"Oh. Right. No problem. The crack is at the warehouse in Brooklyn. We'll set up a time and—"

"Right *now*. Tonight," she demanded. "I'm going to send your little boy toy to fetch our drugs, while you and I negotiate some more. When I have my *oxi*, you get a nice, big bag of cash and a ride back to Chinatown."

"Can't do that," Matt said.

"Talking out of turn, you naughty boy," Dragon Lady said, playfully slapping his wrist.

"No, I mean she's in charge," Matt said. "I can't let you in because Boss Cosi is the only one who has the security codes for the warehouse."

Matt was lying, but I understood his motive. He knew whoever remained here with Dragon Lady would face the most danger, and he didn't want it to be me. I suspected Matt also knew (or at least hoped) that cops were watching the warehouse and would swoop in as soon as I arrived.

Dragon Lady ran a long, ebony fingernail along Matt's forearm. "Oh, such a problem! What to do? What to do?" she cooed.

"Look. I'll get your drugs," I said, rising. "You stay and have fun with Matt. But don't play rough. I may need him later."

I hated to leave the father of my daughter alone with that man-eater, but as Sully said, Matt was a big boy. And what choice did I have? Anyway, I had problems of my own.

Once again, I was shoved into the back of a stuffy van, blindfolded and handcuffed, though this time Dragon Lady's boys handled me with a gentle touch. And with each passing minute, my anxiety mounted.

What would happen when we arrived at the warehouse? Would Mike's men be there? Or would I be alone with Moustache Man and his pal, Balikbayan Boy?

I remembered my little old Chinatown cab driver, Mr. Jun Hon. *Size does not matter,* he'd said. Okay, so I didn't have his black belt. What I had was a black blindfold! But I also had a half-decent brain, and Mr. Hon basically said it all came down to strategy. I had to find a way to turn my enemy's strength against him.

That's it. I'm not waiting to be rescued. I'm rescuing myself!

Somewhere along the Brooklyn-Queens Expressway, I figured out what my enemy's strength was. Like so many people who wield power, they maintained control over me by keeping me in the dark—and that was how I'd beat them.

I ran the scheme in my mind a dozen times, counting the steps, measuring the distance. By the time the van rolled into Matt's warehouse parking lot, I was ready.

The engine died and the back door opened. My captor removed the handcuffs, then the blindfold. I rubbed my eyes to clear them. When I looked up, I realized I'd caught my first break of this very long day. Moustache Man had decided not to take this ride. I was alone with Balikbayan Boy, who was short, stocky, and muscular, but not nearly as formidable as Moustache Man.

"Let's go," Box Boy said, waving a handgun.

Okay, he's armed. That's a setback, but not unexpected. I have to try anyway, for Matt's sake as much as my own.

I hopped out of the van. Pretending to smooth the skirt of my dress, I scanned the area for any sign of a police presence, but saw nothing beyond the dark façades of silent buildings and the oily black water of the bay

Box Boy seemed nervous, too, and I hoped he didn't have an itchy trigger finger. Before we crossed the shadowy parking lot, I extended my hand.

"I need the keys."

Box Boy had Matt's set in his possession. He'd used them to open the fence's padlocked gate. Now he fumbled in the pocket of his tight denims with one hand, while the other still gripped the wavering weapon.

Finally, he thrust the keys into my hand. Now came the hard part. I had to time things just right, judge the distance perfectly. My life depended on it.

Box Boy remained behind me as we approached the steel security door. That was fine. My plan relied on where he was looking, not where he was standing. I took a few more measured steps, my shoes clacking on the dew-damp pavement.

Almost time . . . Just another second . . . Another step . . .

"Up there!" I cried, pointing. "Someone's on the roof!"

Box Boy looked up, directly into the sleeping halogen bulbs. I closed my own eyes to preserve night vision and took that final step. The motion detector did the rest. Box Boy cried out and threw his arm over his face to block the sudden brilliance.

How do you like that, Box Boy?! Your blindfold is darkness. Well, mine is light!

He howled again when I kicked him where I knew it would hurt the most. I heard the gun clatter to the pavement and I bolted for the gate.

I didn't make it five feet before I blundered into a wall of muscle. I lashed out, swinging madly, until I saw dark silk, a spotless white shirt, a bow tie.

"Chill, Coffee Lady!" Franco said, taking hold of my arms. "It's okay! You're safe now."

A group of uniformed police officers dashed by us. Under the halogen's bright spot, two cops hauled Balikbayan Boy to his feet, while a third read him his rights.

"We have to hurry. She still has Matt," I told Franco.

"Who's she?"

"The Dragon Lady! She's holding Matt hostage!"

Franco frowned. The police were dragging Box Boy across the parking lot to a waiting police cruiser. Franco stopped them.

"Where's this lady's partner?" His voice rumbled with menace.

The youth sneered. "I'm not saying nothing, and you'll never pind him."

"I already know where Matt is," I shot back. "He's in the basement of a happy house on Roosevelt Avenue, in Little Manila."

Franco seized the back of Box Boy's neck and pulled him close.

"Listen, kid. If I were you, I'd get in front of this. Judges like punks who cooperate, and the mandatory sentence for kidnapping, hostage taking, and drug running?" Franco shook his head. "You don't want to know."

"No way, dude," Box Boy insisted. "I'm no rat pink."

"How about we forget the accessory stuff and book this guy as the mastermind," Franco called to the other cops.

"I'll testify that the whole drug scheme was your idea," I told him.

"Then it's bye-bye for life." Still gripping the youth by his neck, Franco pointed to the sky with his other hand. "Take your last look at the moon, 'cause you can't see the sky from a maximum security cell."

"Okay, okay," Box Boy whined. "We'll do a deal. I'll talk."

"Smart man," Franco said, releasing him at last. "Start with an address."

Fifty-three

The drive from Brooklyn to Queens was like one of those nightmares where you're trying to get somewhere but you can't make any progress.

Before we boarded his SUV, Franco was on the phone to the precinct in Jackson Heights. The conversation continued on the BQE, all the way past the Brooklyn Bridge.

That's where we hit our first snag—a multicar accident!

"I need to borrow your phone," I told Franco.

Dante answered on the first ring. "Boss! I've been trying to reach you for the last half hour!"

"I got separated from my phone. What did you find out?"

"You were right about the Cloud. Nadine ran the remote download—"

"And—"

"We found everything," Dante replied. "Josh made a mask of Gwen Fischer. And we found something else."

"What?"

"Josh created a file called 'Changing Lanes.' Inside we found a comic written and drawn by Josh. It's called *The Revenger* and the hero is a guy who wears masks to trick the police and get even with wrongdoers. But these aren't really stories, boss, they're blueprints for the murders.

"Josh shows how he stole the truck, then ran over the plastic surgeon and Lilly Beth, too. He even storyboarded Helen's murder, with *The Revenger* disguised as a doctor. This is the proof we needed to nail Josh and clear Gwen."

"Call Detective Buckman. He needs to know," I told Dante.

I knew Mad Max had two reasons to be pleased. Not only did we find the person who ran down Lilly Beth, that person also happened to be wealthy—rich enough, if civilly sued, to pay for the pain he'd inflicted on Lilly and her family.

As I ended the call, I realized we hadn't moved an inch since I first dialed up Dante—and we were still miles from Little Manila!

Franco sensed my mad panic, but instead of trying to talk me down, he slapped a magnetic bubble light on the roof. Then he revved up his siren. Inside of a minute, the tide of traffic magically parted.

We hit a second snag on Roosevelt, less than a block from Amina's Kitchenette. Roosevelt Avenue was blocked by a wall of flashing emergency lights. A half-dozen police cars were scattered about, and I saw a pair of fire trucks, too.

My heart nearly stopped when a wailing ambulance flew by in the opposite direction. Still a block from the maelstrom, I released my seat belt and popped open the door.

"Hold up, Coffee Lady!" Franco shouted.

But I was already racing toward the commotion. I reached a police line and tore right through the tape. A young cop yelled for me to stop, but I kept going. A moment later, I was surrounded by police and firemen.

Smoke poured out of the front door of a karaoke parlor. A slight whiff started my nose burning. *Tear gas.* A garage door beside the club was open, and cops emerged, pushing handcuffed men and a scantily-clad young women ahead of them.

"Matt! Matt, where are you?" I called.

Tears blurred my vision and I rubbed my eyes to clear

them—and that's when I spied my partner. He was wrapped in a blanket, sitting alone on the curb beside a fire truck.

"Matt! Over here!"

This time he heard me and rose to his feet. We met in the middle of the street and fell into each other's arms.

"You're okay!" I cried. "Oh, thank you, God!"

He dabbed at his raw, red eyes. "I was crazy scared for you, Clare. Are you all right?"

"Absolutely," I said, still clinging to him. "Just another fun Friday night in NYC."

Suddenly we both sagged under the weight of heavy arms. The last time I'd been in a group hug, Franco had initiated it. But when I looked up, it was Mike Quinn pulling us into a three-way.

Fifty-Four

A short time later, we were in my duplex kitchen again, downing coffee and leftover slices of groom's cake. Quinn's team followed through with the mop up, processing the Dragon Lady and her minions, but he wanted to make sure we got home okay.

Quinn also mentioned that he was waiting for some kind of important confirmation. When a call came through, he appeared relieved by the message.

"You'll be happy about this, Allegro," he said after hanging up. "Looks like you can start adding those Brazil stamps to your passport again."

"You're joking, right?"

"Just confirmed. A DEA fast-action team took out your drug lord and his gang. They'd been working off your intelligence all week, and your friend Nino—"

"Not Nino!" Matt cried. "He's just a poor, innocent farmer. Don't tell me—"

"Take it easy. Nino is giving us full cooperation."

Matt paused. "Is that code? Is he an 'asset' now?"

"It's better than a prisoner."

"I'm just glad this whole thing's over," Matt said, rising to hit the sack. "Nothing against you two, but I cannot wait to move back to my Sutton Place apartment. Bree's flying in tomorrow, and I plan to be at the airport with a big, fat, ridiculously expensive bouquet."

"Good night, Allegro." Quinn stood, held out his hand. "I'm happy you're glad."

"Thanks," Matt said, clasping his hand. "I mean it. *Thanks.* That new boss of yours should be happy, too."

"New boss?" I said.

Matt froze and the room went dead silent. Then Quinn met my eyes, and my spirits sank lower than our roasting room floor.

MIKE made love to me that night like he never had before. The way he touched me, looked at me, the expression in his eyes . . . At one point we both shed tears, and a part of me knew just because of that. But I didn't want to know, so I didn't ask.

The next morning, as I lay in Mike's arms, the rising sun brought an end to our brief oasis, shedding light on the hard truth I didn't want to face. The sacrifice Matt had mentioned, the one I'd have to make, was about to begin.

Mike's explanation was terse but clear: The U.S. attorney who'd lured him to D.C. for a job offer had wanted him on a special task force so badly that he'd brokered a deal.

In the dead of night, when my ex-husband and I had been under arrest by the DEA, that federal attorney went to the mountaintop to help Mike help us—but with one caveat: Mike had to join the attorney's D.C. team.

"In other words," I whispered, "you're leaving me."

"I'm *not* leaving you. Get that straight."

"But you're taking a job in Washington."

"It was the only way . . ."

"How could it be?"

Mike paused, took a breath. "Do you know who made that

phone call in the dead of night? The man who put the fear of God into those federal agents?"

"Who?"

"It was the attorney general, Clare."

"The attorney general," I rasped. "Of the United States of America? The man in charge of the NSA, CIA, DEA—"

"That's right, all the A's."

"The *attorney general* demanded those agents release me and Matt to your custody?"

"And you were—but you don't get favors from a deity without paying tribute."

"You're the tribute!"

"It's a one-year special assignment. Sully's taking over the day-to-day of my squad. My captain's agreed to the arrangement. The PD's holding my place for me. I'll check in as much as I can."

"And that's your plan for us?" My voice was barely there. "Don't you want me to move with you?"

"Clare," he said, "Your whole life is here. It's who you are. You can't leave. You've told me that."

"But Mike—" I couldn't stop them any longer; the tears were spilling out.

"The year will go by fast, sweetheart. I promise." He tightened his arms around me, pressed his lips to my head. "I'll come back to you as often as I can—and you're welcome to visit me as much as you like. But until this year's assignment is over, that's the most I can give you."

I didn't know what to say, and that's when he reminded me—

"Just a short time ago, didn't you tell me that you needed more time?"

I closed my eyes. *Oh, god.*

"Well, now you have it . . ."

It's one of Murphy's Laws, isn't it? You only get what you want when you don't want it anymore.

The hardest part for me was knowing how this miserable situation had come about. Mike had agreed to the deal because he cared for me. It was our closeness that made him accept a job that would keep us apart.

Could time and distance erode feelings as powerful as that? I hoped and prayed that wouldn't happen. But I knew it could, and Mike was probably asking the very same question about me.

Digging deep, I searched for an answer to this impossible situation. I knew God worked in his own time—not to mention mysterious ways. But I'd always trusted His plan, even when my own choices had tested the heck out of me.

"At some point in their lives," I finally said, "parents are supposed to start learning from their children."

"Are we there yet?"

"Joy and Franco are a lot farther apart than you and I will be." Somewhere in the tears, I found a smile. "On the other hand, you don't Tweet. And you're not even on Facebook."

He touched my wet cheek, his expression raw but real. "I love you, Clare Cosi."

"Hold that thought."

"I will," Mike promised. "Just remember, the train from D.C. to New York goes both ways."

Epilogue

THE following Tuesday, I kissed Mike Quinn good-bye on the platform at Penn Station. After watching his train depart, I wiped away my tears and returned to my Village Blend.

Lilly Beth was now conscious and out of the ICU. According to the text message I'd received from Terry, she was craving a good cup of coffee, so I prepared a very special thermos of Ambrosia, and headed across town to the hospital.

No surprise, I found Detective Buckman at her bedside. Pausing in the doorway, I watched the two of them with deep curiosity.

Lilly was cocooned in a torso-to-ankles cast. Strapped to a tilt bed set on vertical, she was lifted to an almost standing position. Her arms were free but badly bruised from IV needles. Despite her condition, she was actually smiling.

Max was in the process of cutting Lilly Beth a big slice of her mother's light-as-a-cloud chiffon ube cake. "Got to say, this is the first neon blue cake I ever saw," he told her. "Come to think of it, I once drove a Buick this color. What does UB stand for anyway? Ultra blue?"

Lilly's laugh was a song to my ears. "I told you before, Detective Buckman—"

"And I told you before, the name is Max."

"It's not a *U* and *B* cake, Max. It's an *ube* cake. An ube is a purple yam that gives the cake its color."

"YOU-BEE cake," he said, passing her the slice.

"Ooo-bee," Lilly repeated. "You must have it by now. I've said it like five times."

"Yeah, I know," he said sheepishly. "I just like watching you say it."

Lilly Beth's eyes widened at that—and she finally noticed me in the doorway. Brushing away a tear, I moved to gently hug my friend, and for the next hour, she, Max, and I shared Ambrosia and sweet pieces of lavender-blue cloud.

When a team of physicians came by to examine Lilly, Max and I stepped out, and I suggested we talk in the patients' lounge.

"I hear Quinn took that D.C. job, after all," Buckman began, studying me.

"He did," I confirmed.

"So how are you holding up?"

"I'm fine."

"Fine?"

"Yeah, Max . . ." I tapped my watch. "After three hours and eleven minutes, no problem. Come midnight, my answer may be different."

"Well, I was beginning to wonder. I mean, two whole days and you haven't once pestered me for an update on our case. A guy could think you lost interest."

I smiled and told him the truth. I hadn't lost interest in our case. I simply trusted that he was motivated enough to nail the thing shut—which he did. With uniformed backup, Buckman had picked up Josh Fowler on Saturday night at JFK, just as the young man was about to board the redeye to Paris. By then, Max and his team had reviewed the evidence recovered from the computer at Five Points and built a strong case.

Of course, Buckman wanted more than proof of a theory. He wanted a confession; and in the quiet of the empty hospital lounge, he confided to me how he got it.

At first, Josh claimed innocence, even after Buckman played the role of sympathetic cop. "I told the kid I understood his pain over losing his best friend, Meredith, *yada, yada*, but he still didn't open up. Fortunately, I had an ace up my sleeve."

The ace was Josh's comic, *The Revenger*, in which he actually drew up and dramatized the details of Dr. Land's murder, of Lilly's hit-and-run, even how he planned Helen's death in Central Park.

"I showed Josh the printouts we made of his graphic novel, told him I'd read it, thought it was a masterpiece. If *The Revenger* was allowed to be published, it would *surely* become one of the most famous comics of all time." Buckman paused, and I knew why.

"That's when you delivered the coup de grace."

Buckman nodded. He told Josh that *The Revenger* comic would never get published, instead it was destined to be destroyed. Of course, Josh freaked, demanding to know why the police would do such a horrible thing.

"It's your own defense attorneys who will have the comic destroyed," Buckman claimed. "They'll see it as evidence, not art. They'll want to bury it."

Of course, *The Revenger* comic was Josh's emotional button, and Buckman pressed it hard in the interview room. He knew Josh's comic was marked as evidence and would not be destroyed. But Josh believed Buckman and, desperate to preserve his art, he confessed everything without a lawyer present, including exactly how he got the dark inspiration for these "hit-and-run murders"—attending one of John Fairway's Two Wheels Good rallies.

"There's one thing I'd still like to know," I said. "How did Josh even find Lilly Beth? I mean, Helen's detectives couldn't locate her. How did he?"

"An act of God. Or bad luck," Buckman replied.

Apparently, on a visit to see Dante at the Village Blend, Josh recognized Lilly while she was sitting at a café table, working with me. Years before, Josh had accompanied Meredith to Dr. Land's cosmetic surgery center, holding her hand on the way in. He'd seen Lilly that day. Seeing her again in the Blend had sealed her fate. He added Meredith's "Filipino nurse" to his hit list.

"Now Josh had three people to kill," Buckman continued, "but he still needed one thing—"

"Someone to take the fall," I finished, and knowing the timing, I'd already guessed who and how. "Josh saw Meredith's mother arguing with Dr. Land's ex-wife, Gwen Fischer, at the mayor's Gracie Mansion birthday bash, right?"

"That's right. Josh figured police would easily buy a woman killing her ex-husband, and the argument at the party with Helen made their animosity public. As far as a motive to kill Lilly, Josh figured the police would assume Gwen was angered by some aspect of an affair her ex-husband had with his Filipino nurse—not true, but a theory that both you and I had considered, too."

According to Buckman, Josh swiped Gwen's wineglass that night to plant as evidence. He found the Smile Train website, downloaded photos of Gwen, and used his 3D sculpting software and artistic talents to make a lifelike mask of her. When he was ready to strike, he stole a van from a vendor in Chinatown and used it to run down Dr. Land. Then Josh stashed it in a parking garage until he needed it again.

For his next strike, Josh planned a double event, intending to kill both Lilly Beth and Helen on the same night.

"But how did Josh know Lilly would be at the Blend that evening? Did Dante tell him?"

Buckman nodded. "Remember, that night Josh was going to help—"

"Prime the truck, of course!"

Dante had discussed Friday's Muffin Muse schedule with Josh. They were going to put the base coat on the truck late in the evening—after Lilly and I showed off the truck to Matt. So Josh knew where Lilly would be, and when to strike. He also learned Helen was attending a fund-raiser nearby at Cooper Union that same evening, so the timing was perfect.

"Josh planned to draw Mrs. Bailey-Burke into the street with a fake phone call," Buckman explained, "just like that phony call he used to lure Dr. Fischer away from the wedding. Of course, things didn't work out that way."

Apparently everything fell apart after Josh ran Lilly down and he got stuck in the ultimate New York leveler—traffic. On Thompson Street, a police cruiser appeared at the end of the block and Josh got spooked. He ditched the van, leaving the glass behind to finger Dr. Fischer, deciding to kill Helen another day, and another way.

Unfortunately, the prints on the glass were smudged and Gwen was never arrested. Then Helen publicly slapped Gwen Fischer in the face at the Brooklyn truck-painting party, and Josh was inspired to try again, with an even bolder plan. He'd lifted Dr. Fischer's purse at a coffeehouse, which held her car keys. He stole her car and ran over Helen in Central Park after luring her to the perfect spot with a fake phone message—the same method he'd used to get Gwen away from the party, making her look guilty.

For the second time, Josh wore that creepy Gwen mask he'd created. But this time he used the patsy's car, and there were witnesses, so Dr. Fischer was charged with murder. That's when Josh burned the mask, wiped his files off the Five Points computers, and bought a plane ticket to Paris.

"Why Paris?" I asked. "Random or another reason?"

"A very specific reason," Buckman said, "and the real reason this all took place. Josh had made a tentative deal with a French magazine to publish the comic he'd created with the late Meredith Burke. But their offer was made based on photocopies. To publish, Josh had to produce the original art and the legal rights to Meredith's contribution.

"Meredith's mother, Helen, was the only obstacle. She had

possession of the artwork and refused to release what she saw as an embarrassment: her daughter's frank portrayal of her tormented childhood."

I sighed, understanding. Josh's motive came down to much more than revenge. "With Helen dead, he thought his troubles were over. Yes, he avenged his best friend, but he also killed the woman holding his artwork hostage."

Buckman nodded. "Josh told me his plan was to travel to a better place. He was moving to France to become a famous comic book artist." Pausing, he scratched his silver-gray temple. "The kid is talented, and maybe that comic he created with Meredith was brilliant. But the poor girl's death twisted something inside him."

Like Lilly's jars, I thought. *All the good things inside Josh got emptied out.*

"It's a terrible waste," I said. "Instead of enlightening the world with his art, Josh Fowler used his creativity to spread anger, hate—all the dark things within him."

Buckman reminded me that Josh would have a long time to consider his mistakes. And he would leave prison a poorer man, too. John Fairway, esquire, had been talking to Lilly's mother every day since Josh was arrested.

"I think Fairway's convinced the woman to file a civil suit on her daughter's behalf," Buckman said.

"You mean Fairway's intent all along was to get in on a fat lawsuit? No wonder he was always lurking." I shook my head. "All that reconnaissance his Two Wheels Good people do on vehicular accidents. It actually boils down to—"

"Ambulance chasing. Yep. But then, 'follow the money' is an old saw. And since Josh has deep pockets, and Lilly's going to need money to cover expenses, it all works out for John Fairway and for Lilly's family."

"What about the papers I found in Lilly Beth's bedroom?" I was uneasy about bringing this up, but I had to. "Those medical records of Meredith's, what are you going to do with them?"

Buckman shrugged. "File them. That's where they'll be

forever. In the evidence file, for anyone to act on if they choose to . . ."

Silence fell between us.

We both knew the facts. Dr. Land and Helen Bailey-Burke were dead, and it seemed unlikely that anyone would have an interest in digging up those records and pursuing any kind of case with them. Even if they did, most people probably would agree that whatever Lilly had done wrong, she'd suffered enough punishment for it.

Buckman checked his watch. "I hope the docs are finished with my Lilly. She might want another slab of that blue cake. I know I do."

"Hey, Max."

"Yeah?"

"Did you just say '*my* Lilly'?"

"Gee, nothing gets by you, does it, Cosi?"

"CLARE, dear, I have news!"

Three weeks after my sit-down with Buckman, I rose early to pack a Pullman and roast enough fresh coffee to cover a busy weekend. Just before noon, Madame swept in and waved me over to her favorite sidewalk table.

The summer sun was warm on our faces, the cooling kiss of an Atlantic breeze carrying salt-tinged air through our yawning French doors.

Over iced mocha frappes and my fresh-baked Coffee Cake Streusel Muffins, my former mother-in-law finally shared her announcement: "Otto and I have secured a new angel for Esther's summer outreach program!"

I smiled at this, but it was hardly a revelation. "You already found two patrons," I reminded her. "The audio-video stream is up and running on the truck, and Esther's holding her first Village Blend poetry slam upstairs next Saturday."

"I know, dear, and I can hardly wait!" Madame's ube-colored eyes hadn't sparkled this brightly in years. "But our new patron is an award-winning filmmaker who wishes to make Esther's mobile muse and the inner city kids she inspires the subject of a short documentary. He's calling it *Poetry in Motion* and plans to enter it in several international festivals, isn't that wonderful?"

Esther at the Oscars? Short documentary category? Yeah, I could see it . . .

After knocking glass mugs, we caught up on news of Joy, who was planning a fall visit home, and Matt, who just took off for a three-week stint of regional coffee hunting.

Despite Quinn's confidence in Brazil's "safe" status, Matt thought Indonesia was a better idea (as did I). Timor, Sulawesi, Papua New Guinea, and the Island of Java were all sharing the same harvesting season, and as far as I knew, not one of those countries was harboring an *oxi* drug lord with a grudge.

"Billy, my man!"

"Dante, whassup!"

Madame and I paused in our discussion to witness a small miracle. The boy with the dragon tattoo strode into the Village Blend with a new delivery of his grandmother's warm egg custard tarts (our fastest-selling new item), and my *artista* barista slapped hands with him.

Madame tilted her silver pageboy. "They're getting along now?"

"Famously."

The first time Billy Li delivered the tarts, things were tense between the young men, until Billy asked Dante about a few of the many designs on his arms. (Franco had been right. Tattoo talk really was the way to a potential delinquent's heart.)

Both guys had designed their own elaborate body art, and by the end of their "tats" discussion, Dante was inviting Billy to stop by the Five Points Arts Collective.

With Josh gone (for a long, *long* time), Dante was in the market for a new apprentice. "Now Billy's helping Dante on a Battery Park mural," I said. "And he's developing his own proposal for a 'Dragon and Lion Dance' installation in City Hall Park for the next Lunar New Year."

According to Tucker, Billy even responded well to those pointers on serving Village Blend beans.

"Well," I told Tuck, "when Billy gets tired of delivering his *yeh-yeh*'s tarts, let's try him out behind the counter." After all, I reasoned, given his grandmother's DNA, Billy couldn't be all bad, and I might even get something out of it—like that Jimmy's Kitchen recipe for warm custard sauce.

Madame, on the other hand, enjoyed the possibility of a new artist in her barista family. Clapping her hands, she suggested we have *another* truck-painting party. "I'll get the permits," she promised, "and we'll hold it in front of the Blend this time."

"A block party sounds perfect to me . . ." Our turf war with Kaylie was history, and Dante was already working up a fresh parody painting for the truck, one that wouldn't remind us of Lilly's brutal hit-and-run.

Madame sighed, noting all that had happened since that terrible Friday. "The older I get, the more I see it . . ."

"What?"

"Blessings in disguise."

Taking in the cloudless blue dome above, I didn't dispute her, although few people would ever characterize a nearly fatal hit-and-run as a blessing. And yet . . . if Lilly hadn't been hit, one day the burden of her secret may have become too much for her.

To my mind, Buckman himself had posed the most difficult question in this case: *When Josh recognized Lilly at the Village Blend was it "bad luck" or "an act of God"?*

Given the new direction Max Buckman's life was taking, I knew how he'd answer it. As for me, I couldn't stop thinking about all those jars Lilly had filled with dark coffee beans. Every last one had been emptied of its colorful contents and refilled with blackness—an appropriate color, given Lilly's internal struggles with guilt. But there was an important difference between Lilly's darkness and Josh's, and that difference was prayer, the desire to find a way back to the light.

Seeing Lilly out of her coma these past few weeks, with Paz and Max and her mom around her, I knew she was on her way.

On the other hand, I found myself wondering if Madame's "blessings in disguise" idea could be applied to the other half of my Little Manila drama—the lambanog-pushing, hair-flipping Dragon Lady.

With the woman's properties and businesses seized by the government and a hefty financial award sure to be granted to Lilly in a civil suit, I had no doubt Amina Salaysay would be able to purchase the building that her beloved little restaurant had occupied for over two decades.

That fact actually made me see what Matt and I had gone through with new eyes. Would I call finding millions of dollars of Brazilian crack in our coffee bags a blessing? *Uh, no.* But that little problem did end up preventing a deadly drug from hitting our city's streets, and an already monstrous woman from growing into Godzilla with false eyelashes.

Finally, Madame's curiosity took another turn. "Now that Lilly's hit-and-run case is closed," she said in a sly little voice, "is that nice detective still visiting the hospital?"

"More than that," I said. "Max Buckman and Lilly Beth Tanga are officially a couple."

"Really?"

"Oh, yes . . ." I explained how Lilly had woken from her coma to find a strange man playing Go Fish with her young son, a man who seemed to know everything about her, who now makes her laugh every five minutes, appears absolutely taken with Pinoy food (*especially* ube cake), and insists on bringing her fresh flowers every day.

"Well, I don't know many women who could resist that!" Madame said.

"There's only one downside," I noted.

"Oh, dear. What's that?"

"Max's vintage GTO is being neglected. He's too busy retrofitting Lilly's wheelchair."

A short time later, I checked in with Tucker, who assured me all was well for the next few days.

"We're fine, sweetie. Now get your assets in gear or you'll miss your ride!"

Nancy tapped her watch. "To quote Taboo, 'Your train! Your train!' "

Esther slapped a hand to her forehead. "It's *Tattoo*, and it's 'de plane, de plane.' "

"Huh?" Nancy appeared puzzled.

Tucker patted her hand. "Esther's right. I mean, you were trying to quote the opening of that kitschy old TV show *Fantasy Island*, weren't you?"

"Holy Smokin' Rockets, is that where it's from? I always thought it was an ad for Amtrak."

Well, Nance wasn't totally wrong, because the Acela Express was where I was heading, by way of yellow cab to Penn Station. Mike Quinn texted me earlier with info on the hotel room he'd booked.

True to his word, Mike had come back to New York for two weekends in a row. But Esther had been right when she'd defined "in love" as passive and "loving" as active. They really were distinctive parts of life as well as speech, like the difference between theory and practicum.

I knew this year would be my practicum with Mike Quinn, and this weekend was my turn to make the effort—although, really, how much effort was it to join the man you love at the Ritz?

Dinner in Georgetown, Mike texted. Champagne chilling.

Can't wait to CU, I texted back and waved good-bye to my kids.

"Be good!" I called before reciting the silent prayer of every mother, manager (and upright sleuth) since time began.

Please don't kill each other!

Recipes & Tips from the Village Blend

Visit Cleo Coyle's virtual Village Blend at
www.CoffeehouseMystery.com
to download even more recipes including:

* Ube Cake *(a beautiful blue-violet Filipino dessert)*
* Blue Velvet Muffins *(inspired by the Ube Cake)*
* Easy Pound Cake Swirled with Nutella
* Strawberry Cheesecake Muffins
* Caramel Latte Cupcakes
* Maple Bacon Cupcakes
* Mostly Frosting Cupcakes (*with whipped "flour frosting"*)
* Dreamy (Low-Fat) Mocha Muffins (*with ricotta*)
* Chocolate Fudge Frosting (*sans butter or cream*)
* Easy Frozen Yogurt Bites (*from your favorite flavored yogurts*)
* *Champorado (chocolate rice pudding, a favorite Pinoy breakfast)*
* Forbidden Chocolate Muffins *(inspired by the* Champorado*)*
* Cakelets and Cream Sandwiches
* Black Bean Brownies *(you'll taste chocolate not beans!)*
* *Ensaymada (a delicious Filipino brioche)*
* and more . . .

Recipes

True well-being is found in happiness, not in prosperity.

—FILIPINO PROVERB

Clare Cosi's Blueberry Muffin Tops

Nothing builds up the appetite for cozy comfort foods like a DEA *interrogation, and the morning after her arrest by the Feds, Clare craved a big stack of blueberry pancakes. Unfortunately, pancakes require attention to the griddle—the pour, the flip, the juggling act of keeping everything warm. With Quinn and Matteo about to go for each other's throats, Clare found herself with the same hands-free goal as your typical harried parent, attempting to fix breakfast while keeping potential combatants apart.*

The solution? Muffin tops! Much like a pancake, Clare's muffin top batter is a basic quick bread with the added tanginess and nutrition of yogurt. For fat, Clare chose healthy canola oil. For flavor, she balanced the tartness of lemon zest with a sweet kiss of vanilla, and all those luscious, juicy blueberries.

Best of all, these muffin tops could be dropped on a sheet pan and baked all at once, so Clare would have time to brew up a fresh pot of coffee—and make sure all the sharp utensils were off the table.

Makes about 20 muffin tops (depending on size)

1¾ cups all-purpose flour
½ cup sugar
½ teaspoon salt
2 teaspoons baking powder
½ teaspoon baking soda
1½ cups whole, fresh blueberries
(if using frozen, roll lightly in flour first)
2 large eggs
⅓ cup canola or vegetable oil
½ cup whole milk
½ cup plain yogurt
2 teaspoons vanilla
1 teaspoon lemon zest
Confectioners' sugar, to dust tops after baking and cooling (optional)

Step 1—Mix ingredients: Measure out flour, sugar, salt, baking powder, and baking soda into a mixing bowl. Whisk to blend well, then add the blueberries and lightly toss to coat the berries. (Do not crush them, keep them whole.) In a separate bowl, crack in the eggs and beat lightly with fork. Add oil, milk, yogurt, vanilla, and lemon zest. Stir well. Finally, pour the wet ingredients into the dry and gently stir, only enough to blend into a lumpy batter. Do not overmix or you'll develop the gluten in the flour and your muffin tops will be tough instead of tender. Place the bowl in the fridge to chill for ten minutes.

Step 2—Preheat oven and prepare pan: While the batter is chilling, preheat oven to 350° F. Line a baking sheet with parchment paper (some blueberries will leak a bit and this will save time on clean up). When oven is ready, remove batter from fridge and drop by heaping tablespoons onto the baking sheet. You want rounds of about 2 inches. These will double in size after baking, so leave room between.

Step 3—Bake: Depending on your oven and the kind of baking sheets you're using, the baking time may be between 12 and 15 minutes. Rounds will rise in the center, resembling muffin tops, and should be golden in color. Serve the muffin tops warm with butter or allow them to cool on a rack and finish with a dusting of powdered (confectioners') sugar.

Note on Cooling: Do not allow the muffin tops to cool on the hot pan. The bottoms may end up steaming and become tough. Cool them on a wire rack.

How to Store: To store your tops, allow them to cool completely (otherwise moisture will condense and you'll get a soggy product). Wrap in plastic or place in an airtight container and store in refrigerator. They'll keep several days this way.

Easy Hong Kong–Style Egg Custard Tarts

After tasting Mrs. Li's egg custard tarts, Clare developed her own recipe using muffin pans. For authentic tarts, you can't beat Chinatown's bakers, but these are a very close second. Unlike English custard recipes, which include nutmeg or other spices, Chinese egg custard uses only a trace of vanilla. The overall flavor is wonderfully pure—sweet, eggy, and absolutely delicious. Traditionally, Hong Kong–style egg custard tarts are served and eaten warm, but Clare also enjoys these chilled, especially on warm summer days.

Makes 12 tarts

For filling:

4 large eggs
4 egg yolks (save the egg whites for brushing crusts)
2/3 cup whole milk

2/3 cup sugar
1/2 teaspoon salt
1/2 teaspoon vanilla

For tart shells (options):

Make your own (recipe follows)
or 12 premade tart crusts
or 2 premade pie crusts
or 1 box of frozen puff pastry dough

Step 1—Create filling: First preheat your oven to 325° F. Gently whisk together filling ingredients until sugar and salt are dissolved and eggs are blended into the mixture. Do not over whisk or allow to froth up too much. Run the mixture through a sieve. (Do not skip this sieving step.)

Step 2—Muffin Pan Tart Shells: Unroll two premade pie crusts or thaw and unfold frozen puff pastry and stamp or cut out large circles. Generously coat muffin cups with nonstick spray or grease them well with butter or shortening. Tuck the dough circles into each cup. The dough does not need to reach up to the rim, but it does need to rise at least halfway up the cup. Turn the reserved egg whites into an egg wash by adding a few drops of water and whisking with a fork. Brush the whites across the top edges of the crusts—this will protect them and help them turn golden brown. Once your strained filling is ready, pour into the tart shells, about two thirds full. Do not fill all the way.

Step 3—Bake: About 25 to 30 minutes is the most you'll want to bake these. Do not overcook. The centers should resemble creamy custard and not be hard and rubbery. Tarts are done when the filling sets (is no longer wobbly). A toothpick inserted should stand up on its own. Allow to cool before removing from the tins. Use a butter knife to gently pry the crust free. These tarts are traditionally served and eaten warm, but they're just as good after being chilled. To store, loosely wrap tarts in plastic or wax paper and refrigerate.

CLARE'S QUICK TART CRUSTS

Makes 12 small tart shells or 1 large tart crust

1¼ cup all-purpose flour
½ teaspoon salt
1 tablespoon granulated sugar
6 tablespoons butter (chilled)
¼ cup vegetable shortening
2–3 tablespoons hot water, or as needed

Sift the flour, salt, and sugar into a bowl. Cut the butter into small pieces and add in the shortening. Using the tips of your fingers, work the fats into the flour until it resembles coarse crumbs. Add the hot water and continue working and kneading until it comes together into a smooth dough. Pat the dough into a large ball, flatten the ball into a disc, and wrap the disc in plastic or wax paper. Refrigerate for thirty minutes, then dust a surface with flour and roll flat. Stamp out circles and press into tart molds or muffin pan tins. Bake as directed in the Easy Hong Kong–Style Egg Custard Tart recipe previous to this one.

Clare Cosi's Oatmeal Cookie Muffins

Because these muffins smell and taste like his mom's oatmeal cookies, they're a favorite of Detective Mike Quinn's—and lately his boss's, New York's one and only police commissioner. Redolent with the flavors of brown sugar, cinnamon, and raisins, Clare's muffins are also packed with nutrition and fiber. She developed the recipe one morning while making steel-cut Irish oatmeal for Mike, although she more often uses rolled oats for this recipe. Don't know the difference between steel-cut, rolled, and quick-cooking oats? Jump ahead for a little tutorial. Whichever you use, however, the overnight soak in buttermilk turns them into a delicious ingredient.

Makes 6 standard muffins

1 cup buttermilk (low-fat is fine)
½ cup rolled oats (not instant or quick-cooking, see note 1)
1 egg
½ cup dark brown sugar
2 tablespoons canola (or vegetable) oil
1 teaspoon cinnamon
1 teaspoon vanilla
¼ teaspoon salt
½ cup raisins
1 cup all-purpose white or white whole wheat flour (see note 2)
½ teaspoon baking powder
½ teaspoon baking soda

Step 1—Soak oats overnight: Very easy. Combine buttermilk and oats in a bowl or plastic container. Cover and place in refrigerator overnight (or at least 6 hours before making muffins).

Step 2—Make batter: Crack egg into a bowl and beat lightly with a fork. Add buttermilk and oat mixture (from Step 1), dark brown sugar, oil, cinnamon, vanilla, salt, and raisins. Stir well to combine. Now add flour, baking powder, and baking soda, and stir to create a lumpy dough. Do not overmix at this stage or you'll develop the gluten in the flour and your muffins will be tough instead of tender.

Step 3—Bake: Preheat oven to 375° F. Line muffin cups with paper liners and lightly coat the papers and top of your muffin pan with nonstick cooking spray. (This dough is low in fat and may stick to your paper liners if you don't lightly coat them with nonstick spray.) Drop dough into muffin cups, filling to top. Bake for 15 to 20 minutes or until top of muffin is firm to the touch and a toothpick inserted comes out clean. Remove pan from oven. Remove muffins promptly to prevent bottoms from steaming and becoming tough. Finish cooling on a rack.

Note on Oats: You can use "steel-cut" oats for this recipe, such as McCann's Irish Oatmeal. Steel-cut oats will give your muffin a chewier, nuttier texture, as if you've added chopped walnuts to the muffin. The rolled oats (like Quaker Old-Fashioned) will give your muffins a softer, cake-like texture. Look for steel-cut oats wherever cereal and oatmeal are sold.

Note on Flour: To add even more nutrition and fiber, replace the all-purpose white flour with white whole wheat flour. A lighter whole wheat flour will give you the benefits of whole grain but with a taste and texture closer to white flour. You can also substitute white whole wheat flour for all-purpose flour at a 1:1 ratio. While this won't work for cake or puff pastry, you can get good results using it in cookies, muffins, brownies, quick breads, and yeast breads. (If you have trouble finding this product, try the King Arthur flour website.)

AN OAT BY ANY OTHER NAME

Do you know the difference between (1) steel-cut oats, (2) rolled oats, and (3) quick-cooking oats? Is one "healthier" than the other? Can you substitute one for another in a recipe? And what is the actual health benefit of eating whole grains like oats?

Here are a few answers: (1) Steel-cut oats are whole oats that have been chopped up a bit. (2) Rolled oats are whole oats that have been steamed and rolled flat, which allows them to cook faster than steel-cut oats. (3) Quick-cooking oats are rolled oats that have been chopped up even further so they'll cook even faster. All three of these oats carry nearly the same amount of fiber and nutrition. The primary difference among them is in how they're cut.

As for recipes, do not substitute. Any recipe that specifies a certain kind of oats is attempting to create a specific texture in the product, so substituting one type for another will produce less than optimum results.

On the subject of health benefits, there are many. In addition to vitamins and minerals, fiber-rich whole grains like oats take longer to break down in your body, which means your glucose levels will remain constant instead of shooting up and crashing down, so you won't be craving another snack an hour later. With a warm cup of joe, one of these muffins is deliciously filling, easily curbing the appetite between meals.

(Low-Fat) Strawberry Shortcake Muffins

A favorite of Esther's Muffin Muse customers, these babies offer the taste of a strawberry shortcake but with far less fat. The canola oil and low-fat milk make this a guilt-free breakfast or coffee break snack. If you'd like to make it richer, simply replace the low-fat milk with whole milk, half-and-half, or heavy cream. However you decide to bake them, Esther and Clare hope you'll eat them with joy!

Makes 6 standard muffins

4–5 ounces ripe strawberries (This equals about 4 medium, 3 large, or 8 small berries. When chopped, they should measure about ⅔ cup.)
1 tablespoon + ¼ cup granulated sugar
1 egg
2 tablespoons canola (or vegetable) oil
1 teaspoon vanilla
¼ teaspoon salt
⅓ cup low-fat milk (2% milk gives great results; for richer-tasting muffins, use whole milk, half-and-half, or cream)
1 cup all-purpose flour
½ teaspoon baking powder
½ teaspoon baking soda

Step 1—Prep oven, pan, and berries: Preheat oven to 350° F. Line six muffin cups with paper holders and lightly coat the papers with nonstick spray. (This is a low-fat recipe, so if you don't coat the papers, the muffins may stick.) Wash your strawberries and gently pat them dry with a paper towel. (It's okay if they're still damp.) Hull them (see how in note following recipe) and chop them into small, uniform pieces. You'll retain more of the juices if you slice them over a bowl. Once chopped, the strawberries should fill ⅔ cup and no more. Sprinkle berries with 1 tablespoon sugar, mix, and set bowl aside.

Step 2—Make batter with one-bowl mixing method: Crack egg into a mixing bowl and gently beat with a whisk or fork. Add ¼ cup sugar, oil, vanilla, and salt, and whisk until well blended. Add milk and chopped strawberries from Step 1. Be sure to include any strawberry juices that may have accumulated at the bottom of the strawberry bowl. Stir to blend.

Step 3—Add dry ingredients: Measure flour and pour into the bowl with your wet ingredients. Sprinkle baking powder and baking soda evenly over the flour. With a spoon or spatula, mix the dry and wet ingredients to form a lumpy batter. Do not overmix at this stage or your muffins will be tough instead of tender. Just be sure to blend the flour completely into the batter.

Step 4—Bake: This batter will make 6 standard muffins, so divide it up evenly among your paper-lined cups. (Be sure to coat those papers with nonstick spray). Bake for 25 to 30 minutes. The muffins are not done baking until the tops have turned golden brown.

Step 5—Cooling and storing: Allow the muffins to cool for five minutes in the pan. Remove and finish cooling on a wire rack. Once they're completely cool, you can wrap them in plastic and store them in the refrigerator. A little butter, a cuppa joe, and you're set for breakfast, a coffee break, or late-night snack.

Note: To hull strawberries, pinch off the green stem. Using a small, sharp knife, cut around the berry's crown (or move the berry in a circular motion against the blade). Remove the fibrous, white conical-shaped core, leaving as much fruit intact as possible.

Nutella-Swirled Banana Muffins

Another Muffin Muse favorite, these warm banana muffins are swirled with Nutella, a delicious spread made of chocolate and hazelnuts. Nutella originated in Italy, where the hazelnut is king. Now available all over the world, jars of Nutella are usually shelved where your grocer sells peanut butter. If it's not available to you, or you'd simply like to make your own natural version, try Clare's recipe for homemade Nutella, which follows.

Makes 12 standard muffins

1¼ cups sugar
⅓ cup vegetable or canola oil
3 bananas (well ripened)
2 large eggs
2 teaspoons vanilla
½ teaspoon salt
½ teaspoon cinnamon
½ teaspoon nutmeg
2 cups flour
1 teaspoon baking powder
½ teaspoon baking soda
½ cup chopped hazelnuts, toasted (optional, see note on toasting)
½ cup of Nutella (chocolate hazelnut spread)

Step 1—Prep pan: First preheat oven to 350° F. Lightly coat top of muffin pans with nonstick cooking spray. This prevents the muffin tops from sticking. Next, line muffin cups with paper liners.

Step 2—Make batter: In a large bowl, measure out the sugar, oil, two of the ripe bananas (just slice into bowl), eggs, vanilla, salt, cinnamon, and nutmeg. With an electric mixer, beat the assembled ingredients until smooth, about one minute. Now add the flour, baking powder, and baking soda to the batter. Beat again with an electric mixer until batter is smooth. Be sure not to overmix at this stage or you'll develop the gluten in the flour and your muffins will be tough instead of tender.

Step 3—Final fold-ins: If including optional hazelnuts, fold in now, using a spoon or spatula. With a fork, roughly mash up the final ripe banana and fold in the mashed banana, as well. (This final banana addition really boosts the flavor in the muffin.)

Step 4—Swirl and bake: To finish follow these steps: (a) Fill each muffin cup about one third of the way with batter. (b) Drop a dollop of Nutella in and swirl to marble the batter with a knife or toothpick. (c) Finish filling each cup nearly to the top with more batter. (d) Add a final dollop of Nutella on top and marble it into the batter by swirling in a circular motion. Bake for 20 to 25 minutes. To test doneness, insert a toothpick into the middle of a muffin. If it comes out with no wet batter clinging to it, the muffins are done. Remove muffins promptly from the hot pans to prevent the bottoms from steaming and making the muffins tough.

Note: To toast nuts, simply spread them on a baking sheet and warm them in a 350° F oven for 8 to 10 minutes. Stir a few times to prevent scorching.

HOW TO MAKE YOUR OWN NUTELLA

Nutella is a chocolate hazelnut spread that originated in Italy. It's delicious spread on baguettes, toast, graham crackers, and shortbread cookies. You can swirl it into muffins and quick breads. For a fast, five-minute microwave fudge recipe, which uses Nutella, drop by Cleo

Coyle's online coffeehouse: www.CoffeehouseMystery.com. To make your own version of Nutella, follow these directions.

Makes about 1 cup

8 ounces (about 2 cups) hazelnuts, shelled and skins removed
4 tablespoons + 2 teaspoons canola oil
(hazelnut oil is even better, if you can find it)
½ cup unsweetened cocoa powder
1 cup confectioners' sugar
⅛ teaspoon salt
½ teaspoon vanilla extract

Toast hazelnuts about ten minutes in a 350° F oven, stirring once or twice to prevent burning. They're not finished until you smell the aroma of toasting nuts. Grind toasted nuts in a small food processor until they reach the consistency of thick peanut butter (about 5 minutes of processing). If you're having trouble getting the nuts to change over from sandy to viscous (like peanut butter), then cheat and add 1 to 2 teaspoons of oil and continue grinding. In a separate bowl, whisk together the cocoa, sugar, and salt. Add these to the food processor with the nuts. Measure in the vanilla and 4 tablespoons of the oil. Process everything until it's well blended (one to two minutes). If it seems too thick, then add a little more oil and process again until the mixture reaches a smooth, peanut butter–like consistency that's easy to stir and spread. Store in the refrigerator in a sealed glass jar or covered container.

(Healthified) Blueberry Pie Bars

These little squares taste just like bites of blueberry pie. They're so delicious and nutritious, the Muffin Muse couldn't keep them in stock. Fruit crumb bars have been around for years, of course, but this recipe adds dietary fiber via oats. The addition of applesauce to the ingredient list even cuts down on the amount of fat (butter) in this type of recipe. Just brew up a fresh pot of coffee while they're baking, and . . . eat with blueberry joy!

Makes a 9-inch square pan

For blueberry filling:

3 cups fresh or frozen blueberries
1 tablespoon flour
2 tablespoons white granulated sugar
½ teaspoon cinnamon

For crust and topping:

5 tablespoons butter, softened
¾ cup light brown sugar, packed
2 tablespoons unsweetened applesauce
1 large egg
1 teaspoon vanilla
¼ teaspoon salt
1 cup quick-cooking rolled oats (see note)
1½ cup all-purpose flour
2 teaspoons baking powder
½ teaspoon baking soda

Note: Be sure to use quick-cooking oats and not old-fashioned, steel-cut, or instant. To learn the differences among these oats, read An Oat By Any Other Name on page 339.

Step 1—Prep pan and make filling: Preheat your oven to 350° F and prep 9-inch square pan by lining bottom with parchment paper that hangs over the edge of two sides, creating handles. Toss blueberries in a bowl with flour, brown sugar, and cinnamon and set aside.

Step 2—Mix dough: With an electric mixer, cream butter and sugar. Add applesauce, egg, vanilla, and salt. Mix until blended. Finally add oats, all-purpose flour, and baking powder and baking soda. When the dough comes together (it will be soft and sticky), stop the mixer. Do not overmix.

Step 3—Assemble: Press a little more than half of the dough into the prepared square pan with your fingertips, until it completely covers the pan bottom. Spread the blueberry filling over the crust and break the remaining dough into small pieces over the top. Bake for about 30 to 40 minutes, or until top is slightly brown.

Bars are easier to cut (and they will keep their shape better) if you allow them to cool. So let the pastry cool in the pan, then run a butter knife around the sides to free up any sticky bits. Lift by those parchment paper handles, transferring the entire pastry square to a flat surface for further cooling. Cut into rectangular bars or bite-sized squares. Store in the refrigerator.

Clare Cosi's Classic Coffee Cake Muffins with Streusel Topping and Vanilla Glaze

These truly are classic muffins, and they're especially delicious paired with coffee. Clare was only too happy to share a fresh-baked batch of them with Madame at the story's end, right before she hopped on train to Washington, D.C.

Makes 12 muffins

For muffins:

1½ cups streusel filling and topping (easy recipe follows)
½ cup butter (1 stick), softened

½ cup granulated sugar
½ cup light brown sugar
¾ teaspoon salt
½ teaspoon cinnamon
1½ teaspoons vanilla
2 large eggs, lightly beaten with fork
¾ cup sour cream
¼ cup brewed coffee or espresso, cooled (see note)
2 cups all-purpose flour
1½ teaspoons baking powder
½ teaspoon baking soda

Note: Whole milk or buttermilk (regular or light) may be substituted for the coffee.

For Vanilla Glaze (optional):

2 tablespoons butter
1 cup powdered sugar
½ teaspoon vanilla extract (for a whiter glaze, use clear vanilla)
1 tablespoon milk (more or less)

Step 1—Preheat, prep pans, mix dry ingredients: First make the streusel filling and topping (recipe follows). Then preheat your oven to 350° F and place paper liners in 12 muffin cups.

Step 2—One-bowl mixing method: In a large bowl, use an electric mixer to cream the softened butter and sugars. When light and fluffy, beat in the salt, cinnamon, vanilla, eggs, sour cream, and cooled coffee or espresso. Continue beating for another minute. Stop the mixer and measure in the flour. Sprinkle the baking powder and baking soda over the flour. Mix everything until you have a batter that is smooth. Do not overmix or you'll develop the gluten in the flour and your muffins will be tough instead of tender.

Step 3—Layer muffin cups and bake: You will now need the streusel topping that you prepared ahead. Into your paper-lined muffin cups, drop a generous dollop of batter. Sprinkle streusel onto the batter and top with more batter. Finish with a generous sprinkling of streusel. Bake for 18 to 20 minutes. Muffins are done when a toothpick inserted comes out with no wet batter clinging to it. Remove from oven and take muffins out of the hot pan promptly or the bottoms may steam and toughen.

Step 4 (optional)—Glaze the cooled muffins: In a small saucepan, over medium-low heat, melt the butter. Sift in the powdered sugar (or sift the sugar first and then add). When all of the sugar is melted into the butter, remove from heat and stir in vanilla. Finally stir in the milk, a little at a time, until the glaze is the right consistency to drizzle over the muffins. To finish the muffins, dip a fork in the warm glaze mixture and drizzle it in a back-and-forth motion over the cooled muffin tops.

HOW TO MAKE STREUSEL (CRUMB) TOPPING FOR ANY MUFFIN OR COFFEE CAKE

Makes about 1½ cups of streusel

½ cup all-purpose flour
½ cup light brown sugar
1 teaspoon cinnamon
5 tablespoons butter (unsalted is best), cubed

Food processor: Place all ingredients in the processor and pulse until you see coarse crumbs.

By hand: Using your hands and/or a fork or pastry blender, work the butter into the dry ingredient until you see coarse crumbs.

Store any extra in the refrigerator.

Easy Iced Mocha

Makes one 8-ounce serving

1/3 cup brewed coffee (4 coffee ice cubes)
1/3 cup milk (low-fat is fine)
2 teaspoons sugar (or more if you like your drinks sweeter)
1/4 teaspoon vanilla extract
1/4 teaspoon unsweetened cocoa powder
Whipped cream
Chocolate curls (see how to make below)

Fill an ice cube tray with leftover coffee and freeze. Remove four coffee ice cubes (per 8-ounce serving) and place in blender. Add milk, sugar, vanilla extract, and cocoa. Pulse the blender to chop the coffee ice cubes into fine particles. You can create a very icy drink with small ice chips (like a frozen margarita) or you can run the blender full speed until the mixture is completely liquefied yet still cold and frothy. The drink is delicious either way and a great use for your leftover joe. To finish, pour this frosty refresher into a glass mug, top with whipped cream and chocolate curls (see below).

HOW TO MAKE CHOCOLATE CURLS

To create chocolate curls, start with a block of room-temperature chocolate. Using a vegetable peeler, scrape down the block, and you'll see curls of chocolate peel away. Chocolate curls make a wonderful garnish for coffee drinks, hot cocoa, cakes, cupcakes, and puddings. Or use them to decorate a dessert plate. Chill or even freeze the curls for more sturdiness and longer life on a serving plate or dessert table.

Clare Cosi's Orange-Vanilla "Creamsicle" Coffee Cake

The Muffin Muse served a more elaborate version of this cake at the deputy mayor's food-truck catered wedding reception. This version is much simpler. Clare came up with it during her years raising Joy in New Jersey, when she wrote her In the Kitchen with Clare *column for a local paper. It's an easy coffee cake that's so moist and rich it tastes like a pound cake, yet it bakes up quickly in a single-layer pan. It requires no special skill to bake or glaze and only dirties one bowl. Now that's cooking with joy!*

Makes a 9-inch pan

½ cup butter (1 stick), softened
1 cup granulated sugar
2 large eggs
¼ cup whole milk
½ cup orange juice (with pulp or not, your choice)
1 teaspoon pure vanilla extract
¼ teaspoon salt
1 tablespoon orange zest (grated peel from 1 medium orange)
1¾ cups all-purpose flour
2 teaspoons baking powder

For Orange-Vanilla Glaze:

Makes 1 cup of glaze, enough to liberally cover one 9-inch cake

2 tablespoons butter
2 tablespoons whole milk
2 cups confectioners' (powdered or icing) sugar
1 teaspoon pure vanilla extract
2 tablespoons orange juice (Be sure to add separately)

Step 1—Make batter with one-bowl mixing method: First preheat oven to 350° F. Using an electric mixer, cream butter and sugar in a mixing bowl. Stop the mixer. Add in eggs, milk, orange juice, vanilla, salt, and orange zest. Continue mixing until well blended. Now add the flour and baking powder. Continue mixing only enough to blend ingredients. The batter will be somewhat thick (although not as thick as cookie dough). Just be sure not to overmix or you will develop the gluten in the flour and your cake will be tough instead of tender.

Step 2—Prepare pan and bake: Generously butter the bottom and sides of a 9-inch cake pan. Bake for about 25 to 35 minutes. To check for doneness, insert a toothpick into the cake's center. When it comes out clean (with no batter on it), the cake is done. Cool the cake in the pan but on a rack so air can circulate under the bottom of the hot pan. Do not attempt to remove the cake from the pan until the top of your cake is cool to the touch.

Step 3—Remove cake from pan and glaze: Wait for the cake to cool (about 30 minutes out of the oven or it may stick on you). Run a knife around the pan's edge. Place a flat plate over the top of the pan and carefully flip it. Gently tap the pan bottom to loosen the cake. When you've removed the cake this way, it's (obviously) upside down. Flip it once more so that it's upright on your serving plate. Now it's time to drizzle the entire cake with Clare's easy Orange-Vanilla Glaze.

Warning: First, Clare wants to warn you *not* to dump everything into your saucepan at once when you make the glaze. Follow these steps as written or your glaze will curdle when your milk and orange juice meet!

Step 4—Create sugar paste: Place butter and milk in a saucepan over low heat. When butter has melted, stir in the confectioners' sugar, a little at a time, until dissolved. The mixture will be thick and pasty.

Step 5—Add vanilla and orange juice: Remove the pan from heat. Add vanilla and orange juice. Stir well to blend. Return pan to low heat, tilt pan, and whisk well until smooth. This may take a minute.

Note: This mixture should never boil or you may get a scorched taste in your glaze.

Step 6—Glaze cake: While glaze is still warm, drizzle over cooled cake. Clare transfers the warm glaze to a glass measuring cup and pours a thin stream in a zigzag motion across the cake until it's completely iced.

Clare Cosi's "Melt-and-Mix" Double-Chocolate Espresso-Glazed Loaf Cake

Yes, this is the very cake Matteo and Quinn fought over—well, the last slice anyway. But Clare has learned her lesson. The next time she finds herself sharing a household with a hot-headed coffee hunter and a stewing detective, she's making two of everything!

Makes two cakes using loaf pans of 8½ x 4½ x 2 inches

¾ cup (1½ stick) butter, sliced into small pieces
½ cup vegetable or canola oil
2 cups granulated sugar
6 ounces semi-sweet chocolate, chopped
½ cup brewed coffee or espresso
½ cup whole milk
3 cups all-purpose flour
½ cup unsweetened cocoa powder
2½ teaspoons baking powder
½ teaspoon baking soda
½ teaspoon kosher salt

¾ cup sour cream
2 teaspoons vanilla
3 eggs, room temperature
1 cup semi-sweet chocolate chips
Chocolate Espresso Glaze (recipe follows)

Step 1—Prep oven and pans: First preheat oven to 300 degrees F. Butter bottom and sides of two loaf pans (size 8½ x 4½ x 2-inch) and create parchment paper slings. The handles of these slings will be used to lift the baked cakes out of their pans. Here's how to make the slings: Trim a length of paper in each pan so that the bottom is covered and excess paper extends beyond the long sides to create handles. The butter will help the paper stick to the pan's sides. For a tight fit, put sharp folds in the paper at the pan's corners.

Step 2—Easy "melt-and-mix" method: Into a saucepan combine the sliced up butter, oil, sugar, chocolate, coffee, and milk. Stir over *low* heat until chocolate is melted and all ingredients are smoothly blended together. (Do not allow this mixture to boil or you'll end up with a scorched taste to your chocolate.) You can also use a microwave to melt these ingredients, but be sure to use a microwave-safe bowl and heat in 30 second bursts, stirring between each burst to prevent chocolate from burning. Set aside to cool.

Step 3—Finish batter: Into a separate bowl, sift together the flour, cocoa powder, baking powder, baking soda, and salt. Stir in the cooled chocolate mixture, the sour cream, vanilla, and eggs. Beat with an electric mixer, scraping down the bowl until all ingredients form a smooth batter. (Do not over-mix) Finally, fold in the chocolate chips.

Step 4—Bake and cool: Divide the batter evenly between your two lined loaf pans. Bake for about 70–80 minutes (time will depend on your oven). Remove from oven. Allow cakes to cool 10 minutes in the pan, and then use the parchment paper handles to lift the cakes out. Let the cakes cool on a rack for another 30 minutes before slicing. Do not glaze until completely cool.

Step 5—Glaze and serve: While the cakes are cooling, mix up the Chocolate Espresso Glaze (recipe follows). Spoon generously over each *completely cooled* cake top. Use the back of your spoon to spread the glaze evenly. Be sure to push excess glaze over the edges for a nice drizzly effect down the cake sides. Serve slices with dollops of Whipped Coffee Cream (recipe follows).

Chocolate Espresso Glaze

This glaze pairs beautifully with chocolate, mocha, and coffee-flavored cakes, muffins, cupcakes, and croissants. For a frosting-like layer, spoon the glaze over the tops of your cakes and cupcakes then use the back of the spoon to smooth it. Or use a fork to drizzle the glaze back-and-forth across your pastry. Either way, it's a stunning and delicious finish to your baked goodies.

Makes about 1 cup

1 cup semi-sweet chocolate chips (or 4 ounces of block chocolate, chopped)
¼ cup brewed coffee or espresso
2 tablespoons butter
1 teaspoon vanilla
½ teaspoon instant espresso powder
1 Tablespoon corn syrup (light or vanilla)
1 cup confectioners' sugar

Place chocolate chips (or 4 ounces of chopped block chocolate) into a mixing bowl and set aside. Over low heat, bring the following ingredients to a simmer in a small saucepan: coffee or espresso, butter, vanilla, instant espresso powder, and corn syrup. Pour the simmering liquid over your chocolate chips (or chopped chocolate) and stir until all chocolate is melted and the liquid is smooth. Finally add in 1 cup of confectioners' sugar and whisk until the glaze is completely smooth and shiny (with no lumps). You can spoon it over your cake and use the back of the spoon to smooth the glaze into an even layer. Or you can use a fork and a back-and-forth motion for a drizzling effect. Glaze will be wet at first and should set in about an hour.

Whipped Coffee Cream

⅔ cup heavy cream, well chilled
*1 tablespoon brewed coffee, cooled**
1–2 tablespoons confectioners' sugar, sifted

Note: For vanilla cream, replace coffee with 1 teaspoon of pure vanilla extract (use clear extract for a prettier, whiter cream)

For best results pre-chill your mixing bowl and beaters. Using an electric mixer, whip the cream until frothy and thick. Slow the mixer and beat in the *cooled* coffee and sugar. Increase speed and continue whipping until firm peaks form. Keep chilled in refrigerator. Dollop over slices of the cake before serving.

Clare's Cappuccino Chiffon Cake for Mike

Clare's "household for three" had its challenges, and on the night Mike Quinn finally grew weary of Matteo's carnitas burritos, Clare whispered sweet foodie promises in his ear, namely a special roasted chicken dinner that would end in this "light-as-air" Cappuccino Chiffon Cake with Whipped Cream Frosting.

"A forkful of this cake," she cooed, "should fill your mouth with the most delicate flavors, then dissolve on your tongue as if you've bitten into a cloud from heaven."

Clare shares two variations for frosting this chiffon cake—vanilla or mocha—and she suggests finishing it with a generous sprinkling of dark and white chocolate curls.

Makes two 8-inch round layer cakes

4 extra-large egg yolks, room temperature
(keep egg whites for next step)
2 teaspoons instant espresso powder
⅓ cup brewed coffee
¼ cup canola or vegetable oil
½ teaspoon vanilla extract
½ teaspoon salt
⅓ cup + 6 tablespoons granulated sugar
1¼ cups cake flour, sift before measuring
1½ teaspoons baking powder
4 extra-large egg whites
¼ teaspoon cream of tartar
Whipped Cream Frosting (vanilla or mocha)
Chocolate curls (dark and white)

Step 1—Prep oven and pans: First, preheat oven to 350° F. Line the bottom of two nonstick cake pans with parchment paper, and coat the paper lightly with nonstick spray. Separate the eggs. You will need both the yolks and whites in this recipe.

Step 2—One-bowl mixing method: In a large bowl, dissolve the instant espresso powder into the brewed coffee (if the coffee is very hot, wait until it cools before proceeding). Add the oil, egg yolks, vanilla, salt, and sugar. Beat well with an electric mixer, at least 3 minutes. Stop mixer and add flour. Sprinkle baking powder evenly over the flour. On a lower speed of your mixer, blend until a smooth batter forms, but do not overmix at this stage.

Step 3—Lighten batter with whipped egg whites: Choose a very clean glass, ceramic, or metal bowl for this next step. (For best results do not use plastic. Grease clings to plastic and this will prevent you from properly whipping the whites.) Using an electric mixer, beat egg whites and cream of tartar on high speed until frothy. Gradually add in the 6 tablespoons of sugar and beat until you see stiff, glossy peaks. Very gently, fold these glossy, sweetened egg whites into the batter mixture from Step 1. Divide your final chiffon batter between your two cake pans.

Step 4—Bake: In your well-preheated oven, bake for 25 to 30 minutes or until tops spring back when lightly touched. Remove cake pans from oven and transfer to a wire rack. Allow cakes to cool for at least 30 minutes before removing from pans. To remove cake layers from pans, wait until *completely cool*, then carefully run a knife around the sides of each pan and invert cakes onto plates. Peel away the parchment paper on the bottoms.

Step 5—Big finish: Frost with Clare's Whipped Cream Frosting (see next recipe). Decorate this frosted cake liberally with dark and white chocolate curls to finish. For instructions on how to create chocolate curls, turn to page 349.

Clare Cosi's Whipped Cream Frosting

2½ cups heavy whipping cream, well chilled
5 tablespoons granulated sugar
2¾ teaspoons cornstarch
1 teaspoon vanilla extract (use clear vanilla for whiter results)

Note: For a Mocha Whipped Cream variation, replace the vanilla with ½ teaspoon instant espresso powder and 3 tablespoons unsweetened cocoa powder.

Step 1—Create the stabilizer: First place mixing bowl and beaters in the refrigerator. Chilling will give you better results in the next step. In a small saucepan combine the sugar and cornstarch. Pour in ½ cup of the cream. Bring the mixture to a simmer over medium heat, whisking continually until the mixture thickens (about 2 minutes). Remove from heat and whisk in the vanilla. Transfer mixture to a bowl and allow to come to room temperature—to accelerate the cooling, place the bowl in the fridge or freezer.

Step 2—Whip up frosting: In a large pre-chilled mixing bowl, whip the remaining (well chilled) 2¼ cups of cream with an electric mixer until frothy and slightly thickened. Slow the mixer and beat in the stabilizing cream from Step 1 then increase the speed to high and whip until firm peaks form.

Warning: Before frosting any cake, be sure it is completely cooled or else you'll melt this frosting. Store any unused frosting or uneaten cake in the refrigerator.

Clare's Roasted Chicken with Rosemary and Lime for Mike

Rosemary and lemon may be a classic flavor combo for chicken, but Clare saw a beautiful green mountain of plump, juicy limes at her local market and decided to bring their refreshing summer flavor to a gently roasted bird. Mike Quinn flipped for it, and she made good on her promise, roasting this chicken for him the Sunday before he hopped the Acela Express down to Washington. With a side of her Fully-Loaded Colcannon and a slice of Chiffon Cappuccino Cake for dessert, Mike swore he'd be back for a visit the very next weekend—and he was.

4–6 pound whole chicken
5–6 fresh limes (medium size)
1 tablespoon sea salt
½ teaspoon white pepper
6 cloves garlic
2 tablespoons chopped, fresh rosemary
1 teaspoon poultry seasoning
3 tablespoons olive oil (divided)

Step 1—Prep meat: First preheat your oven to 350° F. Allow the chicken to reach room temperature (20 to 30 minutes outside the refrigerator). Rinse the chicken and pat dry. If your limes were in the refrigerator, warm them to room temperature, as well.

Step 2—Stuff the bird: Quarter one lime and place the sections inside the chicken cavity, along with a dash of sea salt and white pepper. Close the cavity. (Use a simple wooden skewer for this.)

Step 3—Create the rosemary-lime slurry: Place the sea salt into a small bowl and smash the garlic on it. Mix in the freshly squeezed juice of 2 to 3 limes (enough to measure about ¼ cup). Add the chopped rosemary, poultry seasoning, white pepper, and 2 tablespoons of the olive oil. Now rub this slurry all over the bird and place breast side up on the greased rack.

Step 4—Roast: Lightly coat the top of your broiler pan or roasting rack with the final tablespoon of olive oil. (For easier cleanup, I also like to cover the bottom portion of my pan with aluminum foil.) Place your pan in the center of your oven for about 25 minutes per pound, giving a bird of 6 pounds about 2½ hours of cooking time; a bird of 4 pounds about an hour and forty minutes. You're watching for the thickest part of the thigh to reach an internal temperature of 165° F.

Step 5—Finish: Once cooked, allow the chicken to stand for 15 minutes before carving. To keep it warm, tent foil over the bird. This resting period is important. If you cut into the bird right out of the oven, the juices will run out and your chicken will be dry instead of succulent, which is almost as bad, in Clare's opinion, as missing a clue.

Clare's Fully-Loaded Colcannon for Mike

Growing up in a big, Irish-American family, Mike Quinn ate colcannon on a regular basis. The dish takes its name from the Gaelic word cál ceannann, *meaning "white-headed cabbage"—and kale or cabbage is in the traditional recipe, along with potatoes, onions (or scallions, chives, or leeks), and cream and/or butter.*

Clare often made the traditional version for Mike, but for this recipe, she decided to give it an Italian kiss of olive oil; a warm, sweet hug of garlic; and a big old American-style finish of gooey melted cheddar and smoky crumbled bacon. Like a "fully-loaded" baked potato, she's loaded Mike's colcannon with comfort-food flavor.

Makes about 6 cups

1 pound red potatoes, cut into uniform pieces
2 slices thick-cut bacon, chopped (or four regular bacon slices)
1 tablespoon olive oil
2 cloves garlic, chopped
1 large onion, chopped
½ head cabbage, sliced thin (approximately 6 cups)
1 cup milk
1 tablespoon butter
½ teaspoon salt
¼ teaspoon white pepper
⅔ cup cheddar cheese, shredded

Step 1—Cook the potatoes: Steam the sliced up red potatoes until cooked through, about 15 to 20 minutes. Clare uses a simple collapsible steamer basket in a deep pot. Remove the pot from heat, drain any extra water, and cover to keep the potatoes warm.

Step 2—Render bacon and sauté veggies: While potatoes are steaming, chop bacon into ½-inch pieces and cook over a very low heat to render the fat. When bacon is brown, remove from pan and set aside. Turn the heat to medium, and add the olive oil to the drippings in the pan. Then add the garlic and onions and cook until the onions are translucent, about 3 minutes. Add cabbage and continue cooking another 5 minutes, stirring often.

Step 3—Simmer: Reduce heat to low. Stir in milk, butter, salt, and white pepper; cover and cook until the cabbage is tender, about 8 minutes.

Step 4—Finish: Add the hot cabbage mixture in with the potatoes. Mash with a metal potato masher or large fork until the ingredients are blended. Fold in the cheese and cover the pot until the cheese is melted. Serve topped with crumbled bacon bits.

Dominic Chin's "Chitalian" Chicken (or Shrimp) Lo Mein

Clare Cosi snagged this recipe from City Councilman Dominic Chin. With an Italian mom and a Chinese dad, Dom famously grew up on one grandmother's biscotti and the other's moon cakes. As for this recipe, according to Dom, mein *means noodles in Cantonese, and* lo mein *means "stirred noodles," which refers to the method of stirring them into the pan at the end of the cooking process.*

Because Chinese lo mein noodles are flat and wheat-based, Italian linguine, spaghetti, or "thick spaghetti" (Dom's favorite for this recipe) are good substitutes, which is the Italian part of this Chinese-inspired dish. Cooking time is under 30 minutes, and to make life easier, Clare suggests using a frozen veggie mix so you don't have to spend time cleaning and cutting.

Both Clare and Dom have a final word of advice for cooks in a hurry: Do not skip the prep step! Marinating the chicken (or shrimp) boosts the flavor enormously in this dish, and it's very easy. The "Chinglish" marinade recipe follows this one, and you can use it in plenty of other recipes, too. May you cook it with love, and eat it with joy!

Makes 4 servings

1 pound marinated chicken, chopped (or whole shrimp, marinade directions follow)
1 cup of dried spaghetti, linguine, or fettuccini (about ⅓ of a 16-ounce package)
2 tablespoons soy sauce
1 teaspoon ginger (dried powder from the spice aisle)
½ teaspoon dried/powdered chicken bouillon
Dash of ground white pepper
2 tablespoons hot tap water
(or scoop out water from noodle pot)
1 tablespoon oil, either sesame or peanut oil
(if you can't find, use canola)
1 yellow onion, finely chopped
2 cloves garlic, finely chopped
1 green onion (scallion), finely chopped
*3 cups (about ¾ of a 1-lb bag) frozen peas and carrots (or "Asian-style" frozen veggie mix)**

Note: 1 large chicken breast or 4 chicken thighs will equal about 1 pound of meat, which is the amount needed for this recipe.

The frozen vegetables can be increased to 4 cups or reduced to 2, depending on your taste.

Step 1—Marinate the chicken (or shrimp): See Dom's easy "Chinglish" marinade recipe for chicken or shrimp, following this one. When ready to use, remove the chicken pieces (or shrimp) from the marinade liquid and *drain well.* If using shrimp, be sure to peel them and *drain well.*

Warning: Do not add sopping wet chicken or shrimp to hot oil or you'll create dangerous hissing and spitting of hot oil! (Also, be sure to discard the marinade liquid; do not reuse.)

Step 2—Cook the noodles: Follow the package directions; do not overcook. Rinse in cold water to prevent sticking, drain well, and set aside.

Step 3—Prepare finishing spices: Mix together soy sauce, ginger, chicken bouillon, and white pepper. Stir in 2 tablespoons hot tap water—or do what Dom does: scoop the hot water right out of the pot of cooking noodles. Set aside for end of cooking process.

Step 4—Sauté onion, garlic, and chicken: Heat the oil in a large skillet (or wok) over medium-high heat until good and hot. Add the chopped yellow onion and garlic. After about five minutes, when the chopped onions appear translucent, stir in the green onion and chicken pieces. Stir often until chicken is no longer pink. Create a well by pushing chicken pieces to outer rim of pan.

Step 5—Add veggies: Add the frozen vegetables into the center of the "chicken well" and cook, uncovered, for about 8 minutes, stirring often. Do a taste test on the veggies to make sure they're thawed, hot, and ready to eat. When the veggies are ready, fold in the chicken.

Step 6—Put the "lo" in the lo mein: Stir the cooked noodles into the pan and pour the little bowl of finishing spices (that you made in Step 3) over everything. Mix well to distribute flavors and cook for another few minutes to make sure everything is nice and hot. Taste and adjust final seasonings to your liking; maybe you'll want a splash more of soy sauce or sprinkling of white pepper, and enjoy!

Easy "Chinglish" Chicken or Shrimp Marinade

Dom Chin developed this recipe in college when he couldn't find the traditional Shaoxing rice wine, second only to soy sauce in Chinese cooking. As Dom told Clare, marinating the chicken (or shrimp) makes all the difference in the flavor of any stir-fry dish. Never skip this step. It's very easy. Just toss a few ingredients together into a plastic container, add the chicken or shrimp, snap on the lid, throw it in the fridge for a few hours (or even overnight), and you're ready to cook with joy!

Makes 4 servings

2 tablespoons grape juice (see note at end of recipe)
2 tablespoons rice wine vinegar (or white vinegar)
¼ cup vegetable or canola oil
1 teaspoon soy sauce
1 teaspoon corn starch
Generous pinch of white pepper

Into a plastic container with a lid, mix all ingredients until well blended. Add in the chicken pieces or whole shrimp (see previous recipe) and toss well to coat. Snap on the lid and refrigerate for 3 hours. (You can certainly marinate longer, even overnight, if more convenient for your schedule.) Dom's "Chinglish" marinated chicken or shrimp is delicious and can be used in any basic stir-fry recipe. To make his lo mein, see recipe preceding this one.

Special Note on Two of Dom Chin's "Chinglish" Ingredients: The grape juice and vinegar make a delicious substitution for the more traditional Shaoxing wine, a rice wine so commonly used in Chinese cooking that it's second only to soy sauce. This wine has a specific taste profile and is difficult to find in most American markets, but if you can locate a bottle, replace the grape juice and vinegar with ¼ cup of the wine instead.

Matteo Allegro's Carnitas *("Little Meats")*

When Matt decided to keep an eye on Clare after the Red Hook shooting, he did what any practical tough guy would do: He went grocery shopping. The first menu item he prepared was carnitas, a traditional Mexican braised pork dish that's savory, rich, delicious—and very versatile. Once prepared, carnitas (or "little meats" in Spanish) are ready to heat and eat in many different ways.

Mix them with Matteo Allegro's Easy Mexican-Style Black Beans (see recipe on page 367), and leftover rice for tasty burritos, shred and mix the pork with cheese for meaty quesadillas, fry them up with eggs for a great bacon substitute, stuff them into a taco with your favorite fillings, or simply enjoy fried carnitas between two slabs of crusty Italian bread. And don't throw away those pot stickings (fond, *as Joy would call it) unless you want to miss one rich and tasty red sauce (see below for that recipe).*

Makes 12 servings

2–3 pounds boneless pork shoulder or butt, cut into 2 to 3-inch cubes (do not trim fat)
8–10 cloves garlic, peeled
1 teaspoon ground cumin
1 teaspoon kosher or sea salt
½ teaspoon white pepper

Step 1: Place the pork in a large Dutch oven or heavy pot which heats evenly. Add the garlic, cumin, salt, pepper, and enough water to just cover the meat. Bring the pot to a boil, then quickly reduce the heat to a slow simmer. Simmer uncovered for two hours. Don't touch the meat and don't stir the pot.

Step 2: After two hours, increase the heat to medium-high while stirring (very) occasionally and turning the pieces. Continue to cook for about 45 minutes, or until all of the liquid has evaporated, leaving only the rendered pork fat. Let the meat sizzle in this fat long enough to brown at the edges, turning pieces gently and only as needed, because they'll be eager to fall apart.

Step 3: Remove the finished carnitas, let them cool in a separate bowl until room temperature, then store in an airtight container. Reheat carnitas as needed, for use in tacos, burritos, etc. The braised and fried meat will stay fresh in the refrigerator for up to two weeks.

Matteo's Carnitas' Fond *Spaghetti Sauce*

Matt made this sauce for Clare the night he confessed his little secret. Clare inhaled it, of course, because it's one of her favorite dishes. For years, she's considered this sauce a culinary bonus whenever she cooks up Matt's carnitas (page 365). The sauce makes excellent use of the amazing pork pot stickings (what French chefs like Clare's daughter call fond*), which are left over after making Matt's "little meats." A bit of sautéing, a little deglazing, and you're on your way to one mouthwatering bowl of pasta.*

Serves 6

2 tablespoons extra virgin olive oil
1 small onion, chopped

2–4 cloves of garlic, minced
28-oz can of Italian-style peeled tomatoes, hand crushed
1 tablespoon dried oregano
⅛ teaspoon sea salt
¼ teaspoon ground black pepper
¼ cup red or white wine
1 pound pasta (Matt suggests thick spaghetti or linguine)
¼ cup Romano cheese, grated

Step 1—Sauté veggies: In a medium saucepan, heat oil over medium heat. Add onion and sauté until translucent. Add garlic and gently sauté until lightly caramelized. Add tomatoes and season with oregano, salt, and pepper.

Step 2—Deglaze the *fond*: Using the wine, deglaze the carnitas pot, scraping the bottom and sides to collect the *fond* (pot stickings). Transfer this mixture to the saucepan of tomato sauce in Step 1. Reduce heat under the sauce and simmer for approximately 20 minutes.

Step 3—Finish on pasta: Prepare pasta according to instructions on package. Pour sauce over cooked pasta; toss until pasta is well covered. Top with grated Romano cheese.

Matteo Allegro's Easy Mexican-Style Black Beans

Black beans are full of fiber and nutrition, and Matt's recipe is both easy and delicious. Serve these as a side dish, add to burrito or taco filling, or mound it warm on a plate, top with grated cheese (Monterey Jack, Co-Jack, white cheddar, or queso blanco), and cover to melt.

Why doesn't Matt call these beans "refried"? As he once noted to Clare, the name "refried" is based on a bad translation. The prefix "re," as used by Mexicans, should be translated as "very" or "well" and not with a meaning of repetition. The Mexican name of this dish, therefore, is frijoles refritos *and should be translated into English as "well-fried" and not "refried" beans.*

Serves 6

2 tablespoons olive oil
6 garlic cloves, finely chopped
2 large jalapeño chilis, seeded and chopped
½ teaspoon ground cumin
2 (15 ounce) cans black beans, rinsed and drained
1 cup chicken broth (low-salt is best)
Salt and pepper (to taste)
Fresh lime juice
Chopped fresh cilantro (optional)

In a large saucepan, heat the oil on a medium-high setting. Add chopped garlic, chilis, and cumin. Sauté these for only about two minutes. Add beans and broth and cook 10 to 15 more minutes, uncovered, stirring frequently to prevent burning. The beans are done when most of the liquid evaporates and the mixture dramatically thickens up. If you like, mash with a fork at the end of the cooking process, and season to taste with salt and pepper. Before serving, Matteo finishes his with a squeeze of fresh lime and a sprinkling of cilantro. Clare likes to grate a soft cheese over the top, as well. "Cover it for a minute to allow the warmth to melt the cheese," she says, "and eat with joy!

Clare Cosi's Taco Cups, aka Muffin-Pan Quiches

These little taco cups were one of Joy's favorite meals growing up, which thrilled budget-minded mom Clare because the dish relied on leftovers—and she could easily make dozens of variations. For instance, she'd replace the taco filling with crumbled bacon and shredded Gruyere and have a mini quiche Lorraine. Or she'd go vegetarian with sautéed mushrooms, onions, and mozzarella. She'd pair shredded chicken with Monterey Jack, chunks of ham and green pepper with Swiss, and leftover hamburgers from a backyard cookout with white cheddar. The only limit is your imagination—and the leftovers in your fridge.

Makes 6 Mini Taco Cups or Muffin-Pan Quiches

2 soft flour tortillas, at least 8-inches in diameter
½ cup filling (leftover taco filling, or see more veggie and meat filling ideas at the end of this recipe)
½ cup shredded cheese (cheddar, or see ideas at the end of the recipe)
2 eggs
⅓ cup low-fat milk
¼ teaspoon salt
Pinch of ground pepper (black or white)
Your favorite taco toppings (salsa, guacamole, sour cream, etc.)

Step 1—Tuck tortilla crusts: Preheat oven to 350° F. Cut each tortilla into quarters. Place paper cupcake liners into each of the 6 muffin cups. Tuck each tortilla quarter into each muffin cup.

Step 2—Fill cups: Divide your taco filling (or the meat or veggie filling of your choice; see ideas below) into each of the six muffin cups. On top of each cup, place a bit of shredded cheese.

Step 3—Finish with egg-milk mixture: Whisk together eggs, milk, salt, pepper. Divide this liquid evenly among the muffin cups. (During baking this mixture will rise and inflate like a popover so the liquid should fill only about half of each cup.)

Step 4—Bake and garnish: Bake in preheated oven for 20 to 25 minutes. Remove and top with your favorite garnishes, such as sour cream, salsa, and/or guacamole.

ALTERNATE TACO CUP FILLING IDEAS

Meat: Traditional taco fillings (ground meat, chicken, or shredded pork), crumbled bacon, chopped sausage, cubed ham, pepperoni, shredded smoked salmon

Veggie: Sautéed onions and mushrooms, sautéed spinach and garlic, chopped steamed broccoli, sweet bell peppers sautéed in olive oil with onions

Cheese: Swiss, cheddar, Monterey Jack, Colby, queso blanco, Gruyere, Asiago, mozzarella, provolone, or a combo of 2 or more

Additional Suggestions: Mini Quiche Lorraine Cup (crumbled bacon and shredded Gruyere or Swiss), Mini Spinach Quiche Cup, Mini Broccoli and Cheddar Cup, Mini Cheeseburger Cup, Mini Pepper and Onion Cup